NON-PLAYER CHARACTER

VEO CORVA

First published in 2021 by Witch Key Fiction
Copyright © 2021 Veo Corva

ISBN: 978-1-9161009-7-8

Veo Corva
Website: https://veocorva.xyz

Witch Key Fiction
Website: https://witchkeyfiction.xyz

Cover art by Vanessa Schiefer / Art of Hellebarde
Website: https://www.theartofhellebarde.com/

Chapter header art by Tais Yastremska

Proofread by Angelica Fyfe

Many thanks to the supporters of the
Non-Player Character Kickstarter campaign.

For Scott, Nick, and Rob, my first adventuring companions who faced the terrors of the Underwater Bird King and his birthday party with me.

For Angelica and Kerry, the best players anyone could ask for (except for and maybe because of their aggressive collection of pets).

And for Joh, who has been part of every adventure I've had in this world and others and is the best damn goblin player in existence.

CONTENTS

For Content Warnings, please go to the last page.

YSSAMBER OCEAN
NOTT
UXRN
VOLANTHIS
UTHORN OCEAN
TORMALAN
ALIT -UNDULAR
PRYNN OCEAN
EVANDER
MISTCURL
YSSAMBER OCEAN
THE MISTEMBRA ISLES

SPECTRE BAY
DRAGON'S DEEP
MIHILIT-DALATH
STITCHFALL MOUNTAINS
LUNDANAR
TUROVELLIS
THE WOUND
WELDWOODS
UMALTHEE COAST
THE SPIRAL PLANAR RIFT
YSSAMBER OCEAN
MISTCURL
AND THE
REGION AROUND
MIHILIT-DALATH

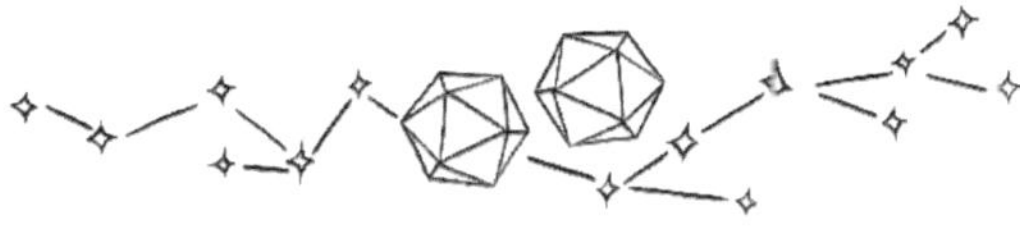

CHAPTER ONE

I was standing on a stranger's doorstep and wishing my feet were nailed to the ground. Even now, I could feel the build-up of pressure in my chest. The restlessness growing in my legs made me jiggle slightly on the spot.

I was a champion of accidental 'ding-dong-ditch'. I would go somewhere new, ring the bell, and the next thing I knew I was sprinting to my car with my hood up and the sense that the wolves were on my heels. It was a hard instinct to resist.

The house, with its mossy hip-height stone fence and cheerful yellow walls, seemed to loom over me with all the frightening charisma of a haunted mansion rather than the cosy terraced house it was.

So yes. I wanted to run. And under any normal circumstances, I would have.

But this time was different. There was a friend waiting inside, and there was a game that was going to change my life.

That's what he'd promised me, anyway, when we were on a raid in the Arcadia: Redux Online. I had been knee-deep in skeletons and taking a beating, crouched under my shield, when he sent a blast of golden energy across the floor, setting me free.

'Oh my god.' I'd pulled a glowing silver potion from one of the bone piles scattered around me. Or my in-game avatar had, anyway, but the lines on this kind of thing get blurry after a few thousand hours of gameplay. 'This is a potion of experience! This is the best thing to happen to me all week!'

'Haha, yeah!' Arries had laughed. He had the voice of a natural encourager, the kind of person who could cheerfully talk you into anything without ever seeming like he was trying to. Which was something I really liked about him but should probably have put me more on guard.

He'd already talked me into voice chat ('it'll be so much more convenient than typing while we play!') and joining his in-game guild ('I'll get you better gear from the guild equipment and you can finally do that sixteen player raid!'), and though it seemed insane whenever I thought back, I'd given him my phone number ('we can text each other whenever we're online!') which I think was three more things than anyone had talked me into ever.

Truthfully, he might not have gotten past my guard even so if he hadn't been asexual, like me, and aromantic besides. Easier to befriend someone I knew wasn't likely to use my contact details to bombard me with dick pics.

We even lived in the same town. I think it excited him that we could meet in person one day. I wasn't so sure, which was why in two years I'd never suggested it. I was 32 and not worried about being an object of prey; I just wasn't great at 'in-person'.

Arries' laughter had faded into silence, which was always a warning sign. 'Wait — this was really the best thing to happen to you all week?'

I had stared at the game, trying to see this robed-and-hooded lizardman healer as anything more than pixels on a screen. 'When you say it like *that*, it sounds sad,' I'd said.

His character had raised his hands. 'XP potions *are* ultra-rare and amazing,' he said.

'Right,' I'd said.

'So I'm not suggesting that you couldn't have had a week full of fun and thrills ...'

I had frowned at the screen. 'I don't like the way you say "thrills".'

'... Have you, though?'

☆ 2 ☆

'Arries!' I had conked him on the head with the pommel of my sword. 'Yes, my week of guiding bored customers through a lifeless tourist trap museum has been exhilarating.' I'd paused. 'It doesn't matter. I don't need anything more thrilling than this.'

'Okay,' he'd said, like he was talking me down from a ledge. 'Wanna trigger the boss fight?'

'Sure,' I had replied. But it had niggled at me. And twenty minutes and several resurrections later, when we were sitting on the mountainous form of the fallen undead yeti and were dividing the spoils, I said, 'You work full-time and still play A:RO four hours a day.'

'Yeah?'

I had chewed my lip, staring at the screen. 'So this game is your whole life, too.' I'd winced at the sound of my own voice. I'd sounded defensive, and I hated sounding defensive. I wanted to be the kind of person who could let things go. Who could breeze through life unaffected.

I was not breezy, however. Not then, and not now. If I was weather, I'd be suffocating still air or gale force winds, with no in-between. Maybe that was good, though. Mum was the kind of person people described as breezy, but she was also the kind of person who got parking tickets every week and had four psychics in her phone contacts.

'I wouldn't say it's my whole life,' Arries had said 'I socialise a lot. You know: parties. Game nights. I'm in a lot of clubs, too.'

'You go clubbing?' I'd boggled, trying to paint a picture of this guy I'd known for two years through the world's third most popular online roleplaying game and match it up with the kind of person who got into a lot of clubs.

'No, clubs. You know — tennis, bowling. I'm in a knitting group, too.'

'Right, that makes sense.' I'd wiped a bit of sweat from my brow. Sweating made me feel uncomfortable, like I was being watched — or worse, smelled. Which you might think wouldn't matter when the person I was talking to was at the other end of an internet connection, but you'd be underestimating my ability to worry.

We'd discussed the loot a bit more, Arries giving me all his biggest weapons and spikiest armour, me giving him all the magic scrolls I'd collected. A pause, then: 'Tar?'

'Yeah?'

'Are you, you know ... happy?'

'My therapist thinks so,' I'd said. Then, because I hated lying: 'That was a joke, by the way.'

'A joke because you don't have a therapist or a joke because you have one and she thinks you're unhappy?'

'Kind of both,' I'd admitted. 'I'm meant to have a therapist but I kind of hate her. Her job seems to consist entirely of trying to make me do things I don't want to do.'

'Like what?'

'Like talk about my feelings,' I'd said. 'Which we are somehow doing. Now. Instead of playing.'

'Sorry, I didn't mean to — look, do you want to join my TTRPG group?'

'Your what?'

'Tabletop Role-playing Game,' he'd said, and his voice took on a reverence I'd only heard when people talked about god. 'Tar, it's the real deal.'

'You're going to have to explain more than that,' I'd said. 'I'm not sure I know what the 'fake' deal is either.'

'It's like *Lairs & Lizards*. You've heard of that, right? It's ... it's another world. Another life, you know? Like A:RO, except you can do anything. Anything at all. But it's still fun, because there are consequences and like ... story. Like a cross between a book and an MMO.' MMOs being games like A:RO, where you role-played alongside other players.

I had heard of *Lairs & Lizards*. It conjured to mind thick rulebooks and dice rolls and people acting out their characters. I didn't know how I felt about that.

'I already have both of those things,' I'd said.

☆ 4 ☆

'This is better,' he'd said. 'This is a game that'll change your life.'

And somehow, a week later I'd donned my glasses, my A:RO hoodie and my least ratty jeans, tied my ash-blonde hair into a tail, and glared at my own reflection. Pale-skinned, round-faced, rounder-bodied. As ready as I'd ever be.

I'd left the house where I lodged in my small room, and now I was standing on the doorstep of Arries' mysterious 'lair master' which he assured me was not even a tenth as kinky as it sounded.

Because even though I hated change, I was ready for it. I wanted 'the real deal'. I wanted escapism on a higher level than online fantasy games could give me.

Needed it, really.

So, when a shadow passed across the frosted glass inserts and the door clicked with the sound of a key turning in the lock, I tensed but I didn't flee as my prey animal 'fight or flight' instincts urged me to.

The door swung open and there was a guy I'd never seen before, somehow taking up the entire doorway with his smile. I flinched from the intensity of it. He looked late twenties, which was only a handful of years younger than me but it felt like centuries. He was short and broad, with jewel brown skin and short black hair in a twist-out style.

He was also wearing an A:RO hoodie, the twin of my own.

'TarAntula?' He said, and being greeted by my username forced a smile from me.

'It's just Tar, IRL,' I said, and his smile somehow got even bigger.

'I feel like I should hug you. Can I hug you?'

I laughed. 'I'd rather you didn't,' I said, because I was certain that I was even now becoming disgustingly sticky with what I called 'the social sweats'.

If he thought I was sweaty, he didn't say it. He said, 'Come in! Come in! The *actual* TarAntula, in the flesh, at my actual lair master's house. Shoes go there,' he said, as casually as if he lived here, but I knew he didn't. It was shared between the lair master and one of the players.

I toed off my shoes, stumbling as I did. Arries grabbed my elbow to save me from face-planting directly into the wall. He quickly released me when I'd stabilised.

I wasn't normally clumsy but I was so damn nervous.

'You okay?' he said. I didn't think he was talking about my near-miss with a concussion. Even though I'd never seen his face before, everything about his expression seemed familiar — it was a look of friendly concern that perfectly matched the voice of my best friend.

I'd never really had IRL friends before. It was a strange feeling — terrifying, but not terrible. Maybe this whole 'in real life' thing would work out. 'I don't know,' I said, because my chest was tight and I was sweaty and my thoughts were jumping between flatline and defibrillator. 'Can we pretend that I am?'

'Fake it 'til you make it,' he said, his smile toned down to something more gentle. 'Yeah, we can do. And you will be. Okay, I mean. I've got a good feeling about this.'

'About me?'

'About the party — the TTRPG adventuring party.' And he got a sort of glint in his eyes. 'I get the feeling you're going to be *exactly* what we need.'

'You need an anxious recluse?'

He gestured that I follow him down a spotless pastel-blue corridor that wouldn't look out of place in a showhome. All the doors were closed. It smelled of cinnamon and roses, likely from the diffusers plugged in at the wall.

'We need a new perspective,' said Arries. 'An outsider.'

'An outsider,' I repeated. I crossed my arms because it made me feel safer even though I'd been told it made me look unfriendly. I could handle that. I'd been an outsider in every situation I'd ever been in. I couldn't imagine this being any different.

☆ 6 ☆

Arries opened the door at the end of the corridor and stepped inside, sweeping his hand to encompass the room. 'Everyone, meet Tar. Tar, welcome to Kin, and the Amethyst Hand.'

I got one quick look at a dice-scattered table and the four unfamiliar figures seated at it before my gaze dropped to my feet and I was seized by the urge to run.

CHAPTER TWO

I backed up, bumping into the doorframe. Though I kept my gaze low, I could *feel* their eyes on me, like someone had turned several searchlights in my direction.

I didn't want to look like a frightened rabbit, so I raised my gaze, but I couldn't quite bear to meet any of their eyes yet. They all looked roughly my age. I took in the room. Modern floral wallpaper in bold patterns. The longest wall fully lined with bookshelves stuffed with board games and guidebooks. A worn, long table of dark oak surrounded by padded chairs, bringing to mind a conference room.

'Nice to meet you,' I mumbled, as I had been trained to as a little kid, but what I wanted to say was, *'There's been some sort of mistake, I'm not supposed to mix with people.'*

'I suppose,' said a woman sitting behind a dragon art screen. She had shoulder-length black box braids tipped with gold beads. Her dark eyes weighed me in a way I didn't like, and she was impressive in an elegant, angular way, like a ballerina. She wore a knitted cardigan in a mixture of reds, blues, and greens, autumnal and beautiful against her cool umber skin. The sleeves were rolled up neatly to the elbow. A purple wheelchair was tucked into the corner beside her.

Another woman tossed her ombre beach curls and leaned forward, resting her hands on the table. She was pale and pink-cheeked, with lean, muscled arms and a hard grey gaze. 'Don't fucking listen to Pauline; she's not a people person. And possibly not a human at all, but some kind of rule-obsessed cyborg.' She was wearing what looked like a blue tennis dress, branded leggings, and another hand-knitted cardigan, this one deep red. There was the start of a knitting project on the table beside her; I wondered if she went to the same club as Arries.

'Hanna.' The first woman, Pauline, could take a tone that was only one step above a growl. She frowned at the other woman.

A big guy nearly my equal in fatness turned in his seat, putting his elbow on the back of the chair and smiling to one side in what could only be called a smirk. His skin was the colour of aged parchment and his eyes were brown and full of mirth. His hair was black, short on the sides, and combed back. 'Better sit down before a fight breaks out. Unless you'd find that amusing; I know I would.' He gestured to the seat between him and a guy with his hood up, and although I hated being walled in by strangers I couldn't see a non-awkward way out of it. I edged in between him and the other guy — as narrow-boned as the first guy was broad.

'I'm Kenta,' said the first. 'Ken is fine.' He looked like the kind of person who liked to shake hands, but perhaps he could read my nerves in the tight set of my shoulders, because he didn't attempt that hated social nicety.

'Tar,' I replied, before remembering that Arries had already introduced me.

'Short for Tara?'

I stiffened at the traditionally feminine name.

'Short for TarAntula!' Arries said excitedly, taking the seat across from me.

I didn't usually tell people my full name. It led to assumptions, some of them woefully accurate. 'Just Tar,' I said. 'They/Them.'

Kenta looked chagrined. 'Oh! Right, Arries said.'

I resisted the urge to touch my chest and reassure myself that there were no breasts there. I knew I was still read as feminine in most contexts. It was a look I liked. I wasn't so much trans masc as agender. But being misgendered still made my skin itch in a way I didn't like.

I glanced at the man sitting on my other side, but his head was lowered, his expression hard to read between the waterfall of thick pink-and-black locs obscuring the side of his face and the white hoodie he wore with hood drawn. His skin was a cool, dark brown. As I watched, his long fingers drummed on an open binder thick with character stats and spells; more paper than anyone else had in front of them, except possibly Pauline, as I couldn't see behind her special screen. I sort of wanted to ask him about it, but as he hadn't spoken yet, I couldn't see how I would.

'Rex, are you going to introduce yourself?' Arries' tone was patronisingly encouraging. I grimaced in sympathy.

'It seems that you just did,' he replied. He turned his head toward me so that he could look at me without really looking at me, which was honestly a relief. He had a sharp jaw-line and high cheekbones. 'Sorry. Welcome to the party.'

I dipped my head in acknowledgement. Without really thinking about it, I started rubbing my legs, which relieved some of my restlessness.

'Do you need help making a character?' Pauline asked. 'I'm willing to assist you. Or I have a pre-generated character you can play if you'd prefer. An NPC I was planning to introduce.' A Non-Player Character, or the background and side characters of a game that were part of the game world rather than player-controlled.

It was a relief that the terminology was so similar to video games. Made it feel less like I was diving headfirst into a pool of unknown depth.

'I um ... I've actually already made a character,' I said. 'If that's all right?'

There was a beat before Pauline said, 'Of course.' I tried to hide my embarrassment. I wondered if this was a TTRPG faux pas. Even among other geeks, I was the awkward one ... 'Mind if I take a look?'

I handed Pauline my character sheet and supporting materials, thicker than anyone but Rex's. Not so much because I was playing a complicated character as that I wanted to make sure I had everything I'd need ready.

'You didn't find the rules confusing?' Arries looked impressed. 'I always find the rules confusing.'

'Beginners usually struggle,' said Kenta. 'You must be smart.'

I didn't think I was especially unintelligent, but I was also pretty sure it was more down to the week I'd spent poring over the rulebook and drawing up character build ideas than any inherent cleverness. I'd been frustrated that as it was a 'homebrew' or homemade game, there weren't any character builds or guides online.

'Or a total nerd, like Rex and P,' said Hanna, as if she could read it on my skin. 'No offense to you other nerds.'

'We can be both,' said Rex, flipping through his binder.

'Hanna ... you're playing *Kin* too.' Kenta rolled his eyes.

Hanna shrugged. 'I'm only playing because *Pauline* is my housemate and she runs the game. Besides, a cool person can play a TTRPG and still be cool. Nerdiness is inherent. You fucking nerds were already in too deep before we started. And rules nerd is on a whole other level. That's the bottom of the pile.' She bared her teeth at me. 'Don't worry. I'm great with nerds.'

'And children, I bet,' I said, then blinked as she burst into laughter. She laughed like a bear might laugh, throwing her head back and guffawing.

'Fucking *burn,*' she said, one hand on her chest. 'I'll remember that.' But the words held no venom. If anything, she looked pleased.

What a terrifying woman. Yet, I already kind of liked her. It would be easy to tell what she was thinking, considering she clearly didn't bother to filter at all.

'So what's your build like?' This from Rex, beside me. His voice was mellow and hesitant.

'Healer!' Arries jumped in before I could say anything. 'I am barely holding this team together with one heal spell.'

'Oh my *god*, do we need a healer,' said Hanna. 'We're always *this close* from a total party kill.'

'Because you keep getting us into fights we can't win,' said Kenta.

'No. Because P won't balance the fights for a party without healers!'

'You're not dead yet,' Pauline murmured, still looking through my sheet.

'I didn't take any healing spells,' I said. I looked at Pauline to see if this would be a problem, just as she finished the last sheet.

'This is good,' she said. 'You even wrote some backstory I can work with. Most of them have barely glanced at the rules.' She passed it all back to me.

'I definitely *glanced* at the rules,' said Kenta, spreading his hands.

Hanna rolled her eyes. 'What's the point of having a lair master if I have to learn the rules?'

'I make the story,' said Pauline, face impassive.

'The *players* make the story,' said Hanna.

'Both can be true,' said Arries, looking anxiously between the two.

I looked around the group. With all their fast-paced bickering, there was a feeling of family about this group. I got the sense they had known each other a long time, and I liked that, but it was hard not to feel like an intruder.

There was a lot here I liked. The room, with its wall lined with alphabetically organised board game shelves and an entire bookcase devoted to RPG books of all kinds. The way all the chairs around this long table were padded desk chairs, as if this whole room was set up specifically for this.

But liking it didn't make me feel any more comfortable, or feel any less like I needed to bolt. I kept my exit strategy in my mind — I'd told my mum to call me in an hour. If I couldn't cope, I would use that call to make my excuses.

'Are you a spellcaster?' Rex asked quietly while Hanna and Pauline's standoff continued over Arries' head. His words distracted me from the increasingly knotty feeling in my brain.

I smoothed my hands over my carefully crafted character sheet. When I'd been building it, it had seemed like the most incredible character in the world. I'd customised everything the game allowed, sucked in by the depth and complexity you could build into a character just by following the basic rules. I'd been excited to become them, however briefly, and at his question I could feel stats and backstory bubbling up. 'Actually, I'm playing a —'

'No meta-gaming!' Pauline's voice was sharp. Her head whipped around to face me. She looked like she'd been mid-argument with Hanna.

The words dried up in my mouth.

'*Fuck*, Pauline. Don't scare them.' Hanna rolled her eyes.

Pauline inclined her head. 'Sorry. I don't allow meta-gaming — using outside, out-of-character knowledge in-game. Your introduction will be more natural if the other players know nothing of your character until you're introduced. Speaking of which: you might as well forget all the names you just learned because you're only allowed to refer to each other by your in-character names.'

'Are all TTRPGs as strict as this?' I asked.

'Pauline's a natural dictator,' said Kenta. 'We're very lucky to have her here.'

'Instead of in Parliament,' said Hanna.

Arries smiled encouragingly. 'Don't listen to them. Pauline's lovely.'

'Deep down,' said Kenta.

Beside me, I heard Rex murmur, 'She's the best. Only the axe murderer LMs ever are.'

It was hard to keep up with their pace and energy, but I liked it. I smiled nervously around the table, not meeting anyone's eyes.

'We have a rule, by the way,' Pauline said. 'You can leave the table whenever you need to. Just stand up and I'll pause the game. If you need to quit early, just let me know. We don't need a reason.'

'It's for me,' Rex said in a low voice. 'I'm autistic. Sometimes I just need to go.'

'Oh! Me too.' I didn't know what to make of that. I hadn't had much to do with other neurodivergent people. Just Arries, who had ADHD and no anxiety to speak of, so we had as much in common as not. A seed of hope planted in my belly. Maybe I could fit in here. Maybe.

Rex smiled to one side, turning over a page in his binder. 'Tap my binder if you want to go early,' he said. 'I'll get us out.'

Pauline's watch beeped; she casually muted it, but the whole table fell silent. I glanced at my phone: 12pm, the official start time. I took out my bag of dice — seven odd little polyhedrons — and spilled them onto the table. I'd spent a full week deciding which set of dice to get. They came in so many beautiful colours, and there were even shops online that custom-made them with flowers or plants trapped in the resin. I'd decided to be in-theme with my character and had done just that, getting a crystal-clear set of dice with tiny spirals of moss inside.

Pauline took a long breath. When she next spoke, her voice was even and calm.

'Barely escaped from the betrayal at the Obsidian Palace, the Amethyst Hand slog through a swamp: wounded, pursued, and uncertain who to trust. The shapeshifter posing as Queen Ivemaya has taken control of Uxrn, and you decided that your only hope was to disappear, and make your way through the Long Marsh to the kingdom of Tormalan. Night is falling ...'

As she wove a story recapping the group's most recent adventures, I could feel it coming alive in my mind's eye. The players started to chime in with their own actions — what they wanted to do now, in the present, occasionally rolling dice to resolve actions. But I could barely process the mechanics of the game. It was all background noise to the story — to the adventurers of the Amethyst Hand, who I was soon to meet.

I let myself sink into the character of Astaran, witch of the Silver Grove, waiting for Pauline to signal my entrance, and hoping desperately that I wasn't about to screw this up.

CHAPTER THREE

I watched from the trees as the outsiders passed below.

Their steps were heavy and laden in the bog; they were unable to handle the thick swamp muck. I wondered whether they would be eaten by the grove guardians. I wondered whether I should care. And yet I was concerned; not for their lives, but for the danger they brought. Weapons hung from their belts or were strapped to their backs. Though obscured under heavy cloaks, I could hear the jingle of mail and the creak of leather. Armour, then, as well.

My grip tightened on the claw gifted to me by The Old One before she passed: a curved sickle taken from a cruel farmer who'd been poisoning the local wildlife in a scheme for gold and glory, honed over the years and given a handle of blessed ash. I didn't want to fight these people — they were numerous and of unknown strength and power. But I could not let them pass unchallenged if they meant us harm.

And sadly, many did, these days.

I followed them from the trees, watching closely.

(Pauline: Astaran, make a stealth check. Roll a d20 and add your Stealth die — yeah, for you that's a d6. So the twenty-sided die and the six-sided one.)

(Me: 18? Is that good?)

'Are we there yet?' said the smallest one. She was maybe four feet tall, with deer-like legs and doe-like ears and features. A feykin, most likely. She was also pale purple. Her black hair was in a long twisting plait that came over one shoulder. I could see a flash of opulent dark fabric under her cloak, and though the others carried weapons, she had a flute hanging from her belt.

'No.' replied one of her companions The man wasn't especially large, but was broad, and by the bulk of his cloak, armoured as well. He rubbed his chin tiredly. If he had any extraplanar traits at all, I couldn't detect them. A rare thing to see. 'We're obviously not there yet, and we obviously weren't there yet the last hundred times you asked. The gods have terrible punishments for complainers.'

'Not any gods I've heard of,' said the peach-furred fox-man on the man's other side. Another feykin. His large, wedge-shaped ears twitched, taking in the surroundings. He had a bright shine in his eyes and his stance was far less beleaguered than the others in spite of his heavy golden plate armour. Though there was just as much mud climbing his shins, he seemed as cheerful as if he were taking a stroll through the woods.

'Maybe not your Gods, Arries, but *my* god definitely does.'

(Me: I thought we weren't allowed to use our real names?)

(Arries: I get special dispensation. When you have a name this good, you use it as much as possible.)

(Hanna: Arries comes from a nerd lineage. His mum's a Tolkien scholar and his dad's an anime weeb.)

The feykin woman sighed and pressed her hand to her forehead, like a noblewoman in full-swoon. 'I can't go on any longer. Carry me, Kendallien!'

'You'll get mud on my cloak.'

'There's *already* mud on your cloak.'

'I'll carry you,' said Arries. He offered the feykin a hand, which she took, and he lifted her onto his shoulders.

'See? At least someone has respect for the leader of this party.'

'You're not the leader,' said the final member of their group. He'd been silent until now and had barely drawn my eye, but now I noticed that his hood was misshapen. I could just make out a sharp chin and dark brown skin.

'Who talks us into jobs and out of tight situations? Who is always the first person to submit a strategy?'

'Leadership doesn't default to whoever is shouting the loudest,' he replied. He glanced up at the treeline, and for a moment I froze, certain that his gaze had landed on me. But all he said was, 'It's getting dark. We need to set up camp for the night.'

(Rex: Natural 20 on Perception!)

(Me: Does that mean he sees me?)

I tensed. I did not want these outsiders chopping wood and destroying trees. As the broad one took a hatchet from his belt, I knew that it was time to act.

I dropped down from the tree, landing lightly atop a rock, free of the mud. My claw was loose in one hand and with the other I summoned a wind that threw back their hoods.

Immediately, a rope snaked around my ankle.

(Pauline: Astaran, roll Agility. That's your Agility skill die plus a D20)

(Me: Oh no. I rolled a 1 on the D20 — is that bad?)

'Aargh!' I tried to skip away but it tightened and hoisted me into the air so that I was dangling from a tree by my ankle.

I could see the hooded one clearly now as his hood fell away. His hands sparkled with arcane energy and his eyes glowed an eerie blue, wisps of ethereal energy floating at the edges of his eyes. It was clear now that what had been hidden under his hood were two curling ram's horns, each embedded with crystalline imagery the same ethereal blue, then fading into ghostly points as if only half-corporeal. His ears were pointed and again faded at the tips and a lizard-like tail lashed the ground behind him — with similarly crystalline scales and ghostly edges — and he bared fanged teeth while he concentrated on his spell. A voidkin.

The broad one, Kendallien, immediately strode forward and placed the tip of his hatchet against my throat. 'Can I kill them?' he asked mildly. 'I'd really like to kill them.'

'Not yet! We don't even know who they are!' Hanley, the little bard, scrambled down from the golden-armoured feykin to peer up at me. 'Who are you?' She asked. 'Why did you attack us?'

I stared pointedly at Kendallien until he huffed and eased up with his hatchet. 'I didn't attack you. I wanted to see who you are. You're trespassers in this sacred Grove!'

Hanley looked down at the mud climbing her thighs. *This* place is sacred? Are we looking at the same place?'

'Would you let me down?'

'Please Ram?' Arries, the armoured foxman asked. 'It looks uncomfortable.'

'Bleeding heart,' Kendallien muttered.

The voidkin met my eyes with his. 'No sudden moves,' he warned. With a sudden slicing motion with his hands, the rope released me.

(Me: I rolled a 21 on Agility!)

I twisted in the air and just managed to get my feet under me, stumbling slightly. Hanley put out a hand to steady me. I flinched at her touch, but she seemed to mean well.

'We're the Amethyst Hand, defenders of Vanthis,' she told me. Something about the way she said the words, some trick of her voice, made the words sound laden with destiny.

'For hire,' Kendallien added with a dark chuckle.

Hanley gave him a narrow look. 'We ... are on an important mission.' She looked me up and down. 'There's a great threat to nature in this area —'

Arries' furry brow furrowed. 'There is?'

'— and we need to pass safely through this swamp to deal with it.' She looked me up and down. 'You look like you know the area. Perhaps you could guide us?'

(Me: Do I believe her?)

(Pauline: Hanley, roll Liar)

(Hanna: 28)

(Me: That's crazy!)

(Hanna: I'm very careful with my skill points)

(Pauline: Astaran, make a Social Instinct check opposed to Hanley's Liar.)

(Me: Okay, I rolled okay on the fate die but my skill die — oh no. 14?)

I considered her words, searching them for dishonesty. I had no reason to trust these people, but thus far they had done me no harm. 'What evil?' I asked.

'I don't completely know, but our instructions are clear.'

'Instructions from who?

Hanley hesitated a moment. 'A priest of Lunala,' she said, naming a forest guardian god — one of the fey ones, I thought.

(Me: Do I still believe her?)

(Pauline: She rolled high. You do.)

'All right,' I said. 'I'll show you the way through the swamp. But I warn you: this land is sacred. And the creatures in it are not all peaceful.' I glanced around us. 'Tread lightly.'

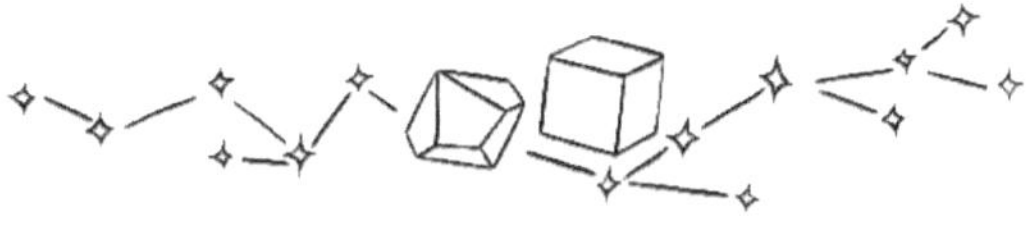

CHAPTER FOUR

I was surprised by how fun the game was. I felt completely immersed despite not knowing where they were in the story or one hundred percent understanding the rules. All the study and character planning I'd done had helped a lot but I still felt a little out of my depth.

I looked around at the others. They laughed and smiled while they packed away their character sheets and dice. I hoped they couldn't tell that I was drenched in sweat. Although I'd enjoyed myself, my entire body ached from sitting tense and rigidly for four hours of play. It was the longest I think I'd ever spent in an IRL social situation, and by the end of the game I hadn't been able to stop myself from rocking in my seat to ease the nervous energy built up inside of me. Somehow it had still passed quickly.

Kenta nudged me with his elbow, making me jump. 'So how'd you find it?' he asked, clearly not realising the panic spiral this unexpected contact had sent me down.

'Um, good,' I said. 'I like how creative it is.' I tried to tell myself to calm down, that just because I'd been touched once didn't mean that it would happen again, that it was only a small thing that a neurotypical person probably wouldn't even notice. But I still felt panicked about the whole thing.

'You did a good job adjusting to the way different traits are labelled,' Rex said. 'It's hard to adjust from games with fantasy "races" to one where you just identify people by their most noticeable magical traits.'

Like how Hanley had been feykin because fauns were associated with the Fey Plane of the Glamouring, or how Ram had been Voidkin because of the voidshadow highlights to his appearance. In Kin, people could have traits from multiple sources, and they could be caused by curses, circumstances of birth, or any number of other things, not just heritage. Made it easier to customise your character, too. 'Oh, I like that about it,' I said. 'I spent a lot of time on character creation so I think I absorbed that bit of the lore okay.'

'Haven't scared you off yet, then?' Kenta grinned and pat my shoulder. 'It's good to have new blood.' His hand felt heavy.

He was just being friendly, I told myself, even though it made me feel sick and cornered, made the air feel too thick to breathe. There was nothing sleazy or inappropriate about his behaviour, but I was exhausted after four hours playing a new game with several strangers and I no longer had the capacity to pretend to be neurotypical. Masking my autism always wore me out, doubly so when I was also flooded with social anxiety. I tried to smile and say something reassuring but no words would come.

I glanced at Arries but he was excitedly miming out the battle we'd had to Hanna, who rolled her eyes but was barely concealing a smile.

'*Ken.* You can't just touch people, we've been over this.' I glanced around at Rex. He'd put his hood down during the game, revealing that his locs had been pulled into a neat tail that hung over one shoulder. His shoulders were hunched defensively as he glared at Kenta, making eye contact for the first time that I could tell the entire afternoon.

'I thought that was just with you?' Kenta said.

'It's with everyone.'

'Are you — ah, sorry.' He looked sheepish as he registered my expression for the first time. 'I forget sometimes that not everyone's like me. I'll do better. I'm getting a drink — anyone want anything?'

Rex and I shook our heads and Kenta got up and headed into Pauline's kitchen. Pauline looked up from the notes she was writing up to call sharply, 'And this time don't break anything!'

'You okay?' Rex asked quietly. Again, avoiding my eyes. I was struck by how soft his voice was — when he was playing, he spoke with a lot more conviction and confidence, but now he seemed to shrink into himself. 'It's okay to just get up and leave if you need to. Nobody'll hold it against you, and Pauline's surprisingly chill about that kind of thing.'

I nodded and drew a shuddering breath. 'I was hoping to get through today without any awkwardness.'

He shrugged. 'You're not that bad.'

Pauline winced as she stood up and took a few steps to the wall of board games. It looked like the movement was painful, but she threw a smile over her shoulder. 'Anyone for beer and board games now?' she asked. 'We can order takeaway — *healthy* takeaway,' she said with a glare at Hanna.

'I'm plenty healthy,' Hanna muttered. She was easily the most athletic-looking person in the room.

I wasn't prepared for this. I scooped my dice into their pouch and stood up. 'I actually have somewhere I need to be,' I said. 'Um — but thank you. I'd definitely like to come again, if — you know —'

'We're not gonna give up our witch!' said Arries. He gave me a concerned look. 'Are you sure you won't stay? Pauline has a really good selection of games.'

I nodded — well, more of a sharp jerk of my head. 'I'm sure. Thanks though. Uh ... bye.' I edged past Kenta.

Arries stood up. 'I'll see you out.'

'It's okay, I'm going anyway,' said Rex.

'Thanks Rex — oh! Tar! I'll send you a link to the party chatroom. Thanks for coming!'

I nodded again and ducked out the door, Rex on my heels. He had a black backpack slung over one shoulder — I noticed the A:RO logo on it but was now far too nervous to ask.

'You don't have to go on the chatroom if you don't want to,' he said. He quickly slid on his shoes, still tied. They were thick high-tops with white soles and purple fabric. 'And they don't really mind whether we stay for beer and board games — well, Arries does, but he just wants to surround himself with everyone he loves all the time.'

'Do um — do you go on the chatroom?' I asked. I knelt to put on my shoes and he hovered awkwardly, waiting for me to finish.

He dipped his head. 'Yeah. Yeah. I like these guys, but I find it easier when I'm not ... I find it easier online.'

I smiled tightly. 'I get that.' I stood up and he let us out. We both paused on the doorstep. 'See you next week,' I said.

He nodded, again not meeting my eyes, and we both walked in different directions away from Pauline's house.

I got an email from Arries not long later with a link to a chatroom labelled 'The Amethyst Hand'. My thumb hovered over it a moment, then I switched off my screen and headed for my little beat-up Nissan Micra and from there, home.

'Home' was a lodger's room in a semi-detached house on the outskirts of Goosey. I walked down a street with sad yellow grass and sweaty trees, looking for the cherry-blossom pink house I'd lived in for the last 2 years.

I intended to vanish into my room. My encounters with my host and her daughter were infrequent and I intended to keep it that way. I never knew what to say to them and didn't want them to think I didn't like them. It seemed easier to keep my distance than to fumble through conversation and accidentally offend them. But as I came through the door, there was a scene I couldn't easily skirt.

Saanvi, a woman with tired eyes, russet-brown skin, and a crow-black pixie cut, was on her knees wrestling with her six year-old daughter who was, I realised with a start, only wearing underwear.

'It's a fancy dress party, Riya! You need to be *dressed* for a fancy dress party!'

★ 24 ★

'No!' Riya clenched her fists and dodged her mother's attempt to pull a spiderman costume over her head.

'You need a costume, sweetheart!'

I edged toward the stairs.

'I *have* a costume,' Riya shouted. 'I'm a BABY!'

Saanvi saw me and a look of pained embarrassment crossed her face. She ushered her daughter into the sitting room. 'Babies wear *clothes*.'

'Do not!'

I scurried upstairs and closed the door to my bedroom, trying to ignore the tight feeling in my chest that I had handled the situation wrong. My mother would have made a joke. Arries would probably have tried to help — though whether he would have sided with Saanvi or Riya, I didn't know.

Thinking of my mother, I cringed as I flopped onto my bed. I'd cancelled her call earlier — we'd been mid-way through a tricky battle with will-o-wisps and I hadn't wanted to miss anything. I'd sent her a short text in apology, but I knew that wouldn't be enough when I'd specifically asked her to call me.

I put my hands on my head and just ... yelled wordlessly from the bed, letting out all the pressure and build-up in my chest. Not as loud as I wanted to; Saanvi was used to the occasional outburst from me, but I still didn't want to startle her or Riya.

Eventually, the cry died out. I felt a little better. I looked around my room — curtained, cool, with a galaxy-coloured bedspread and books piled up along the walls. Some clothes were scattered across the bed beneath me — the remnants of my early-morning outfit panic. It all looked and smelled so perfectly of home — my own bed, my own books, my own desk, my own A:RO posters on the walls. I'd hoped to just go home and spend the entire evening on A:RO, trying not to obsess over every last awkward thing I'd said and done at the game, but I knew I owed it to my mum to give her a call.

She picked up on the first ring. 'That was very rude of you, darling.'

I gazed at the smooth white ceiling of my bedroom. 'Sorry, mum.'

'I've always been puzzled by this sort of behaviour in you. I was so careful to have you in July, but you're not like any Cancer sign I've ever known. Always so independent, so withdrawn. Anyone would think you were an Aquarius.'

I rolled my eyes at the phone, but I didn't take the bait — every few months my mum tried to trick me into letting her hold court over my star sign, the minute details of my birth, and what her psychics had told her about me. Sometimes I corrected her out of irritation without thinking, and I got sucked right in. But today I was apologising, which put me in a generous enough mood that she could talk all the nonsense she wanted without getting a rise out of me.

'What was so important you wanted to arrange a phone call, anyway? You weren't,' her voice turned stern, something that sounded out of place in her breezy, gossipy voice. 'You *weren't* trying to escape another date, were you?'

'No! Mum, I don't date anymore —'

'Because I really think you need to develop a more graceful exit strategy than having your mum call you and maybe you should give these young men and women more of a chance —'

'Mum! It wasn't that. I went to play a —' I hesitated, trying to think of how best to explain this to my mum. 'Do you know what a role-playing game is?'

There was a pause at the other end of the line. 'I'm glad you feel comfortable enough to talk about it with me, but I didn't think you were into that kind of thing, darling. It's good to experiment, though —'

'No! Mum. It's ... like Lairs & Lizards? You know ... it's like a board game? Everyone tells a story together about, like ... elves and wizards ...' I hazarded that she might recognise those as fantasy '... and roll dice and stuff?'

'Well — that sounds exactly like your sort of thing, darling. Whyever did you need me to call?'

I hesitated. 'There were people there I didn't know, and I thought, if I panicked ...'

'You met people? Darling, that's wonderful!'

'Yeah,' I said. Although I'd found the game itself to be a dream-like experience, I still wasn't entirely convinced of the 'other people' part of it. They probably all hated me. I'd been so awkward and I'd had to stop Pauline every few minutes to explain the rules ...

'Well, I'm glad you called me, anyway. My astrologer cast my chart today and she could see that there was a particular convergence in my future, so she suggested I do a tarot reading for the specifics, and I really think it might concern you, darling, because ...'

I let my mum tell me all about the reading, even going as far as to confirm or deny recent events in my life, to her delight or disappointment. Although I didn't believe in astrology, or psychics, or whatever new fortune-telling fad my mum favoured at the moment, I felt myself relax as she spoke. I sort of liked how she was always looking forward, how confident of her own destiny she was. My mum knew who she was and she knew where she was going — and she made sure her psychics confirmed it.

Me, I felt adrift at any point in my life. Like I didn't know where or why anything in my life happened, like someone else had pre-plotted my every step, and had done a patchy job of it.

I liked that for the space of a conversation, I didn't have to say much. And I could pretend, however briefly, that there was any sort of excitement or adventure in my future.

The evening after she hung up wasn't kind to me. I felt wrung out, bruised inside and out, with lungs that were squeezed too thin. I'd never been very good at processing emotions, and now, with nothing to distract me from *feeling* everything that had happened that day, it was like standing in oncoming traffic.

There was nothing I could do but crawl under a duvet and try to pick up the pieces of myself in the morning.

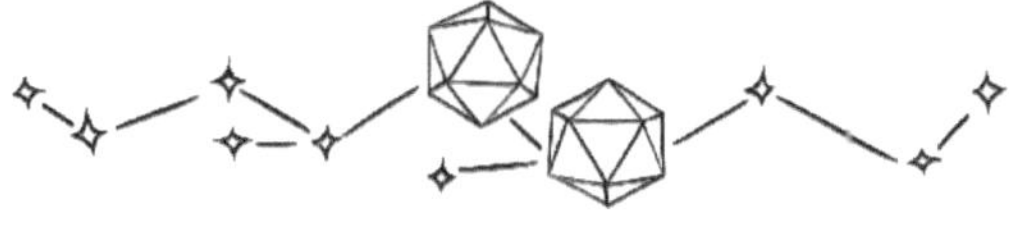

CHAPTER FIVE

'Welcome to the Elfred Bevin Museum, commemorating Goosey's most famous mayor, Elfred Hywel Ieuan Bevin. Please, allow me to guide you on a journey into Goosey's past.'

I bared my teeth at the small huddle of poncho-wearing tourists waiting at reception. I hated this moment, when I had to introduce myself to the unsuspecting customers and give them the most boring tour of their lives. They were sure to feel disappointed, and it was incredibly awkward the way I had to just walk up to them and begin my spiel. But I wore my uniform of khaki trousers and Bevin-Museum blue polo like armour, and my script was my shield. All I had to do was drag them after me, recite my lines, and wait for the next gaggle of Goosey-visitors to arrive.

They looked, to me, like any other tourists — just as frazzled and windswept, with that classic English summer look of rained-on and sweaty. I kept up a smile that made my cheeks hurt and guided them through Bevin's life of inane and sometimes odd achievement.

'In 1956, Elfred Bevin was the first mayor of Goosey ever elected who hadn't been born in Goosey. In fact, Bevin was born in Blyth-on-Wye, a full fifty miles away in Wales. This caused a controversy that would change Goosey council politics for years to come ...

'As well as a baker, Bevin was a savvy businessman. Cornish pasties were growing in popularity at the time, and he seized his opportunity. He saw a key niche in the market and seized it, modifying the Cornish recipe by replacing onion with radish and selling his pasties with a mustard relish. The Goosey Pasty is now local legend and no longer sold in bakeries, but you can try one here at the Bevin Museum's on-site historical café ...

'In 1972, Bevin wanted to put Goosey on the map by investing in space travel. The resulting fire in the engine shed spread across 5 acres of land, but the ashy soil proved to be the perfect environment for the rare Goosey-blue thistle, which had gone nearly extinct but in the aftermath of the fire, exploded in numbers ...'

The tourists ahhed and yawned by turn as I showed them Bevin's characteristic '*Bore Da*' tea pot which he'd hand-turned himself, and let them see Bevin's bright-feathered fishing lure collection, notable because he'd entered every fishing competition for ten years and never caught a single fish. I showed them a diorama of Bevin's space engine shed and let them each take a clipping from the museum's Goosey-blue thistle greenhouse. It felt like we were animatronics moving along on rails and reciting our pre-scripted lines, as did the next group, and the next group. Nobody was ever unexpected: even when small children were added to the mix, all that changed was that there was sniffling and tears from them and hissed warnings and mumbled reassurances from the parents.

When I got home after my five-hour shift, it felt like twenty. My brain was full of unfamiliar faces and the strain of being watched by so many eyes. My face hurt from hours of my mummer's grin. All I wanted was to play A:RO and forget the day had ever existed.

And I did, for a while, racking up XP on solo missions and killing beasts in the Summerglades in the hope of getting some useful loot. Arries wasn't online — probably at his knitting group — and it struck me that I wanted to talk to someone. I was exhausted from a day at work, but I didn't think I'd said a single non-scripted thing all day. And A:RO, as much as I loved it, was very repetitive — taking the same actions over and over again in the attempt to level up.

I rubbed my eyes and flopped back on my bed. disturbing the hoodies I'd left strewn across it. The last time I felt like I'd had anything new to say had been at the *Kin* game. Was that pathetic?

But it had been so creative and *so* vivid. In those few hours, I had somehow shaped myself into an entirely different person. To be honest, it had been a relief not to be *me*, however briefly.

And I still had no idea when the next one was.

I picked up my phone and let my thumb hover over the link in Arries' text, as I had done so many times over the last few days. It seemed ridiculous that I should seek these people out. They were already friends: I was an outsider. I was there to make up the numbers.

I remembered Arries thanking me for coming and Pauline inviting me to stay for games. I thought about Rex talking to me with eyes lowered, as casually as if all conversations were held that way. *'I like these guys,'* he'd said. *'But I find it easier when I'm not ... I find it easier online.'*

Me too, I thought.

I opened the link.

Five minutes and a frustrating login process later, and I had a username and a fuzzy spider to finish it off.

And the chat, as I scrolled down to catch up, was not at all what I had been expecting.

❀**Hanna:** I've locked myself into this bathroom and I'm not coming out until I'm *sure* she's gone.

❀**Hanna:** This is a fucking nightmare

❀**Hanna:** I can't believe you let me do this.

Kenta: It's not that bad.

❀Hanna: It *is* that bad! She's *MARRIED*. To a *MAN*.

❀Hanna: God, she was so nice about it too. Hot *AND* nice. And straight. Ugh. I could die right now.

Arries: You don't know she's straight.

❀Hanna: Who would marry a man if they had a choice?

Arries: That's biphobic, Han. And sexist.

Kenta: I'm trying my best to find a man to marry, personally.

❀Hanna: Right, sorry. That was shitty of me.

❀Hanna: You're allergic to commitment, Ken, you're not *trying* anything.

❀Hanna: AND MY SKIRT WAS TUCKED INTO MY LEGGINGS

❀Hanna: You're all a load of filthy enablers, every one of you.

Arries: You asked us to encourage you!

❀Hanna: Except for Rex, my only *true* friend

Rex♛: Pass through this world like a ghost, Hanna

❀Hanna: That is exactly the kind of freaky antisocial advice I should have taken, Rex.

Rex♛: It's all the younger siblings. I am a fount of brotherly wisdom.

I decided to jump in. It felt like the kind of private thing that would be rude for me to join, but at the same time, Hanna seemed to be holding court.

Tar♧: I have a lot of experience dodging people in cafés and restaurants

Arries: Tar!

Kenta: Oh man, I really thought we'd scared you off.

Rex♛: You. You thought YOU had scared them off.

Kenta: I'm not taking full credit for scariness

Kenta: I mean, look at Hanna

✿Hanna: Ken: go fuck yourself. Tar, I welcome your wisdom.

Tar♧: If she isn't sitting by the bathroom, just get out as quickly as possible. Walk straight out of the building.

✿Hanna: YES. I will do that. Wisdom accepted: the rest of you are still on my shitlist.

Arries: :(

Kenta: Is there a prize for being number one on that list?

Rex♛: I wouldn't know. I'M not on it.

❀Hanna: OK

❀Hanna: OK, I'm out

Pauline: Perhaps now we can go back on-topic?

Arries: P!

❀Hanna: God, you were here, too?

❀Hanna: Is there anyone I know who wasn't present for my brutal rejection?

Rex♛: Just the Amethyst Hand and God. If God wasn't busy.

❀Hanna: Weird

Kenta: Tar, I don't know if you saw the chat, but we were choosing a date for the next session. Any dates you can't do?

Tar⬡: No, my life is an empty void

Rex♛: relatable

Arries: Tar! :((

❀Hanna: Dark

Pauline: Perfect. Then it sounds like it'll be the 10th at 7pm. See you all then.

I smiled a little at the screen. It *had* felt like a safe distance. And it was nice that Hanna felt like she could go to the Amethyst Hand for advice and to vent. I made sure my settings

would notify me every time there was a new message in the
chat.

Somehow, it made me feel less isolated in my bedroom.
And it made the next *Kin* session feel a lot closer.

CHAPTER SIX

After a week of chatting on and off in the chatroom with the others, I was again standing on my lair master's doorstep and still resisting the urge to peg it back to my car.

I don't know what it is about my brain that puts me in a constant state of fleeing for my life, but my heart was beating way too fast and my chest was tight and I was pretty sure I'd forgotten everyone's names and also my own.

Currently, I was hovering, which was the first step before running. The prospect of going down a hallway into a closed room to sit around a table with several other people was pressing down on me and thus far I had not knocked, rang the bell, made any noises, or taken any actions such as might cause me to be noticed. Which was difficult because I could feel a bunch of clicking sounds building up in my chest waiting to be released. I would feel so much better if I stimmed ...

I was going to run. I could feel it coming on with the certainty of a hook in the gut drawing me away. I didn't know if I could face sitting on the outside of this group of friends again. I didn't know if I could bring myself to put on the stern voice of Astaran and act like I didn't mind that I wasn't part of this party yet — I was, to them, an NPC of unknown motivations.

NPC: Non-Player Character. It was a phrase that niggled at me, had always gotten under my skin. In games, it wasn't just that NPCs weren't the heroes — they weren't players. They had no active control in their lives. They weren't *real,* the way the players were real. Limited dialogue, limited actions, scripted behaviour. Sometimes I felt like that described me, because I didn't seem to have the words, the initiative, or the strength to direct my own life. Perhaps I was just an NPC in someone else's game.

Finally, my tenuous resolve snapped. I spun away from the door, my hand going to my pocket for my phone. I would make my excuses in the chatroom and —

My forehead hit someone's chin. I squeaked and squeezed my eyes shut and stumbled back, horrified that my gasp had caused me to inhale the person's — admittedly mild and fruity — scent.

'Tar!'

My eyes sprang open. 'I'm so, so sorry —'

'It's okay, I just — um, accidents happen.' It was Rex, looking sheepish. His hood was down today, and he looked exposed and vulnerable in the summer sun. The pink chalk was gone from his locs, leaving them a gleaming black. He wore ripped jeans and a patchy dragon-patterned grey and blue hoodie, the same A:RO backpack slung over one shoulder.

But I was somehow still apologising and feeling a bit manic about it. I had *walked into* someone. I could *smell* him. My *face* had touched his *actual* face. And I knew it was getting weird, how I kept talking, but I couldn't seem to stop the words from coming and he was probably *horrified*, he certainly looked it, and —

'Tar? Do you — could you come sit here, with me, for a minute?' He put his hands in his hoodie pocket, meeting my eyes briefly before looking down again.

The question froze my frantically spinning thoughts. 'I — yeah.'

He walked over to the little stone wall surrounding Pauline's front garden and sat down on it. I was so grateful that something had stopped my never-ending apologising that I sat down next to him without my panic building.

'I usually need a minute,' he said, 'before I go in. I need to ... assemble myself.' He kicked his feet against the wall and added in a murmur, 'Remember how to talk.' He glanced up at me, then away. 'I get it if you need to go, but if you want to stay, you can sit here with me for a while before going in.'

He threaded his fingers and put his hands in his lap, his expression turning inward. He didn't seem to be waiting for an answer, and that alone gave me the room to stay. His head was half-turned away from me, his body language loose-jointed except for a brittleness about the shoulders. His eyelashes were long and dark, resting on his cheeks when his gaze lowered.

I looked away from him, not wanting to be weird. That was a thing I knew I needed to watch — not just that I avoided people's eyes too much, but also that I was too willing to observe when I knew I was unobserved myself. There were so many rules around looking: where you should look, and for how long, and in what way. None of it came naturally to me.

But Rex wasn't looking at me, or talking to me, or asking anything of me that I could tell. He'd made an invitation with no pressure and an easy out.

And somehow that made it easier to stay, and stare at my feet, and think about Astaran, and the Amethyst Hand, and everything I had been looking forward to all week. I rocked a bit while I sat. I was aware of Rex beside me, but his presence wasn't a burden, the way other people often were. He wasn't waiting for me to be something or do something. He was content with this.

After a few minutes, when the whirlwind of my thoughts had at last stilled to a nervous breeze, I looked to Rex.

'Good?' he asked.

I nodded, and, to prove it: 'Yeah. Thanks.'

He smiled briefly. 'Good. Me too.' He looked around at the door and took a shuddering breath. 'Okay. Let's do this.'

When we knocked on the door, Arries was there to greet us — just as he'd been there to greet me last week. 'Rex! Tar!' He gripped the door and leaned out to us, all smiles and sparkling eyes. 'I wasn't sure if you would come!'

I followed him in with a nervous shrug. 'I said I was coming,' I murmured.

'He's talking about me,' Rex said. His high-tops seemed to take a while to untangle, and I could see his lips trembling in embarrassment as he fumbled with the laces.

Arries' smile turned sideways. 'I meant both of you, actually. Can't play without two of my favourite party members!'

'Everyone is your favourite,' said Rex, glancing at me.

'Well ... yeah. But that doesn't make you any less special.'

I smiled and ducked my head as I followed him down the hall.

In Pauline's game room, the scene was much as the week before — a chaos not yet familiar to me. Pauline at the head of the table shuffling through binders, books, and stacks of paper while Hanna baited and heckled; Kenta across from her with his dry humour and relaxed demeanour.

Without really meaning to, I took the same seat I had before; I had always been a creature of habit. Rex took the seat beside me, and Arries again across from us.

Kenta greeted the three of us with an easy 'hello' and turned back to Pauline. 'Good week?'

'Yeah, did you get time to re-alphabetise your library? That always cheers you right the fuck up,' said Hanna.

'Yes,' Pauline gave Kenta a flicker of a smile. 'And yes,' she said to Hanna, her smile turning into a scowl while Hanna barked a laugh.

'Oh come *on*, P! It's funny! You're so fucking predictable — it's pretty fucking adorable.'

Beside me, Rex murmured, 'Three guesses what Hanna's favourite word is this year.'

'Does it rhyme with ducking?' I replied.

Arries frowned, eyes darting between Hanna and Pauline. 'Predictable isn't always bad. It's reliable. You know, something you can count on.' He gave Pauline an encouraging smile.

'I said it was cute, didn't I?' Hanna made a face at Pauline.

Pauline disappeared behind her lair master's screen. 'I really don't care either way.'

Hanna threaded her hands and leaned forward. 'Sure sounds like you care, P.'

'Get away from my screen, Hanna.'

'Wouldn't you say it sounds like she cares, Ken?' Hanna leaned back in her seat and gestured at Pauline.

'I would, but I don't want Pauline to drop rocks on my head in-game. I think I'll sit this one out.'

'Coward.'

'Very wise.' Pauline's eyes appeared briefly above her screen before she disappeared again.

'Why does P put up with you again?' Rex leaned his chin on his hand.

Hanna grinned. 'I come with the house.'

I checked the time on my phone. Still five minutes until the official start of the game, and I was getting the impression Pauline was an 'on-the-dot' kind of lair master.

Arries caught my eye. 'You okay?' he mouthed, so obviously I didn't know whether to smile or hide.

I nodded and dropped my gaze.

'So why a witch specialist?' Rex suddenly asked.

I glanced at him; his eyes were on his hands, fingers drumming on his character sheet.

I hesitated, wondering how best to phrase it, wondering if it would make me sound strange. 'I like how witches almost always live on the fringe,' I said. 'In all the lore, they're usually loners or in very small, sparse communities that meet infrequently. They don't do people: they spend their time with animals, trees, you know, nature stuff. So that aesthetic appealed.' I paused. His eyes flicked to me, then away again. 'But, um — it's the game mechanics that sold me, if that doesn't make me sound too nerdy.'

'Not at all,' he said, smiling crookedly down at his own binder-load of character sheet. 'I chose a more wizard aesthetic for the same reason. I like how I have to think about everything I do — get creative with my spells, plan ahead.'

'That's what I like about playing a witch!' I said. 'There are so many polymorph options that would be easy to overlook — at first I was thinking heavy hitters and tanks like lions or something, but you can play a giant octopus and just grapple anything in combat, or a giant spider and climb literally any surface, or play a giant toad and swallow a creature whole and carry it, alive, in your belly.'

'You've put a lot of thought into this,' he said approvingly, and I realised that we were actually looking at each other, meeting each other's eyes, and it didn't feel weird. 'Although I'm hearing a theme of "giant animals".'

'Who doesn't like giant animals?' I replied. 'But the small animals are overlooked as well. If you want to be inconspicuous, you can hardly do better than a cat. If you want to get through a locked door, a mouse is perfect. And changing into a regular-sized scorpion makes it a lot more likely that you can sneak up on someone and sting them.'

'This is exactly why I choose the spells I do as well,' said Rex.

'Animate rope?' I asked, my eyebrows raising.

'*Always* useful. All a fireball will do is set something on fire. You can do a hundred things with a good rope trick. I make it a point of honour never to take a spell that only does straight damage. That's what Ken and Arries are for.'

I dipped my head in acknowledgement. 'Well, I look forward to seeing it in-game,' I said.

'Same here.'

An alarm went off on Pauline's phone, quickly silenced. 'It's 7pm,' she said, and the room fell silent, even Hanna cutting off mid-conversation.

CHAPTER SEVEN

'All right.' The hulking man in blood-spattered plate armour braced his foot against the still twitching body of the manticore. 'We've killed your abomination — fine waste of a good man-eater, I'd say — so take us to the nearest city and we'll be out of your weird, shiny hair.'

This was a bit rich coming from a man who appeared to never clean his armour, crusty as it was with blood and gore, but nonetheless I touched my hair self-consciously. I wasn't so unusual around here — I took after astralkin, mostly, with white pearlescent hair shaved on the sides and pulled into a tail, and glitter-dusted skin to match. I also had a glowing aura that tended to flare up when I was embarrassed. I tried to repress that now but judging by the way his eyebrows were raising, I wasn't succeeding. My eyes, though they shone with ethereal light, were cats-eye yellow and spoke to what was probably a feykin connection.

I didn't like thinking about how I looked, and I guess that probably showed — when they'd met me, there were twigs and feathers in my hair and more than a little mud on my clothes. The thing was, I'd rarely had anything to do with *people.* I had guarded my grove and the animals and plants therein. There had never been any need for *people* — not until the Amethyst Hand wandered into my grove.

I was still uncertain how much of their story was truth and how much was lies, but they had been fair in their treatment of me thus far, and helped me dispatch the creature corrupting the grove, as well as being considerate of the land at my request and to their own inconvenience. Not without complaint, of course, but then people *did* complain a lot, in my limited experience.

'I'm grateful for your help,' I said. 'No outsiders have ever done so much good for this sacred grove. Of course I will show you to the city.'

(Me: Do I know the way to the city?)

(Pauline: You would know, as it's local enough and important enough to the safety of your grove.)

'See?' Kendallien turned to grin at the little bard. 'Killing people always leads to good things for us.'

'And *helping* people,' said the fox-eared feykin, Arries, furrowing his brow. When I'd met him, he'd been an upright fox person, but he'd since changed between two forms many times. Now he was a man with warm brown skin and tightly curled hair, elongated canines that peeked with every broad smile, and peach-coloured fox ears and tail.

Kendallien shrugged. 'I'm less sure of that.'

'Come with me,' I said. 'And quietly.'

'Why?' Hanley walked over and gave the manticore's lolling head a good kick with her hoof. 'We've killed your big bad beastie. There's nothing else here you want us to fuck up, is there?'

'Nothing I would allow you to harm,' I said. 'But plenty of things I would allow to harm you. This is *their* grove, after all.'

Hanley looked ready to argue, but the horn-headed one, Ram, held out a calming hand. 'It's fine, Hanley. I've got a spell for this.'

'We ought to harvest materials from the manticore before we go,' I said thoughtfully. 'There's much there it would be a shame to waste.'

'You know how to gut and skin such a beast?' said Ram. 'Because I could certainly make use of the stinger.'

'And I'd like the eyes,' added Kenta. When everyone looked at him, he added, 'What? I just want them. Why does Ram have a monopoly on gore?'

'It's not so different from a mortal beast,' I said. 'It may take some time.'

(Me: How long will it take?)

(Pauline: Depends on how well you roll on your nature check. 2 hours at a minimum.)

(Me: Okay, I'll roll ...)

(Kenta: I'll assist!)

(Me: Okay, that's a 14)

(Pauline: +2 for Kendallien's help. Okay.)

It was bloody work and as the body was cooling fast, we had to pick and choose what we claimed from the body. Kendallien took the eyes, and the heart besides. I took the hide, which would turn aside most weapons and might make good armour if I could find a tanner to make it. Ram took the stinger, after extracting a good portion of its venom and blood.

I found the whole process repulsive. I had skinned many animals over the years — it was wasteful to let rot what could be used — but never something with a humanoid face. This abomination had spoken Common in a long forked tongue and smiled with an oversized human mouth full of yellowed human teeth. It had been a person, in its way; a cruel one who desired only the suffering of others. Its birth, life, and death were all unnatural, and I was glad to see it gone, but it still felt wrong to tear the skin from something that wore a human face.

Once our grisly work was done, we went to a stream to wash before I guided them north, out of the grove, out of the swamp, and toward the city of Sinterlan, which I knew little of but had travelled around many times.

As we walked, Hanley bickered with whoever she could bait into an argument — sometimes Kendallien, who seemed to enjoy the conflict, sometimes Arries, who tried to agree with everything she said just to get out of it, and sometimes

Ram, who she seemed to genuinely dislike and for whom she reserved her sharpest barbs.

Arries and Hanley walked behind me, Kendallien behind them, and Ram trailed at the rear, trying and failing to read as he walked, and stumbling often.

The third time I had to stop and go back to find him, when it became apparent that he was out of hearing range and certainly far from sight. I suggested, somewhat out of desperation: 'Perhaps you would do better to focus only on walking?'

He blinked his dark eyes at me, with their unnerving blue-edged shadows. 'Walking requires very little concentration — and it would be a terrible shame to miss out on reading time, when I have so much reading to do.'

'Little concentration,' I repeated, with a slight cant of my head.

His lips twitched. 'I admit, it's ... it is somewhat easier with a road underfoot rather than all of these roots and shrubs. I'll put away my book for now, out of respect for your guidance. You know this environment far better than I, after all.' He tucked his book into his satchel; it vanished inside with no visible change to the pack itself.

Magic, perhaps. I'd heard of such creations, which held a far greater space internally than they appeared to hold externally. It was something far different than the magic I knew — that was a magic of arcane luxury, where the power I drew from the land was primal and sacred, something I had to tend and grow as surely as if I tended a tree from seed to sapling.

'What are you reading?' I asked over my shoulder as I guided him over root and rock, back to the others of his party. 'Some magic book, I suppose?'

'I, um, I'd rather not say,' he replied. His eyes darted left and right.

'It's only you and I here,' I said. 'But I respect the desire of privacy.'

'Well ... look. And don't tell Hanley.'

He pulled the book out of his bag. It appeared to have a leather cover, but he passed his hand over it and the illusion dropped, revealing a cover with a woman in a flowing dress pining for a topless green centaur. I couldn't read the title — I'd never had the need nor the opportunity to learn — so I found it hard to make sense of the cover. 'What's it about?' I asked.

(Hanna: Oh my god.)

(Kenta: Oh my GOD.)

(Hanna: This whole time Ram's been reading romance?)

(Pauline: Shh. No out of character chatter.)

His brow pinched at my question. 'It's … well, it's a romance novel.'

I stared, uncomprehending. 'A love story?'

'Well, yes.' He paused. 'You … are you literate?'

'I can't read, if that's what you're getting at,' I said. His expression became amorphous, as if he was fighting to keep it calm. 'I didn't know there were love stories.'

'There are books about everything you can imagine, some for the facts, but some just for the pure joy of a story.'

'When my people gather, we tell stories,' I said. I looked at the book and felt a pang of longing. 'We gather rarely, and the stories are always my favourite part.'

'It sounds lonely,' he said.

I blinked and met his eyes. 'I never thought so. But I did miss the stories.'

He nodded, then cleared his throat and looked away. 'Hanley's a storyteller. I'll see if I can convince her to tell one around the campfire tonight, before we make it to the city.'

'I'd like that,' I said. He placed his illusion on the book again and tucked it away, but though it was gone from my sight my thoughts turned to it again and again. A story that one could enjoy privately. A whole world inside one's own mind.

When we caught up to the group, they were setting up camp on a hillside. Kendallien was gutting a boar while Arries set up divine wards and Hanley played a gentle tune on her flute. She set it aside as we arrived.

'Finally! Talk about anything exciting?'

'Not really,' I said, and Ram gave me a grateful look.

'Although I was thinking,' said Ram. 'It's been a while since you gave us a story.'

Hanley grinned. 'I could use the practice — I'm getting fucking rusty and I'd like to make coin doing it when we get to Sinterlan.'

I warmed myself by the fire while Hanley considered her choice of story. I looked for Ram, but he was again on the edge of the group, gazing out across the plains to the city, sprawled and twinkling in the distance.

I found myself wishing that he would sit at the fire as well.

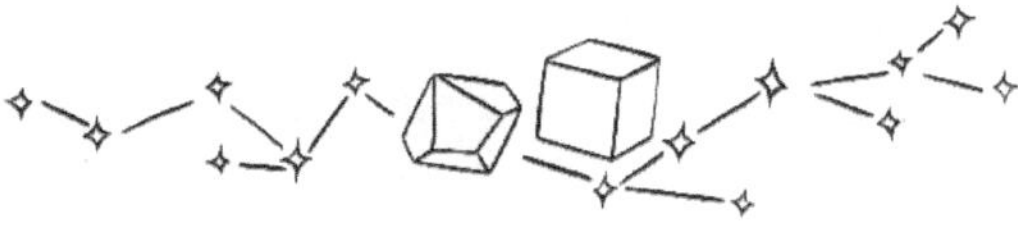

CHAPTER EIGHT

'And as blood gurgles from the courier's mouth, he looks down to see an arrowhead protruding from his chest ... and that's where we'll leave it tonight.' Pauline's lips quirked as everyone started talking at once.

'Nooo!' Arries put his hands on his face. 'You can't stop there! What does the note say? Who was The Man of Many Names sending the note to?'

'I read the letter,' said Hanna. 'I immediately take it, and I read it — what does it say?'

'You'll find out next session,' said Pauline.

Hanna groaned. 'Come on, P — bullshit! Just a little hint?'

'It's almost ten — game time is over. Anyone staying for beer and board games?'

'I'll get the drinks,' said Kenta. He looked down at me. 'Can I tempt you?'

'I — uh, I don't drink,' I said truthfully, though right now I was struggling to come down from the game. Such an enormous amount of story and character development had been crammed into a few short hours and I needed a moment to re-orientate myself for the real world.

I froze as I realised what I'd just said. It had never in my life worked out when I told people I didn't drink. They would ask questions — demand an explanation, for which my only answer could be that I didn't like it. Then they would try to persuade me, or coerce me, or insist I didn't know what I was talking about. It was one of the simplest ways of accidentally ostracising myself I'd ever found. My eyes moved from Arries, to Hanna, to Pauline, to Kenta, but nobody seemed moved to say anything about it. Hanna raised her eyebrows at me.

'Do you want to stay for board games, at least?' Pauline asked, still not looking up from her notes

'Uh.' I wondered how best to extricate myself this time. I didn't think I could keep using the amorphous 'I have somewhere to be'.

'Oh *please* stay,' said Arries. 'Pauline has some *really* fun games.'

'I'm leaving,' said Rex. He stood up and nodded to Pauline without lifting his gaze.

'Somewhere to be?' Hanna asked waspishly.

He shrugged. 'See you next week. Thanks again, P.'

As he pushed his chair back to get out, his gaze met mine. He flicked his eyes at the door, then back at me.

'I'm leaving, too,' I said quickly. Sometimes, in situations like this, it felt like my brain moved too slowly to keep up, but I was going to seize an opportunity when it was offered. I grabbed my backpack and followed Rex to the door. 'It was a really good game,' I said as I left.

'You're a good player,' said Pauline. She smiled, so quickly I almost didn't catch it, and it made me feel a lot better about leaving. I wasn't ostracising myself. I wasn't the odd one out. I was just being like Rex.

'See you in A:RO tomorrow morning!' Arries said. I nodded and ducked out the door after Rex.

My mind was still whirling as we put on our shoes. The relief I'd felt when Pauline smiled was fading fast. Every awkward moment, every miscommunication, every odd thing I'd said and done during the evening was coming back to me in a way that made my limbs tremble. The euphoria of a social event gone well was replaced with a growing, choking horror.

'So ... you play A:RO?'

I flinched at Rex's voice, startled from my spiralling thoughts. 'Uh ... yeah. I, um — I play with Arries, mostly.'

'What's your main?'

'I play a Sun Elf Knight. You?'

'I jump between a Moon Elf Assassin and ...' his lips twisted wryly. '... a Half-Demon Warlock.'

I smiled, letting the moment push my worry to the back of my mind — though not entirely gone. 'So Ram, basically.'

He shrugged. 'I guess I see myself as a cool dark spellcaster. Do you play often?'

I weighed my sad truth against a boring lie. 'Daily. I think I've mentioned the void of my existence before.'

'You did. I play a lot too.'

'Maybe I'll see you around sometime?'

'Maybe you already have.' He opened the door and held it for me to walk through. 'It's entirely possible. We're both on the UK servers. It's weird to think we might have partied up sometime and not realised.'

'Probably not,' I said. This was one of those times where I was supposed to just nod and laugh, but it was nearly impossible for me to let an incorrect impression stand. 'I mostly solo, except when Arries is on. I hardly ever party up with strangers.'

Outside, the evening was dark and blissfully cool after the scorching heatwave during the day. We hesitated on the doorstep, both caught in the awkwardness of a final goodbye. Rex smiled, almost meeting my eyes. He seemed more relaxed than I'd seen him before, his shoulders lower, a sort of brightness in his usually guarded eyes. Some of the tightness in my chest eased.

'We could add each other on A:RO.' I surprised myself with the hopefulness in my voice. I offered Rex a shaky smile staring somewhere in the vicinity of his shoulder.

'I don't know. Maybe. It ... it seems like it might be a lot of pressure. No offense!' He raised his hands. 'I barely play with Arries, and he's probably my best friend.'

☆ 50 ☆

'Arries is everyone's best friend,' I said, and his lips twitched at that. Maybe Rex, like me, wondered what kind of alien creature Arries must be to be so generous with his friendship.

Another awkward beat where neither of us seemed to know what to say. 'See you next week.' He dipped his head, pulled up his hood, and walked away from Pauline's house. After a moment, I followed and climbed into my car.

On the drive home, I started to feel it. I gritted my teeth and whined under my breath, glad of the dubious privacy of my car. I could feel the too-sharp sting of elation and tried to hold onto it to ward off the walls of my mind from closing around me.

I pulled up outside the house and killed the engine. I rested my forehead against the wheel, closing my eyes. I tried to focus on my breathing, but my thoughts kept turning over every interaction from the party. In particular, I kept going back again and again to the last few minutes with Rex. It had seemed so natural and comfortable at the time, but now the memory made my skin crawl.

I went to my room as swiftly as I could, eyes low to avoid catching Saanvi or Riya's eyes. I didn't think I could bear to be thought strange by anyone else.

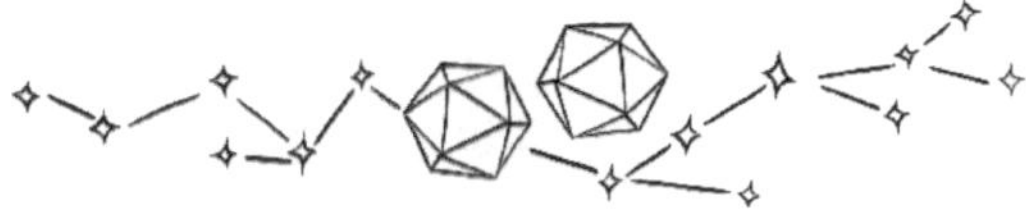

CHAPTER NINE

The next afternoon, as I headed to the kitchen to make up some lunch, I found Saanvi pacing by the front door. Her hair was unusually frazzled, and she was dressed for work in a rumpled suit. 'I know it's late notice,' she said into her phone. 'But I really ... no ... no, I understand. Of course.'

She hung up and stared at her phone, shoulders slumping. She looked so ... defeated. It was wrong — like we'd somehow fallen into an alternate universe. Because of *course* Saanvi must have bad days, but I'd never seen one. She was a single mother AND a tech manager, and every day she walked out the door in an ironed suit with a briefcase tucked under her arm.

But now she looked scruffy and frustrated and probably in need of help.

She hadn't seen me yet. I could probably sneak back into my room and she'd have no idea that I had been there. Even if she did see me, it would hardly weigh on her. That was how this had worked for a couple years now — I contained myself to my room. We rarely crossed paths, and didn't chat when we did. Maybe that was strange, but to me, it had always been a comfort. It was hard coming home after a day of customer service, even customer service on a script. Knowing that Saanvi wouldn't ask for small talk from me made this house a refuge I didn't think I'd get as a lodger anywhere else. And I got the feeling Saanvi was okay with the arrangement as well.

But though I swayed back on the stairs, ready to make my escape, I couldn't quite bring myself to run. Saanvi had been good to me. And yeah, I mean, I paid for this quiet space in her house, but ... you can't live in someone's house and not know them at least a little, no matter how hard you try.

And it's hard not to care about the people you know.

'Any —' I cleared my throat as I came down the stairs. 'Uh, anything I can help with?'

'I'm fine,' said Saanvi, but the creases in her suit said otherwise. For me, it would be nothing, but for Saanvi it was tantamount to a sign on her forehead that read 'CRISIS' in all caps.

Saanvi sighed. 'Well — mostly fine. Well ... ahh.' She wrung her hands nervously — like actually wrung her hands, as if she was afraid of me.

Me. The person who got a fight-or-flight response every time I rang a doorbell.

I assumed an expression I hoped projected calmness. 'What is it?'

Saanvi ran a hand through her hair. 'I ... I need to ask a favour. And you can say no! I can't believe I'm even asking this ...'

I raised my hands. 'Saanvi. It's fine. I'm not going to get offended. I asked to help, right?' Somehow, Saanvi's nerves were making me feel calmer. I knew how to deal with anxious people. I knew how un-intimidating we were.

Saanvi was still talking, '... It's not even appropriate, you're already *paying* to live here, I can't just expect you to drop everything and help me, you're my lodger not an au pair ...'

'Saanvi.'

Saanvi took a deep breath. 'Something's come up at work. Something urgent. And I hate to ask, but I don't know who else — ahh.' She pinched her brow between her fingers. 'Would you be able to watch Riya for me for a few hours?'

A beat passed where all I could do was blink stupidly at her, as if she'd just flicked me on the nose or something. 'That's it? Yeah, I'll watch Riya.'

Saanvi straightened. 'You will? She can be difficult.' She looked at me with concern, like she thought she was tricking me.

'We get on okay, I think,' I said, having no idea whether that was true. 'And, I mean, I live here, Saanvi. I barely leave the house. I don't mind if you want me to babysit sometimes. It's not so far out of my way.'

'I won't ask again —'

'It's fine,' I said.

Saanvi's eyes filled with gratitude and she rushed into the lounge. 'Riya! Tar's gonna look after you for a few hours, okay?'

I could just hear Riya's small voice reply with a very discouraging, 'Who?' before Saanvi was saying her goodbyes. She rushed out the door with a laptop case on her shoulder and a briefcase in her hand, calling 'Thank you!' as the door slammed shut behind her.

I walked into the lounge. Riya sat with her back against the sofa and a jigsaw splayed out before her. She had a piece in one hand, a pair of scissors in the other.

'Are you allowed to use scissors?' I asked. That was a thing, right? That small kids shouldn't have scissors? I had no idea at what age that stopped being a thing.

Riya gazed at me solemnly. 'Are you?'

I really had no answer to that. I walked toward the kitchen. 'What do you want for lunch?'

'Salad!' Riya said decisively, snipping the edge off of one of the pieces.

Salad?

'You can have anything,' I said, a little desperately.

Riya narrowed her eyes. 'Salad.'

'Okay.' I nodded, then nodded again. 'Right. Okay.' I walked into the kitchen, then walked back out again. 'Riya?'

'Mm?'

'What do you usually put in salad?'

Riya put aside her scissors with a sigh and walked past me into the kitchen. *'Salad.'*

Later, we sat in front of the TV watching *Pippa Parrot,* a surprisingly sarcastic show for kids. We each had a large salad bowl in our lap of mostly grapes with some loose bits of rocket, cucumber and carrot. 'This salad is actually pretty good,' I said, spearing a grape with my fork.

Riya nodded solemnly, her eyes never leaving the TV.

'Do you have any video games, or ...?'

Riya raised her eyebrows and I swear, I had no idea children as young as six (was she six?) could look so withering.

'Sorry. You're watching.'

After a few minutes, I asked, 'So do they fall down laughing at the end of every episode, or were these just weird episodes?'

'They always laugh. Sometimes they don't fall over.'

'Intense.'

When Saanvi came back, Riya was asleep on the sofa while I hate-shopped for jeans on my phone.

'It went well?'

I looked at Riya, whose face was squished awkwardly on the arm of the sofa. 'Yeah,' I said, surprised by the truth of the words. 'I'm happy to do it again sometime.'

CHAPTER TEN

Impossible though it had seemed when I first stood on Pauline's doorstep, *Kin* became part of my routine. My days became more than a blur of tourists and canned lines while I waited to play ARO. Every Friday or Saturday at 7pm, I would inhabit Astaran of the Silver Grove, who was gradually becoming accepted into the notorious Amethyst Hand.

There, I would laugh with Hanley and Kendallien, help Arries keep the party intact, and discuss magic and loneliness with the ever-mysterious figure of Ram. But I was becoming part of the group in real life as well, a transition so gentle that I barely noticed how close we were really becoming.

Weeks passed without me noticing. Then months. I stopped being the newbie and became part of the team. They treated me like I'd always been there. I started to feel like it.

Hanna always wanted to know about the funniest tourists I'd seen that day, and Kenta and I had started up a daily scrabble match to try to win a bet with Hanna. Arries and I still talked daily on A:RO, but it became much more personal now that we shared the same friends. He would keep me updated on all the others and answer any questions I had been too nervous to ask.

Even Pauline, with all of her abruptness, would check in with me every couple of days. She seemed concerned about my health — I'd let slip in the chat that my diet was largely ready meals and tins of soup. We started to talk watching cheesy TV fantasy series together — it turned out Pauline absolutely devoured any kind of fantasy media. The way she talked about it was amazing — for all she was the most creative person I knew, she had killer critical thinking and would dismantle all the creative decisions to me casually over breakfast each morning.

Only Rex was hard to pin-down, a fleeting figure in the chatroom, ever-present but always lurking in silence, or being called away on unspecified business. He would pipe up to quip or post pictures of his cat, boast about his younger siblings, or offer his somewhat cynical advice, but otherwise chose to fade into the background. And that was okay, even if it was a bit disappointing.

I got back from work one day too tired to face cooking a meal. I ordered pizza and flitted up and down the stairs like a ghost when the doorbell rang, whisking my greasy prize back to my room. I opened it on my desk and reclined in my seat while A:RO loaded, letting the dramatic music swell around me.

A phone symbol blinked in the corner of my screen. I let a cheesy bite slide down my throat, then accepted the call. 'Hey Arries.'

'Hiya! I didn't think you'd be on today. Aren't you meant to be visiting your mum?'

I took another bite, giving me a moment to think before responding. I didn't want to talk about my mum, about how hard I found it to visit her. She lived in a cramped flat in a busy city, where there was nowhere to park. I had to get the train whenever I visited and navigated the city alone. All perfectly regular things for a human to do — other than me. I felt ... fuzzy ... whenever I thought about making the trip. Flashing between static and clear, like a TV losing signal.

'I rescheduled,' I said, which wasn't true. I hadn't gotten up the energy to call, or deal with the situation in any way. Did that make me an awful child? I looked at my phone and contemplated calling her, but hearing her disappointment was more than I knew how to deal with right now, and she never understood why I couldn't just *do* the things that other people did. I could text her, but then she would know something was up, and she would immediately call me anyway.

'Again?'

I let my silence speak for me. For a moment, Arries didn't say anything either. I wondered if he was thinking: *You haven't seen her in three months and she only lives an hour away?* I wondered if he thought I was being pathetic, or lazy, or callous. Maybe I was being all of those things. I only knew that I couldn't face the cold horror and sickly brain static of making the journey.

After a moment, Arries said, 'I'm sorry, Tar. I know you want to go. Are you feeling, uh, *unwell* again?' He said the word in a way that clearly meant 'in your brain'.

'Yeah.'

'Is there anything I can do to help?'

I exhaled long and slow. 'I just want to be distracted right now.'

'Right. Right! I can do that.'

We played for a while. I wasn't as lively on the chat as I usually was, but Arries could fill awkward silences single-handedly, and soon I could feel myself loosening up. We'd just slain the slimy wyrmlings in the Wyrm's Eyrie quest when I heard a knock at my door. 'BRB, Arries.'

'Sure.'

I took off my headset and went to the door, puzzled. Saanvi rarely disturbed me, unless I'd gotten a parcel in the post or something. When I opened the door, it took me a moment to look down into the face of Riya. She was wearing Spiderman pyjamas with the shirt on backward — I'd heard her shouting before that the spider went on the *front*, and she'd refused to wear it any other way since. The tag stuck up under her chin. In her hands was a still-wet painting in thick, dripping strokes.

She offered it to me silently. I looked at it. 'The Bedroom Monster' it read in a balloonish hand, imitating Saanvi's neat pencil handwriting at the top of the page. It portrayed a blue person and a small green girl holding hands.

She looked at me, as if waiting for something. I didn't know what to say, and I didn't want to break the silence, but it seemed wrong to send her away empty-handed. I offered her a pizza slice. She accepted it with a nod and padded back to her bedroom.

'Back!' I said. Arries' big lizardman character was doing a sort of jig. He went back to all-business as I spoke.

'Great. What was it?'

'Riya.' I glanced at the moist painting on the desk. 'She made a painting of us together.'

'Aww! Did you tell her it was great? You were nice about it, right?' Arries' tone was light, but I could detect his anxiety that I would somehow crush a young child. 'Children need lots of encouragement.'

'We didn't really speak,' I said. 'But I gave her a piece of pizza.'

'That's ... uh, did she seem happy?'

'She seemed satisfied, yeah. Artists are supposed to be paid for their work, right?'

'I ... guess.'

We returned to gameplay as normal, but every now and then I glanced at Riya's painting and smiled.

☆☆☆

❀Hanna: It's my birthday on Thursday!

Arries: OMG happy birthday, Hanna!

Kenta: Merry Birthmas

❀Hanna: THANK you.

Pauline: I assume you have the usual plans to debauch yourself.

❀Hanna: Oh yeah. I am going to get extremely debauched.

❀Hanna: I've got big plans for Saturday.

Arries: You're still coming to Kin, right?

❀Hanna: Oh yeah. I don't trust P with my character.

Tar❀t: Happy birthday for Thursday! Why don't you trust P?

Kenta: There was … an incident.

Tar❀t: Ominous.

❀Hanna: Hanley got killed the last time I missed a session!

Arries: I don't think P meant anything by it …

❀Hanna: I got back to a session that started with a desperate race to a temple to resurrect me.

Pauline: That was unfortunate, but Hanley was fine.

❀Hanna: You were punishing me!

❀Hanna: Why else would you kill my character when I wasn't even there.

Pauline: It's a game run on dice and chance. These things happen.

✽**Hanna:** It's a game run by YOU.

Kenta: It did seem kinda like a punishment.

Pauline: Your character didn't die when you missed a session.

Kenta: No, but I did lose all my equipment.

Pauline: By chance.

Tar✿: So what I'm hearing is: don't miss sessions.

Pauline: Of course. It would be rude to miss a session.

Tar✿: Wow.

✽**Hanna:** See?

✽**Hanna:** Anyway

✽**Hanna:** Even though I'm seeing you Friday for the game

✽**Hanna:** And even though I'm gonna celebrate properly on Saturday

✽**Hanna:** I kinda wanna see you nerds to celebrate on the actual day.

✽**Hanna:** And since none of you will get fucking sloshed with me

Kenta: I refuse to get a beer belly

Arries: I like to be clear thinking

Pauline: I'll drink but I'm not a degenerate

Tar⬚: Not my thing

❀Hanna: Right

❀Hanna: I thought we could go out and do something fun?

❀Hanna: What do nerds do for special occasions? Laserquest?

Arries: OMG I LOVE Laserquest

Pauline: Not great for me. Spaces are too tight for the chair.

❀Hanna: Sure. Well, what do you suggest?

Pauline: I really enjoy escape rooms?

❀Hanna: What's that?

Rex♜: You know when P locks us in a dungeon and sets off a timer and we have to solve a puzzle before the time runs out?

Kenta: Hey Rex. You lurking?

Rex♜: Always

Rex♜: Anyway, escape rooms are like that but IRL. We get "locked" in a room and run through a scenario and have to solve a series of puzzles to escape.

Kenta: Basically the most P thing ever

❀Hanna: That actually sounds good!

❀Hanna: In a nerd way

Kenta: We get it! You're cooler than us.

❀Hanna: Okay. Could someone get that booked?

Pauline: Of course. I'll send the details once confirmed. Who's going?

Arries: Me!

Kenta: Me

Rex♛: I don't think so

Arries: Reeeex

Rex♛: I'm not feeling very social

❀Hanna: When do you ever?

Rex♛: Sorry, Hanna. Hope you have a great time.

Arries: Tar?

My fingers hovered over the keyboard, frozen in the moment before I gave one of my usual excuses. I knew I would get away with it — probably even more easily than Rex, since there was more trust there so they felt more able to push.

But the escape room sounded fun. Another game, another story, and this time *we* would really get to be the heroes.

And I liked Hanna. I liked all the other players.

I just had to somehow make it there and into the room, where it would be too late to run away.

It was getting easier. Every week, it got easier. Arries to care how I was feeling. Rex to understand. Hanna and Kenta to make me laugh. Pauline to keep me grounded and give me something to focus on. Friends. Something I'd never really had, thanks to my habit of freezing or fleeing when faced with people.

Tarö: I might come

✿Hanna: !!!!!

Kenta: ???

Arries: :D :D :D

Pauline: Excellent. I'll book for five then. I believe it will come to £20 each.

I made a face at the screen. That was expensive, but I didn't want to admit it.

Arries: Ouch. Okay.

✿Hanna: I'm not worth £20, Arries?

Arries: Of course you are. :D

Kenta: I'm undecided on that front

✿Hanna: Hey!

Kenta: But I'm still coming

Pauline: I'll message back in a few hours with the details.

I logged off from the chat and folded trembling hands in my lap. But for once I didn't feel overwhelmed by my fear — I felt elated, like I'd been filled with air and light. These people were genuinely excited to see me, and the escape room sounded like the kind of activity that would keep us all focused and engaged and save me from the small talk I'd mostly avoided thanks to Pauline's tight *Kin* schedule.

I was going to celebrate a friend's birthday.

Later, when I was lying in bed online shopping for a good present for Hanna — my plan was a necklace that said 'Bard' in flourishing font, which I hoped would appeal to the secret nerd in her without offending her outer athlete — my phone buzzed with a notification from the chatroom app.

A private message from Rex.

Rex♛: Why did you decide to go?

Rex♛: Not that I think it's a bad idea — I think it's a good idea

Rex♛: It's just

Rex♛: You've never gone to anything but Kin

I paused, running a finger across my lip as I considered my response. I didn't like my motivations being questioned, generally. It made me feel examined, and like someone was going to discover my crazy at any moment.

But this was Rex, who would help me escape after every *Kin* session, and who sat with me in Pauline's front garden until I felt like I could go in. I couldn't see what he got from that — we weren't close like me and Arries — except that he understood and didn't want to leave me to flounder. He was kind. So though I normally squirmed under any kind of scrutiny, I didn't think that was what was happening right now.

Tar🐾: I think I want to be more than Kin friends

Tar🐾: Before that thought was scary but now ... I'm willing to try

Rex♛: That's really brave of you

Rex♛: I mean

Rex♛: Not because they're bad people — they are the best people

Rex♛: Just because it's hard to do. Connecting with people.

Tar🐾: Oh, I know

Tar🐾: I guess I'll see you at the game?

Rex♛: Yeah

Rex♛: See you then

Rex♛: I hope you crush the escape room record

Tar🐾: Me too. I could use an actual talent

Rex♛: You're already really talented, Tar.

Rex♛: Anyway. Good night.

His status greyed out to offline, leaving me alone with the messages. I stared at them for a long time, wondering what

Thursday would hold, and wishing Rex would be there to join us.

'Silly,' I muttered to the blue-white glow of the phone screen. 'I'm being silly.'

I put my phone on charge, closed my eyes, and tried to fall asleep.

They were the best people, and soon I'd meet them without even a character sheet to use as a shield. And somehow, that was more exciting than terrifying.

CHAPTER ELEVEN

I arrived at the escape room and was saved from my usual routine of fighting myself to enter the building because the group was waiting outside.

Pauline was already there, with Kenta standing with one hand on the handles of her chair, both chatting with Arries, who lounged against the steep ramp leading up to the crumbling Victorian terraced house. A faded sign in faux metal-worked type declared this to be 'LOCK AND KEY: Escape Rooms For All Abilities'.

Well. That was reassuring. I was doubtful of my own puzzle skills, but somehow I didn't think Pauline had chosen the beginner's room for us.

'Tar!' Arries waved enthusiastically.

Everyone's eyes moved to me. I blushed. 'Uh. Hiya.'

'We're discussing strategy while we wait for the birthday girl,' said Kenta. 'Pauline thinks someone needs to be in charge of note-taking.'

I joined the circle of conversation, crossing my arms to mitigate how exposed I felt in this new situation. 'Will that be necessary? Can't we just all write down notes?' I didn't like to think of someone missing out on puzzling because they were stuck nannying a notebook.

Pauline tilted her head to one side as she considered me. Her eyes narrowed. 'Escape rooms are timed. They require communication, strategy, and speed. If everyone is writing down notes, there could be duplicates: wasted time. People won't know which codes have been tried with which puzzles: more wasted time. Notes will get lost, things that are shouted out will be missed. Without a central hub of information, there can be no order. And without order, we will fumble around like pigeons in the dark.'

'Pigeons.' Kenta snickered.

Pauline's gaze was still locked on me. 'Do you want to win this, Tar?'

I don't know how she did it, but I felt my chest swell. 'Yes. Of course.'

Pauline nodded. 'Good. Then bring all your notes to me.'

I blinked. 'You want to take the notes?'

'I don't trust anyone else to do it. It's not like Rex is here.'

My eyebrows lifted. 'You'd trust Rex?'

Arries said, 'Have you seen his binder?' as if that explained everything.

Kenta chuckled. 'Anyone who's put as much effort into tracking their character as Rex can handle note-taking, no problem.'

'Singing my praises again? I'm touched.' Rex strode over, shoulders high and hood up again.

My breath caught in my throat.

'OH MY GOD, Rex!' Arries launched at Rex, arms wide, then stopped as Rex flinched away. 'Oh ... uh. Can I hug you?'

Rex looked up. His lips quirked. 'Just this once,' he said, giving Arries a stiff pat-pat-pat hug that Arries returned with enthusiasm.

'I didn't book for you, Rex.' Pauline's voice was harsh, but her scowl lacked enthusiasm.

Rex looked down, shuffling his feet. 'I'm sorry, P. Is there room for me, though?'

Pauline sighed heavily. 'The room goes up to six, so yes. You'll owe everyone a couple pounds each, though.'

Rex smiled tightly. 'Thanks, P. I'll pay everyone back right away.' He proceeded to divvy up his change, pressing cold coins into my palm. I released a haggard breath as he moved on.

Arries followed my gaze. 'I'm pleased he's here, too,' he said quietly. 'He doesn't get out much. I worry about him, sometimes.'

I glanced at Arries. 'I don't get out much either,' I said. 'It's not so bad.'

'Yeah. I worry about you, too.' He nudged my shoulder gently, and because it was Arries and it was very brief, I didn't mind.

'Probably wise,' I murmured. My eyes went back to Rex, now being firmly lectured by Pauline on the virtues of RSVPing. To my surprise, he met my eyes. He smiled wryly, then we both looked away.

'Listen up, nerds!' Hanna strode toward us across the parking lot, arms spread. 'Your fearless leader has arrived!'

Kenta whooped and clapped his hands, which Arries joined in with. Pauline rolled her eyes.

'Congratulations on your continued existence,' I said.

Hanna pressed a hand to her heart. 'Thank you. I know you'd all be lost without me. So! I'm the leader of this team. Listen up to my directions and we'll win this thing!' She paused, looking at Rex.

Rex shrugged. 'What?'

'No complaints? You're going to finally admit that I'm the leader?'

Rex smiled and looked at his shoes. 'Today.'

Hanna's smile turned wolfish. She punched the air. 'All right! So we need a plan. Any suggestions, crew?'

'Pauline's got a lot of ideas,' said Kenta.

'Great! Then as team leader, I appoint Pauline chief strategist. Listen to her and we'll win this thing.'

Pauline checked her watch. She was the only one present who had one. '10 minutes until we start. We're all here. Let's go inside to strategise.'

Without any idea which puzzles or scenario we were facing, I didn't think there was a lot of strategy possible, but Pauline had a surprising number of suggestions — largely based around using our time efficiently and not treading the same path twice. A single note-keeper, keys left in locks, opened doors left ajar. If you're stuck on a puzzle, tag out to someone else. Don't try the same codes twice (apparently clues are only used once in escape rooms). If a clue or puzzle seems incomplete or missing essential components, then pause it and return later when more of it may have been unlocked.

We sat in the reception of the escape room on brightly-coloured sofas with walls decorated with keys and clocks. My sofa was red and I clutched a 'LOCK AND KEY' cushion a little too tightly, but it made me feel safe. Rex perched on the arm next to me. He looked tenser than usual, his shoulders high and head ducked, but a smile flickered across his lips when Pauline started quizzing Arries on her tips.

'Once a lair master, always a lair master,' he murmured, and I couldn't help but smile as well.

'She does look like she's about to make us all queue for combat,' I said.

'Quick! Make a Mind check against forgetfulness.'

I snickered.

'Tar! What do you do when you find a new key?'

I straightened, fumbling for an answer that would satisfy her.

When Pauline was done enumerating her tips and was sure we all remembered them, Hanna squeezed her shoulder. 'I knew I was right to pick you for strategy,' she said.

Rex raised his eyebrows. 'I mean, it was Ken who suggested —'

'I'm a NATURAL leader,' Hanna said loudly while Kenta chuckled.

The escape room host, a bespectacled and bearded guy wearing a plaid shirt and a nervous smile, greeted us warmly when we arrived and plied us with puzzles to occupy us while he reset the room from the last group. We read riddles aloud to each other. While I enjoyed our waiting time, it didn't fill me with confidence that we would do well once we entered the room.

Hanna would confidently state wrong answers which Kenta would deride but wouldn't offer alternatives to. Arries didn't want to offer any solutions until everyone else had already tried, and Rex was silent during the exchanges. I don't think I was much better — being wrong made me feel very vulnerable, so it was hard to suggest something when I had no way of knowing how it would be received.

And as everyone talked, I fixated on my shortcomings. While I wasn't terrible at logic puzzles in general, I did very badly whenever there was any ambiguity in the question. A poorly worded puzzle would quickly stump me where the more flexible members of our team had no problem.

When our host, Adam, arrived to introduce us to the puzzle, I was sweating and hoping desperately that nobody had noticed — although how could they not when I was clearly drenched and disgusting and probably smelled terrible? This always happened to me in social situations and I really didn't know how to deal with it — I swear I was *not* normally sweaty, but something about talking to other people turned my pores into fountains.

Adam looked eager to let us into the room. As he walked us down the corridor, he gave us a LM-like spiel that instantly both put me at ease and got me excited to start. 'The story so far,' he began, clasping his hands. 'Your friend Professor Dumont disappeared several weeks ago and you heard nothing from him until now, when you receive a mysterious letter with a none-too-subtle hidden message ...'

Then we were let into a room with an ornately locked door at the other side and let loose on the puzzle. The scenario was that we had to find and destroy Professor Dumont's artefact and escape before the thugs returned in an hour's time to collect it. The room was beautifully appointed with the feel of an old-timey professor's study, with furniture with lots of secret compartments and mechanisms and even a hidden door that led to a second room. We split into individuals and pairs to solve puzzles, following Pauline's advice that we should switch puzzles if it was clear we weren't going to make any progress.

Arries and I tackled a cupboard full of keys with clearly coded labels — each room label had one or two numbers in the place of letters. While he listed the relevant rooms and numbers, I examined the cupboard itself, looking for hidden latches or mechanisms. My fingers brushed a keyhole on the bottom of the frame. I crouched down to get a look at it from underneath.

'Uh ... Tar?' Arries looked up from his notes.

'There's a keyhole here,' I said, feeling pleased to have already contributed *something* to the team, however small. 'I guess now it's time to work out which of these keys goes to it.'

Arries and I decoded the keys but couldn't work out which key was the correct one — it felt like we were missing something. We took our puzzle to Pauline, who was keeping a number code connected with a key symbol which Kenta and Hanna had unlocked. 'Does that number mean anything to you?' she asked.

Arries and I grinned at each other. '47,' said Arries.

'Or BATHROOM,' I said. The 47 replaced the A and T on the label.

We unlocked a secret compartment behind the cabinet and found a mechanical puzzle requiring cogs of varying sizes that Pauline and Rex had been collecting from around the room. And that puzzle led to another puzzle, which led to a secret compartment which led to a code that let us through a secret door. All the while, the time was ticking down on the screen hanging on the wall.

Kenta called Arries to help with a map puzzle, while Pauline and Hanna worked on the morse code a phone dial was giving them. I joined Rex at Professor Dumont's journal, which we'd recently unlocked.

'Any progress?' I asked.

Rex glanced up at me, then away. 'Not yet,' he said. 'Which is especially embarrassing when you realise what it is.' He handed me the journal.

I flicked through page after page of arcane diagrams, each with X's marked at different points of the shapes. 'Is this ... what, a spellbook?' I couldn't help but smile. 'That's your bread and butter, right?'

Rex exhaled, a sound somewhere between a laugh and a sigh. 'You would think,' he said. 'They clearly correspond to the diagram marked here,' he showed me something like a summoning circle marked on the top of the table, obscured by sheaves of blank parchment. 'And I think Pauline and Ken have collected a bunch of items that are supposed to be placed at the marked points on it. But there's a missing code or something — all the pages are numbered, and we need to find out which page number is the correct one. I mean — I could try working through the book trying out each combination —'

'But there isn't enough time,' I agreed. I looked around at the others, still deep into their own puzzles. 'Well, either they'll discover the page number and run it over to us, or it's still out here somewhere to find. We may as well start searching for it.'

He glanced up and met my eyes, offering another wry smile. For a moment, my lungs felt too thin to draw breath. He was, it suddenly struck me, very beautiful. I had noticed before, of course, but in a detached way, like looking at a painting. Now, I was so aware that it was hard to look at him, but also impossible to look away.

His expression was hard to read, his dark-eyed gaze wavering on mine. His lips twisted to one side and he dropped his gaze. 'Whatever you say, Tar.' His locs fell forward, obscuring his face.

Oh no. I didn't like this. I didn't like that I was noticing it, noticing him. It was a rare occurrence for me and had never ended well.

And he'd already made it clear he didn't want to see me outside of *Kin*.

I found it even harder to make eye contact after that. I alternated between stuttering and mumbling, and I felt my face grow hot whenever we spoke. It was unbearable.

If Rex noticed, he didn't say anything about it. He helped me search the remaining items that hadn't been used in a puzzle for hidden compartments or codes we'd missed. We worked in such close proximity that I was terrified of bumping into him and I held my breath a lot of the time — I hated smelling people at the best of times, but when it was someone I was maybe possibly developing feelings for, it just made the whole thing creepy as well as uncomfortable.

When at last we found a reference to the page number stuck to the base of a drawer someone had passed by, it all ended fast: we set up the "ritual" according to the book, covered the eyes of the skeleton, and a key shot out from the coffin Professor Dumont had been trying to protect.

'I've got it!' Hanna yelled, snatching it up and rushing for the exit.

The rest of us looked to Pauline, who scowled. 'What're you looking at me, for? It's time to go!'

We all shoved out after Hanna, with Pauline bringing up the rear. When the door closed behind us, Escape Room Adam greeted us with applause. 'You did good!' he said. 'You made it out in time!'

'Did we make it out in a *good* time? Better than other people?' Hanna's fists clenched, her eyes sparkling with a competitive spirit I found utterly alien.

Adam's pleasant expression grew thoughtful. 'Uh ... maybe? We don't record times or anything.'

Hanna's shoulders dropped an inch. 'I thought this was timed?'

'There's a time *limit*,' Adam explained. 'But it's not a competition. We just want people to have a good time and immerse themselves in the story.'

While Hanna tsked, Arries leapt in, 'We had a really good time! It's all really well made — everything is so clever!'

'Yeah, what he said.' Kenta gave Adam a thumbs-up.

I had also enjoyed the escape room but found this whole interaction cringe-worthy. Surely Adam just wanted us to leave?

I glanced at Rex, who had his hood up and head down, as usual. He caught my eye and gave me a nearly imperceptible shrug, the ghost of a smile passing quickly across his lips.

I looked away, uncomfortable with the way my stomach flipped. I needed to get a grip. This was not something I should pursue. It couldn't end well.

Adam smiled around. If the conversation made him uncomfortable, it didn't show. He looked pleased.

I relaxed a little. I knew I could be over-sensitive to stuff like this.

'Actually,' said Adam. 'We try to give out little prizes for people who make it out in time. Just stuff we pick up at car boot sales, nothing special. Something to remember the experience by. Do you want the nerdy prize or the regular prize?' He had a half-smile that made me certain he knew which we would pick.

I guess he'd just watched us nerd our way around his escape room, so that wasn't terribly surprising.

'Hanna?' I said. All eyes had turned to her. I swear I could *feel* the telepathic weight of the group trying to get her to choose the nerdy option in spite of her disdain for all things geek.

Hanna rolled her eyes. 'The nerd option,' she said. 'For my nerdy-ass friends.' She gave me a scowl that couldn't quite disguise her smile. She'd had a good time.

'All right. You'll like these. I think they were a pretty good find.'

To my utter surprise, he withdrew a dice pouch from his pocket and revealed a set of translucent blue poly dice. They sparkled as they caught the light, flecked in a rainbow of colours. 'They're crystal,' he said, offering them to us. 'Not sure what kind. Couldn't pass them up. I'll be honest — it was hard to add them to the prizes. I feel like they'd really suit my healer.'

'You play TTRPGs?' Arries sounded eager.

'Yep. Next best thing to an escape room,' he replied with a wink.

He seemed nice, but on that we'd have to disagree. Nothing was better than *Kin*.

'So ... who gets them?' Arries asked Hanna, his eyes wide.

'One each. Maybe give the spare to that weird kid in your house,' Hanna said, looking at me. She loved every update I made on Riya. 'Inspire a new generation of nerds.'

My mouth pulled to one side. 'It's your birthday,' I said. 'Shouldn't you keep the spare?'

'One each,' she repeated firmly. 'We all played a fair part. Don't get all weird on me, it's just dice.'

I nodded, and she winked. 'Thanks everyone for coming out. And thanks, P, for organising it all.' She gave Pauline a rare smile lacking in sarcasm, and Pauline looked down at her hands, an expression so shy that it looked out of place on her face.

Hanna distributed the dice, pressing a cold d4 and d8 into my hand. 'The d4, for the skill die of all your tiny beasties,' she said, referencing my habit of shapeshifting into small and unusual animals in the game via my polymorph spell.

I studied the die as she handed out the rest. A tiny, glittering pyramid, with a surprising weight. It seemed unlikely that it could be a *balanced* die, but it was beautiful nonetheless. Besides, Adam had been right; I *did* want to remember today.

Rex lightly brushed my shoulder as we went through the door. 'Sorry,' he murmured. Then he looked up. 'It was fun today.'

His eyes were so dark. We both made so little eye contact that it startled me every time; the moment of connection, the surprising warmth of his gaze. It was a level of intensity that I usually tried to avoid, but with Rex it was hard to look away.

I managed to nod. 'We were a good team,' I agreed. 'Um, see you tomorrow.'

'Tomorrow,' he agreed and strode off into the evening air while the others gathered outside.

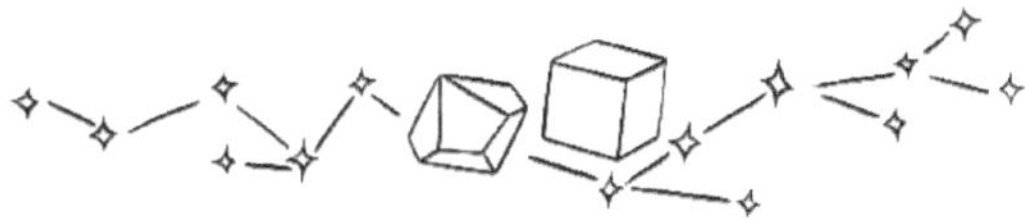

CHAPTER TWELVE

'What was that?' Kenta's voice was close to my ear.

I jumped. 'What the hell, Ken!' I was too startled to be meek, besides which Kenta was very familiar with my dislike of close contact by now.

'Yeah, what the hell, Ken!' Hanna agreed loudly, before returning to her conversation with Pauline.

Arries elbowed him. 'Kenta.'

'Sorry. Yeah. Tar needs personal space. I keep forgetting that.'

'*Everyone* needs personal space,' Arries corrected. 'Some people just put up with it when you don't ask them first.'

'Wow. Okay. If we're done calling me out, I'd like to repeat my earlier question. What was that, Tar?'

Arries' eyebrows furrowed. 'What was what?'

'*That.*' Kenta flapped his hands at me, then lowered his voice. 'With Tar. And Rex.'

I felt my traitorous cheeks heating up. 'Nothing,' I said while my skin flushed in betrayal of my words. 'I really have no idea what you're talking about.'

'No, there's definitely *something.*' Arries watched me thoughtfully. Then he straightened and rounded on Kenta. 'Doesn't mean we can hound them about it!'

'Who's hounding? I'm not hounding. I'm a cat person.'

'Ken.'

Kenta rubbed his chin sheepishly. 'Look, I don't want to be, like, invasive. But if you want to talk about it, I'm here.'

'Ditto,' said Arries.

I stared at my feet, my mind turning. I'd never really been the kind of person who *talked* about things. Real things. I could discuss video games or books, you know, *topics*, but when it came to emotional stuff ... I barely had a grip on things myself. I'd never had anyone I trusted enough to talk things through with.

I'd always been envious of the easy communication between friends though. If nothing else, it would be amazing to have someone to help me work through the thoughts and feelings that confused even me.

'I, um.' I cleared my throat, eyes still on my shoes. 'I might be developing a crush, but don't worry, I've got a handle on it.' That was a wild lie. 'It'll pass, probably.' I had never known a crush to pass.

The thing was, I wasn't attracted to people the way most people were. I didn't look at someone and want them based on what I saw. It was based on what I knew, what they were like. It was based on whatever relationship we had built. And it didn't happen often.

I didn't want to sleep with Rex. I wanted him to notice me. I wanted to talk to him, and laugh with him, and spend time with him. I wanted to feel like he was drawn to me, the way I was drawn to him.

'"It'll pass",' Kenta echoed. His eyebrows raised. 'Wow. You're a real romantic.'

I looked up just long enough to scowl at Kenta. 'Look, he's made it clear that he's not interested.'

'Has he?' Arries seemed surprised. 'You mean, you told him how you feel?'

I remembered our conversation on Pauline's doorstep. 'Well ... I asked him if he wanted to party up in A:RO sometime and he said he found it awkward to spend time with *Kin* people outside of the game. I think that's pretty clear.'

Arries nodded. 'That's fair.'

'What?' Kenta blustered a moment. 'No! That's not fair. That's barely even tangentially related to telling him how you feel, or him telling you he's not interested. Rex's a freak who only leaves his bedroom for *Kin* and gets all hyper-ventilate-y at the thought of socialising.'

My blush deepened. 'Okay, this is turning into a call-out and I'm not enjoying it.'

'And Rex isn't a freak,' Arries said. 'He's just ... shy.'

'We're talking about Rex being a freak?' Hanna and Pauline joined our little circle. 'Oh man, I have *so* many thoughts.'

'Be nice, Hanna.' Pauline frowned at her.

Hanna shook her head. 'It's my birthday! I'm allowed to be mean to my friends on my *birthday*. Besides, I love the little hermit.'

'Hanna.'

I'd been anxious about sharing my feelings with Arries and Kenta. I definitely wasn't going to do it with Hanna. 'Look, it's getting late. I should head home. Happy birthday, Hanna.' I gave her a brief smile. 'See you all tomorrow.'

I headed for my car. 'Tar!' Kenta trotted after me.

I paused, wondering whether I'd forgotten something, but Kenta said, 'I know it's not my business, and I'm a terrible gossip sometimes but ... Rex hasn't ever come out with us before, and I've known him for years.' He raised his eyebrows. 'I wonder what's changed?'

I nodded, too surprised to manage more than that. It was a heavy thought, and one that I didn't quite know how to feel about.

No, that's not true. I knew exactly how I felt about it. I felt light and buoyant and tense at the same time, like I was full of too much air.

And that was bad, because the main obstacle in this ... this whatever this was, wasn't Rex.

It was me.

When I got home, my mind still whirling from all that had happened that day, I found Saanvi and Riya doing a puzzle scattered across the sitting room floor.

Saanvi looked up as I walked in. 'Sorry — this isn't in the way, is it?'

I shook my head. 'No, not at all. Do you mind if I use the kitchen?'

'Go ahead.'

I fixed myself a light dinner of vegetables and rice, listening to Saanvi's gentle conversation with her daughter as they worked on the puzzle.

My own mother could not be described as gentle. She was frantic and weird, always talking, always pushing. It had always seemed like there was no common ground between us; like we were standing on opposing cliffs, facing off across an abyss of misunderstanding. But I still recognised a mirror of our relationship in Saanvi and Riya as they talked and chuckled their way through their puzzle.

Whatever our differences, my mother had always loved me and wanted the best for me. I remembered evening tarot readings by candlelight, my mother holding my hands as she read my future.

I scooped my dinner into a bowl and was heading upstairs when Saanvi got a phone call. She strode into the hallway, blocking my exit. I looked down at Riya, carefully turning every puzzle piece upside down so the colours didn't show.

'That must be hard mode,' I said, crouching down opposite her — which wasn't extremely comfortable with a bowl of food in my hands, but I didn't teeter too much and it wouldn't be for long.

She gazed solemnly at the puzzle before her. 'Peeking is cheating,' she said. 'What's in your bowl?'

'Vegetables and rice,' I said.

She leaned forward to peer into my bowl. 'I like those,' she said, before returning to her mission of preventing puzzle cheating.

I didn't speak child very well or really know how to interact with Riya at all, but she was an easygoing sort of person so I didn't think I could get it very wrong. 'Do you want some?' I asked.

Riya's head shot up. She looked surprised to be asked. Her mouth twisted to one side, then the other. 'Hmm ... yes please.'

Riya scrambled off to get a bowl and fork, and when she returned I transferred a small portion from my bowl. It didn't look like a lot to me and had barely interfered with my own serving, but Riya gasped and said, 'Ooh, that's a lot!' in a pleased way.

Though I could feel the tension building in me, I still had nowhere else to go. As I cast around for something else to say, I remembered the spare crystal die. 'Hey, Riya. You like games, right?'

She nodded. 'I like pounce-and-seek, and snakes-and-ladders, and the one where you give each other money and everyone yells a lot.'

I paused. 'Monopoly?'

Riya shrugged and took a bite of her rice.

'Well ... I have a very special die,' I said. 'For very special games. And it's for you.' I held up the crystal d8, which sparkled in the light.

Riya's mouth made a perfect 'O'. 'It's got extra sides!'

'It's got 8 sides,' I said. 'It's called a d8. It's used in games of pretend called Tabletop Roleplaying Games, or TTRPGs for short.'

'A lot of letters,' Riya said, frowning.

'Uh. Yeah, actually. Could definitely be shorter ... well, the one I play is called *Kin*.' I dropped the die into Riya's hand.

She stared at it. 'Will you play it with me?'

I felt a pinch of panic. Could I run a game? I wasn't very experienced ... but then, Riya was seven. 'I can show you my rulebook sometime,' I said. 'Then if you want to play, we can give it a go.'

Riya considered. 'I like rules,' she said. And that seemed to be that.

We ate on the floor, Riya still working on the puzzle, until Saanvi returned. Her eyebrows quirked as I scrambled to my feet, feeling vaguely guilty. I wasn't completely sure on the rules of engagement with Riya and Saanvi — I'd baby-sat Riya a few times, but that probably didn't mean I could just barge into family time.

'Sorry, Saanvi,' I started breathlessly.

Saanvi waved away my apology. 'Don't look so panicked, Tar. I'm glad Riya had someone to play with while I was busy.' Her eyes swept to the little bowl beside her daughter. 'And it was kind of you to share your dinner, though I'm sure she bullied you into it.'

'Oh, uh — it's fine, honestly. I had a big serving.' I headed for the door, and hesitated a moment. 'Uh, bye Riya.'

Riya picked up her bowl. 'I'm going with Tar,' she announced, but her mother caught her around the waist. 'Tar has other things to do,' Saanvi told her. 'Besides, we haven't finished the puzzle.'

'The puzzle!' Riya agreed excitedly, and as I ascended the stairs unfollowed, I assumed she settled back into it.

As I closed my bedroom door behind me, the weight of the entire day pressed on me. Anxieties that I had been forcefully holding at bay overwhelmed my defenses, nearly bowling me over. I flopped onto my bed, cringing as I ran over every awkward moment, every perceived mistake and faux pas. I knew this was an unhealthy behaviour, that I should shake off these thoughts and do something more productive, but I couldn't seem to unstick my mind from this slideshow of amplified embarrassment. I grew sweaty and nauseated and felt a fist clenched in my chest. I growled and clutched my face and rolled on the bed as if in the grip of a nightmare, though I was fully awake.

When it passed, I was tired but oddly focused, my mind caught around one specific memory: *'Rex hasn't ever come out with us before,'* Kenta had said. *'I wonder what's changed?'*

It was the one memory that didn't make me squirm.

I picked up my phone, clicking through my chatrooms until I found my recent messages with Rex.

Tar♟: Me too. I could use an actual talent

Rex♛: You're already really talented, Tar.

I stared at the message, hoping it would reveal Rex's mind to me. But all I could see was the Rex I already knew — withdrawn, encouraging, unreadable.

I took the crystal d4 from my pocket, admiring it for a moment. It was cloudier than some of the others, with little internal cracks and fissures, but it was smooth and cold to the touch. Somehow, it made the memories of the day less painful. We'd worked well as a team and got out in good time, and everyone had been enthusiastic in their praise. It had been a good day.

I set the die on my bedside table and, after a moment's hesitation, called my mother.

'Tar, darling? Is everything all right?'

'I just wanted to ... wait.' There was a little mechanical hum on the other end of the line, followed by a long exhale. 'Mum! Are you vaping?'

'It's called an e-cigarette,' she said. 'They're very safe.'

'You don't even smoke!'

'Of course not. But e-cigarettes can be used in cleansing rituals, you know. A pure mist, much like incense. Very good for the soul.'

'Where the hell did you hear that? No, nevermind.' I clamped down on my sudden irritation. It was hardly the weirdest fad my mother had jumped on. 'Mum ... I was wondering. You always said I'm destined for great things. And

... and I feel like I'm failing at even regular things. Normal stuff, like friends and relationships and work. I'm not talented. I'm not anything special. And I just want to know why you say that.'

My mother went unexpectedly quiet on the other end of the line. As the seconds stretched, I prompted, 'Mum?'

'I wish I could say it was written in the stars at your birth,' she said quietly. A chill ran down my spine as I realised: it was just something she said. It didn't mean anything, even to my mother who believed in destiny. 'But the truth is, there was nothing miraculous about your birth, except that it brought *you* into the world. I named you Tarot because I wanted you to choose your own future and not be at the whim of fate the way the rest of us are.'

My mother's dramatics usually made me roll my eyes, but she sounded so sincere that I found myself caught up in her words.

She continued, 'But you struggled. You struggled so much, and I didn't know how to help you. Not just with your gender, not just with your sexuality. With life. Sometimes I felt like I was one of the problems; just another person who didn't understand you. But I wanted to. I wanted it so badly.'

She drew a shuddering breath. 'But in spite of it all, you grew into this amazing person. Creative and strong in ways I never expected. Able to look at the world and see things nobody else does. Truth-telling in ways that sometimes make me think you have the gift. You can see so far into people, Tar, when you're not afraid of them. When you're not telling yourself you're a different species.

'You weren't born with it. You trained hard for it. And it's those things — your creativity, your strength, and your hard-won empathy that told me, even when you were a little kid, that you would do great things one day.' She paused. 'Does that answer your question?'

It was hard to speak past the lump in my throat. 'Yeah, mum. Thanks.'

For a moment, the line was silent as we both processed the conversation. It was more intense than any conversation I could remember having with my mother that wasn't also a fight. But it also made me feel closer to her. I don't know that it reassured me that my mother thought I would be able to fight my way to greatness. I don't think she completely understood me, either. I didn't think of myself as a different species. Sometimes, I just felt like people had shoved me into that box. But it did make me feel seen, and cared for, and like someone was in my corner. And right now, that was enough.

'So, um.' I cleared my throat. 'What have you been up to recently?'

And my mother became completely animated again. She launched into a conversation about her recent meeting with her psychic and I couldn't help but laugh at her enthusiasm. Later, when I said goodnight, I felt a lot better than I had when I'd first called.

I put out the lights and turned over in bed. The die on my bedside table glowed faintly in the dark. Sleepily, I wondered what it had been treated with. Then my body grew heavy and sleep overtook me and the day at last came to a close.

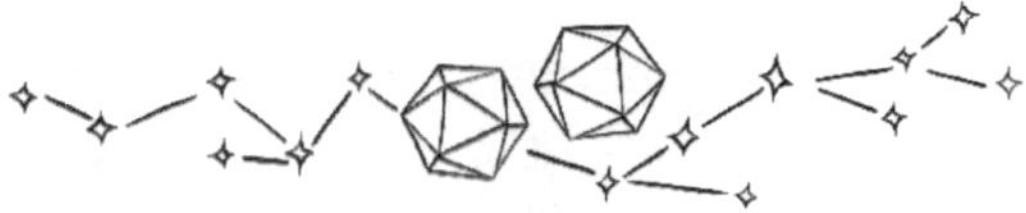

CHAPTER THIRTEEN

I awoke groggily, startled by moisture on my cheek. I rolled over, my bedding crinkling oddly, squinting against the unexpectedly bright light. My entire body ached as if I'd run a marathon the day before, and a headache nearly split my head in two.

I blinked, wiping the moisture from my face, as my eyes slowly adjusted. I had a terrible sense of wrongness. Everything seemed too open.

I reached out beside me and felt leaves. I lurched upright. I was in a forest clearing, shrubs and leaf litter all around me, dew on my cheeks and on my glasses. Mixed among the silver-barked trees were thick, fleshy stalks in blues, greens, and purples, holding up glittering caps with thick fibrous undersides. Toadstools the size of trees. 'No,' I whispered. I staggered to my feet, wincing at the pain in my muscles.

This could not be happening. This was ... some sort of weird dream. I looked down at myself — I was wearing robes? Or a long tunic? Blue and split around my legs, with comfortable leggings and soft-soled leather boots. My glasses were unfamiliar; round and wire-rimmed. I had leather pauldrons buckled to my shoulders and crossing my chest, plus leather bracers and padding on my legs. Armour, of a sort. My hands were pale and near-white, the skin oddly sparkly. A sickle lay in the leaves beside me. I flinched as a luminous purple beetle the size of a mouse scurried over the carved wooden handle to disappear into the leaf litter.

A suspicion struck me. I reached up and felt my head. My fingertips ran along rough shaved sides to tug at a short tail at the back. Hair utterly unlike my own, but still utterly familiar to me.

I had dreamed of being Astaran many times, but never this vividly. And never with such a startling clarity of mind. It had never *frightened* me.

Somehow, I had gone to sleep as a regular human and woken up as an astralkin. If this *was* awake ...

Something stirred in the leaves to my left. I watched as a huge fox person sat up, clutching his head. He had a small rune beside his left eye — a pronoun-marking rune, from the game. 'Owww,' he said, wrinkling his muzzle. His armour gleamed, silver against gold, with a sun emblazoned on his chest.

He looked different than I'd envisioned him when we played — his fur was more defined and a more vibrant peach, his muzzle longer, his armour a different design — but I couldn't mistake that voice.

'Arries?'

He looked at me, then gasped, bearing long white teeth. 'Tar? Or is it Astaran? God, why does my head hurt like this?'

'Arries, you're, uh ... look at your hands.'

'Hmm?' He held out his hands. 'What the flip? Oh my god, I'm Arries! I mean, Feykin Arries, not Human Arries!' He got to his feet, panting at the effort of lifting so much metal. 'I have a *tail!*' He swished back and forth to prove his point. It was longer and slimmer than I had imagined it, but still incredibly plush. 'Wait ... can I ...? Tar!' He shrank down, fur receding, until he looked nearly exactly like his normal self, but with fox ears and tail. The armour shrank with him. He stared down at his human hands as if he didn't recognise them. '... Woah.'

'Holy Fuck. *Ken.* Nooo.' Hanna's voice crew our attention. She was now 4ft tall. Her face was the same, but with a doe-like nose and ears, her skin purple and dusted with freckles. She had a rune denoting her gender as well, as I suspected would all the others. Her bottom half was fawn-like with trousers that didn't obscure her hooved feet. Her short, smooth tail twitched.

Beside her, Kenta looked roughly himself — except that his face was smeared with a fearsome black paint, and he wore armour crusted in blood and entrails.

'This is so much worse than I ever imagined it.' Kenta touched the armour gingerly with one finger. It came away with a thick paste of dried blood. He shuddered. 'Ughhh. *Awful.*'

My head throbbed again. I felt like my brain was being squeezed in a vice. I doubled over, clutching my head. 'Oh god. Does anyone else feel like someone is using their brain like a stress ball?'

A chorus of agreement followed my question. Kenta said, 'I also want to puke from the smell of me. This is the worst way I've ever woken up, and that's really saying something.'

'Same.' A woman in a silken silver cloak and grey robes staggered to her feet. The hood, embroidered in strange runes, was pinned to her thick hair, which was dark as the night sky and shimmered with just as many stars. More shimmered like glittery freckles against her cool brown skin. A large pearlescent-white eye tattoo marked her forehead. She stood slightly hunched over, clearly in pain, and utterly familiar even through the smudgy kohl around her eyes.

It was not a look I had ever imagined Pauline wearing, but it was obviously and unmistakably her.

'P!' Arries rushed over to her, armour clonking. 'Are you all right?'

'Apart from a pain in my head to complement the pain in my abdomen? Fine.'

Arries offered her a thick, armour-plated arm for support, which she took and leaned against, gritting her teeth in a pain snarl.

'This is a very weird dream,' I said.

'I was just thinking the same thing,' said Arries.

Hanna shrugged. 'Oh, well it's pretty normal for me.'

'Really?' Kenta looked skeptical.

'No!' Hanna threw up her hands. 'I'm four feet tall! I have *hooves!* This is fucking crazy!'

'I don't think it's a dream,' said Pauline, and the truth of her words rang within me.

'Of course it's a dream!' said Hanna. 'What the fuck else could it be?'

'It *has* to be a dream,' said Kenta. 'If it's not a dream, then this is *actually blood* and I refuse to believe that.'

I looked down at my hands, at the strange paleness of my skin, the silvery sheen of my fingernails. 'I've never had a dream this vivid,' I said slowly. My voice shook over the words. 'And when I'm lucid in a dream, nobody else knows it's a dream.'

'Where's Rex?' Pauline said. She looked around us. 'The rest of us are here. Why isn't he?'

'I'm here.' Rex's voice was tired. He parted a thick shrub wall and stepped through, a lizard-like tail sweeping the ground behind him and leaving a trail of blue-edged shadow with the movement. He looked like himself — same face, same build — but voidkin now. His eyes were filled with the ethereal blue energy of Ram, and his locs faded to ghostly blue at the edges. Curling ram's horns and sneaky scales disappearing into his hairline. Black nails and shadowed eyes. I didn't know how to deal with the blending of these two people I had come to know so well — Ram, the mysterious wizard with a soft side, and Rex, my reclusive *Kin* friend.

For a moment, all I could do was stare at him. He could have walked ready-made out of a daydream. So could *I*, for that matter. So could we all.

This was a dream. It had to be a dream.

'Help me down?' said Pauline. Arries gently obliged, helping Pauline settle on the floor. She took a deep, steadying breath. 'Okay,' she said. 'Each of us thinks this might just be an incredibly vivid dream. Let's run through our options. When I am dreaming, space is distorted. That tree over there looks ...' she paused. 'Maybe fifteen steps away. Arries?'

'On it.' Arries walked to the tree, counting loudly, until he stood beside it. 'That was thirteen steps, P.'

Pauline's lips thinned, and she nodded. 'That sounds plausible.'

Hanna elbowed Kenta. It thunked against his armor.

'Hey!'

'Pinch me,' she demanded.

'You just elbowed me. That had to hurt.'

'Pinch me, damnit!'

Kenta leaned down and pinched the flesh on her outstretched arm between his gauntleted fingers.

'FUCK!' Hanna tried to shove Kenta away, but couldn't budge his plate-armoured bulk — especially not from waist-height. 'That was fucking hard, Ken!'

'I'm wearing gauntlets! I can't feel pressure!'

Hanna smoothed over the skin where Kenta had pinched her. 'This is going to bruise.' She looked around at the group, eyes suddenly wide. 'I don't think this is a dream, guys.'

'That doesn't prove anything for the rest of us,' said Pauline. 'What else is a signifier?'

'In my dreams, uh ... I can never dial anything on my phone,' I said. 'Every time I try to dial 999, it doesn't work. My fingers fumble the numbers.'

There was a pause. 'How often do you have to dial 999 in dreams?' asked Pauline.

I crossed my arms, avoiding their eyes. 'It comes up,' is all I said. People got weird about it whenever I talked about how frequently I had nightmares. It was, as far as I knew, an anxiety thing — my body was so full of nerves and adrenaline that my dreams interpreted it as constant danger.

'Well we can't test that without a phone,' said Pauline. She paused. 'Does anyone have phones?'

Everyone replied in the negative. We went through things as a group then — Hanna could never count to a hundred,

Kenta was never wearing trousers, Arries could click his heels and hover. Nothing came back a dream, but somehow nobody was quite convinced. Even though we could all feel the chill of the breeze when it picked up, even though we all had twigs and leaves stuck in our hair, even though the blood on Kenta's armour was sticky and hard to get off our hands.

'People don't bleed, in my dreams,' said Rex.

Kenta looked taken aback. 'What the actual ever-loving hell, Rex?'

'No, it's not —'

Hanna raised her eyebrows. 'I knew you were a freak but — '

Rex pressed his fingers to his temples. 'I have a lot of nightmares, okay?'

He looked tense, already closing in on himself. I knew how hard it was to reveal that kind of weirdness. And while I didn't think Hanna or Kenta actually meant to insult him, I knew the words cut just as deep as if they did.

And the thing was … he wasn't *wrong*.

'Nobody ever bleeds in my dreams either,' I said. Everyone turned to look at me. 'And it comes up a lot for me too. Think about it — does it for any of you?'

After a moment, there were a lot of shaken heads. 'I don't really know,' Arries said. 'I don't really have nightmares. Or if I do, I don't remember them.'

I smiled tightly. 'Lucky,' I said.

'Look, I'll test it,' said Rex. 'Kenta, give me your axe.'

Kenta shook his head, raising his hands. 'You do *not* want this thing touching your bloodstream,' he said. 'You'll probably catch consumption from it or something.'

'You're a nurse,' said Arries. 'Are you legally allowed to say things like "catch consumption"?'

'This is a very medieval situation!'

'You can have my knife,' said Hanna. She unsheathed it with a short, metallic swish from her belt, then held it up to Rex, handle-first.

Rex pulled back his sleeve, revealing neat, pale scars laddering his skin.

My mouth went dry and my stomach lurched.

'Rex ...' Pauline gripped Rex's wrist, the one holding the knife.

Arries came up on Rex's other side, resting a hand on his shoulder. 'I had no idea, buddy.'

Rex shook his head. 'It's not recent. When I was a teenager ... it doesn't matter.'

'It matters,' says Pauline.

'We can't ask you to do that to yourself,' said Kenta.

Hanna was conspicuously silent, staring at Rex with a softer expression than I had ever seen on her face.

I took a deep breath and stepped forward. Kenta was right; we couldn't ask him to do that. And I didn't want to ask any of them to do it, either. 'I'll do it,' I said, holding my hand out for the knife.

Rex looked at me uncertainly. 'Tar ... it's nothing, really.'

'Then it won't matter if I do it instead,' I said, as practically as I could. Truthfully, I was terrified of cutting myself. I dealt well with pain when I received it, but the expectation of it was almost more painful. I kept all that tucked away inside though. Pauline released Rex and gave me a nod; after a moment, Rex handed me the knife.

'Outside of the arm will do the least harm,' he said.

I nodded and tested the knife with my thumb. I could barely brush against it before it started to snick against my skin. Shit — this was a hell of a lot sharper than a kitchen knife.

Did I draw it lightly across my skin, because it was so sharp? Or did I do it as quickly as possible because I was already losing my nerve? Could I do both? Could you be light and fast? Was that a thing?

'Tar. Hey.' Kenta walked over and snapped his fingers, drawing me out of my spiral. I blinked up at him, the knife still in my hands. 'Do you want me to help you?' he asked. 'I'm a nurse. I won't cut deep.'

Cut deep. The words seemed to echo in my mind. Slowly, I nodded. Kenta reached for the knife.

Something rustled in the trees nearby. I tensed; everyone turned to look. Nobody reached for their weapons, because god, who reaches for a weapon?

Pushing aside a hip-height cluster of blue toadstools and silver-leafed shrubs came a little girl — jewel-brown skin, messy black curls, and pointed elven ears. Her tongue was sticking out on one side of her mouth in a look of comical determination. Her blue tunic and leggings were already grass-stained, and a crushed velvet cloak trailed behind her. Her eyes swept the group, then locked onto me.

I froze. My chest went tight.

Hanna lowered her fists, which she must have raised in anticipation. 'Whose kid is this?'

But I already knew.

That kid was Riya.

This was my dream or it was no dream at all.

I opened my mouth to say as much, but then Kenta swiped the blade across my arm and everything went black.

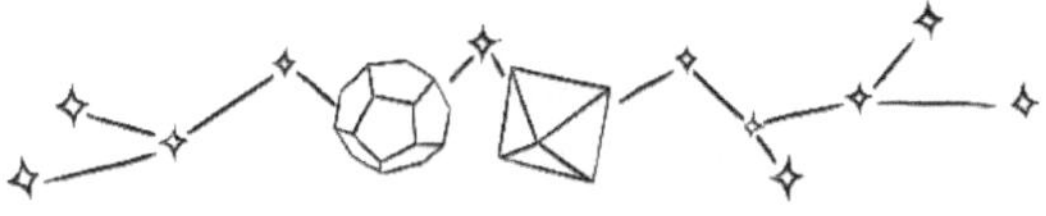

CHAPTER FOURTEEN

When I opened my eyes again Riya was crying and Hanna was shouting and Arries' fox ears were twitching as he leaned over me. 'Oh my god, Tar! Oh my god, are you okay? It's going to be okay!'

He was gripping my wrists. The back of my arm bled sluggishly. It wasn't a bad cut — I must have fainted. 'Arries,' I said, but the words came out muzzy and mumbled. 'It's fine.'

But Arries was still fussing over me and staring at the wound. Then his hands felt oddly warm, like a burst of sunlight, quickly followed by a bloom of golden energy that illuminated my arm. The skin of the wound itched; it felt like it was being gently pinched closed. I watched the skin seal before my eyes.

All at once, everyone fell silent. Even Riya seemed too stunned to cry.

'Arries,' said Rex, the first to break the silence. 'Did you just Healer's Touch?'

Arries released my arm and scrambled back. 'I don't know — did I? I was just really worried about you and then I felt —'

'Warm?' I said.

He stared at me with wide dark eyes. 'Exactly.'

'So do we have the same powers as our characters, then?' Hanna asked. 'Could I play a song and force you to dance?'

Kenta was shaking his head. 'No. Nope. This can't be happening.'

Riya tugged at my sleeve. 'Tar?' She said my name like a question.

I tried to smile. 'Yeah, it's me, Riya. Just, uh ... shinier.'

'I'm a Lord of the Rings,' Riya told me solemnly. She looked shaken to me — more shaken than I had ever seen her. She was a kid made of confidence and surety and weirdness, but this was too strange even for her.

I needed to hold things together for her. If I acted like things weren't scary, maybe that would give her confidence.

Because looking at her now, twisting her hands in front of her, it suddenly occurred to me that we needed to get back — that we needed to get *her* back. She was a seven year-old kid who needed her mother. Saanvi must be going crazy right now wondering where she was.

'Yeah,' I told her. 'You're an elf, like in Lord of the Rings.' Actually, that wasn't such a crazy thing to say. Elves were included in feykin mechanics ...

God, why was I thinking about mechanics right now? I wasn't playing *Kin*, I was *living* it.

Riya looked soothed by the words, anyway. She brought her hands up to her ears and ran her thumbs over the pointed tips.

'So you know this kid?' Hanna said, jerking her head in Riya's direction.

I nodded. 'She's the daughter of the lady I lodge with.'

'I don't recognise her,' said Rex.

'Well, yeah, you've never been to Tar's house,' said Kenta. 'None of us have.'

But Rex was shaking his head. 'You don't understand — there are no new faces in dreams. It's all people you've encountered, and I have really good facial recall. I have never seen her before.'

Pauline sighed. 'I think we need to proceed as if this isn't a dream. It's passed every test, and now there's a little girl who needs our help.'

Needs our help. The words resonated inside me, deep and kind of sickening. Riya wasn't a thirty-something year-old who daydreamed about living in a fantasy world. Riya was a child.

Panic started to build again, tighter and more crushing than before. I knew I was Riya's only contact here, the only familiar face. I knew I needed to hold it together for her. But my breathing was already starting to judder and jump and the world was starting to spin and no amount of breathing exercises was going to help me when each inhale felt utterly devoid of oxygen.

'Arries.' I heard Pauline's voice, unusually gentle but still with that snap of authority. 'Look after the kid.'

'Will you be —?'

'Now, please.'

Arries clinked past in a blur of golden plate armour. Then I felt cool hands on my wrists. I flinched at the touch, but the pressure was reassuring. Though one hand rested over the healed-over wound, I felt no pain from it. 'I need to sit down,' said Pauline. 'Can you sit down with me?'

I nodded, unable to look at her. Together, we lowered to the ground. Pauline kept her grip on my wrists.

'What's the girl's name?' she asked.

I opened my mouth but no words would come out. I tried again. '... Riya,' I said after a pause.

'And what's her mother's name?' Pauline asked.

Her mother? 'Saanvi,' I said. It felt like a name from a long time ago, but saying it grounded me a little. I was answering questions; I hadn't suffocated yet. I wasn't dying, I reminded myself. I only felt like I was. This was what panic felt like.

'Ken? Can you and Hanna go look for the mother, Saanvi?'

Kenta didn't answer.

'Ken. Hey. Earth to Ken!' Someone, Hanna probably, snapped their fingers. 'Shit. He's panicking too. I'll go on my own, P.'

'No, take Rex. You're okay, Rex?'

'I'm here, I'm alive, and I am too numb to panic properly,' came Rex's cool response.

'Good enough!' cried Hanna. 'Come on, let's go find this kid's mum.'

I don't know how long passed after that. I closed my eyes and focused on my breathing, and now it seemed to help. Pauline still manacled my wrists, but I felt more tethered than trapped.

This was my friend. These were my friends. There was no-one I would rather be lost in a fantasy world with. I wouldn't have to get Riya home on my own.

When I opened my eyes, I realised Pauline had let go of my wrists. She spoke quietly to Kenta, who sat on the ground with his arms around his knees, far too anxious to be either the bloodthirsty cleric of the game or the loud, friendly player I knew. Arries and Riya were playing tic-tac-toe with sticks in the dirt.

'How do you keep winning?!' Arries asked.

Riya gave him a solemn look. 'You need to get three in a row,' she told him. He caught my eye and winked.

I looked down at my lap. I was wearing Astaran's clothes, almost exactly as I'd envisioned them. Patched brown leggings pocked with grass stains and mud spatters. I was wearing a top of mostly rags wrapped around my torso like bandages, and a woollen blue tunic-like garment over the top. My skin was my skin, but paler and freckled with sparkling stardust. I wondered if, on a full moon, my aura would flare into a bright glow, as I'd written into my character sheet.

Exactly as I'd envisioned it, yet simultaneously so much more real. I lucid-dreamed fairly regularly. I was used to vivid dreams. But this — the scratch of the coarse wool against my arms, the thick ridges of the patches on my leggings, the way my pearl-white hair hurt if I tugged on it — this was more detailed, more sensory, than anything I could have come up with.

This was real. And maybe that would make me freak out if I thought too hard about it. But I needed to deal with it, regardless.

I got up and walked over to Arries and Riya.

'You okay?' Arries asked. His eyes, still dark brown and reminiscent of the human I knew, were creased with concern.

I nodded, because actually saying the words seemed like a lot. 'How about you, Riya?' I asked.

Riya pursed her lips. 'Winning is boring.'

Arries looked crushed.

Riya stood up and walked over to stand next to him. Even with her stood up and him sitting down, she had to get on tip-toe to pat his shoulder. 'You'll get better,' she said, consolingly.

She seemed to be coping okay. She was only seven — this couldn't be that strange to her, right? The whole world was still pretty new to her.

But she was only *seven* — she needed a parent. She needed her mum. She needed to be cared for and looked after.

God, if only I was *capable* of that. I wasn't even capable of caring for myself! But I needed to try.

'Are you hungry? Cold? Tired?' I tried.

Riya stared at me a moment. 'I want cabbage.'

I don't know how it was that I was literally standing in a fantasy world straight out of the combined imaginations of my TTRPG group but somehow it was this that had me spluttering in disbelief. 'You ... what?'

'I'm hungry and I want cabbage,' she clarified, yet I felt no closer to understanding the words coming out of her mouth.

'Riya ... I don't think I have cabbage.'

Riya frowned.

'But!' I raised my hand. 'I'm pretty sure I have some rations or something. I know Astaran had some left over ...' I knelt down beside her and unslung the satchel swinging at my side. 'Uhh ... I think Ken was carrying most of the supplies, but here.' I reached into the bag, sorting through what I carried. Bundles of dried flowers, a few little fabric-wrapped parcels, and ...

I paused as my fingers brushed smooth crystal. I pulled out the small pyramid, which glittered in the early light.

My d4, from the escape room.

Nothing else here was from home. No phone, no clothes. Just this.

Riya leaned close to examine it. 'I have mine too,' she said, pulling the d8 out of her pocket. She clinked it against mine, as if in a toast.

I looked around at the others. I was willing to bet they had their dice, too. And that Rex and Hanna wouldn't find Saanvi anywhere in these woods.

Riya sighed and shifted from foot to foot.

Later. We would work out what that meant later.

I put the die away, pulled out a little cheesecloth-wrapped parcel, and undid the twine. Inside was a hunk of mature but serviceable cheese, some spiced bread loaf that was mercifully still soft, and a little pot of what smelled like a fruit chutney. There were a few hairy carrots among them.

I kind of smiled to see them. I remembered buying rations but not specifically how Pauline had described them. Was this what she had envisioned for us?

I offered the spread to Riya. 'Have whatever you want,' I said, my mind going back to our general supplies. I was pretty sure we had a magical cooler with supplies for a week or two ... that had to be more than enough for whatever we were doing here, right? Or at least enough to get to the nearest town, I didn't think any of our travel had taken us more than a week without pitstops.

So we had our characters' supplies. We had our characters' bodies ... sort of. We had our characters' abilities, if Arries' recent miracle was anything to go by. Would the people of this world remember us? Those of us who correlated to the Amethyst Hand, anyway?

And what did that make Pauline, who had played every NPC we ever encountered in this world but resembled none of them. What did it make Riya, who knew nothing of this world at all?

I watched Riya carefully dip a carrot into the chutney then crunch it with an approving look. I was lucky she was such a weird kid ...

Rustling came from the edge of the clearing. I stood up, hands flexing nervously, completely unprepared for what we would do if we got attacked by an owlbeast or a gillyteeth or any of *Kin*'s monsters. I wasn't Astaran of the Silver Grove, I was a local museum guide wearing their clothes. Could I attack one with my sickle? An image of the open maw of an owlbeast filled my vision, the teeth dripping with drool and gore. No, that didn't seem likely ...

But then a purple feykin emerged from between the bushes, cursing, followed by a sheepish-looking Rex.

I hurried over. 'Did you find her? Saanvi?' I didn't expect them to, but I couldn't let go of the hope. It would be so much better for both of them if Saanvi had somehow come here with us.

Hanna shook her head. 'We found some, like, blue wolves — don't fucking panic, Tar, they ran when they saw us. We made a goddamn racket, but we didn't find her or any sign of her.'

Rex gave me a worried look. 'She might not have come with us. What do we even all have in common?'

Hanna shrugged. 'Everyone but the kid is in P's game.'

'It's the dice,' I said, more abruptly than I intended. I fished the d4 out of my pocket again. 'I gave one to Riya. I bet you have yours, too.'

Hanna and Rex felt their pockets and produced their dice.

'Well ... fuck,' Hanna said.

Rex tried to tuck his hair behind his ear, grimacing as he bumped his knuckles against his ram horns. 'We can't just sit around here in a forest. We need to discuss this. We need shelter, and we need help.'

I nodded. 'I'll see if we can ... I don't know. Have a meeting? To decide what happens next?'

Hanna snorted. 'You don't need to say it like it's a question. None of us have a fucking clue what's going on right now. You're as sure of yourself as anyone is going to be.' She reached up and gave me a swift, hard punch in the arm. I was still so stunned by everything that I barely flinched.

So we rounded everyone up. Arries and Hanna started a campfire. We all knew that Rex possessed the magic to start it, but nobody acknowledged that out loud; perhaps it was still too strange. Or perhaps, like me, they didn't want to think about what might happen if we started playing with fire magic.

As Hanna struck the flint against her dagger and the wadded up grass and leaves flared into flame, we all looked to Pauline. This was her world, created whole-cloth from her own mind. Surely she, out of everyone, would know what to do.

But Pauline only stared into the flames, drawing her knees to her chest.

CHAPTER FIFTEEN

I wasn't sure our group had ever been this quiet. Hanna had no acerbic remarks, and Arries had no encouragement. Pauline wasn't calling anyone to order, and Kenta had still barely spoken since we'd arrived, looking oddly small for such a large and normally boisterous man. Perhaps Rex and I were quiet, but we always were. He sat across the fire from me and caught my eye, then flicked his gaze to the others around us. I knew he, too, was disturbed by the silence of our friends.

It was Riya who broke the silence first. She'd been watching Hanna and Arries build the fire with the same intense concentration she gave to everything. Now she picked up a stick and pointed it toward the fire. 'Can I help?'

Arries shook his head. 'I don't think so, Riya. Fire is dangerous —'

'— Not if you know what you're doing,' said Hanna. 'Come here, kid. I'll show you how it works, but you gotta promise not to mess with fire unless one of us is around, okay? Fire'll fuck you up.'

I flinched at the words, which I was certain Riya couldn't have encountered before, but she only nodded solemnly.

'Okay. Hold still.' Hanna came and stood behind her, gripping her hand which was holding the stick. She was only a matter of inches taller than Riya, but she nonetheless looked almost motherly as she guided the seven year-old through stoking the fire, turning the logs, and helped her add kindling so she could see the difference between kindling and fuel. Each movement sent a flurry of sparks up into the air.

It was calming to see, even though it was, in some ways, a reminder of how very far we were from home. This was a side of Hanna I would never normally see. And while she was still extremely Hanna about it, telling Riya grim stories of horrific burns and warning her that 'fire looks cool but it fucking hurts when you touch it', it was an alien experience.

After a while, Hanna and Riya sat back and the silence returned: oppressive, numbing.

Everyone was too stunned to handle this, but we couldn't sit here forever. We needed a plan. Rex caught my eye again. He lifted his eyebrows at me, as if asking my permission. I dipped my head in assent. We would handle this together.

'All right,' I said. 'We need a plan. P, who do we talk to, to ... I don't know, teleport?'

'Planeshift,' Rex said immediately. 'There's gotta be a powerful wizard somewhere who could send us home.'

Pauline stirred, resting her chin on her knees. It was still unsettling that she had taken on the appearance of a fantasy character as well, and not one we recognised. The eye marked on her forehead seemed to shimmer in the firelight. 'There are several who could planeshift us that I can think of, but why they would help us, I'm not sure. I never intended our world to be connected to Vanthis. It wasn't even a passing fancy for me. It's possible that a planeshift wouldn't be enough. And what's more ... the mage would have to be at least vaguely familiar with the plane they shift us to.'

'So we describe it to them,' said Hanna. She helped Riya turn a log, which resulted in a cloud of ash and sparks. Riya laughed and flinched back, while Hanna covered Riya's eyes with her other hand. 'It's not like it's fucking difficult. Cars, internet, space travel, T Swift ... I think we can give them the gist.'

Pauline didn't look convinced.

I ran my hands up and down my legs, the tension starting to seep through to me. I knew it was an autistic stim and that some people found it unnerving, but I really needed it right now. 'We need some kind of plan,' I said. 'This is as good as any.'

'I need to go home.' Kenta spoke for the first time since we'd first arrived. His voice was hoarse. He'd unbuckled his armour while the campfire had been set up; it now sat in a heap against a rock a ways away. He glanced at it quickly now, then away again.

Arries nodded. He'd kept his armour on and seemed to be adjusting to it fast. 'Hey. We know, buddy.' He leaned over and squeezed his shoulder. 'We'll work it out.'

Kenta shook his head. 'You don't understand.' His voice was little more than a murmur, almost swallowed by the crackling campfire.

There was a pause as we all took in the words. I continued to rub my hands on my legs, turning it into a light rock. Maybe I couldn't understand. This situation was stressful, but ... in many ways, wasn't it what I'd always dreamed of? Even my friends were here with me. Yet I didn't like the insinuation that he knew what I was thinking. *I* barely knew what I was thinking.

'Maybe you can explain it, then,' said Arries. His gentleness continued to astonish me. He had no bottom to his patience.

Kenta reached for the holy symbol at his throat. He tapped the symbol there, of the interlocking circles within a diamond. He cast a rueful look at Pauline as he did. Then he ripped it from his neck and threw it into the dark.

Pauline frowned, then tensed, her eyes widening. 'Oh. Oh Ken —'

'She's real, isn't she?' he said.

Pauline inclined her head in an unwilling nod. 'As Arries was able to cast Healer's Touch, we must assume that the gods are as real here as the magic.'

Understanding washed over me in a sickly wave. We had long speculated as to the name and nature of Kendallien's mysterious goddess. While we had never received confirmation, nobody had ever guessed that Kendallien, who craved violence and bloodshed, worshipped someone gentle and kind.

But Kenta was not Kendallien any more than I was Astaran. Kenta was a man of laughter and hugs and loud proclamations. He worried about making other people uncomfortable, even though he didn't really understand people as sensitive as me or Rex. Being a bit lacking in subtlety was a far cry from the character he played in-game.

'Shit,' I said, earning me a stern look from Riya. Perhaps she was more exposed to profanity than I'd assumed. 'What, can she make you —?'

Kenta shook his head. 'She can't *make* me do anything. But she can punish me for displeasing her, and send her other disciples to finish the job.' He snapped a twig between his fingers and tossed it into the fire. 'I always thought it was a fun challenge in playing the character.'

In my mind's eye, I envisioned a shadowy giant watching us through the clouds. Her gaze fixed on Kenta. She reached out with a clawed hand to snatch him away ...

Terrifying enough to be in a strange and dangerous world far from home. Far worse to be at the mercy of all-powerful beings who watched our every move.

I thought of some of the cults we had encountered in the game, or heard rumours about. Each led by a dark or strange god. Eldinithar, the Fey King, a shapeshifter who trapped people in elaborate and dangerous illusions for his own enjoyment. Ikkim, the Thorn Mother, who demanded suffering and whose disciples fed humans and creatures to the vast carnivorous plant that was the goddess' worldly avatar. Loshora, the Cruel Wind, who was said to be the voice of self-hatred in people's ear and whose followers were victims of her creed of redemption through pain and rejection.

There had been others, but none we had encountered followers of in-game yet. And none but the Thorn Mother really matched the violence Kendallien seemed to revel in. But the idea of Kenta having to answer to these gods or any like them was intolerable.

Sweat beaded on Kenta's forehead. He crossed his arms, staring deeper into the fire.

'Who is she?' Rex asked softly.

Kenta shook his head. 'I ... I don't want to say it out loud.' He glanced at Pauline.

Her eyes were full of sympathy. 'Alis-Umor,' she said softly. A breeze kicked up, sending a flurry of leaves across the clearing. 'The Blood Drinker.'

'The Blood Drinker,' I repeated automatically, more for the feel of the words than anything. It wasn't a name I had come across in our games so far, but the others tensed at the words.

'Isn't she a vampire, or something?' Hanna asked.

'Or something,' Kenta murmured, drawing his knees to his chest.

Pauline stared down at her lap, hands opening and closing. 'She's a goddess. Most commonly depicted as a red shadow. She derives her power from violence committed in her name, though there are stories of her draining the blood from sacrificed victims. She ...' Pauline cleared her throat. 'Doesn't give up her disciples easily.'

'Oh Ken,' I breathed, overwhelmed by sympathy. What must it feel like to be tied to something like that?

Kenta didn't say anything.

'Hey,' Arries gripped his shoulder with one gauntleted hand. 'We can get through this. We're practically trained to deal with this world. And we have help.'

'Do we?'

'We have P. She knows this world inside and out,' he insisted. Pauline looked down and didn't answer. 'And we have Sunara.'

Arries played a holy warrior, pledged to the sun goddess, Sunara, a being of warmth and growth. In the game, Arries had had several visions of her. A woman of healing flame who occasionally offered Arries guidance, and from whom Arries derived his healing powers.

If the gods were real, then in a way, it had been Sunara who had healed my arm.

But Sunara had never directly been involved in anything in the game. We couldn't expect her to swoop down from the sky and save us then, and somehow I doubted this would be any different.

'Your plan is to pray me away from my shitty god?' Kenta said. In spite of his fear, he almost smiled.

Arries smiled. 'For a start.'

For me, being Astaran had always been a dream, but now I wondered what that could really mean. Kenta was bound to a goddess of cruelty. Any of us might be at the mercy of our magic, or our characters' backstories. What made for a good game didn't necessarily make for a good life.

But surely, if we were here, it was better to be our characters than to be our regular selves?

'We should be using our abilities,' said Pauline. She started snapping her fingers, as she often did when she was agitated and thinking. It had the same energy as pacing. 'We should at least be testing them! Tar — you took the Pathfinder spell, right? You should be able to identify our location and our next step. So where are we?'

I started to panic. 'I don't know how to —' I stopped, my chest tight, but not from panic.

Because I did know how to do it. I could see it in my mind's eye, as if I had done it thousands of times before. The shape of my hands in the air, the feel of my breath filling my chest, the sensation of drawing energy up through the ground and into my body in order to fuel the spell.

I stood up. Almost without thinking, I lifted my hands, tracing the shapes in the air even as I pulled tingling energy into myself with a twist of my mind. Sparkling light followed my fingertips, spreading to form something more complex than I was really making, but which matched the sigils in my mind. The light flashed, then faded, shrinking into a small orb in my closing fist.

The wonder of that moment would stay with me. The moment magic became part of me.

'We're in the Mycoforest, Turovellis,' I said, the certainty filling me. In my mind's eye I could see a map of glowing lines and sweeping shapes, the words rippling into focus. 'Near Lundanar, in Mistcurl, in Mistembra.' I kept my fist closed, the orb insubstantial but tingling against my palm. Once I opened it, the orb would direct us on a path, but I wasn't sure of our chosen destination.

I looked around at my friends, a little uncomfortable with the shock on their faces. My cheeks warmed and I ducked my head.

'Uh. Tar?' Hanna's eyebrows raised. 'You're glowing.'

My head snapped back up. 'I'm —?' I held up my hands, careful not to release the orb. My skin, already oddly sparkly, was now limned with a pink-edged white glow that flickered and shifted like flame.

Oh my god. The aura blush. I'd given Astaran an aura of light that appeared at moments of high emotion. It had seemed cute at the time, but now that I had *my* embarrassment broadcast in glowing light, I found I *did not care for it.*

I tried to tamp down on my embarrassment, but my aura only flared brighter the more nervous I became.

Arries touched my elbow and took me aside. He transformed into his werefox form, growing large enough to block me from the view of the others. 'Hey. It doesn't matter.'

I nodded. Tears stung at my eyes, and I didn't trust my voice not to shake. Ridiculous. I was being ridiculous.

It was just ... I'd always hated being noticed. Feared it, even. Especially when I was anxious, or embarrassed. And now I had a built in 'look at me' function for whenever I felt the most vulnerable.

I tried not to focus on the glow. Arries was hiding me from view; I had just cast a spell for the first time in my life. I was in a world of magic. I didn't want anxiety to ruin that.

Focus on my breaths; in for three, held for three, out for three. Focus on the feeling of the air in my chest. Focus on the tingling sensation in my palm.

Magic.

I flicked my gaze up to Arries, who stepped aside so I could rejoin the group.

'Lundanar,' said Hanna. 'We've been there, right? The bee people?'

'The people with bees,' said Pauline.

Hanna made a face.

My mouth was dry. I swallowed hard then said, 'Do we have a map?'

We all looked at Arries, who normally carried the group storage in the form of the Sack of Safekeeping. 'What? I have the Sack here, but I don't think ...' He picked it up and showed it to us. A thick leather sack buckled at the top with a narrow belt, the bottom studded with iron fixings, the leather itself etched with runes that looked ordinary enough but glittered a little out of the corner of the eye. He shook it; it flopped limply.

'Nothing in there,' said Arries. He opened it up and put his arm inside. 'There's just not — wait.' He withdrew his arm, now with a rolled-up scroll of parchment in hand. 'P ...?'

Pauline shook her head, looking torn between laughter and exasperation. 'It's extra-planar storage. It only appears empty.'

Arries stared at the scroll in one hand and the Sack in the other. 'I knew that, I just ... always imagined it all kind of piled up in there somehow.'

'It's piled up *somewhere,*' said Rex. 'Well — now we know we have all our characters' equipment, at least.'

I got up and went to kneel beside Arries. He spread the map out onto the ground in front of us, pushing the leaf mulch aside to clear a space.

It didn't look so different from the map Pauline had created for us. She'd used a computer program to produce it, but this one looked far more hand-made — the ink was faded in places, the edges stained. The shapes were sometimes drawn in a shakier hand, and there were little blotches at the edges of some of the illustrations, as if the artist had accidentally dripped paint onto it. It was more detailed, too. It was nonetheless reassuringly familiar. I couldn't help but touch the edge of it; the parchment had a crisp but leathery feel.

'There,' I said, pointing out Turovellis. A cluster of trees and mushrooms. 'That's where we are right now. And I think ...' I tapped my lip, then pointed. 'That way? Is south. So we could head to Lundanar and plan our next steps from there. It's the nearest settlement.'

The orb fizzed in my hand, waiting to be released. I kept my fist closed. I didn't know for sure how much magic I had at my disposal. This spell might be all I got. The in-game mechanics of using Action Points and Energy Points to work out how much you could do and in what order didn't seem that applicable to this extremely real world.

The others came nearer, Hanna tapping Riya on the shoulder and gesturing for her to come too. We crowded around the map, some kneeling, some peering over the heads of those who knelt. It was all a lot closer than I knew how to handle; Pauline sat to one side of me, and of course she needed to sit and that was fine, but then I couldn't scoot to the other side because Hanna was there with Riya leaning over her back. Kenta stood behind Arries, bracing a hand on his armoured shoulder as he leaned over for a better look. Even Rex came to join us; he didn't crowd me but stood behind Pauline, giving her a respectful distance in spite of his obvious curiosity.

'Shouldn't we head for Mihilit-dalath?' said Rex. He gestured at the map, too far to point, but he'd referenced the nearest city — one we'd visited before as a group, but never spent much time in. Said to have originated from the fey plane of The Glamouring, it was now a bustling multi-cultural city with a flourishing magical community. It'd be a good place to start if we needed to find someone to planeshift us back to the real world.

I beat a drum beat against the sides of my legs. The real world. Even as I thought it, it felt uncomfortable, like I was lying to myself. Vanthis was already startlingly real.

Pauline shook her head. 'There's a teleportation circle in the mage's tower in Lundanar. I think it's closer. And we can go to any of the major cities, if Mihilit-dalath isn't our best option.'

Teleportation. Just the word made my stomach kick with nausea. 'Couldn't we just … I don't know, catch a wyvern ride or something instead?' I tried to keep my voice calm.

'I doubt we'll find riding beasts available somewhere as small as Lundanar,' Pauline said. 'Teleportation is our best bet, if we can get permission.'

If we could get permission. I hoped we wouldn't. I didn't want to teleport, *I didn't want to teleport,* and yet I couldn't bring the words forth from my mouth, trapped by my obligation to Riya, by the necessity of finding a way home, by the shame of my fear.

I glanced at Rex, who shrugged, biting his lip. In the game, he and Hanna often went to parlay with mages for access to their teleportation circles. It was never easy and often required our group doing some kind of quest or favour.

We were not in a position to be doing any quests right now, even ignoring the fact that we had a seven year-old kid in tow.

But it's not like Pauline didn't know that. She had planned out every encounter, every quest, every favour.

Rex bit his lip and looked to me.

Me.

As if I knew anything at all.

As if I wasn't terrified just at the suggestion of teleportation.

But I guess I did have a magic spell clenched in my fist.

'We'll let the Pathfinder spell decide,' I said. It would point us to the fastest route to Mihilit-dalath, if that was what I desired.

I did desire that. Didn't I?

I opened my hand and the orb floated up, flickering and sparking like an odd-coloured flame, then darted off through the trees, leaving an afterburn of light that was already beginning to fade.

We all checked the direction.

Pauline nodded. 'Lundanar,' she said. 'That's our next step.'

'Tomorrow,' said Arries, looking anxiously at the high sun — all the more dramatic here in this little clearing in the thick canopy of trees. Our deliberations had taken longer than I'd realised.

'So what do we do now?' asked Kenta. He still sounded a little hoarse, but I noted determination in his gaze. This plan gave him hope; we had a path ahead of us to get home.

The same plan made my nausea rise in my throat.

'Now we set up camp and protect it as well as we can,' said Pauline. She sounded bleak. 'Because the Mycoforest is full of ferymars and they could very easily kill us in our sleep if we don't.'

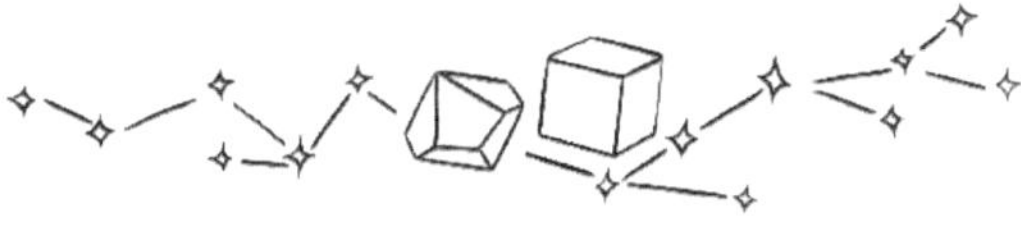

CHAPTER SIXTEEN

Ferymars. I'd never encountered them in-game, but I knew the others had. To me, they were only a description on the pages of the *Kin* guidebook. Large, hyena-like beasts with fungi growing along their spines. Able to root into the ground and spring up elsewhere. Blank-eyed and slavering.

Beautiful and terrible. Something I would love to watch on TV but certainly didn't want to meet close up.

The teleportation fell from my mind, becoming background fear to this new and frightening threat.

'Okay,' said Rex. His voice was rough and cracked with anxiety. 'All right. Just got to learn to use magic before sunset or we'll all be eaten by ferymars. No pressure.' His tail swished and whapped me in the leg. I yelped.

'Oh shit! I'm sorry.' He took three quick steps back. He held up his hands in a conciliatory gesture, eyes low.

I tried to smile, though I was feeling overwhelmed by the interaction. 'I didn't mind,' I said. 'It was just surprising.' I didn't want him to feel bad for something he couldn't help. And though I appreciated that he understood I didn't like being touched, if there was anyone here I wouldn't mind being touched by, it was Rex.

God, was that creepy of me?

We scattered around the clearing and got to work. Arries helped Kenta clean and don his armour, getting the supplies from the Sack. Riya sat on the ground with Pauline, who kept her occupied by asking her to identify various rocks and leaves around the clearing. Hanna set up our small two-man tent and was now assembling her flute from the small case she carried in her pack.

'Arries? How did magic work for you?' I asked.

He shrugged as he continued to work at Kenta's armour, buckling the breastplate at the shoulders. He'd transformed into his larger, stronger werefox form. 'I just ... willed it to happen. It was instinct. Ken, I'm sorry this is taking so long — it's harder with claws than I thought it would be. Oh right!' He shrank back down to his human form, fur and muzzle receding in one smooth motion. 'Much better.'

I paused a moment, taking in the transition. It would certainly take me a while to get used to watching a friend shapeshift.

I glanced at Rex. 'Healer's Touch isn't technically a spell, is it?'

'Oh, it is. Arries just has it granted from his goddess for flavour. But the instinct thing ... I mean, if we have our characters' abilities ...' He looked down at his hands. They looked utterly like and unlike Rex's hands. They were as long-fingered as I remembered, but the back of his hands and wrists were speckled with clusters of scales, and the fingertips faded to a spectral blue. 'I guess ... just a small spell, maybe ...?' He reached up into the air and drew three quick runes. Light followed his fingers, leaving a glowing trail that hovered for just a moment before the spell kicked in. The runes flared, then flew to his open palms, which glowed with the same shifting vari-colour light. He threw up his hands, and the light separated into several globes of light which floated around him, as buoyant and swerving as bubbles.

'Will'o'wisp,' I whispered, naming the spell. It bathed the clearing in a mosaic rainbow more beautiful than I had ever envisioned during the game. I heard the others go quiet for a moment.

Hanna whooped. 'Fuck yeah, Rex!'

Rex's own eyes were wide. He made a small gesture, and one of the orbs drifted over to me. Hesitantly, I reached up and touched my fingertip to the surface. There was no sensation at all; my hands passed through it without any obstruction, no heat or cold. As insubstantial as it was beautiful.

I glanced at Rex. 'How?'

He shrugged, and gave a light, nervous laugh. 'I just ... knew. I remember the runes, the breathing, everything about how to cast. When I wanted to do it, I just ... could.'

I nodded. Casting the Pathfinder spell had been much the same for me. But if this was really how it worked — if we really had all the abilities of our characters — I wondered ...

I closed my eyes and breathed deeply, holding the image of a creature in my mind and imagining myself transforming into it. Instinct took over. Energy came up through the earth, through the air, permeating my body. I drew three quick runes in the air.

I rolled forward onto all fours, my body rippling in one smooth motion. My muscles itched, as did the base of my spine. My vision sharpened even as the colours culled. And then the ground was crunching beneath my paws, and my tail swept the air, and I was gazing up at a Rex who was staggering back with shock writ across his face.

'Shit, Tar! Give a guy some warning ...' He was clutching his heart, but he looked at me with wonder.

I yawned, baring my huge sabre-like teeth. I couldn't see myself, but I knew what I looked like, because I had brought it into reality from my mind. Because I could *feel* the truth of it.

I was a pearlescent white sabre-tooth tiger. I had enormous, mitt-like paws and a faintly glowing aura. My astralkin heritage showed true in my shape unless I specifically willed it otherwise, just as it was in the game.

I flexed my paws, feeling the earth and mulch crunch between my toes. A shiver ran through me. This was real.

Magic was real. I laughed, and it came out in a deep, raspy *cough-cough* sound.

Rex laughed as well, holding out his hands and approaching me as if I were really a large animal, and not a museum tour guide in the shape of one. 'Tar, this is ...'

'God, they really did it.' I glanced aside, to where Hanna helped Pauline to her feet. Pauline was hunched over her middle and the movement clearly caused her pain. 'Tar ... you're a witch. Really a witch.'

My ears twitched and my stumpy tail wagged nervously as it hit me: if magic was real for us, then it was real for the whole world. All the terrors and dangers our characters had faced in the game? We would have to face the same thing.

I thought, for a moment, that I would freeze up over it. My muscles tightened and I could feel the primal urge to flee, all the stronger inside my powerful sabrecat form. But there was no car here for me to lock myself inside until the shaking stopped. There was no little room in Saanvi's house to retreat to, no A:RO to drown myself in.

As bizarre as it was, being brought here, into the life of the character I'd imagined, had stripped me of the ability to hide in fantasy. I was living in fantasy now. There was nothing I could do but continue to be me.

Something touched my flank; I flinched away, snarling back over my shoulder without meaning to, only to see Riya stumble back with a shriek.

I immediately felt ashamed. Riya was even more lost here than we were, and she was counting on us. I might be wearing the shape of a wild animal, but that didn't mean I could act like one.

Arries caught Riya, and steadied her with one strong gauntleted hand. 'It's okay,' he said. 'It's just Tar. They don't like being touched, so it makes them jump.'

I tried to look contrite, hanging my head. After a moment, with Arries standing protectively over her, Riya reached again for my side and sunk her small hand into my fur. I didn't like being touched any more as a sabrecat than I had as a human. I could feel the fibres of my fur twisting and shifting, and my muscles twitched at the touch. But I wasn't going to deny her the chance to do something wonderful in a situation that must be scaring her.

After a moment, she smoothed my fur back into place and stepped back. 'You're spiky,' she said.

I flicked my ears at her.

She nodded as if I'd said something, and added, 'You make a good kitty.'

Arries leaned forward. 'Uh .. Tar? May I ...?'

I sighed and boffed my head against his hand. He made a little squeal of delight. After a moment, the others came and stroked my fur as well, touching my ears, my flank, the spot between my shoulders. All but Rex, who hung back.

'This is incredible,' said Kenta. 'I just want to give you a big bear hug!'

I made a tiny growl in the back of my throat. It was nonetheless rich with threat.

Arries elbowed him, and he stepped back. 'But I wouldn't! Obviously!' He held up his hands in surrender.

When they were done, I felt more tense than ever. I had loved the sensation of being a sabrecat, but I didn't like them looking at me like I was an animal and not a person. I barely had to think about it before my fur and muscles melted away in a ripple of magic. Then I was once again Tar — in cosplay as Astaran, maybe, but still just me.

'So magic works,' said Hanna. She grinned at Rex. 'Let's get to work!'

Somehow, my transformation had eased everyone else's tension, or at least given them something wondrous to focus on instead of the shock of our situation. Rex set about putting up an alarm ward around the immediate clearing, drawing a ghostly thread from the air and carefully stretching it from tree to tree until we were enclosed by it. A few short runes and incantations in a language we didn't understand later, and the thread shimmered and was gone.

Hanna took out her flute and tried a few quick notes. The first was shaky, the second sharp, but after that she quickly played a quick ditty. She grinned at Kenta. 'The flute skills didn't transfer, but luckily I had flute skills back home. Ten years of being yelled at by Mrs Ito for my 'bad concert posture' weren't wasted after all.'

Kenta shook his head. 'Didn't you have a crush on your flute teacher?'

'That makes two reasons it wasn't wasted.'

She winked and went to draw a circle around the tent, tracing runes into the dirt with a stick and then assembling her flute and playing a strange, ethereal tune as she walked around it. Soon the canvas walls of the tent took on a strange sheen when viewed out of the corner of the eye.

Alterdimensional Extension. A spell which she got a lot of use out of in the game; it expanded the internal dimensions of the target. In the game, it turned our two-person tent into a ten-person one. For a time, at least.

Though in-game she most often used it for setting up magic tricks like pulling rabbits out of hats.

'That's a day on each spell, right?' I said as she finished and Rex returned to the group.

Hanna was sitting half-in, half-out of her shack — it would disappear if she left its confines. 'Or maybe it was ten hours?'

'It's a day,' said Pauline firmly. 'Kenta, can you cast Divine Guardian? Otherwise we'll have to leave someone on watch.'

Another spell often cast during camping in the game. It created a watchful spirit that would warn us of impending danger, and attack anything that approached us with intent to harm.

Kenta was sitting beside the campfire, his hatchets bare and resting across his crossed legs. He shook his head. 'I'll take first watch,' he said. 'It's ... it's better I don't ...' He trailed off.

Pauline's expression shifted from misgiving to understanding. She nodded.

The others gradually disappeared into the tent, until it was just me and Kenta. 'Better not to what?' I asked quietly.

Kenta looked down at the weapons in his lap. 'Draw attention to myself,' he said. And though I didn't completely know what he meant, I shuddered all the same. When you took spells in *Kin,* you chose a source for that magic. Rex's came from the runes themselves, which made the spells more complex but also more stable. My magic came from nature, channelled through runes like Rex's, but requiring less complicated casting. But Kenta's magic came from a god — and not a kind one, either.

Alis-Umor, the Blood Drinker. A red shadow that fed on torment ...

No. I don't think I'd want to draw attention to myself, either.

'I'll take next watch,' I told him. 'I have darksight, so.'

I hoped I did, anyway. As of yet, everything looked pretty normal.

Kenta nodded. 'I'll wake you in four.'

And with that, I left him at the campfire and cucked into the Alterdimensional tent, passing through the flap with only the tiniest bit of static. From inside, I could see through the canvas as if it was translucent gauze. It seemed poor protection from the outside world, but it was more sheltered from the wind and at least nothing would be able to see *in.*

Hanna and Pauline spoke quietly, already having spread out their bedrolls. Riya snoozed beside them, looking small and lost under the tent's thin canvas and the flickering campfire light. Arries unbuckled his armour, preparing for sleep. Rex unrolled his bedroll at the other end.

The extended tent was large enough for ten people to sleep in, if we all tetris'd in top-to-toe. Or at least that was what Pauline had said in-game — there were only six of us in here now and it was already looking extremely tight. I frowned at

Pauline — her space estimation was fatphobic, especially considering Hanna and Riya were so small. There was no way ten of *me* would fit in this tent.

I went to the Sack of Safekeeping, sitting open beside Pauline, and reached in. The strap of my bedroll hooked onto my fingers, and I pulled the bedroll free.

Already I could feel the closeness of them all.

I went to the far end toward Rex, hoping he wouldn't be offended if I put my bedroll over there as well. It was the least cramped part of the tent at the moment — or certainly, that's what I told myself.

As I approached, he picked up his bedroll and I nearly froze in terror. God, I'd already made him uncomfortable. But he caught my expression and quickly said, 'I was saving a spot on the edge for you. I get the feeling you'll find it even harder to sleep cheek-to-cheek with people than I do.' He put his bedroll nearly a full person's gap away from the spot it had first rested, offering me that expanded space.

My cheeks heated. For a moment I just stared at him. His eyes were cast low, his mouth twisted to one side, like he'd been caught doing something embarrassing.

I spread my bedroll in the offered spot, feeling strange and light. 'Thank you,' I said. I couldn't quite look at him now. He felt oddly close, though he'd left a sizable gap between us. Even though he wasn't looking at me, I felt more seen than I ever had before.

I fussed with my armour, unbuckling the pauldrons, bracers, and legs. It felt like it was taking too long, and I carefully avoided looking at anyone.

I lay down, using my cloak as a blanket. I pulled it up to my chin. I felt exposed on the ground, somehow, so I pulled up my knees, which made me feel a little safer.

Rex lay down across from me, and for a moment, our gazes locked. I swallowed hard, my mouth suddenly dry.

I wanted to say something. I wanted to tell him that if I had to be lost in another world, I was glad it was with him. I wanted to thank him, not for this small thing, but for every small thing he had done to make me feel safe and seen. I wanted to take this too-large feeling inside my chest and show it to him.

But behind him, Arries lay down to sleep, his armour shucked. Hanna shifted on her bedroll, murmuring to Pauline. I felt frozen by all the listeners pressed so close to us.

Rex's lips pulled to one side — in a grimace, maybe. I couldn't quite tell. 'Goodnight, Tar,' he said. He turned over and went still, leaving me in the flickering, dappled half-light of the tent.

After a while, my darksight kicked in, shifting the world into shades of silver and blue. A more ethereal, more beautiful way to view the world than I had ever known.

I closed my eyes to bring back the dark and fell into a fitful sleep.

CHAPTER SEVENTEEN

Somehow we made it through the night safely, but the threat of the ferymars still followed us into morning. None of us wanted to get into a fight, and everyone agreed that we needed a better grip on strategy, spells, even our equipment.

Rex and Pauline found two courses of gender balance potions among our supplies in the Sack of Safekeeping, ending a quiet fear both had been harbouring. The potions were labelled either 'For Ram' or simply with the same eye tattoo that Pauline had. Pauline seemed confident that gender balance potions were at least as good as hormone replacement therapy was on Earth, but with fewer side effects. Rex complained about the taste, but said it was worlds better than an injection.

There were other necessities too, including potions to stop monthly bleeding, some of which I quietly added to my own satchel. The last thing I wanted *ever* was to menstruate, but the idea of doing so while adventuring in a fantasy world was especially galling. We didn't find any meds, which meant Rex and I would have to go without our anxiety and depression meds. Worse, there was no pain relief for Pauline. When we found out, she looked like she would scream, but she went to sit a ways away from the group, her back turned.

'There will be something,' Arries said. 'They have their own brand of medicine here. If we find people, there will be something.'

We could only hope that was true.

Rex, Hanna, and I spent the morning going over our spells, trying to remember what we'd had on our spell lists and whether we knew how to use them, discussing contingencies should things go wrong. I'd spent most of my ability points on polymorphing, so fortunately I didn't have quite as much to remember. But Rex and Hanna both had very long spell lists. Occasionally, Rex would consult Pauline and the two would discuss the specifics. In-game, he'd had Ram keep a spellbook with all his spells written down, and now he was trying to make sense of it — not to remember it so much as to understand it.

At one point, I looked over his shoulder. The runes involved in his spellcasting seemed a lot more complicated than mine. Pages and pages of runes, some of them in complicated diagrams or circles. 'That ... seems like a lot to work through,' I said. I couldn't fathom trying to make sense of it beyond memorising what was needed to cast the spell.

Rex looked up at me with bright eyes. 'It is! But there's a logic to it ... I think it might work similarly to code. It'll take me a while to work through the specifics and I definitely need more books but ... there's something to this.'

His excitement warmed me. I asked him more about it and enjoyed his explanations for a while. At length he grew tense, and I left him be.

As the other main spellcaster of the group, really Kenta could have gone over his spells with us as well, but as casting his spells required calling on Alis-Umor, none of us begrudged him the decision not to.

Arries put Pauline's hair into box braids — she didn't fancy trying to care for it loose in a forest any more than I would with long hair, and Arries had learned a few hair styles from his stylist dad. It was a much more involved and time-consuming process than I had expected, and my eyes wandered to them a few times throughout the long morning.

'You aren't going to ask to touch it or something, are you?' Rex asked, nodding toward Pauline. I couldn't tell whether he was teasing or tense — maybe both.

'Oh ... no,' I said. 'I wouldn't do that.'

Rex nodded and turned a page in his notebook. 'I didn't think you would, but I've been surprised before.'

Definitely tense, as now I could see his shoulders relax a bit.

I felt the urge to apologise, but didn't know what I should say.

'It's good P made a point of including hair care products in the travel kits,' he said, moving on. 'A different LM, and we'd all have been in a much crappier situation right now.'

The morning passed. We fixed our spells in our mind, and Pauline emerged from Arries' handiwork with glittering braids as dark and colourful as the night sky. Now, we travelled with low, comfortable conversation. Riya alternated between walking with Hanna and riding on Arries' broad werefox shoulders — he seemed to prefer his more human form, but happily transformed whenever Riya wanted a lift.

He tried to engage Rex in conversation a few times, but Rex was close-lipped, and Arries soon moved on.

Pauline floated behind Rex on his Arcane Packbeast, a spell that created a translucent pill-shaped container about the size of a computer desk which levitated after Rex, following his every step. It shimmered slightly whenever it caught the light. There was more than enough space for Pauline to sit comfortably there, if a distinct lack of back support, and it could support enough weight to carry Riya as well if needed.

Pauline, however, glared at the passing landscape. I fell back to walk beside her. 'Something on your mind?' I asked.

She glanced up at me. The eye marked on her forehead was still lined in sharp, glittering ink, though she'd scrubbed at it in the morning in the hope of removing it. We had no idea what it might signify. She had her knees up, and the skirts of her grey robes were fanned out neatly around her. She looked a little ashen though, and her mouth was set in a thin line.

'It's nothing, really,' said Pauline. 'It's just ... I don't normally spend this long with people and I can't hide my pain indefinitely.' She grimaced. 'Especially without my meds.'

I nodded, not really sure what to say to that. I wanted to be supportive but didn't have the right script. 'How's the packbeast?' I asked instead.

She gave me a wan smile. 'A very smooth ride, actually. Much smoother than my chair, and I'm delighted it can make the journey across rough terrain without bouncing or vibrating like a car. It's just ...' she trailed off.

I waited, not wanting to press her, but not wanting to cut her off either. I trusted that she would signal to me either way.

'I can only follow Rex,' she said at length. 'And this Packbeast ... it's undignified. It was one of the most frustrating things before I got my electric chair. To have little control over where I go, or when. I'm grateful, of course, to have this. I don't think I could have walked very far.' Her smile turned into a grimace at the thought. 'But even though this is smoother than my chair, and better suited to a forest ... it's not the same.'

'You need your freedom,' I said.

'I do.'

We both lapsed into silence. Only ten feet ahead, Rex walked. The tip of his long tail twitched under the trail of his cloak.

Pauline looked up at the canopy of silver foliage and fibrous mushroom caps, through which sunlight filtered through to dapple our path. 'I don't know this world as well as I thought,' she said. 'Not really. It bothers me.'

'We'll work it out,' I said, in what I hoped was a supportive tone.

Her mouth pressed into a thin line. 'Perhaps.'

I wondered if she felt as exposed out here as I did.

Later, I joined Rex. He'd seemed tense all morning, but he offered me a small smile that put me at ease.

I took a deep breath. 'I think I'm going to try a bird polymorph.'

Rex's brows knit. 'You're going to scout?'

'I was thinking of trying it, yeah.'

He rubbed the back of his neck. 'It seems dangerous to go alone.'

I choked out a laugh. 'Yeah. But we need a scout. Hanna can't cover enough ground and Kenta and Arries have loud, clanking armour.'

One of Rex's long, knife-shaped ears twitched, like an irritated cat. 'I could polymorph too,' he said. 'We could both go.'

I swallowed down a lump in my throat. I was so afraid of scouting but ... 'You shouldn't waste your spells on this,' I said. 'You don't get as many polymorphs per day as I do, if that's even how this works.' None of us had experimented enough with our powers to be sure how closely it mimicked the mechanics we knew. 'Besides, I think it's better you stay here with P and the others.'

Rex's mouth shifted to one side. 'I just ... ferymars. They're not something I'd want to run into alone, you know? And I don't —' He stopped. 'Nevermind.'

His hands clenched at his sides. I didn't know what it meant, or what he'd been about to say.

'They're just big mean dogs,' I said. I drew a shuddering breath and offered a shaky smile. 'I can face big mean dogs.'

I wondered if I sounded any more sure than I felt.

He cast me an uncertain look. 'This isn't something any of us know how to deal with,' he said. 'Separating seems ...'

Silly, foolish, likely to end in my death.

'... You're very brave,' he finished.

I smiled tightly. 'Not a word used to describe me often,' I said.

I thought he would laugh, but he looked very serious. 'I think you'd be surprised,' he said. He looked down. 'Just ... fly right back if there's any trouble.'

'Oh, I will,' I said. 'I don't want to test the hit point system any more than I have already.'

He chuckled a little at that, though it sounded tense.

I took a deep breath and glanced back at where Pauline trailed. 'I won't be long,' I said.

'We'll come looking if you are,' Rex said. He said it as solemnly as a promise.

I drew the same shimmering runes as before in the air. I took a deep breath and drew energy up and into my body — my second polymorph since we'd come to this world. Again, I felt a rippling as if I were liquid, but I also felt ... compressed. Sort of packed in and lightened at the same time. My arms became wings; my body light and feathery. Instinctively, I tread air. My eyes swept the woods. I was a small kestrel, and the sharpness of my vision shocked me, as did the vibrancy and colour. Everything glowed as if lit from inside. There were colours here I would never be able to describe.

I looked at Rex, who stared up at me with a wide grin. I wanted to laugh; a high-pitched shriek came from me instead. The others stopped and looked at me; Arries cheered, as did Riya on his shoulder. None of us yet accustomed to the fact that *magic was real.* And then I swept my wings forward and climbed up into the air, leaving them behind with a breathless speed that made my heart sing.

At first, I feared navigating at this speed, but it seemed this shape came with all the instincts that the body required. I wove in and out of the trees, keeping just below the canopy. I popped up and under branches, dodging and diving with an ease that felt as smooth and natural as cycling. I could feel the air currents through minute changes in my feathers, and began to use them to aid my flight, some which would send me spiralling upward, others which I avoided to keep my path smooth.

It was hard not to lose myself in this. To just spiral up into the sky and focus only on the joy of flight. Wild that there were creatures for which this was as casual an experience as walking. But the group was counting on me, so I searched the land around me with sharp turns of my avian neck.

Movement constantly caught my eye — mice shuffling beneath the leaf litter, small birds clinging to branches or hopping through long grass. There were weasels and stoats stalking the floor, and squirrels and cats climbing the trees and mushroom stalks. I even saw a few rabbits grazing cautiously just beyond their warrens, and a fleet fox trotting through the underbrush in the distance. There were otherworldly creatures too — long-limbed creatures that looked somewhere between a praying mantis and a faerie. Little plantling creatures that trundled along the ground, leaves swaying. Smaller mushrooms that opened bulbous eyes to watch my passing. What I didn't see was anything large — no deer, no wolves, and certainly no ferymars.

Which was a relief, because I wasn't sure how much longer I had in this shape. There were limits to polymorphing — three hours per shape for Astaran. And I only had so many spells to cast in a day. Though I'd frequently circled back to the group to keep in touch and avoid concerning them, my scouting time was coming to an end, and my wings were beginning to ache from the long hours spent in flight.

I caught myself in the air with all the agility of a real kestrel, and turned back, soaring toward where I thought the group must be by now. I beat my wings in a slow, lazy beat intermittent with a smooth glide, letting the air carry me as my shoulders ached from so long holding me aloft.

I was so focused on getting back and giving my weary wings a break that I almost missed the ferymars. Huge, hulking things almost as large as bears but gangly-limbed and with muddy green hide and long, pointy ears. Toadstools grew from the thick ruff of fur following their spine, a riot of colours and shapes, and cluttered around their oddly blank eyes. They moved as a pack, keeping close to the ground and darting from tree to bush to tree, using the environment to mask their progress. My heart seized at the sight of their yellow teeth and huge paws armed with jagged claws. There were five of them, at my count.

I soared over them. One glanced up as I passed, watching me with all-white eyes, but otherwise they paid me no mind. They couldn't do anything about aerial prey.

I made my way past them straight to the group; another fifteen minutes of flight. They were still in roughly the same formation — Arries in front and Kenta coming up behind. Hanna walked with Rex — they juggled balls of light between each other, and the tense mood of the early journey seemed to be forgotten. Riya rode with Pauline, who had curled up on the shimmering packbeast and was letting Riya play with the trail of her cloak.

Arries waved as I approached, his peach-coloured fox tail sweeping the air like an excited animal. It was still uncanny to see him with fox ears and fangs, even in his human form, as he was now, but his smile was just as wide as ever. I landed in front of him, dropping my polymorph just before I hit the ground. I straightened as a human again — or an astralkin, anyway.

'You make a very pretty kestrel,' Arries told me, clapping me on the shoulder with one heavy, gauntleted hand.

'Ow!'

'Oh! Sorry!'

I winced and massaged my shoulder. 'I'm just a bit sore from all that flying.'

And I really was. Somehow that detail had never made it into the *Kin* game system. I could get just as tired when polymorphed as not. And I was willing to bet that getting attacked while polymorphed would hurt just as much, too.

I thought of the huge, gaunt dogs with their blank eyes and long claws. 'There are ferymars ahead,' I said. 'Get the others. We need to prepare.'

CHAPTER EIGHTEEN

We had done this hundreds of times, I reminded myself as Pauline gave out instructions. Maybe we hadn't *actually* done it, but we knew what to do — all the better now that we had Pauline to advise us instead of work against us. It didn't make this any less terrifying.

Hanna set up beside the packbeast, with Pauline holding Riya there. Hanna held her flute with shaking hands. She used music to shape the runes, the same way we drew ours in the air. Riya hugged Pauline around the waist, picking up on the tension. Tears streaked down her cheeks, and though her grip surely caused Pauline immense pain, Pauline didn't complain.

Rex was in the middle, ready to cast spells to encompass the group. Kenta and werefox-form Arries stood further out, ready to fight, though Kenta shook in his armour and even Arries shifted with rarely-seen nerves. In our experiments so far, it didn't seem that physical skills like sword-fighting had come through with us. They'd be relying on their Earth skills.

I tried to run through the spell list we'd worked out this morning, tried to remember what I could cast and in what situations, but my mind was weirdly blank. I didn't know whether I would even remember how to polymorph when faced with the ferymars.

I drummed my hands against my legs. No. It was no good. I had nothing. I went to Pauline. 'Is there something I should cast before they arrive?' My voice was weirdly high and squeaky, for all I was trying to sound calm.

She shook her head. 'Not yet. Maybe once we see them, if you could cast a Hurricane around us, that might drive them off or buy us some more time.' The eye marked on her forehead started to glow with white light. 'We really don't want them getting close — ferymars give off spores that will make us sick, even put us into a stupor.'

'P ...'

Riya looked up, face still wet with tears, and touched Pauline's forehead. 'Your sticker is magic,' she said in a tone of wonder.

'My ...?' Pauline touched her own forehead.

'It's glowing, P.'

Pauline took a shuddering breath. 'I don't know what that means.'

'Neither do I,' I said. I wished we had time to make sense of it. Instead, I looked off in the direction I knew the dogs were approaching from. They couldn't be far out now.

I clenched trembling hands. The idea of fighting was brain-freezingly terrifying, but I would do whatever I had to.

I hoped it wouldn't come to that, and clung to my meager plan.

For a few awful minutes, we stood in silence and waited. I wondered if the others were as frightened as I was. I wondered if their muscles were quivering the way mine were. If they had to clench their teeth to stop their teeth from chattering. A breeze picked up, swirling dead leaves and dust past us and bringing with it a horrible, musky stink.

I saw a flash of white eyes ahead, then again to our left and right. They were trying to close around us. Kenta immediately backed up closer to Pauline and Riya, his axe raised and ready. I heard Rex start to mutter the incantation for a spell. All plans fled my mind.

As the first dog coalesced from the shadows, tall, leather-skinned, and covered in fungi, I strode forward and screamed, as long and loud as I could.

I drew the runes swiftly and pulled energy from the air, as quickly and powerfully as I could. I leapt forward, polymorphing as I did. I rippled and grew, hitting the ground on two enormous clawed feet and snarling down at the first dog. It whimpered and scrambled back, and I heard the others gasp.

Polymorphing was limited by your knowledge of animals, and I knew more than Astaran. An allosaurus, rainbow-hued feathers bristling, was both larger and more terrifying than anything I imagined they were used to seeing. I screeched, an awful, ear-grating sound that echoed across the forest.

Runes lit up in the air all around us, accompanied by the long, clear notes of a flute. Two of the hounds reared up on their hind legs and started slipping and dancing, their paws flailing, their terror at the unnatural movement evident. Then water burst up from the ground in an enormous, roaring wave, spinning around us in a maelstrom.

I steeled myself and bounded through it. The hounds were fleeing, yelping as they did. The ones still dancing struggled awkwardly after them. I watched as they disappeared between the trees, then turned to face the group, each heavy step causing the ground to judder slightly.

The water dissipated, its sudden absence creating a striking silence. Rex lowered his hands; Hanna stopped playing her flute, raising her eyebrows at me.

'Shit, Tar. A dinosaur?' Kenta, lowered his axe. 'I bet we hadn't even queued for combat yet.'

'A critical success on your Threaten roll, for sure!' Hanna laughed and strode toward me to give my haunch a hearty slap. 'I'm so fucking proud of you. That was some real bard thinking.'

'Do we think they'll come back?' asked Arries, casting a wary eye at the treeline.

The eye on Pauline's forehead flared. 'They aren't coming back,' she said. As the light faded, she touched her forehead, looking thoughtful.

The rest of that day's journey passed in relative peace — perhaps aided by my spending much of it in my allosaur shape. Riya rode on my back for most of it. Her little hands were buried in my feathers to hold herself steady, and if she sometimes ripped a few free, I pretended not to notice. It felt safer to keep her close.

At night, we set up camp again and ate around another crackling campfire, which Rex lit with a fire spell in another test of our abilities. It was weird how familiar this group still felt even while one was juggling a ball of flame between his hands and another was a giant fox giving Riya a lap around the camp on his shoulders. These were every bit my friends, no matter how different we might look now.

I played with the grass growing from the forest litter around us, idly using a small witch spell to pour energy into the plant. The grass grew taller and budded seeds under my touch, glowing faintly.

I made that happen. I gently touched the blades as the magic faded. I wondered if I'd ever get used to having these powers.

'So we've survived our first few nights in Vanthis,' said Hanna. 'I'd say that's cause for fucking celebration. Arries — do we have any booze in the Sack?'

Arries glanced at Riya. 'Let's not.'

Hanna tossed a twig into the fire. 'Why not?'

Arries jerked his werefox head in Riya's direction. She was sitting on the Arcane Packbeast, which she had all to herself since Pauline had settled beside the campfire. 'I just don't think it's appropriate.' His voice was almost a whisper.

'I'm not saying we give the kid a glass! I'm not a beast.'

'Debatable,' Kenta murmured, so quiet it almost couldn't be picked up over the crackle of the fire. Hanna and Arries seemed to miss it, but I smiled at him and he returned it with a wry curve of his mouth.

'You okay?' I asked him quietly.

He shrugged and took a swig of the rabbit stew Arries had cooked up for us, though it had been Hanna who lightning-bolted a rabbit. 'It's tense.'

'Well, yeah,' I said.

Kenta shook his head. 'I'm terrified that at any moment, *She* is going to realise I'm here and make me do something terrible — or do something terrible to me if I won't. It was fun in the game, Tar. Really, it was. I just never thought ...' he trailed off.

'I'm so sorry, Ken.' I didn't know what else to say about it. It was awful beyond imagining. 'You, uh, never seemed that anxious, back home.'

Kenta pulled a face. 'I didn't have anything to be anxious about. And now ... here we are.'

'Here we are,' I echoed, feeling lost on his behalf. 'Do you want to talk about it? The anxiety, I mean. I, uh ... have some experience.'

Kenta took a shuddering breath and nodded. 'Yeah. No, that would help. I ... it's been hard. Even wearing the armour. Sometimes it's fine but sometimes it's just so heavy, I can feel it crushing my lungs and it's like I can't breathe.'

I nodded, my frown deepening. 'Ken ... you know, that sounds like a panic attack.'

He shrugged. 'Maybe? I've never had one before but ... I mean, it must be the armour. My chest is so tight I feel like I'm going to die. I only don't say anything because I don't want anyone to freak out, and it eventually goes away.'

It absolutely sounded like a panic attack to me, but I knew how hard it was to accept that your brain was fucking with you. I tried to come up with something practical to focus on. 'Next time it happens, try a breathing exercise. Do you know castle breathing?'

He shook his head.

'I'll explain it. It'll be hard at first but it'll get easier. And if you're worried, you can always come find me and I'll understand and I'll watch you and make sure you won't suffocate, okay?'

'You would do that for me?' he said.

I smiled to one side. 'Yeah. We're friends, aren't we?'

'Yeah.' In the past, he might have slapped me heartily on the back at that, but he only dipped his head and smiled widely. 'Thanks, Tar.'

'No problem. So, the breathing exercise ...'

I walked him through the different breathing patterns my therapist had taught me. I really hoped it would help; I'd had mixed results myself, mostly because I was a little too aware that the breathing wasn't really doing much more than distracting me from my own brain. But sometimes that was all you needed.

By the time we were done, the pot of stew was thoroughly empty and Riya was curled up asleep at Arries' feet. The others started to get ready for bed. 'I'll take first watch,' I said, as Rex started the alarm spell. 'Just let me get Riya settled.'

She barely stirred as I slid my arms under her and cradled her to my chest. She was so small.

I carefully laid her down on a bedroll. Her eyelids fluttered, but she only turned over and curled up as I pulled her cloak more tightly around her. Whatever we decided about Vanthis and our place in it, we had to get her home. God, just the *thought* of Saanvi discovering Riya missing opened up a huge hole in my chest.

I left the tent as the others started disappearing one by one into the hut. Arries, human again and stripped down to the padded clothing he wore beneath his armour, stopped me with a hand on my shoulder. 'Tar ... do you have a minute?'

I tried not to flinch at his touch, but his words made my stomach twist with nerves. I hated it when people asked if they could talk to you instead of just doing it. I understood the idea of it; preparing someone for emotional intensity at worst, making sure you weren't interrupting at best. But it was hard to tell which was which and the anticipation was worse than if he would just come out and tell me something.

'Sure,' I said, staring at the ground. My voice was tighter than I meant it to be, but if Arries noticed, he didn't comment. I crossed my arms, bracing myself and gritting my teeth.

He leaned closer, ears twitching toward me. 'It's Rex,' he said quietly. 'I don't think he's coping well, you know? And he just ... left. Said he needed a walk.'

I blinked at Arries. 'Now? In the dark, with ferymars?'

'I said it was a bad idea too but he didn't listen and he's ... he's in such a weird way, Tar.' He gave me a significant look. 'I think he would listen to you, though.'

I tried to ignore the swoop in my belly at that. This wasn't the time.

I glanced at the hut, where the others were already settling down. 'Could you take first watch, then? At least until I get back?'

Arries nodded. 'I don't want to invade his privacy, you know? It's just —'

'Yeah.'

I thought I might have one last polymorph left. I could feel the magic's potential inside me. I spread my arms and took to the air in a flurry of feathers as a barn owl, my wings near silent in the night.

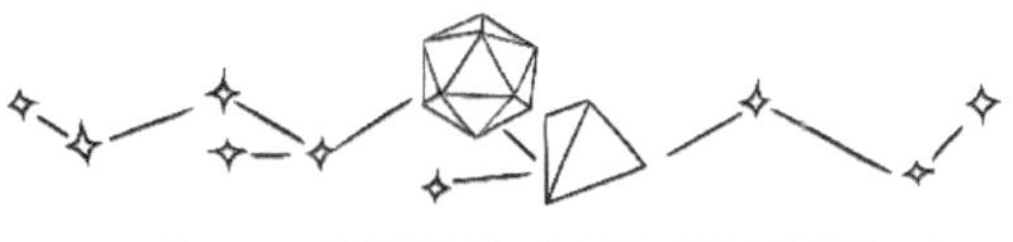

CHAPTER NINETEEN

The owl polymorph was different than the kestrel. A more leisurely flight, less soaring and more swooping. Each beat of my wings felt more buoyant, the finger-like feathers gently kissing the air with barely a stir. My head tick-tocked from side to side as my gaze swept the forest floor for signs of Rex. My vision made the darkening world bright and strange, even more so than with my astralkin darksight.

I heard him rather than saw him. First, glottal clicking sounds. Stimming, probably. Then, a sharp inhale, as loud and cutting as a snake's hiss. I banked on a wing and turned to find him perched on a wide, flat rock. His hood was up and his arms were folded across his stomach. His tail was a blue slash beside him, the tip twitching and curling only a few inches from the ground.

But he was safe. I landed on the bough of a crooked old tree, the wood swaying gently as I feathered my wings to keep my balance and settle.

He glanced up at me, his face unreadable beneath the shadow of his hood, then looked back at the ground. His hands fisted, gripping his cloak in a white-knuckled vice.

I could hear his breathing. Tight and fast. He sounded like he was running for his life even as I watched him sit still and quiet on the rock.

I didn't know how to deal with this. I was always the one panicking, to be honest, and I barely knew how to deal with it myself. But Rex had been there when I needed him so many times. I hooted to catch his attention. He looked up at me, pulling his hood down for a better look. '... Tar?'

I leapt from the bough to swoop down and land a few metres away, the earth crunching beneath my soft-soled boots as I dropped the polymorph. 'Hey, Rex.'

He stood up, looking cornered. I raised my hands in a placating gesture. 'I'm just here so you don't run afoul of some wolves or something.'

He shrugged. 'I'm a wizard now,' he said. His voice was rueful. 'I think I can handle it.'

'All the same,' I said. 'I can keep my distance if you prefer?'

'No. It's ... it's fine.' He sat back down on the flat rock. I could still feel the tension radiating off of him, and I flexed my hands as I went back and forth in my mind over where I should stand or what I should do. I wasn't built to be comforting; sometimes it felt like I wasn't built for much at all. Even the abilities I'd used to protect the group today had been given to me in a weird stroke of fate, rather than being something I had earned.

But I remembered Rex waiting with me outside Pauline's before every session, and how reassuring that had been. Tentatively, I went and sat beside him, giving him plenty of space so he wouldn't feel crowded. Then I looked down at my hands, which I folded in my lap and focused on not wringing or twisting, so as not to radiate a similarly anxious energy.

He didn't say anything. The minutes crawled by, but I kept my peace. I wished I had some wisdom to offer him, like I had for Kenta, but I didn't. So I said nothing, and hoped my company would speak for me.

After a time, his breathing slowed. I glanced up at him; tears made trails down his cheeks. I quickly looked down again, resolving not to mention it.

'I don't know what I'm doing,' he said at length. His voice was brittle, only a thin distance from tears.

I looked up at him, surprised to find his mouth pressed into a quivering line. 'None of us do,' I said. 'We're *living* our TTRPG, for god's sake.'

He shook his head. 'That's not what I ...' He trailed off.

I wanted to press him for a clarification but I knew it wouldn't help. I wanted to lean my shoulder against his, or touch his hand, or offer some kind of physical support. To show him that I was here and I cared, even if my words were failing me. It was an urge I had rarely felt, but I didn't want to invade his space when he was already feeling vulnerable.

So I waited. Eventually, he murmured, 'I can't be around people this long. I feel like I'm losing my mind.'

The quiet intensity of his words struck me. I was feeling the strain of it, too, but then so far I'd spent several hours scouting around in the shape of a bird. 'You could scout with me?' I suggested.

He shook his head. 'P needs the Packbeast.'

I considered. 'Let me talk to P about it? I can probably turn into something she can ride on at least a few times a day. It won't be as smooth a ride as it is on the packbeast, but it'll be better than walking. We can't know what she needs unless we ask.'

Rex nodded slowly. 'Okay. But don't force anything on her —' he paused. 'Never mind, I know you wouldn't.'

I smiled faintly.

We lapsed into silence again. I could feel the strain coming off him, and wondered whether I should leave and give him some space when he whispered, 'I miss my cat. I miss my room, my flat. I thought I wanted this.'

I didn't know what to say to that.

When he was ready, we returned to the camp. I nodded to Arries, who looked relieved to see us. 'I'll take over,' I said.

Rex hovered uncertainly as Arries stretched and went into the tent. 'Will you be okay?'

'Me?' I laughed, though it sounded strained. 'I'll be fine. Staying up way too late alone is my normal operating procedure.' I paused. 'Would you mind taking the spot nearest the edge tonight?'

He offered me a fleeting smile. 'I'd like that. Thanks, Tar.'

'No problem,' I said to his retreating back. The ends of his locs and the tip of his tail glowed beneath the darkening sky.

Left alone I settled next to the dying fire, looking around the forest surrounding us. My darksight cast it in shades of grey and blue, with sparkling silver streaks in the rare place where moonlight pierced the thick canopy.

'Even the dark is different here,' I whispered to the empty night. I didn't really miss home, or at least not yet. But I thought of Saanvi, searching for her missing daughter. I thought of my mother, and what she must think when I didn't answer her calls.

And I thought of Kenta, terrified to be living a fiction he'd created. Pauline, stranded in a world straight out of her imagination but without any of the aids she required to live her life. And Rex, homesick and anxious.

I raised my hand toward the embers of the campfire and sketched a rune, drawing energy from the earth and air. The embers sparked, then flared into flame. I tossed a few of the gathered branches onto it and continued to flare the flame until they caught. The energy of the spell warmed me as much as the fire.

So many problems. So many hurts. And I could barely manage my own nerves, let alone help the others. I thought of my interactions with Kenta and Rex today and my stomach twisted with a nauseating wrench. What did I think I was doing? I was only making things worse.

I swallowed the high-pitched keen growing in my chest and tried to focus on keeping watch. But the world was only grey.

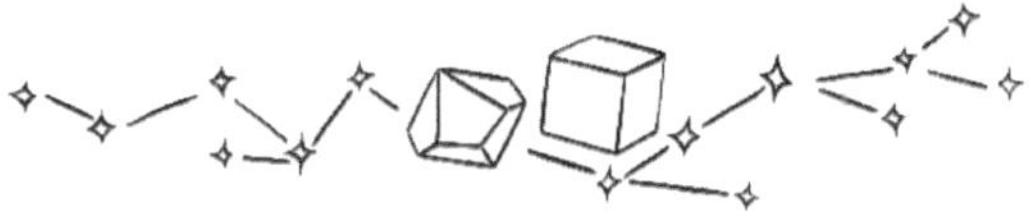

CHAPTER TWENTY

With nothing but the faint crackle of the dying campfire to keep me company, my eyelids began to droop. Even the night-sounds of Turovellis, the trill of birds and the hum of bugs, the spooky rustling in the leaf-litter, was fast becoming background noise.

Perhaps I would have been more afraid had I relied on my old human eyesight, but with the darksight of astralkin, I could see that the strange crinkling nearby was not an approaching predator, but a large beetle. I could see that in all directions, there was little more to fear than a distant stag with a touch of voidshadow at the edges of the antlers and hooves, than owls and bats both Earthly and otherworldly going about their night-time hunts.

My airy assertion that staying up all night was common practice for me was starting to seem foolhardy. There was a big difference between staying up raiding in your favourite MMO and staying awake with nothing to keep your attention. Even this stunning environment only served to lull me, like I was slipping into a dream.

The world began to shift in and out of focus, at times the world of greys and blues before me, at others a vibrant land of pinks and purples that existed only in my mind. I was finding it harder and harder to tell the difference between them. Harder and harder to force my eyes back open.

The sound of clattering metal jolted me awake. I blinked a few times; something had filled the dark clearing with bright, shimmering light, shorting out my darksight.

A fat black creature with overlapping scales and iridescent speckles had its head smushed into our cooking pot, which had been left aside to be cleaned in the morning. It had six clawed flippers and a thick tail with a fin like a trailing iridescent veil. The glow seemed to come from all around it; it was suffused in an almost liquid glow of shifting colours.

I was so startled by its appearance that my mind went blank. I didn't call out a warning, or summon magic into my body. I only stared.

There was a sound of something rasping against metal, the creature shifting a bit, flippers digging into the leaf mulch. Then suddenly they popped their head out. A seal, fat and puppy-like, with rippling iridescent green fins on either side of their head, almost like ears. Another fin stood on their head, following their spine, and a bright green gem the size of my clenched fist resided in their chest. Their eyes were all-black and fixed on my face.

For a moment, we stared at each other. They licked a bit of leftover stew from their jowls.

I had no idea what this thing was. They didn't *look* dangerous though. I got to my feet, still fuzzy-headed with sleep. 'Shoo,' I said, waving my arms at them. 'Go on! Leave!'

They shuffled toward me, fat body rippling across the ground. Their head fin lifted higher as they considered me. They tilted their head to one side and ... baaed.

I had no other word to describe the wordless, grating cry of this creature. I braced myself for them to lunge, or charge, but they only opened and closed their oddly mobile nostrils, then started to snuffle on the ground, clearly searching for more food.

I glanced at the tent, but nobody appeared in the doorway, and I was loathe to wake them for something trivial. I took a few, firm steps toward the creature, waving my arms. 'Shoo!' I tried again. 'Leave! Hsshhh!'

The creature ignored me until I got close, at which point they sat upright, long neck almost reaching my waist in height, and growled, bearing triplet rows of tiny, sharp teeth.

I flinched away as their mouth snapped shut. They stared, enormous black eyes blinking at me thoughtfully, then continued to shuffle around the campsite with their awkward, seal-like gait. Their path would likely take them closer to the tent.

I hesitated. I knew almost nothing about animals, for all my character had nature-based magic. I'd always adored nature documentaries and the like, but I'd never had any pets or really had any idea what to do with an animal when one was in front of me.

I didn't think this thing meant harm? They were just a wild animal. I didn't want to hurt them, either. But I couldn't let them go barrelling into a tent of my sleeping, undefended friends and a sleeping, undefended child.

I picked up my satchel from the dirt beside me and quickly searched through it. I had given Riya the bulk of my personal rations whenever she wanted a snack, but I still found some dried meat and a small hunk of cheese.

'Hey!' I whispered. 'Hssh! Seal!' I had no idea whether magical seal beasts ate either of these things. Their ear fins twitched in my direction at my voice, but they didn't so much as glance at me.

I unwrapped the meat as loudly as I could, remembering Rex talking about his cat coming running at the sound of food packets. The cheesecloth didn't really crinkle much, and the creature didn't come running, but they did float up into the air, flippers gently undulating as if swimming, and tilted over backwards until they were looking at me upside down.

'Okay, so you can levitate,' I said. 'That's great. That's extremely normal and I know just what to do about that.' I tried to remember the kinds of things I'd seen people with pets say. 'Aren't you a clever, pretty thing?' I said, in as talkative and cheerful a tone as I could. 'Aren't you pretty?'

They were pretty. Strange and beautiful, but frightening too, especially now I knew they were a lot more mobile than they had first appeared. Did wild animals care about human voices, or was that only a domestic animal thing?

The creature's nostrils took a large, visible sniff. They twisted in the air until they were upright, and then swam toward me, now graceful and slick where before they had been heavy and cumbersome. They baaed again, more eagerly this time.

I ripped off some of the meat, showed it to them, and threw it out away from the camp as I hard as I could. Their gaze followed the meat. They glanced back at me, head fin perking as if to say, 'Why?', then flowed out after the meat, taking their light with them.

I sagged in relief and settled back on the cold ground.

The tent rustled, and Rex emerged. 'Time for sleep,' he said. He frowned. 'Wow, you do look alert. I thought you'd have been dozing off by now.'

'Uh.' My cheeks heated. Within moments, my aura activated, all the more obvious in the dark.

Rex raised his eyebrows.

I cleared my throat, furious with Past Me once again for their terrible decisions. 'There's a creature wandering around. I don't think they're dangerous, but just keep an —'

The campsite was again bathed in shimmering light. I turned to face the seal creature, which spun gently in the air, dark eyes watching me throughout the awkward cycle.

They baaed again.

'Tar?'

'One sec,' I said. I glared at the seal. 'You want more? Okay, look.' I held out the remainder of the meat and cheese. 'This is everything I have.' I reeled back and threw the parcels as far as I could.

The seal swirled away again.

Rex made a strangled sound.

'What?' I turned back to him. His expression was amused.

'You don't get rid of an animal by feeding it,' he said.

I rubbed my eyes. 'Well, what else was I supposed to do?'

He actively grinned now, baring pointed teeth. 'Nothing,' he said, voice heavy with irony. 'It was your only option.'

I rubbed my eyes. 'I don't care for your tone.'

'But *I'm* really enjoying myself.' He hesitated, smile fading, and added, 'You, uh, you look cute, with your aura glowing.'

I blushed harder, aura flaring. I wished I could sink into the ground and never come back. But after a moment, it occurred to me that Rex's tone was no longer mocking.

'Rex, I —'

A baa at my elbow. I turned to face the seal creature, which now hovered at eye-level.

'I don't have anything else!' I said, exasperated. I raised my empty hands. 'Look —'

They bit me, all three rows of teeth puncturing the skin on my left hand.

'Ouch!' I tried to wrench my hand free but the seal beast was clamping down with painful determination. 'Let — me — go!'

Rex moved in to help, arcane energy sparkling around his hands.

The seal made a muffled growl.

Then: a scream from the tent. The seal immediately fled in a swirl of iridescent fins and bright light, darting away through the trees.

Rex hesitated, then ran for the tent. I clutched my bleeding and much tooth-marked hand and followed.

Inside, everything was in disarray. Kenta thrashed on his bedroll, drenched in sweat. Arries felt around for his absent weapon, which was securely packed in the Sack of Safekeeping. Riya cried and clutched at Hanna, who looked around blearily.

Pauline knelt beside Kenta. 'Hey. Wake up.' She shook his shoulder. 'Ken!' She lightly slapped his cheeks.

Kenta gasped. His eyes sprang open. 'P?'

'It's okay,' she said. 'You're in the tent. We're in Vanthis. Everything is fine.'

'P, I saw Her.' His voice was hoarse. 'She spoke to me.'

'It was just a dream, Kenta,' Hanna said, rubbing her eyes.

His gaze was locked with Pauline's. 'No,' he said. 'No, it was real. A red shadow in the shape of a woman, no eyes, nothing. A red shadow against a backdrop of baking sunlight. She —' He swallowed. 'She said I was a gift from Fate. That she could make use of me. I — I said no.' He started to shake. Pauline reached out and held his hands.

'Then she laughed. The shadow ... swallowed me. Surrounded me. Everywhere it touched, it burned. I felt like I was covered in cuts, the blood sucking right out of me, and —' He shook his head.

'Ken. You're safe now,' Pauline said.

'It was *real*, P.'

She looked around at the group. 'Magical items,' she said. 'Dig them up. I gave you an amulet that prevents scrying. Do you have it?'

My mind went blank. Then I remembered — a necklace with a pink crystal pendant. None of us had worn it, and we hadn't gotten it identified or appraised.

Arries pat his body. 'I think I've got it?' He pulled it from the Sack— the crystal pendant swinging from a thin gold chain. 'This one?'

Pauline gestured, and Arries tossed it to her. She caught it in one hand and held it out to Kenta. 'Put this on,' she said. 'It should prevent Her or anyone else from finding you or messing with your mind.'

He accepted it with shaking hands, pulling it down over his neck. The crystal flashed once as it hit his chest, then faded.

He touched it with two fingertips, but didn't look reassured.

'It will work,' Pauline said.

I looked to Rex. 'Will it?' I whispered.

He shrugged helplessly. 'I guess we'll find out.'

The rest of the night passed quietly. Kenta twitched and murmured in his sleep, but didn't scream again. I slept fitfully myself, my hand healed at a quick touch from Arries, though I couldn't shake the memory of so many teeth digging into my flesh.

I wondered if this experience was really as wonderful as it had first appeared. If, when we finally found our way home, any of us at all would consider staying.

My dreams were full of glittering things swimming through the sky, a large shadow just out of focus behind them.

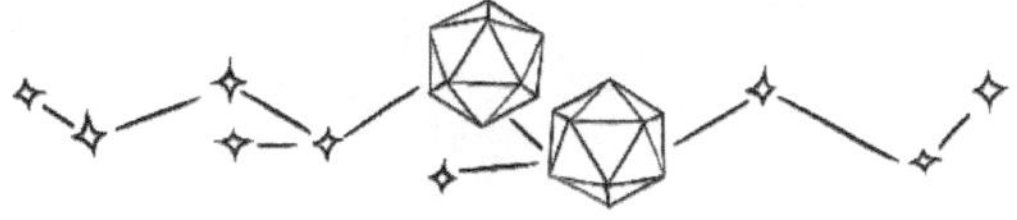

CHAPTER TWENTY-ONE

Our journey continued, hours turning into days. We were attacked only one more time, this time by giant beetles, which werefox Arries quickly saw off by roaring and clanging his sword against his armour. It turned out most predators were interested in easy prey, and didn't want to risk injury on a meal that fought back.

There were other near misses, which Rex and Hanna saw off with clever spells that spun water around us into a shield, or working together to turn the group invisible.

At night, I thought I saw flashes of a familiar shimmering light, but the seal creature didn't appear again. I flexed my left hand and berated myself for feeling disappointed.

We were all getting better at using our abilities. Polymorphing became more natural to me every day. Rex and Hanna experimented with spells and shared notes while they walked. Arries practiced his sword work at camp every night with a reluctant Kenta and healed whatever scrapes and blisters the group had developed throughout the journey.

At times, I saw Pauline's eye tattoo glowing. When I asked about it, she would only shake her head. I decided not to press the matter. It had to be difficult to have gained powers without the blue-print the rest of us had.

Rex and I were finding it increasingly difficult to hide our stimming from the group. Not just when we were stressed, but also just the normal movements and noises that got us through the day. As it happened, nobody said anything about it. Not even Hanna. I began to relax.

Alis-Umor didn't visit Kenta in his dreams again, but he was still tense and skittish. My heart ached to see him like that. Arries prayed for him every night. *His* goddess hadn't visited him in his dreams, but his belief was whole and unshakeable nonetheless.

One night, as we sat in a circle around the campfire, Kenta spoke into the quiet. 'I don't think She knew me.'

I startled at the words, looking up from the luminous flower chain I'd been weaving with idle hands. 'Sorry, she what?'

Kenta leaned back and stretched his legs toward the fire, boots skidding in the dirt. 'She didn't know me. The ... goddess.' In all the time since we'd arrived, he'd not said her name. I wondered if that fear would ever leave him. 'She was surprised by my existence. It seemed like she knew I'm not from Vanthis.' He looked around at each of us in turn. 'If Kendallien didn't exist here before we got here, did any of our characters? I kind of thought, when we got here, that we were continuing our characters' lives. Living the game. But what if those characters never existed? What if this world isn't quite the world we know?'

I hesitated, trying to process this. 'But ... if our characters never existed ... why do we look like this?' I gestured up and down at myself. 'Why do we have all the same items? Why would we be brought here at all?'

Kenta shrugged, staring into the fire.

'She was just fucking with you, or something,' Hanna said. 'It doesn't make any sense.'

I looked to Pauline, sitting beside me. Her eyes were closed. The eye on her forehead started to glow. 'Uh, P?' She didn't respond. Nervously, I touched her shoulder. 'You're glowing again.'

She opened her eyes and they were, for a moment, pure white light. Then both her eyes and tattoo faded back to normal. 'He's right,' she said tiredly. 'This Vanthis isn't quite the Vanthis we knew, or knew us.'

Everyone fell silent a moment.

'Okay, we really need to talk about that eye thing,' Hanna said, pointing at Pauline. 'Because it's getting fucking weird.'

Pauline shook her head. 'I wish I knew. I never made a character like this. I never knew any lore about a third eye like this.' She touched it with her fingertips; it flared lightly, then faded. 'I don't know who I'm supposed to be.'

'More evidence that our characters didn't exist here.' Kenta cracked a twig in half and tossed it into the fire. 'If we are inhabiting our characters, why do we look like ourselves, more or less? Why are Pauline and Riya here as well?'

'Like ourselves,' I repeated, more from echolalia than anything.

He was right. For all we had the abilities and aesthetic of our characters, we were utterly recognisable as ourselves — like actors in very convincing makeup. And my memories were all mine. Astaran's personal skills — their stealthiness, their speed, their knowledge of nature — none of that had passed on to me. Arries trained with his sword because he didn't have his character's in-built training. Hanna could play her flute, but not with Hanley's level of skill, and only because of Hanna's own history with the instrument.

Whatever power had transported us here — and we were all in agreement that the dice had played a part in that — it was not simply a case of us becoming our characters.

But now was the question of Pauline, and her strange magic. I cleared my throat. 'Seems like a kind of divination magic?' I suggested. 'It seems to activate when you need specific knowledge about the world.'

Pauline pursed her lips. 'That's possible.'

'Maybe you have more magic than just that,' Rex said. 'We've all been experimenting and learning our own abilities, but you haven't really tried anything out.'

She nodded slowly. 'Maybe.' I got the sense that she was holding something back, but didn't want to press it.

As our journey continued, we saw things I had barely envisioned with my weak imagination. Many-armed creatures watched us from the trees and mushroom caps, beads and engraved metal tied into their feathers. Huge beasts flew over the canopy, their wingbeats loud enough to make us dive for cover. Each was different from the last: patchwork, colourful creatures with no specific features I could define before they were shadows on the horizon. Giant flowers that bloomed with honey-sweet scent as we neared, baring glowing stamens and deep maws, which Pauline hurried us past with a dire warning not to look.

I also several times saw the strange drifting light that had suffused the seal creature that bit me, but slightly different in tone and with different creatures inside it. Seals, all, but with varying colours and fins. None the speckled black one who'd begged at me before.

Pauline told me they were sealorns, from the Moonsea in the Fey Plane of the Glamouring, though they had been endemic to Vanthis for centuries now and showed a little astralkin nature now themselves. 'People farm them,' she said. 'For meat and leather. They lay eggs, too. Kind of the magical chickens of Vanthis.'

I didn't like to think of someone eating the fat creature that had pestered me that night. 'Aren't they a little aggressive for that?'

She shrugged her delicate shoulders. 'In the wild, maybe. I assume they can be quite tame under the right circumstances.'

I couldn't get the thought out of my head, of the vibrant creature who'd raided our camp being caged up somewhere awaiting slaughter. I knew it wasn't likely that the one *I'd* met would meet such a fate — they had been wild, after all — but then they hadn't been wary of people, either. Maybe they would float their way right into a hunter's trap.

A few nights later, after I put Riya to bed, Hanna and I stayed up to take a watch together. Though it wasn't necessary to have more than one person up, we'd started getting into the habit. It was easier to pass the time in company — and more likely that if someone started to drift off, the other would wake them.

'Something bothering you?' she asked as I glared into the campfire.

'Hmm?'

She rolled her eyes, an action that now caused her deer-like nose to twitch. 'You've been looking like a cat about to hairball for days now. Even more than usual.'

I snorted. 'Flattering, thank you.'

'So? Spit it out.' She shifted, stretching her hooves toward the fire. 'What's on your mind?'

I shook my head. 'What isn't? We're in another universe, we have magical powers, my housemate's kid was magically kidnapped alongside us, and we have no idea how to get home.'

'We have *some* idea.' Hanna tilted her head to one side. 'Do you really want to? Go home?'

'I ...' I struggled to find the words. Did I want to give up my magic? No. Did I want to leave Vanthis, when I had dreamed my whole life of waking up in a fantasy world? Of course not.

But reality was more complicated than that. We had all vanished from Earth without so much as a goodbye. I had no way to contact my mother. The others had no way to speak to their families. Arries was so close with his parents. Rex had four siblings who were as good friends to him as any of us were. The idea that those lives had just ... ended, sat badly with me in a way I had never really considered before.

And more than that ... 'I never really thought that if my dreams came true and I got teleported into a fantasy world, that I would still be *me,* in quite the way I am now.' I snapped a twig and tossed it into the fire. It flashed and was consumed. 'I'm so anxious *all the time.* Still! I'm still ... I don't know.

Boring. Pathetic. Just with added sparkles.' As I spoke, my aura flared, highlighting my embarrassment.

'Yes, aren't you just the worst?' Hanna said. She gave me a disgusted look. 'For fuck's sake, Tar. You're great. If you weren't why would we all waste our time on you?'

I gaped a moment. 'I don't know. You're just being nice?'

Hanna snorted. 'Yeah, that must be it I'm a paragon of fucking politeness, after all.' She frowned at me. 'Tar, are you tearing up?'

I shook my head, turning away from her. 'No.'

'Jesus ... look.' She scooted closer to me, bumping her shoulder against mine. 'Hey. We all feel like that sometimes. And I know your brain gets real screwy about it but you can trust me on this: if I thought you weren't worth my time, I wouldn't bother with you. And if you ever step out of line, I will fucking well let you know. No ambiguity. No passive-aggressiveness.'

I smiled a little at that. 'I guess passive-aggressive isn't really your thing.'

'Damn right. Aggressive-aggressive is the only way to live.' Her grin became a grimace. 'I'll stay. You know, if I get the choice. I didn't daydream about donning a wizard hat or finding a dragon's egg or whatever. This is ... this is beyond dreaming.' Her long, deer-like ears twitched thoughtfully. 'I don't think I could ever give this up. Now that I know it exists.'

'Hard to give up magic,' I agreed.

She shook her head. 'Hard to give up a fresh start.'

The words hung between us a moment, as we both considered what that meant.

'You've probably noticed by now that I don't talk about my family like the others. Well, there's a reason for that. If my gran hadn't left me her house to spite my parents, I'd have nothing at all. And while I'm a total marketing badass, I'd be lying if I said I didn't go home and cry more days than not.'

'You?' I said it before the words even connected with my brain. I couldn't imagine Hanna crying. Hanna was made of steel where I was mostly rust.

'Me. I know you struggle too. And Rex — he can't even hold down a job, poor lad, even though he's intelligent as all hell and would work himself into the ground for an employer that really valued him. And no-one will make allowances for P's needs and flexible working, and — well, you get the picture. It's real fucked up.'

She shook her head. 'I can't tell you the number of times I've wished I could start again. A completely different life, different skills, different career. But Earth is shit for fresh starts, especially in the UK. I'm not rich enough to re-train. And even if I did, I'd miss you lot. We're a co-dependent mess for sure. But this whole magical world thing ... it's kinda taken care of a lot of that.'

'A fresh start, and we're all together,' I said.

'Yeah.'

'So what would you do?' I asked. 'If you stay, I mean.'

She touched her belt, where her flute hung in its case. 'I'd be curious to see whether I could make it as a musician here,' she said. 'I haven't minded sleeping rough out here, and it's not like people have a lot of other entertainment.' She looked down, her cheeks flushing a darker purple.

'I had no idea you wanted to be a musician,' I said. 'You've never really talked about it.'

'You have to be world fucking class on Earth to make anything of it, especially with a flute,' she said. 'And I just ... even if I had the time to practice all day every day, I would never be *that* good. But with work demanding a fuckton of overtime all the time ... I rarely had a moment for it. And I felt pretty guilty about that.'

'But it wasn't your fault.'

She shrugged. 'Guilt is rarely rational.'

'I only find you more impressive, knowing all that,' I said. 'You remain terrifying to me.'

Hanna snorted. 'Good. I don't know if I could bear it if even you thought I was soft and cuddly.'

As ever, Hanna's casual burns didn't leave a mark on me. I smiled.

Her gaze sharpened, looking over my shoulder.

I went cold.

'Tar. Behind you.' Her hand went to the dagger at her belt.

I noticed, too late, the sparkling light surrounding me. Something bit my elbow.

'Ow!' I flinched away, feeling at the light puncture wounds through my sleeve.

The black sealorn blinked up at me with wide eyes, whiskers twitching. A long dark tongue snaked out and licked away from blood from their muzzle.

Hanna drew her dagger and surged to her feet.

'Woah! Hanna!' I raised my hands. 'It's fine. They're the one I was talking about before.'

Hanna wavered, adjusting her grip on the dagger. 'They fucking *bit* you without so much as a hello.'

On my elbow, no less, which was really throbbing now. The sealorn drifted around me until they were hovering over my lap, then all at once the light around them vanished and they plopped like a sack of fat onto my lap.

I winced at the weight of them. They were *heavy* ...

They baaed and rested their chin on my chest, staring up at my chin.

'I think maybe that was their way of saying hello,' I said, staring down into their black button eyes. I glanced at Hanna. 'Oh, put that away. What're you gonna do, kill them?'

'I could do it if I had to,' Hanna said, but she sheathed her dagger and sat back down.

Tentatively, I reached down to try to stroke the sealorn on their head. They immediately snapped at me, so I pulled my hands away. They resettled on my chest.

'Hanna? Do we have any leftovers from dinner?'

Hanna stared at the sealorn. 'You can't be thinking of fucking feeding them after they bit you, Tar. What will that teach them?'

'Not really intending to teach them anything, but they're here because they're hungry.'

Hanna reached out to try and stroke them. Their head whipped around, three layers of teeth snapping closed on the air right where Hanna's fingers had been.

Hanna bared her teeth at the sealorn. 'I'll check my personal rations. Hang on. Riya hasn't gotten through it all yet.'

We spent the rest of our shift giving them bits of dried meat, bread — really anything that didn't seem too risky. The sealorn was delighted and swam around us, turning and twisting in the air for all the world like a seal in the ocean. They still nipped at us — sometimes quite painfully — and reacted aggressively to any attempt to touch them, but it didn't seem to be fear that motivated them and I quickly stopped attempting it. If the sealorn didn't want to be touched, I wasn't going to force them.

The sealorn was still out when Pauline emerged to take her shift. She shaded her eyes against the light. 'Is that ...?'

'Yep. They're back,' I said.

The sealorn swam up to Pauline, flipping upside-down in the air and yawning widely, baring their three rows of teeth.

'Huh.' She started to reach out to them, then thought better of it. 'How long have they been here?'

'Nearly the whole shift,' I said.

'Watch out. They'll fucking bite you for no reason at all.'

Pauline raised her eyebrows. 'Why do you say that with admiration?'

Hanna grinned. 'What can I say? The little goblin has grown on me.'

Pauline frowned at the sealorn. 'Well, they can stay, I guess. I won't bite *them* if they don't bite me.'

Hanna stood up and stretched. 'Right. That's us done, then.' She looked pointedly at me.

I realised that, though my limbs were heavy with exhaustion, I didn't want my shift to end My mind was alive with interest in the sealorn, paying close attention to their behaviour, trying to learn their ways. Their presence was lifting my spirit and making this world magical in a new and uncomplicated way.

But I didn't know how to communicate that to the others. And I *did* need to sleep, however little I might want to.

I ducked into our extended tent, bidding Hanna and Pauline goodnight. I curled up on my bedroll, the sealorn still dancing in my mind's eye, all fluid grace and sparkling light.

When I woke the next morning, Hanna looked haggard but uncharacteristically cheerful. The sealorn, however, was long gone.

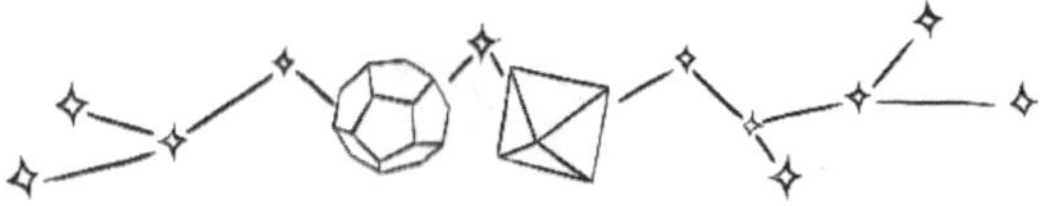

CHAPTER TWENTY-TWO

A few days later, we emerged from the forest onto a meandering road that snaked toward a small town of squat purple houses and brightly-coloured banners that fluttered proudly in the wind. It had been almost two weeks since we first awoke in Vanthis.

I shaded my eyes against the noon-day sun and watched the people scurry about, clearly already deep into the working day. Surrounding the village were fields of what looked from a distance to be large tan pinecones. A glittering black spire rose above the rooftops — the wizard tower, no doubt, which Pauline had suggested contained the teleportation circle we needed to travel to a big city safely. It looked more threatening for the knowledge. I still hadn't brought up my misgivings to the others.

'Lundanar,' Arries said, adjusting Riya where she perched on his broad shoulder. He always transformed into his werefox form to carry her. 'So ... we made it.'

'This is really the game, then,' said Rex. His voice was quiet, though whether from thoughtfulness or sadness, I couldn't tell. I stared at the back of his hooded head. His long black tail swished behind him as he walked. 'We visited Lundanar once.'

Hanna tapped her flute against her leg, looking irritated. 'Obviously it's the fucking game. Or can you light campfires with your mind at home, too?'

'You know what I mean.'

I glanced at Kenta, who looked grim and tired, a look that was fast becoming characteristic. Pauline was quiet, but pulled at her lip thoughtfully.

It made me nervous, how our time in this world was affecting us. Arries seemed his normal cheerful self, but Kenta had completely closed in on himself and Rex, always so steady, was crumbling under the constant pressure. Even Pauline, who was normally so sure of herself, seemed withdrawn and quiet.

Was it affecting me too? Was I more anxious, or more lost? I was definitely anxious but ... ack. It was so hard to judge myself.

I thought, perhaps ... I was better here. Better, but not fixed. I hoped I'd be able to hold myself together just a little longer. Use this ... this whatever it was that being here gave me, to help my friends.

I glanced at the back of my golden-armoured werefox friend. Riya now rode him piggy-back, arms wrapped around his thick neck. His bushy tail made small twitches behind him that I was coming to recognise as contentment.

I guessed, on the other hand, we were all lucky it wasn't up to me to hold us all together.

We passed into the town, instinctively drawing closer as a group. Pauline called to Rex and asked him to dispel the packbeast. I immediately fell in step with her. 'Want an arm?' I asked her.

She nodded. 'Yes, thank you.' She leaned a small amount of her weight onto me. I didn't understand what about leaning on me made standing any easier for her, but I was willing to do whatever I could to make her more comfortable.

I looked around as we walked. I felt like I was in information overload, but in the best way. This was a fantasy village such as I had never dreamed I would *really* visit. The buildings were squat and largely in shades of purple or blue. I could see now that the banners flying from some of the buildings depicted bees and flowers.

Beyond the houses were vast cultivated meadows of flowers with large yellow boxes spread out around them. Some had swarms of bees coming to and fro from them. Others housed much larger bees, easily the size of labradors, which travelled to clustered trees and macromushrooms in the distance. There were people out there too, in wicker bee-keeper masks or lace veils, tending to the boxes. There was the occasional flicker of magical light, though I couldn't quite make it all out.

The townsfolk were a mixed lot: a feykin with a long cat tail and vari-coloured eyes; a voidkin woman and her daughter both carrying baskets, both shrouded in the same aura of shadow; a man with small gull-grey wings folded on his back, chatting animatedly over a picnic in the village square to a man with blue skin and tightly curled white hair. People mostly wore shades of orange, red, or yellow, though I did see the occasional blue sash or green dress. Bright, warm colours — I assumed from the most readily available dyes. People were out hanging laundry or carrying goods, or just on their way somewhere else in town.

I heard baaing, and my heart lifted at the sight of a cluster of glittering sealorns swimming casually down the street. None of them had the black scales and iridescent green fins of my previous visitor, however. They also seemed much milder-tempered, barely glancing up as people passed.

The strangest thing about the town was the way everyone looked at us. Not outright staring, but definitely casting curious glances our way. I realised nobody here was wearing armour, like Kenta or Arries, or carrying weapons as all of us were. It had seemed normal in the game, but now all I could think was how threatening we must look. I wish we'd thought to pack it all away.

Arries transformed back into his more human shape, and flashed his wide smile at anyone and everyone who met his gaze.

'Look for an inn,' Pauline said. 'Seems like a good place to start, get a feel for this place. I'm pretty sure Lundanar has an inn.'

'Pretty sure?' I repeated, surprised by her lack of conviction. I noticed the eye on her forehead wasn't glowing.

I looked around. Someone had set up a small stall of fruit and preserves, and a few people clustered there, haggling with the gentle ease of long acquaintance. A man with a pig nose sat in his front garden tatting lace, frowning and nodding along to the young person with elf ears sitting on a nearby bench and chatting away. I looked down, avoiding the gaze of a young woman as she paused in her work packing up a crate with jars of honey.

Hanna pointed to a painted sign of a stag among flagons of ale. 'Somewhere like that?'

We stopped and Pauline looked it over. 'The Honeyhart ... yes, that must be it,' she said. 'I knew it was animal-themed but I couldn't quite recall.'

Rex frowned. 'It was the Puddle Duck in the game.'

Kenta threw him a sidelong look. 'I keep telling you; this isn't the game.' He hoisted his pack higher up on his shoulder.

The Honeyhart. Close-up, I noticed that the stag's antlers dripped with honey, and that little bees in a rainbow of colours buzzed around it.

A string of children ran by in what looked like a game of tag, giggling and shrieking. I glanced at Riya. She watched the children go with obvious longing.

The inn was a warm-looking affair, a cottage with indigo walls and creeper-shrouded windows. A fox-eared feykin and a woman with a long beard chatted outside. The woman nodded to us, the flowers in her beard rustling. 'Afternoon,' she said. Her voice was light and musical, and her eyes lingered on Pauline.

Arries smiled broadly, which in spite of his plate armour and huge sword was utterly disarming. 'Good afternoon to you as well!'

We filed inside after him, and I dipped a nod to the pair, hoping they wouldn't think us impolite for barging into their town.

Inside, it was a mix of stone floors and warm brick walls. Wildflowers were potted in the centre of every table, and the bar, such as it was, had creepers overspilling their pots to hang down in front of the bar. It had a feel that was somewhere between homey and greenhouse-like, and I instantly liked it. The windows were open, and more of the bees we had seen in the distant fields buzzed around inside in a relaxed manner. They were not all yellow; many were blue, or even green, and they were surprisingly fuzzy. The buzzing was already making me twitch, but I was awed by them and determined to stick it out.

It was mostly deserted, save for an old astralkin woman with glittering blue hair eating a plate of what looked like green scrambled eggs. She talked quietly to a feykin man with silver skin, hair in one thick black plait, and tusks just peeking over his lips. He had an apron around his waist and his sleeves rolled up to the elbow. He glanced at us as we came in, eyes surprised behind his large, wire-framed glasses, and he said something to the old woman before rising and striding over to us.

'Welcome to The Honeyhart,' he said. His voice was a pleasant alto and his small tusks were more obvious when he smiled, revealing the rest of his neat, even teeth. He cast a curious look over our rag-tag group, all bristling with armour and weapons. 'Adventurers, I presume?'

Pauline and Kenta glanced at each other. 'Something like that,' Pauline said. 'We're ... new to the area and more than a little lost. I don't suppose we could get some lunch and hole up here for the night?'

He spread his arms to encompass the empty room. 'We're hardly booked up, but we only have three rooms available. Double beds, though, and with little sofas and room enough on the floor if you don't mind it. Not that there're a lot of other options in these parts, save camping out in the fields.' His eyes passed over each of us in turn; Kenta with eyes downcast and arms crossed over his chest, Arries standing proud with a wide toothy smile, Pauline leaning on my arm, tense but friendly, Ram and Hanna bringing up the rear with Riya. 'I'm Ordeth, by the way. And you are?'

He seemed to address this to Kenta. Kenta glanced up, surprised. 'Just passing through,' he said. I wondered if he, like me, found the idea of claiming our adventuring group's name uncomfortable. We weren't those people, however much we might resemble them. I certainly had no intention of picking up adventuring work here.

Ordeth nodded, looking a little disappointed. No doubt he was expecting more cordiality. Hanna elbowed Kenta.

'Oof!' He glanced at Hanna and then at me, as if I was also at fault. I glared at him then flicked my eyes at Ordeth, embarrassed by the whole situation.

Kenta winced and said, 'Sorry, we're — this is all kind of new to us. I'm Ken. These are my friends.' He introduced each of us. I waved when my name was mentioned, cringing inwardly at my own awkwardness. Kenta shook Ordeth's hand once the introductions were done.

'It's a boxcoin a night per room,' Ordeth said. 'For another five tricoins each, we'll cover board for all three as well.'

I thought of the Sack of Safekeeping Arries carried; with it, a small fortune in hexcoins, gems, and other treasure.

'That'll be fine,' Pauline said. 'Thank you.'

'Let me show you around The Honeyhart, then,' he said. 'You can get your little one settled, and I'll talk to the kitchen about some lunch. Would one of you be able to advise me with that?'

'Uh ... sure.' Kenta shrugged. 'I guess I could.'

Ordeth showed us around. The rooms were just as bright and comfortable as the main inn — green succulents adorned the windowsills, cheerful and plump, and the furnishings were plain but well-maintained. Honestly, I was looking forward to being in even a shared room — it would be a big step up compared to us all trying to squeeze into Hanna's Alterdimensional tent.

After, we kind of spread out across the inn. Rex disappeared into one of the rooms and it seemed likely he wouldn't come out for a while, and Pauline similarly claimed a bed so that she could curl up and try to recover from the walk through town. Kenta chatted with Ordeth at the bar, listing off the various dietary requirements we'd all offered. He looked more himself than he had in days, with the brightness returned to his skin and eyes as he leaned against the bar with his characteristic lazy ease. Arries introduced himself to the old woman, who eagerly told him about her day. He listened with a big smile and rapt attention, and I would be shocked if she didn't come looking for him again tomorrow. Arries had that effect on people.

So it was just me and Riya sitting in the corner. Riya gently felt the leaves of the creeper, a thick and bright-green creature that was just beginning to flower. I suspected it might also be some kind of succulent.

'It'll be nice to sleep with a proper roof,' I said. My insides were already starting to squirm at talking to Riya. I still felt like I had no common ground with kids and no idea where to start.

Riya shrugged. She dipped her fingers in her glass of water and then let the drips fall onto the plant.

She looked ... subdued? Maybe? She was a stoic kid at the best of times so I didn't find her easy to read but ... she must be missing home. Even I was, and this was pretty much my dream come true.

'Riya?'

She glanced up at me.

'How're you feeling?'

She sat back in her chair, raising her knees to her chest. It made me miss being small enough to do that on a dining chair.

I was pretty happy being fat, most days, but my belly did tend to get in the way of things like that.

'I want my Spiderman shirt,' said Riya. 'Mum always puts it on me backwards.'

I nodded. 'Your mum is very funny,' I said.

Riya bared her teeth at me in an approximation of a smile, staring under the table.

'She loves you very much.'

'She tells me that a lot,' Riya said. She rolled her eyes, which made me smile even as my heart clenched painfully. Such a sarcastic expression on a seven year-old.

'We're gonna get you back to her,' I said.

Riya put her cheek on her knees. 'Arries says magic brought us here so we need magic to go back. But you have magic and Hanna has magic, but we aren't home yet.'

God, how to explain the rules of *Kin* to a child? How to explain *any* of this to one? 'Our magic isn't strong enough yet,' I said. 'So we need to find someone with more magic to help us. But we'll get stronger the more we practice, so maybe we'll be able to do it ourselves eventually if we can't find someone to help.'

That seemed possible — I remember Hanna and Rex discussing it. Only a few of us had a shot at getting a planeshift spell, as we'd already put the points in to the prerequisite skills. That was still a few levels from now, and we definitely had no idea how levelling worked in this world. Pauline levelled us up at important milestones in our quests and character development. Would we do tasks and just suddenly find we had more magic? Somehow, it didn't seem likely to work that way.

We'd always been glad that Pauline used that system for the game; More-mainstream TTRPGs had players compete for experience by killing things. It kept us much more in balance and cooperative with each other. It also felt more meaningful and meant we didn't have to rush in to fight every creature we met. It made for a more social and less violent game.

★ 167 ★

But this wasn't a game, even if the game we loved mimicked it well. I had never killed so much as a spider — I wasn't about to go fighting beasts or people. And ideally, I didn't want to end up on any grand quests either.

So we just had to find a wizard powerful enough to send us home, or hope that just living our lives here would be enough to get us where we needed to be.

Riya absorbed all this thoughtfully. 'I have magic,' she said.

I frowned. 'Do you?'

She nodded. 'I saw you make the grass grow, when we were camping.' She closed her eyes and took a few steadying breaths, then reached out and touched the plant at the table. With her other hand, she drew a hazy rune in the air. The plant ... stretched. Like it was waking up from a long slumber. The flowerbuds spiralled open into full bloom, and others sprouted and did the same. Little glimmers of green light hovered in the air a moment, before fading. She leaned back in her chair and brought her knees back up, now with a small, pleased smile.

I stared. 'Witch magic.' I whispered the words, still not completely believing what I was seeing. Riya wasn't in our game. She didn't know anything about *Kin,* and we had never encountered any magical children that I could remember. How could Riya have a witch spell?

There was a lot to unpack about what exactly had happened to us when we came to Vanthis. But right now, Riya was in front of me, waiting for my response to her spell. 'That was really impressive!' I said. 'It's meant to take a really long time to learn how to do that. Lots of adults can't do it.'

She beamed at me. 'I'm very clever though,' she said. 'My teacher always says I have a smart mouth.'

I couldn't help but grin at that. 'Maybe we should practice magic together tomorrow,' I said. 'Since we both know how to make things grow.'

Riya nodded. 'Okay. And if we get good enough, we can magic ourselves home?'

'If we get good enough, we can magic ourselves home,' I agreed. I hoped, for all our sakes, that it would really be that simple.

☆ 169 ☆

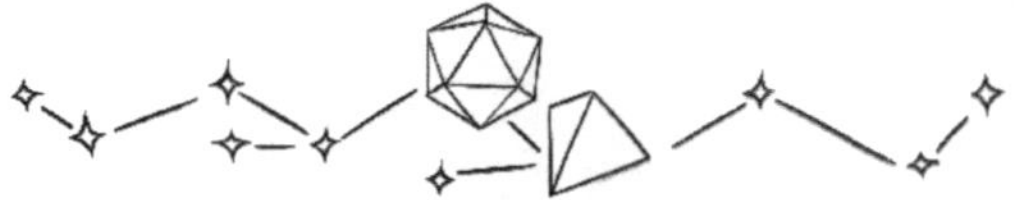

CHAPTER TWENTY-THREE

Night came and, after finally having a day to relax and recover from days of walking, we gradually made our way to bed. Pauline and Arries claimed one room, with Riya going with them. I helped brush her hair before she went and wished her a good night, both relieved and disappointed that she'd chosen Arries over me. Hanna told Kenta he might as well join her, and both of them left over my protests. Kenta actually *winked* at me. So that left me standing outside Rex's room, already feeling deeply embarrassed by the idea of even knocking.

I hovered, hoping somehow Rex would open the door and I could explain the situation to him without interrupting. He'd been so desperate for time alone. I felt ... itchy. Uncomfortable. Like I needed to go wash my face and stare at myself in the mirror and maybe bundle up a towel and scream into it for a little while.

Eventually, the next door over opened and Hanna stepped out, stripped down to her underclothing, which was thankfully long-johns. She saw me and frowned. 'Tar? You're glowing like a fucking lantern.'

I cringed and crossed my arms, as if I could protect myself from her judgement by shielding my body. 'Hi Hanna. Just ... um ...'

She raised her eyebrows. 'Did the hermit kick you out, or are you being a jittery little whippet again?'

God, that felt like a horribly accurate description of me. 'The whippet thing,' I replied glumly.

Hanna shook her head. 'We've got rea. fucking problems, Tar. Might be time to buck up and push past the crazy.'

'If I could do that, don't you think I fucking would have already?' I snapped. I didn't mean to, but I couldn't hear those words, so similar to so many I'd heard before, and not get angry. Anxiety couldn't be fixed by positive thinking or sheer bloody-mindedness. In fact, trying to muscle my way through terrible mental health often made it worse. All I had going for me were my meds, therapy, and years of experience, and I only had access to one of the three right now.

Hanna was not only unruffled by my outburst, but she grinned. 'That's the spirit, Tar.' She walked up and gave me a hearty thump on the arm. God, how was she more annoying now than she was back home? It was like her annoyingness had been compressed into a tighter package and made it more potent. She leaned past me and rapped on Rex's door.

'Don't —'

'G'night, nerd,' she said. She yawned and shuffled toward the washroom.

'Hanna, I —' I whispered furiously, only to be cut off as the door cracked open.

A very rumpled Rex looked at me. His hair was a mess, with some of his locs caught around his horns. There were dark bags under his eyes and his skin had a sheen of sweat. He was wearing the same clothes he had in the cay, though his cloak and hood had been shed, leaving him oddly vulnerable-looking in a blue doublet over a long black shirt and leggings. Without hoodie or cloak, it was very obvious how thin he was — a man so narrow-boned he looked almost bird-like.

'Uh. Tar?'

I wrung my hands. I could feel sweat gathering at the small of my back and behind my knees. I didn't want to be here right now, caught red-handed disturbing Rex. 'It's nothing,' I said. 'Wrong door. Sorry!'

I spun around and started to flee very quickly down the corridor, but Rex stepped out behind me. 'Tar. Stop. It's fine.'

I froze, back ramrod straight, and turned to face him. I opened my mouth, but didn't know what to say. My aura flared around me, betraying my embarrassment.

I'm sorry for being weird.

I'm sorry you have to share a room with me.

I'm sorry we're stuck here and nothing is the same anymore.

He studied me, expression unreadable. 'We're roommates, I take it?'

I nodded. 'I can share with Hanna and Ken —'

He shook his head. 'Come in.' He disappeared into the room, leaving the door open behind him. I took a shuddering breath and followed him in.

The room was much like the others, though the plant on the sill was a purple succulent rather than a vibrant green, and the sofa in here had a worn but pretty embroidery that at first I took for crowns but on a closer look, was actually antlers. There was a little bedside table with a short ironwork candlestick, and little else of note. Rex sat on the sofa, and after a moment's hesitation, I dropped my bag and cloak next to his beside the door and went to perch on the other side.

I noticed the bed was still made and barely creased. Whatever Rex had been doing in here, he hadn't been using it. It made me worry that his rumpled look was self-inflicted rather than the effect of a long nap.

For a moment, we just sat, semi-turned toward one another. Rex's hand rubbed the back of his neck; my hands twisted in my lap. At length, I glanced sidelong at Rex. He stared at his feet. His tail twitched, the tip gently tapping the floor.

'I, um, I'm happy to take the sofa,' I said. 'Whatever you prefer, really. I'm just glad to have a bit more space tonight.'

He inclined his head, like he wasn't really listening.

I hesitated, then reached across the space between us, touching the tips of my fingers to his shoulder.

He startled and his eyes found mine. 'Sorry. Yeah, uh ... I would appreciate the bed if you're okay with it. I'm not ... I don't know.' His mouth trembled, like it was trying to smile but couldn't quite form the shape.

I started to pull away, but he quickly reached up and pressed his hand over mine. 'Thanks.' He stood up.

I didn't know what to say to that, or how to ease the tension radiating off of him in waves. I wanted to. I wanted to be the person he'd been for me on Pauline's doorstep. I wanted to help him feel less alone in this moment, when he was drowning in adrenaline and fear. But I didn't know what to do except bear witness.

He tossed me a pillow, then laid on the bed on top of the covers, one hand out limply in front of him. I placed the cushion and started to unbuckle my leather armour. There were really a lot of straps for it, even though it didn't cover much of my body. I wondered, idly, if I could perhaps keep it in my pack instead of wearing it now that we weren't in imminent danger of being ambushed by ferymars or bears or something. Armour might be a *Kin* staple, but it wasn't very *me*.

I realised, while I struggled with a particularly tough buckle where the little spike had gotten stuck and wouldn't move from the hole, that Rex was watching me. I froze a moment, but I was thoroughly clothed underneath and it's not like I was doing a strip-tease. 'Stuck,' I mumbled, my cheeks heating at the attention. Though this was no more intimate than anything he'd seen during our journey here, somehow it felt it. It was different in a room with just us than it was in a tent with all our friends.

'Do you need —?'

'— No! No, I'm fine.' I continued to struggle with it, yanking hard. It was hard to get a good grip when the buckle was on my shoulder.

Rex sat up. 'I'd like to help.'

How could I argue with that? I inclined my head and waited, head still lowered.

Rex stood in front of me, and I stared at his chest. The doublet fit him well, tapering in at the hips. As stressed as he'd been since he'd arrived, he *looked* like he belonged in Vanthis. It was somewhere his quiet confidence made him look stronger, not something that made him overlooked. He worked at the buckle on my shoulder, long fingers slipping between pauldron and clothing. I held very still.

He slid it from my shoulder. 'Good?' he asked. He didn't step back.

I raised my eyes to meet his. I felt a shock as our gazes locked, but didn't back away. Even edged with blue light, his eyes were familiar to me. One of the few people I could say that about, try as I did to avoid eye contact. We were of a height, and he was so close that there was only a half-step between us. I held my breath, not wanting to smell him, which would seem extremely creepy given my feelings.

His eyes were shadowed by stress, but now something else struck me. He looked at me like he couldn't look away, his lips gently parted like on the verge of saying something. This close, I noticed an incredibly fine dusting of facial hair following his jawline. I wanted to take his face in my hands and sweep my thumb across his cheek. My fingers twitched at the thought.

It was not my habit to touch people without warning. Or to *want* to touch anyone at all. It wasn't a sexual thing, it was just ... he was so beautiful, and sad, and I wanted to be close to him. Wanted him to be close to me.

I needed to say something about it. I couldn't just keep pining after him like an idiot. Either he felt the same and we would work something out, or he didn't and I needed to put space between us and sort my head out.

And he was still looking at me like he was just as trapped as I was.

I swallowed, hard. 'Rex, I ...'

It was like my voice broke a spell. He flinched back and turned aside.

The words fell unspoken from my mouth. His jaw clenched. He looked ... angry? Disappointed? I couldn't tell.

My instinct was to drop my gaze, to drop the whole thing. To go back to the sofa and go to sleep and hope tomorrow I would wake up with a plan to deal with this. But I didn't do that. I cleared my throat. 'Rex.'

He turned, and I stepped right up to him. I didn't try to read into his expression, I just met his eyes and spoke before my nerves could freeze my tongue. 'I like you, Rex. In more than a friend way.' My words kind of squeaked at that point, my lungs suddenly too thin to draw in air. I cleared my throat. 'I hope you feel the same way, because I am already way deeper into this than feels safe.'

Rex's mouth pressed into a thin line. I thought he would turn away without saying anything. I thought his mouth would curl with disgust. But instead, he said, 'It doesn't matter.' Eyes shadowed, tone bitter. Like he was upset that I'd made him say it.

And while I stood there stunned, he went to the bed and laid down with his back to me.

After a moment, I went to the sofa and did the same. My eyes burned, my chest was tight with held in sobs, and my head buzzed with white noise. It was a long time before I fell asleep.

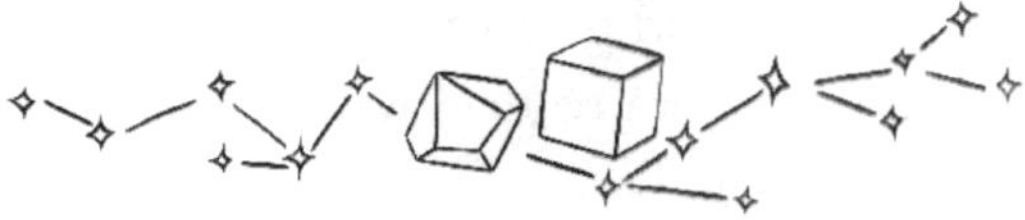

CHAPTER TWENTY-FOUR

When I woke, Rex was gone. I can't say I wasn't relieved. I got my things and headed for the washroom, calling myself a thousand kinds of idiot on the way. I was more than a little panicked when I discovered that instead of a shower there was a big, unplumbed ceramic tub — I knew Pauline had said that Vanthis had plumbing but I guess plumbed tubs was a lot to ask for in a small town.

But as it happened, there was an enchanted jug that produced water to fill it and enchanted black stones that heated said water. I had a comfortable enough clean even as I tried not to think about how I was stewing in my own filth. Plenty of people took baths, I reminded myself, and they were neither stinky nor filthy. This was just a different thing than I was used to, that was all.

It was easy enough to drain and rinse out, thankfully, and when I emerged from the washroom with my hair wet and slicked back and a fresh set of clothing from my pack, I felt significantly more human than I had last night. Or more astralkin, I guess, since that's what I was these days.

I left my things in my room and went downstairs. Ordeth and Kenta chatted at a small table while Riya was on the floor with a watercolour set and a sheaf of paper. 'Morning!' I greeted her, in a voice with such forced cheer that it made me want to grimace.

Riya glanced up at me, then back down at the page. 'I'm doing art.'

After a moment's hesitation, I lowered myself to the ground beside her. I was very aware of my size when I did things like this — I was a relatively fit person, but getting down to the ground and up again was still an effort when you were fat, and I always felt much more visibly fat when I did it. But neither Kenta nor Ordeth so much as blinked at me as I leaned forward to get a look at the rainbow-splattered page in front of Riya. 'So what are you painting?'

'Dinosaur queen,' she said. And sure enough, there was a huge allosaur on the page, rainbow feathers sticking out all over the place. I felt touched, if irked by the misgendering, then noticed the small figure sitting between its shoulders, and the little yellow crown on her head. 'Are you the dinosaur queen?'

Riya shrugged and kept painting, but I thought I caught a smile tucked to one side.

When I stood up, Ordeth smiled at me. 'Good morning. I hope you slept well?'

'Definitely,' I said, though it felt like a weird distinction to make when I was comparing it to sleeping on the forest floor crammed into an enchanted tent.

'Join us, would you?' he said. 'I'll get you some breakfast. Do you take your porridge with fruit?'

I nodded, though truthfully I didn't take my porridge with ... porridge. I normally had toast, cookie crunch, or air for breakfast. I didn't say that though, since it might confuse Ordeth and Kenta would definitely judge me. It was too early in the morning for judgement.

While Ordeth went through the door behind the bar, presumably to talk to the kitchen staff, I eyed up the seats. It was a four person table, so my options were to sit next to Kenta or to sit next to a complete stranger from a different universe.

Kenta raised his eyebrows at my hesitation. 'Choosing the lesser of two evils?'

He said it without rancour, but I cringed nonetheless. 'Congratulations, you're it!' I said, and took the seat beside him. He had his own bowl of porridge, mostly mopped up at this point, but he tapped the spoon against the bowl. The repetitiveness of it instantly made me twitch, each ring of metal against ceramic louder and more piercing. To my suprise, he stopped, and instead put his elbow on the table and rested his chin in his hand, eyes going to the kitchen.

'What do you make of Ordeth?' he asked. He drummed his fingers against his chin thoughtfully.

I shrugged, tracing a whorl in the table surface. 'Nice,' I said. 'I don't really know him.'

Kenta glanced at me sidelong, a smirk playing at his mouth. 'Obviously we don't know him yet,' he said. 'He just ... I don't know. I get a good vibe from him.'

I didn't say anything, since I had no idea what 'a good vibe' meant in this context.

Ordeth returned, and placed a bowl of porridge in front of me along with a wide spoon and a small pot of honey with little pink daisy-like flowers floating on the surface. A cluster of unknown orange fruit brightened the centre of it. It looked, to my surprise, more appetising than cookie crunch. I fished a bit of fruit out and took an experimental bite, then made a face before I could stop myself. Too many new textures and flavours.

Fortunately, Ordeth didn't notice. He leaned forward, hands clasped on the table. 'If you don't mind me asking ... I have a few questions.'

I froze, having been surreptitiously trying to dislodge raspberry seeds from my teeth. Kenta was utterly cool as he replied, 'Oh?'

Ordeth reclasped his hands. He looked a little sheepish. 'Your friend with the eye on her forehead ... is that ornamental?'

'What else would it be?' I asked, my battle with the unknown fruit temporarily forgotten.

He raised his eyebrows. 'The Mark of the Oracle?' He looked between the two of us, clearly not believing our nonplussed expressions. 'The prophesied one? There are pretenders and cultists all over these parts. They come down from Mihilit-dalath.'

I rubbed my eyes, giving myself a moment to take this in. 'There's a prophecy ... about a prophet? That seems a little unnecessary.'

'The Oracle's not a prophet — they're a hero. Are you telling me you really don't know about the Oracle. even though your friend is wearing their symbol?'

Kenta and I exchanged a look. I didn't think he knew what the Oracle was any more than I did. This was a big way reality was differing from the game, and I didn't like that it implicated Pauline in some way.

Ordeth frowned. 'Where are you from?'

Kenta grinned and leaned back, affecting ease. 'Does it matter?'

But Ordeth didn't look at all reassured.

Anxiety gnawed at me. Ordeth was our first ally in Vanthis. He seemed friendly, and since he was an innkeeper I assumed he was unlikely to be a supervillain. And ... it felt wrong to lie. It always did. I wasn't made for misdirection — not even by omission.

'We're from another world — plane,' I said, remembering the terminology. 'We knew about this one, but it's still very new to us. We're trying to get home.'

Ordeth looked troubled. 'And your friend's mark ...?'

'She didn't have it before we got here,' said Kenta. He crossed his arms, looking tense. 'A lot of things changed for us, when we got here. None of us knew that symbol had any relevance.'

I offered Kenta a tight smile, glad he'd decided to tell the truth. But he didn't look any more comfortable for having done it.

Ordeth looked between us as if waiting for a punchline. Maybe our obvious discomfort convinced him, though, because he sighed and slumped back in his seat. 'From another plane ...' he murmured. 'Arcanyl's really playing a joke on me today, aren't they?' He invoked the deity of magic and hidden truths. He shook his head. 'So you'll need a wizard then. A powerful one.'

I nodded. 'That's why we're heading to Mihilit-dalath.' I studied him. He looked nervous, his eyes cast to one side in a way they hadn't been before. I was the last person to judge someone for not wanting to make eye contact, but ... 'You're a wizard, aren't you?'

Ordeth straightened as if a cold poker had been shoved down the back of his shirt. 'Sorry, what?'

Maybe I was wrong but ... 'You mentioned Arcanyl,' I said. 'Aren't they the deity of magic? And you seemed very comfortable with us being from another plane ...'

Ordeth slumped. 'I ... dabble,' he said. 'Nothing dramatic. It would be hard to call me a wizard.'

My gaze moved to the tan cat curled up on the bar, fanning its tail and watching us with bright golden eyes. At my look, it quickly slitted its eyes in a smile.

I tapped the edge of the table, not wanting to push the issue with Ordeth. Surely he had his reasons for keeping it quiet.

Later, we gathered downstairs.

'We need a plan,' Pauline said. 'We need to prepare for the journey, we need supplies, and we need to arrange transport. And I'll be honest,' she took a shuddering breath. 'I am *not* feeling up to it right now.' She did look unusually tense, and her skin was drawn. A fuzzy blue bee buzzed over and investigated her shoulder.

I wondered how much the journey had taken from her, physically and emotionally. I realised how little I really understood about Pauline's disability and how it affected her. I knew it was terrible. I knew it made exertion so painful that she needed to be very careful and take time to recover. But I don't think I'd understood the extent of it. I probably still didn't — or couldn't, because I wasn't experiencing it.

But that floating behind on Rex's packbeast had itself been too much exertion was shocking to me, and I hated myself for not understanding her better. She was my friend, and I owed it to her to show her the respect of educating myself about her condition.

God, that would have been easier while I still had internet access ... I'd find a way.

I looked to Rex, who was staring at the ground, still clearly grappling with anxiety. I looked to Hanna, who always had so much to say but right now could only hover nervously at Pauline's side. The seconds stretched in silence.

'Ken, maybe you could go get us some food?' I said. 'I'll write a list.'

'I'll go with you, if you like,' Ordeth said, from where he sat watching us. The cat was in his lap, purring and boffing its head against his hands. 'They'll fleece you at the market, since you're an outsider. It'll go better if I'm there.'

I smiled encouragingly, though honestly I was surprised by his offer. 'You don't happen to know the fastest way to Mihilit-dalath, do you?'

'I do — you'll want to go to the tower. There's a teleportation circle there, but it's only to be used by pre-arrangement. Usually for the mayor or emergency services.' He looked worried. 'You'll have to convince them —'

'I'll go,' said Rex. Though he said the words quietly, everyone stopped to listen. 'I can talk to them wizard to wizard. I'd teleport us myself but I don't have the runes for the Mihilit-dalath circle.'

'That'd be great, Rex,' Pauline said.

The anxiety I'd been letting fester for days threatened to overwhelm me. 'Isn't there another way?' I asked. 'Is there ... I don't know, a carriage or — or griffins or something we could ride?'

Ordeth shook his head. 'We're not due any riders for another few weeks.'

My feeble hope died in my chest. I crossed my arms over my belly, trying to focus on holding my fear.

If this was the only way, then it was the only way.

'Tar, would you go with him?' Pauline asked.

I wanted to. Somehow, the thought of seeing the circle with Rex made the whole thing less terrifying. And I was glad he was feeling up to helping, but his words the night before held me back. My cheeks heated at the thought.

'It doesn't matter,' he said again in my mind, his mouth twisting downward as he turned away from me, silhouetted in the candlelight.

My mouth parted as I tried, and failed, to find the words to respond.

'Well, shit. You don't have to, Tar.' Hanna dusted off her hands and hopped down from the table on which she was playing. Her hooves struck the ground with a loud clop. 'Rex, you've got the charisma of a hermit, unsurprisingly. I'll go with you — turn on the charm, if your mage-talk doesn't dazzle them.' She gave a jagged smile.

Nobody quite looked at her. In the game, as in real life, Hanna had always had a sort of ... bombastic belligerence. It would be hard to call it charming, but it was undoubtedly persuasive.

Hanna stepping in freed me from the indecision. I took a shaky breath. 'Okay, so I'll make the list and then ... I guess I'll go with the town crew?' I said. 'I'm not sure —'

'Ordeth,' Pauline said. 'Where could I get a wheelchair?'

'Sorry — a wheel chair?'

'A mobility aid,' she clarified. 'For people who cannot reliably walk. You must have disabled villagers here.'

'Oh! Sorry ... I was unfamiliar with the phrasing. I know them as driftchairs.' He looked genuinely embarrassed. 'Yes, there are a few. I think people usually get what they need from the city, but if you have something specific in mind ...' He hesitated.

Pauline raised her eyebrows and waited.

'Well ... there's the town inventor. Pellek Unoran. He takes commissions and he works quick. He might be able to help you, if you wanted something sooner than Mihilt-dalath, but —'

'But?'

He shrugged and crossed his arms, looking defensive. 'He's a little wild. Makes unusual contraptions. You'd probably be safer trying a city artificer.'

'Well, let's give that a try,' she said. 'Rex, could you take me there when you're done at the tower? I hate to ask, but —'

'Of course, P.' Rex gave her a shaky smile. 'I'd be glad to.'

She nodded, her expression a confusion of emotions.

I wrote a list, deciding to go for only a few days of food for the group since we'd be in the city soon enough. I think I did a good job of remembering everyone's tastes and requirements, but I was feeling tense so I checked it three or four times before I finally relinquished it to Kenta and Ordeth.

'Be careful out there,' I said to him.

He chuckled. 'Yeah, I could be jumped by assassins at any moment in the village market!'

'You know what I mean,' I said, but I couldn't put even playful ruefulness into my voice. It was too good to see him laugh again.

And then Pauline and I were alone with Riya. Even Ordeth's cat left.

I almost said something to Pauline, just to break the silence, but I remembered how she'd said she was struggling. Sure enough, she looked more drained than ever after the discussion, and had sat down with her back to a wall and her knees drawn up to her chest. Riya got up and made to take her art over to her, but I took her aside instead.

'What'd you make?' I asked, not wanting to draw attention to Pauline. I felt certain she needed time where she didn't need to pretend for us. While Riya chatted, I guided her upstairs to the bedroom, glancing down at Pauline. She seemed not to notice us, which only strengthened my conviction.

Riya showed me her latest art, and talked about Ordeth's cat, which she seemed very fond of. 'She's very soft,' she told me. 'Mummy won't let me have a pet. Mummy says —' she cut off, falling suddenly silent.

'You okay, kiddo?' I asked.

She nodded, tracing her latest painting with one finger.

I was at a loss, but this was Riya. She was seven years old, and if she needed reassurance I had to do all I could to give it to her. 'Did you hear us planning earlier? Did you understand what we were planning?'

Riya shrugged. 'Getting food and things,' she said.

'That's true,' I said. 'You were paying good attention. But do you know what the food is for?'

She looked up and shook her head.

I smiled encouragingly. 'The food is so that we can find a wizard to send us home. Rex and Hanna are right now getting us transport to the city where hopefully we will find a wizard. We're working on it, Riya.'

Riya's brow furrowed and she pursed her lips. It was an almost comically thoughtful expression. I felt like she'd learned it by watching other people, exaggerating the look. 'So we'll be going home soon?'

My smile faded. 'I don't know. I hope so. But we're trying.'

Riya looked down. 'Okay,' she said.

I wondered if I should reach down and pat her shoulder, or hug her, or any of the things you did to reassure children. She was seven, and she needed to be comforted. Arries and Hanna were both really good about being physically affectionate, and I could tell that Riya needed that far more than I had when I'd been her age. But I also didn't know how to break the barrier between us. The barrier made of every time I hadn't hugged her, of every way in which that wasn't our relationship. How did you become someone who hugged someone else, even a child? What if she hated it?

Just ... ask, I suppose.

'Riya, do you want —?'

A shout came from downstairs.

Riya started to get up, but I held out a hand in warning. 'Stay here, okay? Don't leave until I come get you. It's important.'

There was a sound of glass shattering. Riya's eyes went wide, but she nodded.

I flew down the stairs, wishing I'd worn my armour and kept my sickle on my belt. But this was our first real day of rest, and none of us had expected danger to find us in The Honeyhart.

The first thing I clocked were the people. A man with sepia skin, antlers and a fanged grin and a pale-skinned woman with hair like snakes. They were both hooded, and both held weapons — the man a spear, the woman a sword. Broken glass surrounded them. It looked like they'd bashed a window with a chair.

My chest seized.

This was a real fight.

I wasn't supposed to be here.

I wasn't built for this.

But before I could freeze up, or flee, or scream, I saw Pauline backed up against the opposite wall. She'd thrown a few chairs between her and the approaching people.

She looked terrified.

'We're not gonna hurt you,' the woman said, though she didn't lower her sword. 'Let us check that mark on your head, and we'll be on our way.'

The man nudged her and nodded in my direction.

She glanced at me.

'Stay the hell outta this,' she said.

I clenched my shaking hands into fists and my aura flared around me. They crowded toward Pauline. And I realised it doesn't always have to be flight or freeze for me any more. Not when a friend's life was on the line.

I sketched the runes for Polymorph. I pulled primal energy from the air, from my bones, from the wood of the stairs, and leapt forward. My body shivered and shifted, and I landed with a thunderous crunch of shattered stone.

I snorted and pawed the ground, fixing them in my saurian gaze. I was ten thousand kilograms of angry triceratops. The tips of my horns grazed the ceiling. And I was willing to bet I could terrify these assholes far more successfully than they were threatening Pauline.

'Shit,' the man stumbled back, turning his spear from Pauline to me. 'What void-spawned freak is that?'

But the woman barely glanced toward me. The snakes of her medusa hair hissed, dozens of eyes fixed on Pauline. 'Stay focused, brother.'

I glanced between them, my mind already running through possibilities. If I charged them, I would likely hit Pauline as well — not to mention I'd crash into the wall of Ordeth's inn. God, why had I decided to be so big? I'd thought it would be like the ferymars — I'd look scary and they'd piss themselves and flee. But that didn't look likely.

The man still faced me, back toward Pauline. The woman lunged forward, grabbing for her with her free hand.

Then Pauline did something I didn't expect. She screamed and kicked the woman's knee. It hit with a solid crunch. The woman staggered, sword coming up, but Pauline was already throwing herself to one side.

I lowered my head and ploughed into both intruders, knocking them flat. Instinctually, I lifted my feet to stomp on them, but froze at the sound of their screams. My mind filled with visions of their bones crunching, their bodies pulped. It was unbearable.

Instead, I pulled energy from the earth and shifted my body again, becoming light and agile on eight giant legs. I stared at most of the room at once with multi-faceted eyes, unable to pause and enjoy the new sensation before I arched my thorax and shot a silver-white web at the prone attackers. They screamed at this, too, but I didn't feel remorse this time. I scuttled over to them and lifted them with my foremost legs, wrapping the web around them more tightly until they were tidy little parcels. Their struggles didn't move me. They had attacked my friend. Facing down a giant spider was the least they deserved.

I backed up and looked at Pauline, clicking my mandibles.

She wiped spittle from her mouth. I thought she might have vomited. 'That is terrifying,' she said. Her voice was tight with pain. I outstretched one of my many giant hairy spider legs to help her up, and she took it with barely a flicker of hesitation.

Together, we surveyed the webbed-up intruders. On unspoken agreement, I kept my giant spider shape. I'd be able to re-web them if they got loose, and I think I made an intimidating wingman.

For all Pauline's pain, she was utterly calm and still as she considered the pair before her. 'Why did you want to check this mark?' She touched the eye above her brow; it glittered faintly at her touch.

At once, the pair ceased their wriggling. The woman looked at Pauline with awe; the man unconcealed greed. 'The Oracle,' breathed the woman.

I swayed nervously on the spot. Ordeth had mentioned the Oracle, and been concerned for Pauline. I hadn't realised how quickly his fears would be realised.

But if Pauline needed my support, she gave no sign of it. 'Tell me everything you know about this "Oracle",' she said. 'Or my friend will suck the blood straight out of you.'

... I really hoped they told her everything.

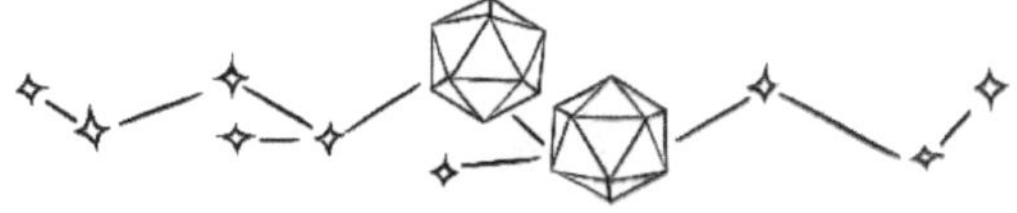

CHAPTER TWENTY-FIVE

I didn't want to suck the blood of either of these people even under the influence of Giant Spider Instincts, but I didn't want them to know that. Instead I leaned forward, clicking my mandibles threateningly. They yelped. The woman's snakes contracted, hiding their heads behind her neck.

'Talk!' said Pauline. And for all she was thin and hunched with pain, she looked for all the world like she might tear them apart if they didn't.

'We serve the Order of the Third Eye,' said the woman with snake hair. She still seemed awed, but there was flint in her words now. 'We seek a rising god from a world beyond our world. They will have powers of truth and knowledge, and their prophecy will determine the fate of Vanthis. What makes you think you are fit to bear their mark?'

A rising god from a world beyond their world.

I didn't even have headspace to unpack that 'rising god' part but ...

A lump formed in my throat.

The Oracle was really Pauline.

And ... if there was a prophecy about her, then maybe this world had been waiting for her a long time.

'I don't,' said Pauline. Her words were clipped; if these cultists had rattled her, she didn't show it. 'I know nothing of your Oracle, and frankly I wouldn't care if you hadn't *made* it my business by attacking me. How did you find me? How did you know about me?'

The woman pressed her mouth into a thin line. The man spat on the floor. 'You'll have naught more from us.'

So they were seeking her, but they didn't owe their loyalty to her? They were *named* after the mark on her forehead, and they wouldn't answer her questions?

There was something really off about this whole situation.

Pauline wrinkled her nose, but it seemed less at the spit than at something more internal. I clicked at her uncertainly.

Just arriving in Vanthis was more than any of us had signed up for when we joined Pauline's game. The idea that there were people actively hunting her was ... well, it was a lot. And for all it *seemed* we had the powers to take down anyone that opposed us ... I didn't think my friends were any more willing to hurt people than I was.

God, I wished I could speak to her right now. It was a minor inconvenience in the game that people couldn't speak while in beast shape, but it was far more frustrating in a real life context. I wanted to take Pauline aside and discuss this with her. I wanted to be able to question these people myself. But I'd lose the ability for a while once I dropped this shape and so far keeping this pair webbed-up was working really well for us.

But to my surprise, Pauline didn't ask another question. Instead she trailed her hands in the air, eyes glowing white and cold while the eye marked on her forehead flashed with vari-coloured light. She shaped six runes in the air. A circle of white fire ran around the group of us, then faded as Pauline returned to normal.

I shook myself, my kaleidoscope vision spinning at the movement. Something inside me had ... shifted.

Pauline smiled, but it looked more like baring her teeth. 'Ah good,' she said. 'You've failed your Mind checks.'

I wasn't sure I liked the sound of that.

The man looked anxious. 'What did you do to us?'

Pauline leaned forward, her expression turning harsh. 'Answer my questions or you'll find out.' she said. 'Who sent you?'

'The Order got a tip-off,' he said quickly. 'Someone in the village.'

'Who sent you?'

The woman clenched her jaw, but the man flinched. 'I don't know her name. The Order has a knight, a faceless helmet bearing that mark on your head. She sends initiates to investigate claims, and pays us well for it.'

'If I let you go, will you tell her?'

'Nnnnnnnnngh,' He gawped, testing his mouth. 'We wwwwwwaaaarghhhhh.' His eyes widened. 'Gods' piss, what did you do to us?'

Something clicked in my mind. There was a spell on Arries' list — Truthsayer. If you failed the Mind check, you were unable to tell a lie within the circle. It couldn't make you talk, but if you did, it had to be the truth.

So these two would rat us out if they had the chance. Not surprising, especially for the woman with snake hair, who seemed to have caught on and glared at Pauline with open hate.

What exactly did the Order of the Third Eye *want* with Pauline, if they were so quick to despise her? Or did they not really believe it was her?

Pauline reached into the pouch at her belt — an enchanted pouch, I realised, as I noted the subtle runework on the leather. From it, she removed a small conch. 'I wonder ...' she said.

She held it up to her mouth and sketched a rune in the air. Again, her third eye lit up as the spell was cast. 'Arries? This is Pauline. We've been attacked at the inn. We've trapped the intruders. You can respond.'

She held the conch to her ear a moment, an expression of concentration on her face as if she was listening. Then she nodded and cast the spell again, to Rex this time.

This was another spell we knew from the game, though none of us had ever been able to cast it. Whisperwind.

What abilities, exactly, did Pauline have?

As if she could sense my thoughts, she glanced at me and said, 'I've been practicing each morning as well. Trial and error testing. Useful to be an LM and have most of the spells committed to memory already.'

It wasn't long before Arries burst in, a gleaming statue of armour and fox ears. He panted as he rushed over, armour clanking. 'What's going on? Are you all right?' His eyes moved to the pair on the floor. 'Who are they?'

'We need to tie them up,' Pauline said. 'Tar, you can drop the polymorph.'

I switched eight legs for two, shaking my head at the sudden switch from kaleidoscope vision to the sharp focus of binocular sight.

We bound and gagged them as best as we could with rope from the Sack of Safekeeping. It was easier than it might otherwise have been thanks to them being pretty well-immobilised by the spider's-web, but I wouldn't call binding struggling people 'pleasant'.

Pauline drew my attention to their wrists. Red eyes, the match of Pauline's, were inked on their inner wrists. They were livid and puffy, almost like recent scars. I supposed this was the sign of their cult. I wondered how Pauline must feel about the connection.

A rising god.

Well, now the rising god was laying on the floor, curled around her stomach. I clenched my fists, overwhelmed by the rush of hatred I felt for the cultists. They had done this to her. They would have done worse, if we hadn't stopped them.

Kenta and Ordeth came in moments after we finished. 'Ah,' Ordeth said, taking in the flipped tables and ropey spider web spooled on the floor. 'I see you've destroyed my inn.'

I immediately flushed and hugged my chest. 'We didn't mean — I'm really sorry —'

'The credit for that goes to these *fine people,*' Pauline cut me off. Even muffled from the floor, her tone was acidic.

'Order of the Third Eye, apparently. You don't happen to know them, do you?'

'Not personally.' He cast a nervous look at the pair. 'I need to check on the others. Don't — don't do anything rash.' There was a squeak of tension in his voice that made me cringe. He was genuinely concerned we might hurt these people.

And ... given the state of his inn, given that I had only moments before been first a triceratops and then a giant spider ... maybe he was right.

And ... god, the rest of the staff. Maybe even his family ... I hadn't thought about who was working behind the scenes, or what they must have thought when these cultists busted in.

The thought made my stomach kick. This wasn't who we were. No matter what abilities we might have in this world, no matter what the dangers were, we needed to be wary of that.

I thought of my mum, somewhere at home wondering why I hadn't been answering her calls. Sometimes it had felt like she didn't understand me at all, but she'd always been certain I would be a good person.

I could remember one such conversation, not long after I'd gotten the job at the Elfred Bevin Museum. I'd managed to catch the train back to my mum's and sat on her sofa with my knees up and a cushion hugged to my chest. At that point, it still felt more like home there than it did in Saanvi's spare bedroom. I tucked my feet under one of her many sparkle-threaded throws, safely ensconced in the same nook of the sofa I'd used for years.

'I just don't think I can do this,' I'd said quietly. Tears made silent tracks down my cheeks. *'It's the perfect job, and I just ... I can't.'* I'd already been in the job two weeks and it wasn't getting easier. The false smiles, the nearness of the visitors, even seeing the same coworkers every day: it was overwhelming. I didn't have room to scream or click or fidget or rock or do any of the things that would help release the pressure building up inside me. And I'd *wanted* this job. I'd

wanted the sleepiness of it. I'd wanted to help archive Elfred Bevin's eclectic artefacts. *'I am a complete failure.'*

My mum had rolled her eyes at me. *'Don't be so melodramatic, darling. Failing a lot doesn't make you a failure, it makes you human. As long as you are kind, you're doing well. The rest of it, we'll work out as we go.'*

As it happened, I had managed to keep my job at the Bevin — the first success in a long series of failed attempts. It wasn't easy, or perfect, and I'd had to reduce my hours and have awful, awkward conversations with my manager over it, but I'd kept it.

And the thing was — my mum was right. My value wasn't measured by my abilities or my success I wouldn't let this sudden shift in situation make me lose sight of that.

I was already trying not to do evil. Maybe, when we got Riya home and could begin to make sense of all this, I would find a way to do active good.

'So we're being attacked now,' said Rex. His voice drew me from my thoughts — I'd been so absorbed, I hadn't noticed him come in. We were all here now, with Rex leaning against the wall and Hanna perched on a tabletop and kicking the leg with the heel of her hoof. He looked flustered — he and Hanna must have run here as well.

I wrung my hands in my lap, staring directly down. I vividly remembered Rex standing before me, shoulders rigid, mouth taut. *'It doesn't matter.'*

I rubbed the sides of my legs and tried to think about other things.

'What's the plan?' said Arries. 'How do we deal with this? We can't have a weird cult chasing P.'

Rex looked down, lips pulling to one side in thought. 'Hanna and I got permission to use the circle.'

Nausea kicked at me. I clenched my jaw.

'Not that they gave it up easily, the miserable sods,' Hanna said. 'We tried to use our clearance as the Amethyst Hand, but they'd never heard of us. Ken's right; we never fucking existed here.'

I glanced at Kenta. His jaw looked tight. He didn't say anything.

'There's an arch-mage of Mihilit-dalath,' Rex said. 'It sounds like if we want an audience, they'll send us there directly.'

'I said we were mercenaries looking for work,' Hanna said. She fidgeted with her flute in her lap. 'When they didn't buy it, I said we're extraplanar travellers and we need passage home. That got their attention. Apparently mages lap up that interdimensional shit.'

'Then the new plan is the old plan,' I said. Everyone looked at me, but I kept my nerve. 'We go to Mihilit-dalath, we get an audience with the arch-mage, and we get them to send us home.' I looked to Riya, who had come downstairs in the aftermath of everything. She perched on the bottom step, a flower cupped in her hand, still sparkling with magical growth. 'We need to get *Riya* home. If we're quick, these Third Eye people won't have any time to track us down.'

Hanna and Kenta nodded. Arries looked worried, and Rex made no sign that he'd heard me at all.

The snake-haired woman made a muffled sound.

'Hush,' Hanna said, and the word had more menace than any of the times she'd screamed profanity at the rest of us. The cultists stilled.

'P?' Arries asked. 'What do you think?'

Pauline stared down at her hands, open in her lap. 'I think getting Riya home is more important than whatever this Oracle business means. We can untangle that later. Rex — will you go with me to that inventor?'

Rex stood up, dusting off his robes. 'Of course.' Blue energy sparkled around his hands. 'But — shouldn't we do something about that tattoo? I can illusion you —?'

Pauline waved a dismissive hand. 'No need to waste a spell. Hanna, could I borrow your scarf?'

Hanna unwound the black scarf with its silver threading from around her waist and handed it to Pauline, who folded it and tied it around her forehead in short order.

'That actually looks really good, P,' said Hanna and then, to my surprise, she blushed.

Ordeth re-emerged, looking tired. 'Everyone's safe,' he said. 'Someone's off to get the constable. Do you want to explain what's happened here?'

Pauline shook her head. 'I wish we could ...'

I gave Ordeth a strained smile. 'I'll try. You know you mentioned the Oracle?'

Ordeth pulled out a chair with shaking hands and slumped into it. 'Arcanyl preserve us. No, go on. I'm listening.'

CHAPTER TWENTY-SIX

It was another five days before we could leave. Pauline's commission from the village inventor would take that long to finish, and she didn't want to go to Mihilit-dalath without it.

We wandered the village or lounged about the inn by turn. I tried not to think about the waiting teleportation circle. We left our armour and weapons behind, in spite of the threat of the Order of the Third Eye. It seemed wrong to frighten the villagers.

Ordeth often accompanied us, explaining things about his home and his world. We talked a lot with him about Earth and the disarray of our arrival. He clarified some things for us, though others remained mysteries. Apparently we were speaking Mistembran, though it felt like English to us. More tricks of whatever magic had brought us here. He had no idea what kind of spells had transformed us, or where our items could have come from. It felt like a risk to trust him with all that, but we didn't really know how the information could be used against us, and we needed the help.

And he was a good friend and host, acclimatising us to Vanthis. He showed us how the bee-singers guided and calmed the bees, using abilities similar to Hanna's to musically manipulate them. The soothing sound of the lute strings mixed with the humming of the bees would stay with me a long time.

Riya and I were invited to meet one of the giant ones. It was called a viryont, a creature that was as fluffy as a pomeranian but three times as big and with huge, multi-faceted eyes. I was afraid of it, but seeing how patiently it responded to Riya's excited pats, I plucked up the courage to touch it. Its hair felt like stiff cotton, and my hand came away coated with pollen, making me sneeze.

Hanna played a small but wild performance at The Honeyhart. Rex created coloured lights to spin around her for added flair, but the small crowd that had gathered in the inn for the evening seemed taken enough by the song. At one point, someone held up a fiddle and Hanna called them over to join her. By the end, they had accumulated a drummer, too, and though Hanna didn't know their songs and they didn't know hers, they managed to follow each other's music and everyone had a blast. It was more joyful than technically proficient, but somehow more beautiful for it. A couple people lined up at the end to thank Hanna and tip her or buy her a drink for her time. She shone with pleasure the entire night.

Arries made fast friends with several of the villagers and was often away from the inn. People came calling for him, or to deliver food in thanks for all sorts of small chores he'd helped with. Taltro, a young man with bat wings sprouting from his arms and a shy smile, came calling with flowers while Arries was out, and Kenta took him aside to let him down gently.

When he called again the next day, asking me where to find Arries, I frowned. 'I thought Ken spoke to you ...?' I said, hoping that was tactful enough.

Taltro nodded and gave me a broad, fanged smile. 'Yes, he was very clear. But friendship is just as good to me.'

He seemed very earnest. I pointed him in Arries' direction, knowing Arries would be glad of another friend.

Pauline read voraciously, borrowing books from Ordeth. She rarely left her room in the days following the attack, but she was hardly idle. When I asked her why she wanted to read so much when she had magical encyclopaedia powers, she actually rolled her eyes at me. 'You're as bad as Hanna,' she said. 'There's so much here to learn. How often am I going to get the chance to read books from another world?' She excitedly recounted everything she'd been reading, which ranged from mythology to science to fiction. It made me want to borrow books from Ordeth, too, but I didn't know how to bring it up.

I wondered if this was what life would be like if we remained in Vanthis. Quiet and cheerful and full of companionship. Sure, we would need to find jobs and somewhere to live, but the possibility of it all — the magic of it — was hard not to cling to. Maybe it would be like Hanna had said. A fresh start, where we could remake ourselves.

Rex continued to practice his spells, which Ordeth often joined him with, shyly sharing his own spellbook and introducing Rex to his cat. The two seemed to have a lot in common, with Ordeth explaining what he knew of the magical theory of Vanthis, while Rex shared the magic he'd been granted on arrival.

Rex was largely normal with me, acting like our conversation in our room that first night had never happened. I tried to do the same, ignoring the ache in my chest and the anxious turn of my belly. Rex was my friend. I was the one who had let my feelings run away with me, and I wasn't going to ruin our friendship over it.

It might have been easier if we weren't still sharing a room, but I didn't know if I could bear to bring it up with any of the others and have to explain why, and Rex didn't bring it up either. I tried not to return to the room until it was late enough that Rex would already be asleep, which ... was not easy, considering he was as much of a night owl as I was. He offered for us to alternate having the bed, but I refused, preferring to keep to what I knew, and as far away from Rex as I could manage.

The last night before we left, when I turned up in the room in the small hours of the morning, Rex was reading by candlelight. He glanced up at my entrance. 'Ordeth lent me some of his books,' he said, showing me the cover of his current one. *A Beginner's Guide to Magical Theory on the Associate Plane.* He took a book off the stack beside him. 'He had a few novels, too. I thought you might like this one.'

I ignored the uncomfortable pang at his attention and gave in to curiosity, accepting the book. It was printed, but bound with a thin leather cover, and generally the pages were much thicker and the binding much looser and more visible than I would expect from a book from Earth. Embossed on the cover was the title: *Alleyn's Astral Adventures,* with a star etched below it.

I opened it. The first page held a synopsis. It was an adventure story about a young person's unexpected journey into the Astralar, the Astral Plane, and the many trials they faced there. I wasn't a big reader, but there was something special about holding a book like this in my hands. The soft cover, the thick, crisp pages; it was incredibly tactile, and made me even more interested in reading it.

'So this is Vanthian fiction?'

He nodded. 'So Ordeth says. He said it was a bit too unrealistic for his tastes, but I thought you might like a bit of escapism, since it's not like you can play A:RO.'

The ache in my heart wasn't going anywhere soon, but I felt warmed all the same. I ran my fingers over the cover, feeling the letters there while I cast around for the right thing to say. I wanted to apologise for my admission the other night. I wanted to thank him for being such a good friend. I wanted to say something wry or funny that would make it seem like everything was okay again.

Something baaed. My gaze snapped to the window.

'Uh. Tar?'

I handed back the book. 'One sec.' I moved to the window, unlatching it and sliding it up, careful not to knock the cheerful plants potted there. The street outside was empty, and too dark to see properly while the candle was lit in here. 'Uh, Rex … could you get the light?'

Rex snapped his fingers and the candle snuffed out. At once, both our eyes started to glow as our darksight kicked in. The room was instantly painted in blue and silver.

Rex raised his eyebrows. 'So?'

I went back to the window. 'I thought I heard the sealorn.'

He came to join me, leaning against the sill. I tried to ignore the way his shoulder brushed mine. 'Aren't there lots of sealorns around here?'

'Not like the one I met.' I frowned out into the night outside the window. It was all as bright and clear now, but I still couldn't make out any sealorns. 'The one I met was, uh … more abrasive.' I smiled a little at the thought of their snappishness and their grating cry.

Another baa, nearer this time. I drew magic in from the air. 'Tar —?'

I polymorphed, trading arms for wings and skin for feathers in a frisson of energy. In owl shape, I hooted and swooped down into the night.

Behind me, I sensed a flare of energy. I glanced back at the other owl following in my wake, dark feathers edged with ghostly blue.

It was easier to search as an owl, for all I had darksight in my human form. My head tick-tocked back and forth, searching the town below. At night, in the strange, colourful vision of an owl, it was beautiful and strange, highlighted with colours such as I could not describe. It sounded different too, every rustle, every cricket chirp bouncing to my ears and calling out their precise locations. I could hear the village sealorns snoring in their coops. I could hear bats on the wing, each one a distracting flurry that called at me to *chase*.

And I heard the gentle swish of a sleek body gliding through the air. I banked and wheeled aside, Rex right on my tail, and spiralled back down into The Honeyhart's garden on the other side of the building. There, suffused in a glittering astral glow, was a familiar black sealorn. They rooted through the bushes, tugging at something I couldn't see.

I dropped my shape as I landed, winded for a moment by the sudden return of human form, so heavy and slow-breathing by comparison. With a pulse of energy, Rex did the same. We glanced at each other. Rex raised his eyebrows.

'This is all you,' he murmured.

I supposed that was true. I took a hesitant step toward the glowing creature. 'Uh ... sealorn?' I said. I wished I had come up with a name for them. The sealorn froze, then pulled their head out of the bush to look at me. The iridescent fins on their head perked up curiously. 'Hey. It's me.' Most of the times we'd encountered the sealorn, we'd been sitting around the campfire, so I motioned to Rex to sit down with me. I sat with one leg out and one leg at an angle.

The sealorn tilted their head. Their seal-like nostrils flared as they sniffed toward me, drifting a little closer.

'I don't have any food this time,' I said, raising my empty hands. The sealorn looked at my empty hands unblinkingly. After a moment, I put them on the ground. 'Sorry.'

The sealorn looked at my hands, then at my face. They swam toward me, undulating through the air. They brought their soft, slitted nose inches from my own. I could feel their breath hot on my face, smelly as a dog's. They fixed their beady eyes on mine.

I was half-convinced they were about to bite my face, but I didn't pull away. The sealorn whuffled at me, snorting hot air into my face, making me blink. Then, they drifted forward and booped their nose against mine.

With a shaking hand, I reached up to stroke their thick neck. The scales were silky and thick, but flexible. They didn't bite me, and leaned into the touch.

'Rex,' I whispered in tones of awe.

'I see it,' he said.

'Is this because of Astaran's Wild Empathy skill?' I asked. The sealorn stopped sparkling and flopped heavily into my lap, still propped up so that its face was level with mine. Their ear fins twitched.

'Can't be,' Rex said. 'Skills didn't transfer. Just the magic. And if they *had* transferred, they wouldn't have bitten you before. Astaran's skill was too high for that.' He paused, and I saw his teeth flash in a brief smile. 'This is all you, Tar.'

All me. That explained why I was so terrified, my mind constantly scrambling for what to do next, how to interpret the behaviour. I had so little experience with animals.

I scratched under the sealorn's chin. They seemed to enjoy it, lifting their head so I had better access. 'Why are you here?' I murmured. Could they really have followed us all the way to Lundanar just for ... what? A few table-scraps? How far did sealorns normally range?

The gem embedded in the sealorn's chest pulsed with a gentle green glow. I wondered what it meant. What *any* of this meant.

I started to pull away. The sealorn's head snapped around, clamping three rows of teeth tightly on my hand. I yelped and tried to pull away but they held me fast. 'Let. Go.' I said through gritted teeth. 'Stop it!'

The sealorn growled, then released me. Then put their head on my chest and bleated pitifully.

I flexed my aching hand. Blood dripped from it.

'That thing has done more damage to you than the cultists,' said Rex. He sounded amused.

'Yeah,' I said. 'I'm well-aware.'

'What are you going to name them?'

'What?' I stared at him.

He thrust his hands into the pockets of his robes. 'I have a cat, remember? I recognise an animal adopting a human when I see it.'

Is that what this was? I had assumed the sealorn was only interested in us as a source of food, but we'd given them very little and they had followed us terribly far. And now, I had nothing to offer them, and they were still blinking up at me forlornly.

My hand was still bleeding, bearing three perfect rings of red punctures.

'Silky,' I said, thinking of the softness of their scales more than the savageness of their bite. I liked that it sounded a little like the mythical shapeshifting seals as well.

The sealorn sighed happily.

'Do you think Ordeth will mind me bringing a sealorn into his inn?'

Rex grinned, baring fanged teeth. 'Only one way to find out.'

CHAPTER TWENTY-SEVEN

The next morning was comfortable chaos as we prepared to leave. Ordeth took the appearance of a wild sealorn in his inn with a kind of amused resignation. 'Nothing is ever boring with you Earth folk,' he'd said, as I tried to stop Silky from eating a potted plant. I'd discovered that Silky was light and buoyant when in the air, and could be fairly easily pulled aside, except that then she'd take vengeance with her teeth if she could.

Her gender, Ordeth had elucidated for us: only female sealorns had gems in their chests. The males, apparently, had them on their backs instead. I wondered, not for the first time, if there were non-binary animals, and whether that affected their lives. I doubted Silky minded what pronouns I used for her though, so there was some comfort in that.

Now, I let Silky tug at a thick bone while I held the other end. She was making a sound somewhere between a trill and a growl, and shook her head aggressively.

Meanwhile, Pauline tried out her new mobility aid: a hexclimber. She sat on a chair with six spider-like legs, each starting out wide and tapering to a point. The chair was made of padded leather and looked comfortable, and there was a bar for her feet to rest on. The arms of the chair glowed with engraved runes, the colours constantly shifting. I noticed the colour scheme was purple, just like her wheelchair back home, and smiled.

Now, Pauline walked the chair around the room with a few quick touches of the runepad on the arm. It moved so fluidly, Pauline could have balanced a glass of water on the arm and it wouldn't have spilled. There were probably robot designers on Earth who would kill for the chance to study its movement.

'How does it feel?' I asked, trying to sound calm even though Silky pulled the bone so hard she nearly pulled my arm out of its socket.

'Pretty good,' she said. 'About as uncomfortable as my wheelchair, but in a different way. Vibrates less, but bounces occasionally.' I hadn't noticed that. She had the hexclimber rock back and forth, which it did smoothly. 'A driftchair would have been smoother — it's like a wheelchair, but it levitates. But it wouldn't handle rough terrain as well. This thing can *actually climb.*' She beamed, the most openly excited I'd ever seen her. 'And it's powered!'

'How much did it cost, P?' Kenta asked.

'Not too much — mobility devices are subsidised in Mistcurl.' She named the country we were in now — part of a cluster of large islands that made up the continent Mistembra.

I'd hardly thought about how the particular country we were in might affect our experience here — it had been hard to look past the fact that we were in a different world entirely.

'I'd like to get a driftchair as well, but for now I'd rather have the extra mobility. There should be some available in Mihilit-dalath, right?' This, she directed to Ordeth where he leaned against the bar, rubbing the belly of his luxuriating cat.

'About that,' Ordeth said. He stepped out from behind the bar, wringing his hands. His cat leapt to his shoulder, her eyes flashing strangely. He'd dropped all pretense of her being a non-magical cat since our conversation a few days prior. 'I was hoping ...' he took a deep breath, 'That you would allow me to accompany you. As a guide.'

A long pause as we took in the words. Ordeth reached up to scratch the ear of his cat, looking more like he was seeking comfort himself than the other way around.

Somehow I was the first to speak. 'Sorry but ... why?'

Ordeth's mouth shifted to one side, tusk peeking out over his lip. 'Well. I don't think you need protection, as your stay here demonstrated, but you don't know Mistcurl. You don't know Vanthis at all. And ... and I can help with that. With the culture, with the people, help you find your way around.'

Pauline raised her eyebrows. 'And your inn ...?' she prompted.

Ordeth shook his head. 'I'm not *needed* here, not really. My family can run it well enough without me — I just happened to be on shift the day you arrived and — well, I asked to be the main contact for you.' He blushed, his silver skin taking on a blue hue on his cheeks. 'I've never met anyone from an uncharted plane before. I feel like ... like if I let you walk out the door without at least *trying* to go with you, I am going to miss out on the kind of story I always dreamed of being a part of.' He crossed his arms and gave us all a sheepish look. 'Besides, I quite like you all. So.'

Pauline and Hanna exchanged a look I couldn't read. Arries put a hand to his heart, clearly touched. Rex's mouth shifted to one side in a not-quite-frown. Kenta looked uncharacteristically soft.

We could use a guide, couldn't we? Ordeth had been nothing but helpful to us, even when our presence had led to his inn being smashed up. He'd been an unexpected friend in a strange land.

But I felt Rex's suspicion, too. *Someone* had told the Order of the Third Eye about us. And we barely knew Ordeth. He was a wizard of unknown power — something he'd tried to hide from us — and we had to be careful about who we trusted. Not just because of the Order, and not just because of Alis-Umor, but because we didn't know who or what had brought us here, or to what end. We didn't know what someone could do with us, or knowledge of Earth.

Ordeth wrung his hands, looking from face to face with evident nerves.

He didn't have a red eye on his wrists. I'd checked, and indeed his sleeves were almost always rolled up to the elbows so it's not like he'd concealed them. I wanted to trust him. I liked him. Much like when I'd met Arries, and when I'd joined the *Kin* group, I'd pretty instantly felt at ease around him. Maybe that was foolish of me, given our circumstances, but I so rarely felt at ease around people that I wanted to trust my gut on this.

More, I sympathised with his motivation. If our situations were reversed — if Ordeth had appeared on Earth — wouldn't I have wanted to go with him, too?

'I think we could use a guide,' I said. 'Right?'

Kenta smiled. 'Yeah. You've already been a huge help.' He looked around at Rex.

Rex shrugged. His tail danced anxiously behind him. 'I don't know. I'm sorry, Ordeth. It feels like a risk.'

Ordeth nodded once, jaw tight.

'Someone did just attack P, like, a few days ago,' Hanna said. 'I'm sorry, buddy. We just can't know who to trust.'

Ordeth took that silently, eyes bright. I could see his dreams being crushed in the slope of his shoulders, and I wanted to protest, but they were right. The only way for this to be fair, was for us all to agree on it.

Pauline tapped her lips. 'Would you consent to a truth spell?' she asked.

Ordeth straightened. 'Yes. Of course!' He looked determined, but also curious. Truthsayer had a lot of prerequisites in the game — perhaps he had never seen it performed.

We all backed up, and Pauline again sketched runes then trailed her hands in the air. A circle of white fire traced around the floor, following her movements, until she and Ordeth were both enclosed. There was a pulse of ... something ... within the circle, ruffling both their hair. The stars in Pauline's braids twinkled; the mark on her forehead glowed with power.

'Do you mean us any harm?' she asked him.

'No,' he responded immediately.

'Are you part of the Order of the Third Eye?'

'No.'

'And did you or would you help them in any way?'

'No.' He was firm.

Pauline nodded, looking relieved. She lifted her hands to dispel the Truthsayer circle, but before she did Ordeth quickly asked: 'Are you really from Earth, on another plane?'

Pauline hesitated. I wonder if she'd failed her Mind check as well this time. Truthsayer affected anyone within the circle, even the caster. 'Yes,' she said.

He nodded grimly, as if confirming something to himself. 'Are you the Oracle?'

Pauline froze. For a moment, they just stared at each other. Pauline licked her lips and said quietly, 'I don't know.'

Then she stepped out of the circle and dispelled it with a snap of her fingers. The fire faded.

The image of her quiet uncertainty would stay with me for a long time. What must it be like, to wonder if you might be a prophesied god?

Ordeth took a shuddering breath. 'All right,' he said. 'Thank you for answering me.'

Pauline shrugged. She backed her hexclimber over to one of the tables. 'I vote for Ordeth to come with us,' she said. 'We could use the help.'

'Me too,' said Hanna. 'He let us fucking magically Truth or Dare him. I think that's proof enough.'

'So that's four against one,' I said, giving a sidelong look at Rex. Rex pursed his lips and looked away, saying nothing. Kenta strode forward to grip Ordeth's arm and welcome him.

From there, we did the final bit of getting ready. Kenta and Rex went to get more supplies. Ordeth packed and made his farewells with his family and the inn staff. His cat, Mileana, would be coming with us. I did my best to introduce Riya and Silky, with Arries on hand to protect Riya should Silky go in for a bite.

Then it was on to the wizard tower, which stuck out like a tall, black tusk over the gentle and colourful village. The bees that hummed and bustled around us as we walked were absent at the base of the tower, as were the flowers and shrubberies we had become so accustomed to. Instead, there were rings of large stones, each carved with glowing runes that gave off an almost crystalline ring.

'Lodestones,' said Ordeth, following my gaze. His cat was cradled in his arms, purring contentedly. 'They draw in magical signals. Towers like the Loten-Tooth catch most of the magical messages that pass through the area.'

'For monitoring?' I asked, not liking the sound of that.

He shrugged. 'Among other things.'

Another thing to worry about. In the game, organisations of magic users were almost always dangerous to interact with. I was glad Rex had already arranged passage for us.

We were greeted by austere, black robed mages, who looked on in disapproval as I coaxed Silky inside with strips of dried meat. I would have been embarrassed if managing Silky didn't take my entire concentration.

Unlike the initial mages, Elemar, the assistant that took us up to the circle itself, seemed quite bubbly and chattered away to Rex about spell preparations. We climbed what felt like an endless amount of stairs, though Pauline's hexclimber took them smoothly, the mechanical legs moving with rapid precision. My anxiety grew as we travelled and the reality of the situation started to press on me. I could no longer ignore the truth of what we were doing.

Very soon, we would have to teleport.

I understood the value of this. That it was essential to getting Riya home in good time.

I understood that it was safe. That it was a common mode of transportation in Vanthis. That maybe even something like it was what had brought us here in the first place.

I was cold with terror at the thought of doing it.

Silky nudged my hand with her soft nose, annoyed by the lack of attention, and I scratched her along her dorsal fin.

We entered the teleportation room. As sparse as the rest of the tower, the onyx walls and slate floors in this room were broken up only by ornate stained-glass windows depicting wizards raising mountains, transforming into dragons, and crowning kings.

I frowned at them. They were beautiful, but the self-aggrandisement was hard to stomach. Did non-wizards see them this way, or was this just how the wizards *wanted* to be seen?

Elemar gestured to the centre of the room, where a wide teleportation circle was; a spell diagram with intricate details and interlocking designs, so complex that I struggled to take it all in at once. It was maybe 5 metres in diameter, traced in lurid green paint.

'I trust you can cast the spell?' Elemar asked, raising his eyebrows.

Rex walked onto the circle, checking over the designs. He seemed to be looking for something, and paused at a section with sigils not in green paint, but blue chalk. 'Looks like the coordinates are there,' he said. 'Yes, we should be fine.'

He nodded and stepped back, standing against the wall.

Rex looked up and motioned for us to join him. The others crowded on, chatting and expressing their anticipation, but I held back. As their feet hit the circle, sparks of green light flew up from the paint where they stepped. I felt sick. I felt the restless urge in my legs to run, run, run.

'Tar?' Arries gave me a worried look, and held out his hand toward me, but I shook my head, not trusting myself to speak.

I just needed a moment, I thought, desperately trying to will myself forward. My aura flared as my shame and frustration grew. Time stretched. I could feel the weight of their gazes, their expectations. Even Silky was on the circle, Hanna occasionally tugging at her tail to stop her from swimming off.

But I couldn't bring myself to take even one more step. My chest was tight, my breathing ragged and painful as if my lungs were gripped in a vice. My pulse was jagged with terror.

It wasn't that I was afraid of teleportation. I was afraid of dying.

'Tar?' Pauline's voice was unusually hesitant.

I shook my head again, still staring at the glowing edge of the spellworked circle, green light sparking up from the lines and runes. Slowly, I sank to the ground, hands crossing my stomach.

I was a witch, I reminded myself. I was magic now. I was strong and powerful in a way I had never been before. There was nothing I needed to be afraid of.

But it didn't matter. The terror inside me wouldn't respond to reason.

The room and its noise faded until all I could see was the circle. I don't know how long I crouched there, shuddering.

I felt a touch at my shoulder, firm and reassuring. 'Hey.' Arries crouched beside me, brows knitted with concern. 'Are you okay?'

I wanted to say something but I couldn't get my lips to part. Minutely, I twitched my head to one side.

'It's just more magic,' said Arries. 'It's no more dangerous than polymorphing, right? And you're fine with that?'

It wasn't the same. It wasn't the same it wasn't the same it wasn't —

Dimly, I heard Arries shift away from me, the weight on my shoulder gone.

Rex's face appeared in front of mine. 'Hey, Tar.'

I didn't have space left in my brain to feel awkward about him.

He wasn't smiling or frowning, but watched me with a calm and level steadiness. 'Everybody left the circle, Tar. They're at the other end of the room, just chatting.'

I could see movement at the edges of my peripheral vision, but I couldn't bring myself to look away from Rex. I didn't give any sign that I'd heard him, but he continued as if I had. 'Do you want to sit down?'

I eased my legs out from under me until I was sitting, and he went with me, kneeling in front of me. He was still on the very edge of the circle, his hands coming forward to rest against the glowing runes. For a while, we just stayed like that. Rex sitting across from me, the long, slow sounds of his breathing gradually catching mine and leading me to do the same.

At length, he said, 'I want to help. I'm going to ask yes or no questions, okay? If you can answer them, nod or say yes. If you can't, I won't ask.'

Yes or no. I focused on my breathing. I could do that. I wanted him to understand. I inclined my head.

'Are you anxious about teleportation?'

I inclined my head.

'Is it because you think it's unsafe?'

No! I shook my head, sharply.

'Do you know how it works?'

Did I? This was a difficult question. I knew how people speculated teleportation would work in our world, and it was that which made my blood run cold and my heart seize inside my chest. I had watched a dozen videos on teleportation in a state of transfixed horror in the past.

Did it work this way here? Did I know anything about how any of this worked at all?

As my silence stretched on, Rex tried again. 'Is it okay if I explain how it works?'

He was so calm and so patient. I looked at his hands, knuckled and pressed against the runes as he leaned toward me. Sparks of green light drifted around them.

I glanced at his face, then away again. 'How does it work?' I asked. The words were quiet, but clear. I was still tense, but didn't feel as crushed. We could talk through this.

'Okay,' he said. 'You know my wizard binder? It held a whole section of notes on magic lore. Teleportation is movement at near instantaneous speed. It's like stepping through a door. It won't change you or touch you in any way, but the speed of the movement — of in one moment being here, and in the next being miles and miles away — can be disconcerting, like missing a step on the stairs. It might even make you feel a bit queasy. But it's just stepping through a door.'

That ... wasn't what I was expecting. I took some time to process it.

Rex leaned forward, his fingers tracing some of the bold, glowing lines on the floor. 'See these runes? They were drawn with a special paint that wizards use for this and similar purposes. Paint for permanent, chalk for temporary. It's wildly expensive. It glows because of the magic running through it — now that it's set up, I couldn't rub it away, see?' He brushed at it.

'It'll be me casting the spell,' he added. 'The magic goes through me into the circle, which opens the door and shunts us through it, metaphorically. Does that make sense?'

It did. But there was a question pushing to escape my lips. 'It doesn't ... take us apart and rebuild us at the other side?'

'It doesn't. It's a door, Tar. I know science fiction would have you believe otherwise but — and I know this sounds crazy, but that's science fiction and this is real magic. That was trying to imagine what was possible without magic. This doesn't have those restraints.'

I nodded. I had already witnessed so many impossible things. Created them, even. If I could turn myself into a triceratops and back with nothing more than an exertion of will and still be me, then surely teleportation in this world had no reason to follow the laws of Earth.

'I'm afraid of dying,' I said quietly, scrunching the fabric of my long tunic between my hands. 'You know, the idea that teleportation takes you apart and reconstructs you on the other side. You die, and a different version of you carries on.'

'I'm not going to convince you either way about what teleportation on Earth might be like,' he said. 'But here, with me, and with my magic, I know that's not how it works.'

He held out a hand to me, palm up. Startled, I met his eyes. They were warm with sympathy. No distance. No dislike.

I took his hand, slim and smooth compared to mine. Slowly, he brought mine down to touch the runes.

'They're cold,' I said, surprised by the chill that radiated through my fingers.

'That's the dormant magic,' he said. 'Are you willing to try the teleportation? It's okay if not; there's no rush.'

I stared at him, helpless to look away from his face as our fingers threaded over the cold spell-worked floor. Even though the memory of my rejected confession was still a painful lump in the pit of my stomach, all I could think was that I had never met anyone like Rex. Nobody as kind, nobody as clever. Nobody who could see me so clearly. Nobody who took dozens of notes on the specifics of magic just because it interested him.

Maybe he didn't care about me the way I'd hoped, but he *did* care. He was my friend. I was still afraid. But I trusted him.

'I can do it,' I said.

He rose with me, our hands still entwined. I couldn't tell whether he was holding onto me or whether I was just clinging to him, but he didn't pull away.

The others were spread out around the room — Pauline studying the stained glass windows, Hanna and Ordeth having a quiet conversation, while Kenta walked Riya and Silky around the room. Arries turned to us with an expression full of brotherly concern.

'I'm fine,' I said.

Arries' brow knitted.

'Well — not fine, maybe. But I'm going anyway.'

He nodded his understanding, expression turning soft.

We had to crowd together to fit onto the circle. I stepped nearer to Rex to give more space, then looked up at him anxiously.

His lips turned up at one side. 'You okay?'

I breathed out, trying to let go of the tension still spiking through my limbs. 'I'm okay,' I said.

He released my hand, reaching past me to trace a glowing rune in the air.

Then light and wind kicked up around us. The ground fell away beneath my feet, and we were falling, falling, falling.

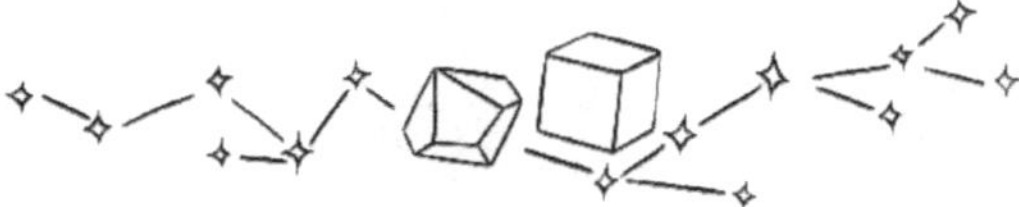

CHAPTER TWENTY-EIGHT

It could only have been a split second of bright, howling wind buffeting us in an empty void, and then our feet were on the ground and I was staggering and only Rex's hand on my shoulder held me in place.

When had he taken my shoulder? He stood close to me, closer than we had when he activated the spell. Even as I thought it, he stepped back.

'That was *not* like stepping through a *fucking* door,' said Hanna. She glared at Rex.

We started to spread out a little around the crystal room.

'Metaphorically it was?' Rex said. His eyes were bright and his skin almost glowed. The blue energy that often burned at the sides of his eyes was gone. His tail twitched and danced behind him, his excitement plain.

'Metaphorically, it was like *falling* through a *trapdoor,'* I said. I clenched my fists at my side to hide their trembling, but Rex's excitement was infectious.

We had *teleported.* And better still, I could remember the sensation of it. It hadn't been quite instantaneous. There had been no breaking apart — my body had felt every sensation.

We were here and safe and alive, and magic was real.

I looked around at the room, which bore little resemblance to the tower at Lundanar. Crystal pillars of aquamarine blue glittered all around us, framing fractal windows that looked half-glass, half-mirror. The floor itself was more crystal, and the teleportation circle here had been carved, not painted.

Hanna stepped forward, her little hooves ringing against the crystal floor with a bell-like sound. 'This place is fucking nuts,' she said.

'We've been here before,' Pauline reminded her. Her hexclimber carried her forward a few steps, slipping slightly on the smooth floor. Already, she was adjusting to the controls. The next step was more stable.

'We've been here in our imaginations,' Kenta said. 'Real life is a whole other thing.'

Ordeth raised his hand. 'For the record, *I've* never been here.'

'Or me,' I added. In my imagination or otherwise. The Amethyst Hand had spent time on Mistcurl long before I'd joined. Silky nudged my hand and rolled in the air, baring her enormous, scaley belly for rubs.

The doors swung open. Three people walked in — a tall feykin with a strong build and antlers, a dragon-like feykin with a sweeping tail and more human face, and a voidkin who would look entirely human if not for the shifting shadows that limned their shape.

The voidkin crossed their arms, their suit-like robes barely creasing from the gesture. Their eyes — black with white irises — were hard. 'We've been sent word that you have ... special circumstances, and require an audience with the arch-mage. Is this correct?' Their scholarly voice was clipped, but they seemed straightforward.

'That's right,' said Kenta. He shared a look with the others, but the voidkin carried on before he could speak.

'Excellent. Please nominate a leader to speak with the arch-mage. The rest of you will be shown to a sitting room to await further instruction.' They looked at Kenta expectantly, but Kenta felt no more able to speak for the group than any of us.

Pauline was easily our leader but ...

'Alone?' Arries asked uncertainly.

The voidkin rolled their eyes. 'You may choose two, I suppose, if you are truly that paranoid. Come now. It won't do to keep the arch-mage waiting.'

Rex caught my eyes. 'It should be you, Tar.'

I cringed. 'What? No! It should be you!' At my emphatic tone, Silky barked, then made a pleased chuff sound as if she found the whole thing very funny.

'Pauline knows magic better than anyone and she makes the sound decisions. But you're both a caster *and* a tank. You're the best one for the job.'

I looked to Arries, the only other person who fit the specification, but he was already nodding. 'Rex's right. It should be you.'

I didn't know if I could agree. But then again, Pauline and I had already fended off a threat together. And realistically, would the arch-mage attack us? If they did, we would be no better off whether it was me or Arries. None of us were really ready for a fight.

Pauline strode over to me, spiderlegs clicking against the floor. 'You don't have to do this if you don't want to,' she said seriously. But I could tell that she wanted me to go with her.

This was what it was to have power, I guess. I could get us out if I had to. I really believed that. My whole TTRPG experience so far had revolved around using my spells to get us out of hazardous situations.

I just ... wasn't so sure I had what it took to speak for the group.

Pauline watched me, a frown pulling at one side of her mouth. She looked ... vulnerable? Somehow? It wasn't something I was used to associating with Pauline. She was so in control. The idea that Pauline could be anxious was anathema to my understanding of her.

'I'll go,' I said. I wouldn't leave her alone with her fear.

She nodded solemnly. 'Thank you.'

I looked to the others. 'Hanna, will you watch Silky for me?'
I tried to nudge Silky toward her, but the sealorn just rolled in
the air, unphased.

'On it.' Hanna rummaged in her pack and brought out a
strip of honeyed jerky. Silky immediately shot toward her,
begging loudly.

The voidkin greeting us took all this in with a curled lip
and narrowed eyes. 'If you're quite finished? Good. The leaders,
come with me. The rest, please follow my companions, Perliot
and Ivexius.' They nodded to the dragon-like feykin and the
antlered feykin respectively. The first smiled; the other
grimaced.

We said our goodbyes as briefly as we could. 'Stay safe,'
Arries said, looking nervously from me to Pauline.

'We'll see you soon,' Rex promised.

'One way or another,' Hanna added darkly.

I tried to take comfort in my friends' words, but my chest
was tight and fluttering.

Pauline and I followed the business-like voidkin, turning
away from the rest of our group to walk down a crystal
corridor lined with tapestries and portraits of intricate detail.
I glanced at Pauline, who adjusted the scarf hiding her eye
mark.

'We haven't introduced ourselves,' she said. 'I'm Pauline. My
astralkin companion is Tar.'

The voidkin sniffed, glancing between the two of us. 'I am
Northosian Cly. You may call me North. I manage the
Verdigris Spire and its staff, and answer to the arch-mage
directly.'

I found my words. 'And the arch-mage's name is ...?'

They narrowed their eyes at me. Their shadow flickered.
'Tellan Vorugar, of course. You expect me to believe you don't
know him?'

We didn't. So Rex's theory was sound — the characters in
the game we had encountered didn't exist in the real Vanthis.

Pauline had seen the world and its structures, but not its people.

'It ... must have slipped my companion's mind,' said Pauline. Her tone was flat, immovable. I wouldn't like to be on the receiving end of that tone — it meant Pauline had been pushed to the limit of her patience. It meant stop pushing or Pauline would drop rocks on our characters' heads.

We went up a staircase. Robed figures strode the corridor or stood to one side chatting beside open doorways. Many of them held books, or armfuls of strange ingredients, or carved staffs with crystal tops or inlays. It was a magical school right out of fiction — Pauline's fiction, to be exact. But it felt more real; the tired looks on some of the mage's faces, their messy hair and stooped shoulders. The laughter and scolding and whispered conversations.

'People learn magic here?' I asked.

North gave me a withering look. 'This isn't a school. Though our patrons and staff make use of the libraries and resources here for their research, rest assured there are no students here to get underfoot.'

We paused as a mage holding copper dowsing rods cut across us, spun on his heel, then started walking in the opposite direction — all without acknowledging our presence with so much as a glance.

'They seem plenty underfoot to me,' Pauline said dryly.

North straightened their cravat. 'Yes. Well.'

I glanced over my shoulder, half-expecting to see the others trailing behind us, or being ushered into one of the many rooms. But though the corridor was busy, it was full of strangers.

After a week of being together at all times, it felt weirdly exposed.

Pauline tapped my shoulder with two fingers, making me jump. 'Ah!'

'Sorry. You okay?'

I nodded. 'Yeah, just ... yes.' Now wasn't the time to go into my weird need to return to the herd, even if I could put that into words that made sense.

We left the crowded corridors behind, entering a room at the end of a quiet hallway lined with strange artefacts in glass cases — a black rose that shivered with blue-edged voidshadow, a suit of armour encrusted with glowing lichen, an old book with an eye on the cover that spun to watch us as we passed. The room itself was like a smaller version of the teleportation room we'd arrived in — crystal walls and floor, glittering mirror-like windows, and a more personal-sized teleportation circle carved into the floor.

North, however, stopped short of the circle, raising a hand to signal us to do the same. 'This way lies the arch-mage's personal suite,' they said. Their eyes, black with white irises, fixed first on me and then on Pauline. 'I will not, however, waste the arch-mage's time. Tell me honestly: who are you and what are you seeking here? The Loten-Tooth steward said only that you claim to be from an uncharted plane and desire the services of the arch-mage. However, you look native enough to me.' They cast their dark eyes over Pauline's astralkin glittering hair and my flaring aura — neither unusual in the Associate Plane. 'Will you allow me to check for illusions?'

I nodded, throwing Pauline a nervous look. Neither of us had magic hiding our natures, but it still felt risky to consent to spells being cast on us. North however quickly traced a line of runes in the air. I imagined dice being rolled across the table, deciding our fates.

Purple energy wreathed us in shadow-edged flames, then faded. It felt like little more than a chill breeze. I smiled in relief, but North had eyes only for Pauline. I followed their gaze; Pauline covered her scarf with her hands, light shining through the fabric and the gaps between her fingers.

'What trickery is this?' North demanded stiffly.

'Nothing, a birthmark —'

They strode forward and seized the edge of the scarf before Pauline could back up. It slipped over her eyes, revealing the shining mark of the Oracle, which glittered even as the glow from the spell faded.

'Well,' they said, stepping back. Their fingers flexed, ready to draw runes. 'That certainly changes things.'

Pauline looked shaken. She pulled the scarf from her face and folded it with small, sharp movements.

'It doesn't change anything.' I stepped between Pauline and North, shielding her with my body. 'Pauline doesn't know anything about your Oracle, except that the mark got us attacked not long after we arrived. We're still not from your Associate Plane, and we still want to go home.'

North raised their eyebrows. 'We'll see,' they said. They took a few steps back and gestured for us to join them on the teleportation circle. 'If you will?'

My misgivings about teleportation were not entirely eased, and were certainly not improved by relying on a stranger who accused us of trickery. But Pauline stepped on, hands shaking as she directed the chair, and I couldn't leave her.

I stepped onto the circle and in a flash we were falling through rushing wind to land hard in a crystal tower overflowing with plants. Creepers climbed the trellis-lined walls, curling and reaching. Large pots teemed with leafy sedges and small trees, and orbs of golden light floated around the top of the room, no doubt nourishing the hungry flora.

Pauline strode closer to the window — this one looking out upon the Crystal City in all its shining splendour. Mihilit-dalath was built from the same crystal as the Verdigris Spire, which glittered in the late morning light. People and vehicles milled through the streets, while winged creatures circled the taller buildings and the large central crystal, larger even than the Spire.

I swallowed, hard. Stunning. And somehow the sight of it made me feel further from home than Lundanar and its squat blue houses ever could.

The wide window seat overlooked a broad balcony and was covered in planters with blooming flowers of all shapes and colours. Gently, Pauline examined a wide purple one which had a shimmering edge — perhaps astral or void in nature.

I was more surprised by the design of the room. Unlike the rest of the tower, it had been adapted to a warmer design — oak panelling on some of the walls and neat wood flooring covering the crystal beneath our feet. so that only the teleportation circle was left exposed. It had turned a cold, clinical environment into something warm and welcoming.

There were two cushioned sofas and matching armchairs in the centre of the room, likely for meetings or entertaining guests, and two closed doors at either side of the room.

North cleared their throat. 'Please, take a seat. The arch-mage will join us shortly.'

I took the far side of the nearest sofa, and after a moment, Pauline powered down her hexclimber and joined me on it, wincing at the movement. I folded my hands in my lap, resisting the urge to twist them or wring the skirt of my tunic. I caught myself kicking my feet and stilled. I needed to remain calm — or at least give the impression of it. North took up an attentive stance to the side, back straight and arms crossed, still looking down at us with a slight frown over their spectacles.

'Hey.' Pauline caught my eyes. 'You okay?'

I nodded, not quite trusting myself to speak. I'd made it this far, hadn't I?

I wondered what to expect from the arch-mage. In our game, the arch-mage had been an elderly feykin with white scaly skin and feathery wings. Our party had been on good terms with her. But the world of the game wasn't quite the world of real life, and I had no idea what to expect.

There was a sound like air being fanned in rhythmic bursts, growing louder. I looked around at the window just in time to see a giant spectral bat climb up onto the balcony, long nose fronds twitching, enormous ears perked forward. Each claw of its wing was easily the length of my forearm, but somehow it looked more friendly than terrifying. Like a large puppy with a funny nose. Fellbats, I remembered they were called. Voidkin creatures.

The bat lowered its head, revealing the figure seated on its shoulders. He dismounted, sliding smoothly down its side, the trailing lengths of his robe falling fluidly into place when he landed. He was feykin — elfin ears and vine-and-flower markings that crept up his neck and onto his cheeks, the petals glowing blue and beautiful against his dark umber skin. His long hair was black with streaks of green, shaved on the sides and braided into neat cornrows and pulled into a half topknot. I had no idea how old he was; he didn't look more than ten years older than us, but it was so hard to tell with planarkin of any kind. Ageing in the Associate Plane, with its many magical influences, was very inconsistent.

He raised a hand in greeting, sleeve falling back to reveal that the vine-and-flower markings also climbed his arms. North inclined their head to him, then turned back to us. 'The arch-mage will see you now.'

He walked in moments later. The fellbat peered in through the window a moment, beady eyes curious, then turned and leapt from the balcony.

'So,' he said. His voice was deep but soft, the kind of voice that naturally put you at ease. Being me, I was instantly suspicious of it. 'You're the leaders of the extraplanars I've been hearing so much about.'

He took in my astralkin aura, and Pauline's sparkling hair. 'Forgive me for saying it, but ... you don't look extraplanar to me.' He drew a string of runes, fingers a blur. Then he threw his hands wide; a circle of light flashed around the seating area. I felt a wave of power rush over me, and tried to resist it, but couldn't.

'I think perhaps now, we can speak honestly with each other,' he said, and now I noticed that his smile had fangs.

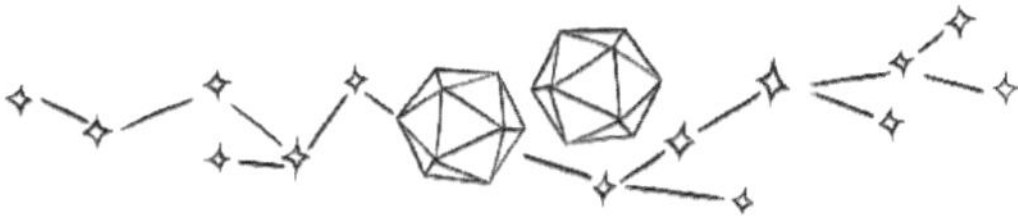

CHAPTER TWENTY-NINE

It had happened so fast, I had half-risen from my seat by the time he was speaking, blood pounding in my ears. The moment the spell had been cast, I'd been sure we were in for a fight. But as I took in the white flame surrounding us, I was pretty sure it had been a Truthsayer spell, like Pauline had cast on the Order of the Third Eye brutes. I had felt the spell hook into my gut in just the same way as it had before.

I glanced at Pauline, and she looked unruffled. I wondered if she had resisted the spell again, just as I'd failed to. Or maybe she thought there was nothing to fear in telling the truth.

Was there? Anything to fear? I mean we would have to tell at least some of the truth if he was going to help us get home but ... there was something about the truth spell hanging over us that made me especially nervous. It made everything more intense. It gave us so little room to tell our story the way we wanted to.

'We were going to be honest with you anyway,' Pauline said.

The arch-mage's brows lifted. 'Then why resist the spell?'

So she had resisted it.

Pauline shrugged. 'Principle, I suppose.'

The arch-mage's gaze shifted to me. But you didn't, now did you? What's your name?'

I started to say 'Tar,' but stumbled over the words and found myself finishing it. 'Tarot Alex Morgan,' I said, only struggling a little.

So half-truths were unlikely to pass muster, according to the spell. Wonderful.

If my name was unusual in Vanthis, he didn't show it. 'From which plane do you hail?'

'Earth,' I said, and I supposed that had to be true.

'There is no such plane,' said the arch-mage.

'There is,' I said. 'We came from it.'

He frowned and tapped his lips. 'What are the properties of your plane?'

I tried to think of something that would make sense. 'Lots of technology and engineering, no magic. No kin.'

'There must be magic, or how did you get here?' he said. 'Please, don't play me for a fool.'

Pauline rested her chin in her hand. 'By your own spell, they can't lie to you,' she said. 'If there's magic, we don't know of it. And we didn't look like this when we left,' she tugged at her hair as an example.

'You weren't human?'

'We were,' I said. 'But not planarkin. No kin traits, no magic.'

'So not an Associate Plane like ours, then,' he mused. He snapped his fingers; the spell flared, then vanished. I felt like a weight had been removed from my mind; the spell was gone. 'I apologise for the force of magic — I needed to verify such an extravagant claim before moving forward. I hope you will find me more polite in its absence.' He bowed, and took the seat opposite us, threading his ringed hands in front of him.

I glanced at North, who had remained silent throughout the encounter but surely had been affected by the spell as well. They caught my stare and raised an eyebrow. I quickly looked away, my cheeks flushing and my aura glowing faintly.

'So what is it you want then?' the arch-mage asked. 'Perhaps we can come to an arrangement.'

'Mr Vorugar,' said Pauline, and this time there was a flicker of surprise from the arch-mage — perhaps the manner of address wasn't traditional here. 'We need to return to our plane. We didn't initiate the planeshift and are unable to get back.'

'Ah yes ... you said you believe your plane to be devoid of magic.'

I frowned, my mind snagging on his use of the word 'believe'.

'What then, were the circumstances of your arrival?' he asked.

'We fell asleep,' said Pauline. 'When we awoke, we had taken the form of various planarkin from your world. We've been here about a month.'

Now North spoke up. 'Yet you seem very confident in your knowledge of us, of our magic, of everything else.'

Pauline's mouth pressed into a thin line. She looked down at her lap. I understood her discomfort — how could we explain that we had been playing a game in this world for the better part of a year? Longer, actually, when you considered how long the rest had been playing before I joined. It made it sound trivial, and made it seem like we didn't see this world as real. Which after a few weeks here, we emphatically did.

Honestly, the world had always felt real to us — it was why Kenta let his 'evil' character be thwarted and led by the rest of the team. It was why we spent so long planning our every move. We wanted the world and its people to thrive. We wanted to be a positive influence.

But that was going to be hard to explain.

I bit my lip a second, then tried anyway 'Pauline could see this world before we came here,' I said. 'She thought she'd imagined it, and us as characters inside it. None of us knew it really existed, or that there was any way to get here. All we know is that we woke up here, in slightly different bodies, and that all that came with us were these,' I fished the d4 out of my pocket, holding it up to the light. Vorugar frowned and leaned forward, clearly interested. 'We each received one the night before we planeshifted, and it's the only item from our world that came with us.'

'May I?' Vorugar held out his hand. I hesitated. This might be our one link home. But the arch-mage was more than powerful enough to take it from me if he wanted to, and if we were seeking his help, we needed to trust him.

I let the die fall onto his open palm.

'Hmm ...' He flexed his fingers; it levitated into the air, hovering a few inches from his hand. It began to glow, as did the hearts of the flowers marked into his skin. 'This is netheril. It comes from the Void Between Planes, and can amplify and store magic. What are the runes on it? I do not recognise the script ...'

I paused. 'Numbers,' I said. 'It's a die, as used in games or gambling.' More evidence that we weren't speaking English, as it felt like we were. It was weird to think it though; I could feel my brain bending at the thought.

'This is a toy in your world?'

I shrugged. 'I don't know. Dice are. I've never seen something made from that material before. I assumed it was a synthetic crystal.'

'Synthetic.' North repeated the word in a clipped tone. They and Vorugar exchanged a fleeting look I found it hard to read.

'Can you help us?' Pauline asked.

'Oh, certainly.' He waved a hand, leaning back in his seat and stretching one arm along the back of the sofa. 'Planeshifting is a science, and a very well-documented one. It will take some working out, and we don't have all the necessary information yet, but that will come with time. We'll also need to discuss what you will give in return, of course,' he smiled slightly. 'As the arch-mage of Mihilit-dalath, my time does not come for free. But don't worry about that for now. Return to your friends; North will help you find lodgings in the city. From there, we will contact you with next steps.'

What we'd give in return. *Next steps.* My stomach clenched and I crossed my hands over it as I turned over those words. I didn't think they meant anything good for us, and I hated the way they mimicked bureaucrats in our world. I felt like he was about to deny my benefits claim.

'Uh, my die?' I said, cringing inwardly at my hesitation.

Vorugar looked nonplussed.

'The netheril,' I clarified.

He extended his hand and dropped the d4 back into my waiting palm. 'Of course.' He smiled.

Nothing about this man was reading right to me. He was all smiles and promises, sure, but nothing concrete. I had no idea what his true thoughts were, except that I doubted they aligned with our goals. But then, I tended to over-read, over-analyse. On Earth, I'd often seen negativity in people that wasn't really there. I looked to Pauline for her input, but Pauline stood and eased herself back into her hexclimber.

'Thank you,' she said. The words only sounded a little stiff. I wondered if she, like I, had gotten an uneasy squirm at the language and tone Vorugar had given us. She had far more experience of battling with shitty bureaucrats than I had. But she only nodded to North, who ushered us back to the teleportation circle.

As the runes lit up around us, I saw Vorugar tap his lips, watching us consideringly. Then we were falling, touching down back in the teleportation chamber. I staggered a little on impact; Pauline reached out to steady me, even though I knew that kind of movement could cause her considerable pain.

'Thanks,' I said.

She nodded and released me, her lips twisted into a frown I don't think was for me.

CHAPTER THIRTY

We were quiet on return to the group. Though Arries was quick to swarm us for hugs and check we were all right, we didn't say much in North's presence, neither of us wanting to properly get into our visit with the arch-mage while they were present. Silky begged me for treats, which I obliged with relief, soothed by the distraction of the sealorn's greedy antics.

Arries made up for our silence by introducing us to the mages North had assigned to them. 'Perliot is a jolly sort,' Arries said, clapping the feykin on the shoulder. 'And Ivexius is very shy but I suspect very kind.'

At this mention, the antlered feykin, Ivexius, grimaced again, but I didn't miss his faint blush. The pair's goodbyes to our group were warmer than I would have expected. Arries never failed to impress.

North had a young feykin — a goblin-like person with green skin, a big, sharp grin, and long pointed ears — see us out into the city. It was more breathtaking up close than it had been through the arch-mage's window. Buildings of blue-green crystal glittered among more normal structures — the wooden fey-like buildings, mostly, as well as some astralkin marble and voidkin slate and burnished wood.

The streets were crystal too, though coated with the dust and grime of constant foot traffic. It was a city bustling with life and business. A centaur-like feykin passed us, looking harried while her bipedal children bounced and laughed on her back. One of them pointed at Silky, clearly excited to see a farm animal in the city. Personally, I was considering getting Silky a harness or something; we only had food to keep her attention, and I was garnering quite the collection of tooth marks from her.

Levitating gondolas full of people or products drifted past, barely stirring the dust in the wake but causing the streets to flash with power beneath the grime. I remembered that Mihilit-dalath was a powered city, the crystal foundations enabling something more like modern technology. But in spite of some superficial similarities to city life here, I felt further from home than ever.

Our guide led us to a comfortable inn only a few blocks away from the Verdigris Spire. The Lodestone Inn wasn't crystal like some of the posher buildings, but I noticed crystals had been embedded in the walls and surrounded the doors and windows, likely so that it could be powered similarly to everything else. It was significantly larger than The Honeyhart, and there were people ranged on tables outside or leaning against the walls and chatting even this early in the afternoon. We followed our guide inside and while Kenta and Ordeth went with him to arrange our lodgings, I took in the scene.

It was a pretty building. Sleeker than I expected from a fantasy inn, with gleaming slate floors and carved stone walls. There were a lot of tables, most with a vase of flowers on them and a glowing crystal besides, giving it a warm, ambient lighting. But it was busy; several of the tables were already occupied, and though it wasn't a raucous atmosphere, it still had that mid-level drone of too many voices going at once. After teleporting not once but twice, after Vorugar and North and 'what we'd give in return', I had no defense against it.

Someone came to stand beside me and I flinched away.

'Hey.' It was Arries, giving me a concerned look. He was in his werefox form, his peach-coloured fur making him look more gentle than beastly. 'You need to step outside or something?'

I nodded quickly and fled outside. Arries called something to the others and followed me out. I went around the outside of the building, away from the tables and seats, put my back to the inn's wall, and sank to the floor.

After a moment, Arries joined me, his armour clinking with the movement. He gave me a sidelong worried look. 'Too many people?' he asked.

Too many people. Too much noise. Too much everything. I nodded and twisted my hands in my lap.

He reached up and scratched the back of his head. 'I like people,' he admitted.

I smiled in spite of myself. 'Yeah, I know.'

'So how'd it go with the arch-mage?'

'Tellan Vorguar ...' I pictured his easy smile, one arm stretched across the back of the sofa. I remembered his tower filled with plants, and the greedy look in his eyes as I handed him the d4. 'You'd like him.'

'You don't?'

I considered. 'I don't know him. But I definitely don't trust him.'

Arries smiled to one side: an oddly friendly look for someone with such pointy teeth. It was nonetheless familiar. 'How can you distrust someone you don't even know?'

This startled a laugh from me. 'God, Arries — do you trust random strangers?'

'Until they give me a reason not to,' he said evenly.

I shook my head. 'That makes no sense.'

'I dunno. It's worked out all right for me so far.'

Somehow listening to Arries be extremely naive about people was centring. I could be back at home, playing A:RO and telling him not to trade random legendary items to strangers on the promise that he'd be paid back later.

I elbowed him in the side. 'You're such a goof, Arries. You think the world is all sunshine and rainbows.'

'I don't think that.' He went quiet for a moment. 'I know I don't look like it at the moment, when I'm wearing this very realistic fursuit,' he gestured at his face. 'but I'm black. I know what the world is. Doesn't mean I don't try to make it better.'

I felt that like a kick in the guts — that I could be so foolish as to overlook Arries' reality, even for a moment.

'Is it weird?' I asked. 'Looking so different? I mean — we all look different but most of us look —'

'More or less the same?' He flexed his hands — gauntlets with claws built in to accommodate his own. His tail twitched on the ground beside him. He sighed and dropped his werefox form, returning to the Arries I knew best — though with added ears and tail. 'You know, at first I was delighted. This is what I've always wanted, right? A furry dream come true.'

'But?'

'But ... yeah. It's weird. My body doesn't work the same way when I'm a werefox. It all feels natural enough to my body, but sometimes it feels wrong to my brain, you know? Sometimes when I see my reflection I'm like "Yes! I finally look on the outside the way I look on the inside." And that's a warm, golden feeling. But sometimes ... sometimes I think where is my mum's nose? Where's my dad's cheekbones? Where's the profile that everyone says reminds them of my great grandma, god rest her soul? It's ... I don't know. It's complicated. It is and isn't how I expected to feel when I was daydreaming about fox peets and fluffy tails. You've probably noticed that I still spend a lot of time in my human shape.'

'I'm sorry,' I said at length, trying to process all that he'd said. Arries was always honest with me about how he was feeling; it was one of the reasons he was so easy to be friends with.

He smiled and shook his head. 'You've got nothing to be sorry about. And I'm not sorry, either. Who wouldn't want to polymorph, if they could? You're loving it right?'

I smiled. 'Yeah. Yeah, I am.'

'Well, then you get it. There's just ... just added stuff. I've been talking to P and Rex about it. Working through what it means.'

I nodded. I hesitated, then rested a hand on his pauldroned shoulder.

'Thanks,' he said, and he honestly sounded touched. Arries might not relate to my touch aversion, but he'd always been careful to be aware of it.

I nodded and waited a few seconds before pulling back. 'Do you want to go back?' The words came out a little hoarse. 'Home, I mean.'

It was the question I'd been wary of asking him. Because of course he wanted to go home. Because he was Arries and there was a whole world of friends and family waiting for him to come back.

Because he was *my* friend, and I couldn't bear the thought of life on Vanthis without him.

Arries sighed and thumped his head back against the wall. 'No. And yes. Do I want to live here? Do I want a life of magic? Yes. God, yes. I used to pray every day in school that a portal would open up and I could jump through it and start my *real* life.' I smiled a little at the thought of a kid Arries, raised on classic fantasy by his nerdy parents, dreaming of magic. 'But my family ... I couldn't choose to never hug my mum again, or play chess with my sister, or listen to live music with my dad. And my friends ... how would I even explain this to them? I don't know.'

'Yeah.' I was quiet. There was only one person I really cared about who wasn't already here with me, and even so, the thought of never seeing her again was too much.

Was that really the choice, though? Were our only options returning to normal life as if nothing had ever happened, or cutting all ties to our former selves and starting new lives in Vanthis? We didn't yet know what going home meant. We didn't know what *any* of this meant. But in the game, planeshifting was a thing you could do on any plane. You could return to Vanthis, if you had the knowledge and skill to do so. So if Earth was truly another plane — if the magic here could get us back — then there had to be a way for us to return.

Right?

Because as strange and fraught as our journey here had been so far ... I wasn't ready to let go of it. Not if I had a choice.

'It's kind of crazy, being here,' I said. 'Seeing all this for real. Living it. I never thought when you invited me to Pauline's game, that it would come to this.'

'I always wondered what made you decide to come,' he said.

'You told me "This is a game that'll change your life".' I smiled at the recollection. 'And I'm a sack of misery at the best of times so I thought "anything is better than this".'

Arries whistled. '"A game that'll change your life" ... wow. Not exactly what I meant.' He smiled, revealing one long fang. Even his human form still had adorable fox accents.

'It did, though,' I said, turning to look at him. 'Before we ever came here, it did. I don't know if I've ever properly thanked you for that.'

Arries smiled. 'We're friends. You don't have to thank me for wanting to hang out with you.'

'All the same, though.'

'All the same.'

Hesitantly, I leaned my head against his shoulder. The metal of his pauldron was comfortingly cold and smooth against my cheek. I was glad to have him. I knew I didn't have many friends, but I was sure that, even if I'd found it easy, I would have struggled to find one as good as Arries. We were all of us lucky that he was so free with his friendship.

It wasn't long before someone came to find us. I expected that; we were all keeping close tabs on each other, given the whole 'lost in a fantasy world' situation. What I wasn't expecting was Rex, tail twitching nervously beneath the hem of his cloak. 'Hey,' he said. His hood was up again, something I had come to recognise as a sign he was feeling exposed.

I leaned away from Arries. 'Hi,' I said.

An awkward pause stretched.

Arries glanced between us, raising an eyebrow. 'Does somebody need us?'

'Uh.' Rex crossed his arms beneath the cloak. 'Well, P is going to sit everyone down and explain what happened with the arch-mage.'

'Great.' Arries stood up, then looked back down at me. 'Wait ... are you okay to go in there?'

I considered myself. I was a lot calmer since Arries had come out to sit with me, but already the thought of entering the inn with its noise and the press of bodies was making my chest squeeze. 'I think I need a few minutes.'

'Well ... what if I stay outside with you?' Rex said. 'I was finding it a bit much in there. You can fill me in while Arries rejoins the group. We could sit here, or take a walk or something.' He didn't quite meet my eyes as he said it, but then I didn't expect him to.

Arries raised his eyebrows at me, clearly wanting me to decide.

'Yeah. Um, I'd like that.'

Arries looked between us. 'And you'll be okay?'

Rex nodded. 'Tar's probably got us covered anyway, but Pauline can Whisperwind me to check in.'

'We'll be fine,' I said. And maybe that was true. The city was full of people, sure, but in the game we were significantly more dangerous than a random person off the street. If we were careful, there shouldn't be anything to fear.

You know, except crowds and loud noises. The usual.

Arries went inside and Rex looked a question at me.

'A walk,' I replied. I started to get up when, to my surprise, he offered me a hand. I took it, and he drew me smoothly to my feet. Stronger than he looked.

His hand was slim and cool. I quickly dropped it. 'Thanks.'

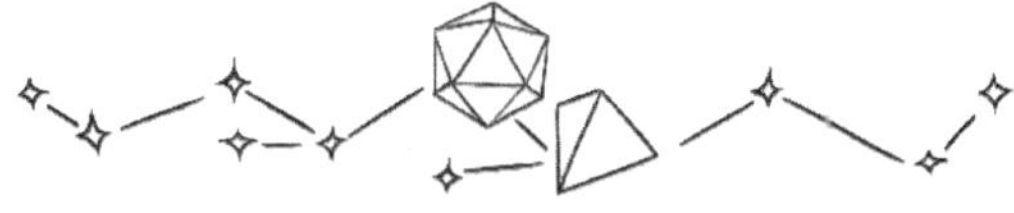

CHAPTER THIRTY-ONE

He flexed his hand then crossed his arms. Together, we strode out into the city streets, the crystal beneath our feet glowing through the thickly-coated dirt. 'I like it here,' he said. He looked up at the crystal-and-wood buildings towering to either side. 'I mean — I think Lundanar is more my speed. But for a city, this is pretty great.'

'I don't get any of those "lost in a labyrinth of people" vibes I get in Earth cities,' I said.

'Yes! Exactly that.' He shook his head. 'Maybe it's just the novelty, I don't know. But there are fewer people by a long way, and the roads are a lot narrower.' He steered us onto a smaller road with less traffic. The crystal road glowed brighter here with less dust choking it, and a pair of voickin fathers ushered their mostly feykin kids down the road.

'We had work training in London at some conference,' I said. 'It was all paid for and I couldn't get out of it. I nearly quit my job in panic but held it together long enough to hop on the train with my co-workers.'

'God, trains ...' Rex made a face at me.

'Hours and hours of trains,' I said. 'I had my laptop with me, which could just about run A:RO, but even so.' We paused in front of a gorgeous crystal building, all rough pillars and archways like it had been carved directly from an enormous block of crystal. 'When we got to London, I was so far beyond running on empty, and it was worse than the train. The station was large and crowded, and the streets were a warren I had no idea how to navigate. We had to catch a taxi and ... I dunno, I just lost it. I didn't even make it to the taxi. I got the next train home.'

'What, right away?'

'Yep.'

Rex shook his head. 'That's wild. So what happened?'

'Honestly? Nothing. Didn't even catch flack about it with work — everyone kept asking me if I was all right, or if I was ill ... I think they were relieved not to have to deal with me, to be honest.'

'God ... I know this probably sounds strange, but you're so impressive sometimes.'

I spluttered a moment. 'I'm sorry?'

We rounded a corner onto what looked like a more residential road. Along one side were terraced houses, most made of a sort of pink terracotta tiling. On the other was a park or garden, blooming with blue-petalled trees with silver bark and blood red flowers with thorny stems. Large fungi sprang up at human height, their voluminous caps glowing cheerfully, blending in with the crystal of the city. It looked wilder than any Earth city park, and I found myself walking toward it. It seemed safe enough — I could see a young astralkin reading under a luminous pink mushroom, and a couple had laid a blanket among some of the flowers, sitting close and talking in low voices interspersed with laughter.

Rex rubbed the back of his neck, looking sheepish. 'Well ... you're not afraid to say "this is too much". I can't count the number of times I've made myself really unwell by pushing myself further than I can go.'

I shook my head. 'I should try harder. Everyone says I should. Maybe I would spend less time in my bedroom if I did.'

'But Tar ... you push plenty hard. When you came to the game at Pauline's ... it was so clear how big a thing that was for you. But you made it happen. It was pushing your limits, sure, but it was worth it for you and it wasn't too much. Then when you went to Hanna's birthday thing ... I've never done anything like that, but I knew if you were going, then maybe I could do it too.' We stopped beneath a silver tree. A gust of wind sent blue leaves swirling past us. Rex smiled to one side. 'If it weren't for you, I wouldn't even be here right now.'

I snorted. 'And we're sure that's a good thing?'

'I'm sure.' His expression turned serious. I stared into his eyes. We were of a height, pretty much, and I was once again struck by the darkness of his eyes, the intensity of his gaze. Something that had been true before he ever set foot in Vanthis. 'I haven't been fair to you, Tar. Coming here has ... it was a lot to deal with. A lot to process, and not a lot of space to process it. But I should never have let that hurt you.'

I went very still. My body was tight with frozen adrenaline while my heart beat way too fast. I couldn't look away from Rex if I wanted to.

His eyes hovered uncertainly on mine. 'You said some things to me, back at The Honeyhart. And ... and it was something I have wanted to hear so badly that I knew, in my heart, that none of this could be real. That it was impossible that I could exist in this place I have dreamed about for so long, with you, and that you could feel about me the way I feel about you.'

My mouth unfroze, but it felt dry. I tried to speak, cleared my throat, and said, 'The way you feel about me?'

He looked down, pressing his lips into a thin line. A muscle worked in his jaw. He looked almost pained. 'I want to be where you are. I want to know what you think. I drive myself crazy sometimes trying to think of a way to start a conversation with you, just to hear your voice. You're so ... wry, and clever, and so attractive you're kind of hard to look at directly. I just ...' he trailed off.

Shyly, half-terrified, I reached out and took his hands in mine.

Rex sighed. 'Tar, my brain is so full of noise. Sometimes the only clear thought I have is you, you, you.'

'Rex ...'

He looked up at me, eyes so full of hope and fear that I thought a slight breeze might shatter him. I squeezed his hands, then released one and touched my fingertips gently to his cheek. 'Is this okay?'

He shivered. 'It's everything I want,' he said.

He leaned his forehead against mine. I flattened my hand against his cheek, brushing my thumb along his cheekbone, then took his hand again. 'You, you, you,' I whispered.

We stood like that a long time.

At length, we found ourselves sitting beneath the tree, me with my back to it, Rex stretched out on the ground. It was the most relaxed I'd ever seen him, arms behind his head and staring up at a two-mooned sky. Every now and then he caught my eye and smiled, and it made me shiver with happiness.

'So this Vorugar guy wants something from us. Why am I not surprised?'

'Hundreds of hours of Pauline making us run quests to get the most inessential items? Nah, you're just prescient.'

He ringed his fingers around his eyes like winged glasses. 'I see all. Well ... I guess P really does see all now.' He let his hands fall. 'What do you think he'll want?'

'He nearly took my d4 once already. I had to remind him to give it back.'

Rex tsked. 'Like a huckster trying to short-change you on the street.'

'Huckster?'

'I stand by it.

I smiled, but looked away, still preoccupied by the thought of Vorugar. 'I don't want to hurt anyone. I dreamed of being an adventurer in a fantasy world for so long but now that I'm here ... I just can't, Rex. Even when those cult weirdos attacked P, I couldn't.'

Rex got up on his elbows. 'Well ... you didn't have to,' he said slowly. 'You found another way. You've always been creative with your magic.'

I crossed my arms over my stomach. 'But what happens when there's no other way? And what happens if I mess up?' I shook my head. 'I can't shake the feeling that Vorugar is looking at us and seeing a free opportunity for violence.'

Rex nudged my foot with his. He was looking at me, expression serious. 'We'll work it out, Tar. I won't let you become a killer if you won't let me, okay?'

I nodded, releasing a ragged breath. 'Okay.'

We spent a few more minutes in the park, enjoying the thick, waxy grass and the blue leaves that swirled around us every time the breeze picked up. But then the expected message came along. Rex sat up, eyes focused on something I couldn't see. 'We're fine. We'll head back now,' he said. He glanced at me, eyes asking a question.

Honestly, I was still pretty overwhelmed, but more from everything that had happened with Rex than the inn at this point. I thought I could probably handle it. 'I'll be all right,' I said. I got to my feet and offered him a hand, pulling him up beside me. He was extremely light. 'Just ... could you stay close?'

He adjusted our hands so that we could walk side by side. 'There's nothing I'd rather do,' he said.

It felt ... different ... walking through the city hand-in-hand. Lighter. I was hyper-aware of Rex's skin against mine, the gentle pressure of his grip. Looking around, I felt more visible, and at first that made me anxious, but then I realised it was all in my mind. This might be an incredible and intimate moment for me, but to everyone else it was a non-event. It was only for us; it was special.

Sometimes, as we walked, his shoulder would bump into mine and we would smile shyly at each other. I couldn't believe that this was my life. That I got to be a witch in a crystal city, and standing so close to this intelligent and kind man was more than a dream come true. I felt full. I felt like I was full of air and might float away at any moment.

We made it back to the inn, which looked no less busy than when we'd left. Hanna and Kenta bookended the door, in an animated argument that abruptly ended as they noticed our approach.

'About fucking time!' Hanna said, stomping a hoof for emphasis. 'We've been waiting a fucking century!'

Kenta took in our threaded hands. 'Feeling ... friendly?' he said, waggling his eyebrows.

Hanna punched him in the side.

'Ow!'

'Don't be a creep, Ken.'

She turned to us. 'P's seen something.'

My breath caught. 'What?'

Hanna pointed at her own forehead. 'Seen something. Third eye shit. Come on!' She jerked her head toward the door and then followed us inside.

Rex pulled closer to me as we pushed into the crowd, following our purple faun friend. I held my breath, like we were diving into deep water. I didn't want to smell the sea of people pressing around me.

To my relief, Hanna led us through the back and to an adjoining housing area with a suite of rooms, which Vorugar had paid for us to have to ourselves. There was a lounge connecting all the rooms, with gauzy curtains drawn, crystal lamps lit, and a neat little seating area with multiple sofas.

As nice as it was, it did nothing to ease my suspicions that Vorugar expected something big in return.

Pauline sat on the lone armchair, knees drawn up to her chest. I remembered that she found it difficult to sit on a sofa with others, lest their fidgeting increased her pain levels. Arries talked to her quietly, looking oddly vulnerable in his human form with his armour removed. We could almost be back home; this was just Arries in some cute cosplay ears, until they moved.

Ordeth was playing with Silky. He rough-housed with her, tickling her neck and pulling his hands out of reach before she could bite him. He was surprisingly quick. His cat sat nearby on the back of Pauline's chair, curled up and with tail twitching gently in contentment.

Riya sat on the floor flicking through a thick tome in a script I didn't recognise, an expression of intense concentration on her face. At our approach, however, she got to her feet and approached me solemnly.

'I've been learning,' she told me.

'Oh yeah?' I said.

Rex squeezed my hand in farewell, and went to join the others on the sofas. Hanna threw herself at an empty sofa and squished around until she was comfortable, and Kenta dropped heavily beside her.

She held up the book to me. 'See?'

I shook my head. 'I can't read that,' I told her. It was a strange script interspersed with runes. It had a garden-like look to it — the script branching like roots, the runes often leaf or flower-like in shape.

She frowned. 'I can read it.' She turned it around and said: 'Elohor mihilit vol etaya. Lor mel ve atar ...'

The words meant nothing to me, and didn't sound like any Earth language I'd ever been exposed to. But Hanna laughed out loud and strode over, gesturing for Riya to hand over the book. 'It's a travel book. A tour guide to Mihilit-dalath. She picked it up and read the first line of the page, nodding. 'Yep. It's in Fey.'

I blinked. 'How do you know?'

Hanna shrugged. 'Well, I can read it, and I'm feykin, and that's the only language my character took.'

'I know another language?' said Riya.

Hanna ruffled her hair, making her grimace. 'That's right, kiddo.'

She started ticking things off on her hands. 'I know English and Urdu and Fey and sort of Welsh.'

I stared. Did this mean I would be able to read Astral? 'Sometimes I feel like I barely know English,' I said.

Riya nodded, as if this was expected, and held out her hands to Hanna for the book, which Hanna gave her.

'Intimidating kid,' Hanna said watching her sit down and continue poring over the travel guide. 'Her mum must be really missing her.'

I felt a sharp jab of guilt at the thought. I'd been here, having the adventure of my life while Saanvi was probably freaking out over the loss of her child. 'They're really close,' I said. 'I can't imagine what she's going through right now.'

Hanna nudged me with her elbow. I flinched, but her expression was kind. 'We'll get her home,' she said. 'Whatever happens, we'll get her home.'

We would. We had to.

I sat down beside Rex, who was chatting quietly to Kenta. 'She hasn't contacted you again?' he said.

'Just that one dream, since I put on the amulet,' Kenta replied. He looked haunted. 'But that was enough.'

Arries leaned forward, elbows resting on his knees. 'You need to find a new god.'

Kenta rolled his eyes. 'Look, Arries, I know you're really fucking psyched to have Sunara real and on your side, but now is not the time for you to evangelise at me.'

'It doesn't have to be Sunara,' he said. 'Think about it. In the game, if you get powers from a god and you want to leave the god, you need to find a new source for your magic. A new god could shield you from your blood goddess too.'

'Simpler than switching to an arcane source,' Rex said. 'There're *a lot* of books involved. Even being transported here with the knowledge, there're a lot of books involved.'

'I —' Kenta stopped, then fell quiet.

Pauline cleared her throat, for all the world like she was calling the table to order at the start of a game. 'I had a vision,' she said. The words echoed around the room as we all fell silent. 'Or something like one.' She touched the eye mark on her forehead, which flared. 'I'm not entirely sure how this works.'

Kenta crossed his arms. 'What did you see?'

'Flashes of things.' She stared into the middle distance, recalling. 'My games room, the table smashed, the room in disarray. Us holding hands and falling through deep water. Vorugar turning away, a full set of polydice in his hands. And through it all, two enormous, alien eyes. One red, and one green, watching everything.' Slowly, she focused back in, looking to each of us in turn.

'Well,' said Hanna. 'Fuck.'

'Is it bad?' said Arries. 'I can't tell whether it was bad or not.'

'I didn't know you could see the future,' I said. 'It hasn't happened before, right?'

Pauline tucked her braids behind her ears. 'I don't think it was bad. Or at least, it didn't *feel* threatening. Just ... alien.' Her mouth twisted to one side. 'And ... it has happened before. Small things. At first, I thought it wasn't any more than idle daydreams. Then ... they started coming true.'

'Things like what?'

Pauline's gaze flicked to me, then away. 'It doesn't matter,' she said.

My gut clenched. Oh, I didn't like *that* at all.

'What's important is that I think this is true. I realise it's not a lot to go on, but be aware that Vorguar may need our dice to send us back, or attempt to take them for his own ends. As for the eyes ...' She shrugged. 'I don't know.'

'Could it be Alis-Umor?' Rex asked. 'Those eyes could be her, watching Ken.'

I glanced at Kenta, who stared at the floor, jaw tight.

'Possibly,' said Pauline. 'I don't think we can rule out that she might still be involved in this somehow.'

We discussed it for a while, going back and forth, asking Ordeth for his input as well. Ultimately though, her images were too brief and too vague to do anything with. It seemed these were the most coherent visions she had yet had — her earlier visions had been briefer still.

I wondered if she was growing more powerful. If Vanthis was changing her in ways beyond what we'd all witnessed upon waking up here. Pauline was more connected to this world than any of us.

The Oracle ...

But at length, Pauline called us to order, and moved us on to more concrete concerns. 'So,' she said. 'Is everyone all caught-up on the situation with the arch-mage?'

Nods and murmurs of agreement rippled through the room. Just like that, we were in player-mode again, not wanting to make too much racket lest our lair master scold us.

'Then you know we need to be prepared for a quest to be offered to us in exchange for Vorugar's help. We need to discuss what that means, and what we're willing to do.'

'I'll be honest,' said Kenta. 'I don't want to do anything. I've got an evil goddess on my back and no powers to speak of.'

'We can *fix* that,' Arries said, and Kenta threw him a glare. 'Ow!'

We all looked at Ordeth, who was shaking out a bleeding hand. 'Uh, Silky. Sorry. I'll be right back — see if the kitchen has any healing salve.' He left the room.

The sealorn landed on the floor and started bouncing around on her belly, sniffing and exploring. She seemed ... okay?

I raised my hand but not very high, not certain how best to add my input.

Pauline tilted her head to one side. 'Yes, Tar? You don't need to raise your hand.'

Hanna snorted, but that was only a little embarrassing. Hanna found everything funny.

'I think I'd be okay with a non-violent quest. Like ... if we need to retrieve some treasure and we can just stealth in. Or I don't know ... he needs an errand running and we just polymorph ourselves and go off to do it.'

'I agree that such a situation would be ideal,' Pauline said. 'But I doubt he'd need random adventurers for that, given the resources he has at his disposal. Whatever it is is likely to be dangerous, unscrupulous, or both.'

I didn't like the sound of that, to put it mildly. And it was all too believable. How many times in the game had we been presented with moral quandaries? People saw adventurers as mercenaries — a chance to achieve their goals on the sly, without risk of consequence. People had asked us to steal, maim, and murder on many occassions.

I wasn't comfortable with any of that. Well, certainly not the maiming and murdering. I guess the stealing kind of depended on what, why, and from whom.

Rex rubbed his chin thoughtfully. 'That's true,' he said. 'I wonder if there might be another option, though.'

Pauline's eyebrows twitched. 'Go on.'

'Go on,' I murmured quietly. Thankfully, nobody reacted.

'Well ... in the game, we were natives to this plane, right? But we're not natives, and Vorugar has been relatively convinced of that, right? He might want something related to Earth from us, or to study us or experiment on us. He is a wizard, after all — for him, knowledge is quite literally power, and we're a unique opportunity to get knowledge of a previously unknown plane.'

'He was extremely interested in my dice,' I said. 'And of the numbers on it ... I don't know, I feel like he might fabricate a reason to take the dice from us — and I'm really sure that we need them to get back.' Everyone nodded; we'd had the concept of a planar anchor for planeshifting hammered into us enough times by Pauline. 'But also ... I don't know. I got the sense that the numbers weren't completely unfamiliar to him. There could be more going on here than we're aware of.'

Hanna drummed her fingers against the arm of the sofa. 'You think he might already know about Earth?'

I shrugged. 'I think he might know more than he's letting on. It's a big coincidence, isn't it? That these dice contain a material known to Vorugar, and that they're the reason we were brought here? Something isn't right.'

Kenta sighed and leaned forward. 'That's ... a really good point, much as I hate the thought. I've played an evil mastermind with the best of them and this whole thing absolutely reeks of some wider plot.' He glanced at Pauline. 'Maybe including your Order of the Third Eye as well. We still don't know how they found us so quickly, or who sent them.'

'You think he could be related?' said Hanna.

Kenta shrugged. 'There's no reason to think he's *not* related, and that's more the point. He's the arch-mage — collecting powerful magic is his thing. And I bet a person prophesied to know everything about Vanthis would be a pretty damn powerful magic to collect.'

We all fell silent for a moment, taking this in. Riya murmured, 'Ello quar deleth!' in a triumphant tone, still poring over the tour guide. I suspected she was just enjoying trying out a new language.

I half-raised my hand again, realised, dropped it, and started speaking, 'So ... what *are* we willing to do, then?'

'He's not fucking getting our dice,' said Hanna.

'We're not going to hurt anyone,' Arries added.

'Okay ... well, that's a good set of boundaries, at least.' Pauline frowned at me. 'Tar?'

I startled. I'd been staring at the drawn curtains, my thoughts elsewhere. 'Sorry. I was just thinking ... what do we want?'

Pauline blinked. 'What?'

I wrung my hands in my lap. 'What do we *want*? We've asked for his assistance in returning to Earth, right? And we can all agree that Riya has to go home, that's not in question. But ... do we? I mean, forever?'

Because I wanted to see my mum again. I wanted to say goodbye to Riya and Saanvi. I wanted to be able to visit them if I could, even if I couldn't live with them anymore. But I didn't know whether I was willing to give up Vanthis. For all it was wild and dangerous, it was also magical. It was beautiful and different and in many ways I felt more at home here than I ever had on Earth.

'I mean ...' Hanna trailed off.

'I need to say goodbye to my mum,' said Arries. 'Have a big family gathering. Visit all my friends. But ... yeah.' He looked down at his hands. Even in human shape, the fingernails gently tapered into claws. 'I ... I don't want to leave here forever. I feel like there's so much left to see and do.'

Kenta's brows knit together, and his lips tugged down into a grimace. 'What, you want to stay in magic land forever, with witches and demons and evil gods?'

I sighed. 'There's ... a lot more to it than that.'

'Is there?' To my surprise, Kenta looked angry. 'What, are we going to play adventurer here? What kind of life could we actually have? Rex, you're a software dev. Hanna, you work in *Marketing*. Those jobs don't exist here.'

Rex scratched the back of his head. 'I mean ... you say that like it's a bad thing.'

'Because it is a bad thing! We don't have homes here. We don't have jobs!'

'We could work it out,' said Rex. 'Just from our player skills alone, there's a lot we could do. I could do small jobs as a wizard to get myself started — scribing scrolls, casting wards, that sort of thing.'

Hanna grinned to one side. 'I'm a fucking bard, Ken. I busked all the time as a teenager in the streets of fucking Goosey — I think I can handle an actual fantasy tavern with no TV and no phones. I'm all the entertainment anyone is going to get.'

'And you think there won't be competition?'

'Oh, I know there will be.' Her grin turned sharp. 'I relish it.'

Kenta turned his gaze to me. I shrugged. 'You know me, Ken. I barely had a home or job on Earth. I can hardly do worse here. If nothing else, I can turn into a bunch of animals. That's gotta be useful for something.'

He looked to Pauline. 'P ... be serious ...'

Pauline folded her hands in her lap. 'I think we're all being serious, Ken. I get your concerns, I really do. But I don't think anyone isn't taking this seriously.'

'And you, then?' he said. 'You want to stay here, too?'

Pauline looked down at her lap. 'There's a chance the healers here will be able to treat my chronic pain,' she said. 'Medicine and healing magic aren't synonymous. They work in different ways, and have different cultures besides. I don't expect a cure.' She pressed her lips into a thin line. 'But if they had better painkillers, a treatment to reduce it, even a little ... I have to try.'

Everyone in the room went quiet. Kenta looked stunned by this response. And it would have been wrong to argue against her. Pauline had had impaired mobility for the whole time I'd known her — and from her own account, for nearly a decade now. Not only were doctors unhelpful, they were often actively harmful in their treatment of her. They would disparage her, gaslight her, and generally mistreat her rather than admit that they didn't know what the source of her pain was or what to do about it. I knew that in the years since her pain had first developed, she'd tried anything and everything in search of pain relief, no matter how wild or hokey.

But healing magic was real — as real as anything else here. Realer, in the sense that there was little that could have convinced me of the reality of this place than the pain of cutting myself followed by the weird itchy-warm feeling of the wound knitting together again in front of my eyes.

The idea that there could be an alternative to living with chronic pain for Pauline — that was a stronger reason to stay than any of us could claim.

'We don't all need to do the same thing,' I said. 'Some of us can go back, some of us can stay. But we all agree that we need to *find* a way back, right?' Nods and murmurs of agreement rippled around the room. 'Okay. Good. So we can still make plans.'

Kenta shook his head, lips pressing into a thin line, but didn't say anything more. I hoped we could all come to an understanding, whether we stayed or went back or some of both. I loved everyone in this group and couldn't bear the thought of hurting any of them. We'd already been through so much together; we would find a way to navigate this too.

'We might not need to choose one or the other,' Rex said. 'If we can get Vorugar to agree to it, the ideal situation would be having the option, right? So let's make that the top priority — a way to travel between Earth and Vanthis. Next priority is I guess ... money? Some way to get set up here, for those who want to?'

'Yeah,' I said. 'That sounds right to me.'

I tried not to think about how moving to Vanthis would be a lot more complicated than moving to another town, or even another country. How difficult communication would be. How confusing it would be to explain. Would I even be able to explain it? Or would my mother — my mother, who had believed anything and everything my whole life — find it too wild a thing? Would she think I'd gone mad — finally snapped from all the anxiety?

Not so long ago, I'd wondered the same thing, after all, and I was actually *living* all this ...

Rex leaned forward, hands on his knees. 'We also need to consider the very real possibility that Vorugar is spying on us, either magically or via proxy. I would, if I was in his position. Very generous of him to arrange lodging for us, for instance.'

'North did that,' I said.

'North is his assistant.'

It was true, and they'd seemed loyal. All the same, North had been very straightforward about their suspicions of us. They were abrasive and unpleasant, but didn't seem ... I don't know, underhanded? It was hard for me to picture them spying on us. It just didn't seem in character for them.

But maybe I was being naive. There was no reason to trust North any more than Vorugar himself.

'What about Ordeth?' said Hanna.

I frowned. 'What about him?' Talking about him behind his back made me uncomfortable; my eyes hovered on the door a moment, as he might return at any moment.

She rolled her eyes. 'He's been very helpful, hasn't he? With no real reason or motive. Pauline was attacked in *his* inn, which he casually abandoned to travel to Mihilit-dalath with a bunch of strangers. Does nobody else find that fucking suspicious?'

'Ordeth's not a spy,' said Kenta. The low intensity of his voice surprised me. It was the first thing he'd said since Pauline brought up healing as a possible treatment.

'How do you fucking know?' said Hanna.

'He's not.'

Pauline gave Kenta a concerned look. 'I like him too,' she said. 'But we should consider the possibility —'

'He's not, all right? God, listen to yourselves! This isn't a fucking tabletop game anymore. These are real people we're dealing with.' He stood up and strode out of the room. We heard the lock turn and click on one of the bedrooms.

For a moment, we were all quiet.

'What the fuck was that?' Hanna asked.

There were a lot of shrugs, but though I kept quiet, I wondered. Ordeth and Kenta had spent a lot of time together since we'd come here. Ordeth was kind and handsome and easily the kind of person Kenta might have feelings for. But even if I was wrong, they were surely becoming friends. And it was hard to think badly of your friends.

Then again, maybe that just meant Kenta knew him better than us. Personally, I didn't think Ordeth meant us any ill-will either.

'So, rooms,' said Hanna. 'You weren't here for it, but we just assumed we'd take the same room formation as before. We've got three rooms: that's one for me, Ken; one for Pauline, Arries, and Riya; and one for you and Rex. Ordeth's got his own room in the building next door. He said he wants to stay and see things through.' She made a face, like that only further proved his guilt. 'Is that cool, or does the fact that you've finally gotten over your "will they, won't they" bullshit changed things?'

'*Hanna.*' I glared at her, blushing from my head to my toes, burning with embarrassment and fury. My aura lit me up like a lantern.

Arries perked up. 'They did what? Are you two a thing now?' He beamed at Rex. 'Oh my god, my two best friends are dating! This is wonderful news! Can I hug you?' he stood up, opening his arms wide.

'No!' I said.

'Definitely not,' said Rex. His hood was up again and he was shrinking into his shoulders. I thought he might cringe so hard he'd planeshift back home.

'Don't be a creep.' Hanna said. 'Also, what the fuck? I thought I was your best friend?'

'You are,' he said happily, sitting back down. He seemed utterly unfazed by her calling him a creep, which I supposed as her best friend kind of made sense.

Pauline looked worried. 'We really could switch. I wouldn't mind if you needed to share with me, Rex —?'

'We're — it's —' Rex started to get flustered. I didn't think I'd ever seen him at a loss for words like this.

'We're fine,' I said sharply. 'Hanna, kindly shut up.'

Hanna whistled. 'Five minutes into a relationship and you're already —'

'Hanna.' Pauline's tone was severe.

Hanna shut up.

I stood up. 'Which room?'

Wordlessly, Pauline pointed to one of the doors on the left. I went in and Rex followed.

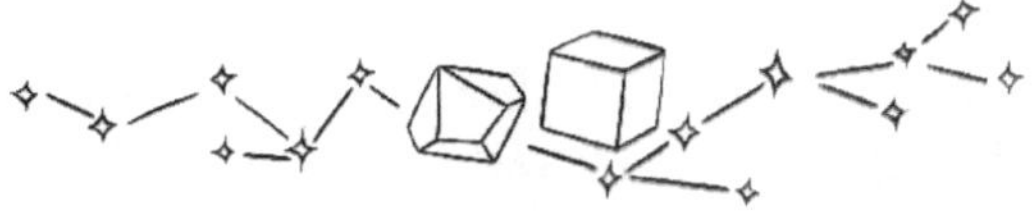

CHAPTER THIRTY-TWO

I closed the door behind us, then leaned against it and sank to the floor. 'Oh my god.'

Rex sat down on the bed, nodding. 'Yep.'

'Oh my god.'

'Mm-hm.' Now he was shaking his head. 'Well ... that was horrifying.'

The room was more opulent than in The Honeyhart. A broad queen-sized bed dominated the room. A body-length mirror with carved oak frame of naked figures stood in the corner. A wardrobe with matching carvings stood at the other end of the room. Two plush purple armchairs faced each other, and the bedside table sported a vase of purple-and-white flowers with stamens that sparkled faintly and I suspected would glow in the dark.

I stared past Rex, still trapped in the previous moment. 'I can't decide what was worse ... literally everything Hanna said or Arries wanting to *hug* us over it ...'

Rex put his head in his hands. 'Would it be bad if I screamed? I want to scream.'

'Would it be bad if I did?'

He threw me a blue cushion from the bed and took one for himself. Almost as one, we pressed our faces into them and started yelling.

It was, somehow, a lot more cathartic than just screaming on my own. Even with the cushion, which kind of ruined things. It worked better when I could be loud.

'What're we going to do now?' he asked. 'We're ... kind of trapped here? I didn't expect to be trapped here. I don't have any books with me except my spellbook, and it's not really the kind of escapism I'm looking for right now.'

I thumped my head back against the door. 'I know. It's what ... barely noon? It's not like it's time to sleep yet.'

We both fell quiet for a moment, reflecting on the situation we'd gotten ourselves into.

'Is this what being in a relationship is like?' Rex asked. 'Just ... constant embarrassment in the company of others?'

I thought back to my brief, disastrous forays into romance. 'Honestly? Mostly yes, in my experience.'

He raised his eyebrows. 'And you're very experienced in these things, are you?'

I smiled. 'Have I ever told you about the time I had my mum call me so I could bail on a date?'

'No?'

'Well ... that's because it wasn't one time. That's how dates went for me.' I shook my head. 'I properly dated two people. Neither for very long ... both wanted more from me than, uh ... than I was comfortable with.'

'Oh.' Rex looked abashed. 'I'm sorry.'

I shrugged, my cheeks heating again. I didn't want to talk about what a horrible datefriend I'd been with Rex. I wanted him to like me and this seemed like dangerous territory. 'Nothing to be sorry about; it is what it is.'

But he was still watching me expectantly. God, I was going to have to talk about this, wasn't I? 'I haven't dated much,' I told him. 'It's ... when I was younger, I didn't know I was ace and relationships seemed impossible to me. Then, when I did know, it only got more difficult. Most people weren't understanding. I had a girlfriend for about five months when I was 25. I was really into her and I thought we were serious but ... I guess she thought I would get over being ace, or something? She got frustrated with me. I had a boyfriend, too, for maybe three months. We didn't see a lot of each other and it ... turned out he was seeing other people without telling me, and that was why he was "okay" with me being ace.' That one still really hurt. I didn't let myself dwell on it. 'All other dating experiments have been a disaster from the get-go, mostly because I'm anxious but also because I'm just ... not that interested in people I don't already know, you know? What's exciting about spending time with a stranger.' I took a deep breath, trying to hold in the maelstrom of emotions swirling inside of me beneath what I'd said. A few short sentences couldn't explain how deeply I'd fallen for Gemma, or how broken I'd been when she broke up with me. Not because I wouldn't have sex, but because I was ace and would never 'want it' the way she would. I'd felt ... horribly broken. Unfixable, even. I'd been more steeled to it when the next relationship rolled around, but being cheated on hadn't occurred to me as a possibility.

Rex nodded. 'Well ... I'm demisexual.' I looked up sharply, and he laughed. 'Yeah, doesn't come up much in regular conversation but ... yeah. I had one serious relationship but I don't think either of us were that happy in it. I hadn't transitioned yet, and he was ... I don't know. Looking for someone a little more outgoing than me, with a lot fewer problems.' He smiled tightly. 'It was a long time ago. I haven't tried to date since. Never really found anyone who interested me, to be honest.'

It was an experience I understood very well. 'So I guess that's all on the table then.'

'All? Oh, definitely not. But it's a good place to start, I think. I didn't know you were ace — that's ... that's a relief to me. I was a little worried about expectations as well.'

I glanced at the bed. Lush silver-and-purple bedding with plump cushions and a pile of blankets at the foot. I smiled. 'Two asexuals were locked in a room, and There Was Only One Bed,' I said.

Rex snorted. 'That's a fanfic, thing, right? Are you about to be overwhelmed by my nearness and seduce me?' He paused. 'I

wouldn't mind being seduced. You know, a bit. Just maybe not
...'

'... not now?' I finished.

'... not now, yeah,' he agreed. 'Not with Hanna chortling evilly next door. Not with Arries waiting to congratulate us on our first kiss, probably.'

He scooted aside and pat the space beside him. 'Are we okay with this?' he asked. 'The only one bed thing? I can sleep on the floor.'

'I'm not going to make you sleep on the floor,' I said, slightly exasperated.

'Why not? I made you sleep on the sofa at The Honeyhart.'

'That's an entirely different level of sacrifice and you know it.'

'I'm trying to be the gentleman here.'

I smiled to one side. 'So am I, though.'

'I guess we'll both have to sleep on the floor then. What a pair of fools we make.'

He flopped back on the bed, knees still hooked over the edge. After a moment, I joined him, resting my hands on my belly. He turned his head to face me, his hair ruffled cutely against the duvet, locs askew, horns catching on the covers. The sight made me feel warm inside.

He smiled. 'You're glowing.'

I blushed.

'No — Tar, I mean you're actually glowing.' He raised a hand and conjured an illusory mirror, into which I could see myself surrounded by a shifting aura of pearlescent light, some of which showed through my skin, like I was a lantern lit by some astral glow. 'Oh god,' I said. 'Is this going to be a thing? Are you always going to know when I think you're cute?'

'You were thinking I'm cute?' His eyes sparked with a faint glow as he smiled to one side, revealing the tip of a fang.

God, was this really happening? Did I really get to be here, laying down next to the kindest, funniest person I'd ever met?

'Yeah, I was thinking that.' I was aware of my aura growing brighter around us.

He grinned and turned to stare up at the ceiling. 'I think you're cute too,' he said. 'I think it a lot, actually. Not in, like, a creepy way —'

'— I didn't think it was creepy, Rex.'

'Okay. Good.'

I sat up.

'Tar?'

I shook my head. 'I'll be honest, this is ... amazing. But it's also a bit overwhelming. And the whole only one bed thing ... I think we're on the same page here about what will and won't be happening tonight but it's still ...'

'... it's still lying in bed with one of my best friends, who I have been crushing on for the better part of a year, and that is A Whole Thing,' Rex said.

God, this aura thing was going to kill me. I was blushing with my whole body. *Fantastic.*

'Yep. Yes. Exactly that. But I was thinking ...'

'Yeah?'

I turned to face him, hooking my ankles over each other. 'Okay, hear me out. You can still polymorph today, right?'

Rex sat up, looking nervous. 'Is this where you reveal a very specific kink to me? Because I don't think I can —'

'CATS.' I closed my eyes. 'I was thinking we could both be cats. Then there would be a lot more room and also I just thought it might be, uh ... fun?'

'Fuck yes.' Before I could explain any further, he was sitting up and sketching runes in the air. 'Okay, so I'll get a few hours of this ...' Within moments, there was a flash of light and Rex was replaced by a lanky Siamese-like cat with dark, flame-edged eyes. He slow-blinked at me.

I laughed and immediately transformed as well, pulling energy to shrink and shift my muscles, bones, and skin. Within milliseconds I was on all fours on the bed, which was suddenly *much* larger and plusher. I cautiously sat down, flicking up my fluffy white tail to curl it around my paws. I slow-blinked back at him in a friendly greeting.

He sniffed toward me, and I politely returned the gesture. He approached slowly, and I waited. He boffed his cheek against mine, an intimate movement that lit up the nerves on one side of my body. Without meaning too, I started to purr, pleased that he felt that comfortable around me.

Except that I felt much more comfortable too. And far, far sleepier. So even though we'd transformed so that we'd have more room on the bed, we found ourselves curled up tightly against one another, my cheek against his side, his paws resting on my head, and we soon fell asleep.

CHAPTER THIRTY-THREE

His polymorph wore off after a few hours, and at first it took my sleepy cat-brain a few moments to really register that. As he sat up, I prrted, eyes still closed, and crawled into his lap, resting my chin on his knee. He scratched the back of my neck and I was already rumbling with a purr when I realised that we had more important things to do and I probably shouldn't spend all day as a cat demanding scritches.

I climbed off him and shifted back, and then we were both sitting on the bed, legs hanging off opposite sides, and he looked just as embarrassed as I felt. 'So ... that was nice?' I said.

He nodded. 'Very inventive use of the spell.'

I blushed at him, and he looked away.

'Let's not tell anyone we did it though.'

'Agreed.'

We stood up and he used magic to straighten our clothes, which were looking really rumpled in spite of the polymorphing. It was an odd experience; it felt like a small invisible hand was tugging on my tunic and patting my hair into place, but I knew Rex couldn't feel any sensation from it so it was more strange than embarrassing.

For a moment we just stared at each other. 'So is that, um, the kind of thing you expected from this relationship?' I asked.

He gave a startled laugh. 'When I was daydreaming back on Earth? No. But honestly I had no idea what to expect from a relationship with you except that whatever it would be, I knew I wanted it.' He took a step closer, until we were nearly chest-to-chest, and settled a hand at the base of my neck, so that he was almost cradling my chin. 'Is this okay?' he asked quietly. He looked nervous, but also his eyes glittered.

I nodded, suddenly tense and warm but for once not from fear. My eyes went to his mouth and I wondered if he would kiss me. To my surprise, I wanted him to. He was so close and so beautiful. Instead, he leaned his forehead against mine. 'You, you, you,' he whispered. His breath tickled my face like a warm breeze. Then he pulled away.

'Come on,' he said. 'I suppose we'd better face the others, given we're still trapped in a fantasy world and we have a little girl counting on us.'

I nodded, trying to centre myself. I was feeling less and less trapped in Vanthis with every passing moment. It was important that I reminded myself what was at stake — that this wasn't an adventure, that it was tearing Saanvi and Riya's family apart — tearing all of our families apart. Until we knew we had a safe way home, we couldn't get comfortable here.

I followed Rex. His hood was down, baring his gleaming ram's horns for all to see, and his tail danced behind him. But he was still Rex. Same face, same hair, same wonderful self. Even if we went back to Earth and couldn't come home, I would still have him. Still have all of these people I had come to love.

I needed to remember that. Because I didn't think for a second that I would be enjoying my time here without them.

As it happened, dinner arrived not long after we emerged. Ordeth joined us, eagerly pointing out his favourite dishes and explaining what each dish contained and how it tasted, as many of them looked completely alien to us. A plate of a pasta-like starchy food in a blue sauce that was vaguely luminous. A large bug that was steamed and buttered, and apparently was a sharing dish to be eaten much like lobster. A large, honeyed squash that was bright pink.

Unfamiliar food was a difficult thing for me to get through — and with eating in front of others added in, I was feeling too nauseated to risk trying anything. I smiled and shook my head whenever something was offered to me, claiming I wasn't hungry, though moments before my stomach had been twisted tight with need.

Arries was sitting beside me, however, and gave me a worried look. 'You ought to eat, Tar. Who knows what we've got to face next?'

When I only shook my head, he turned to Ordeth. The others were already beginning to tuck into their meals, murmuring in excitement about what was offered. 'Do you think they have any bread and cheese?' he asked. 'Just something simple?'

Ordeth raised his eyebrows. 'So you have bread and cheese in your world? Yes, they ought to. I'll go ask the kitchen.' He offered me a reassuring smile, but being noticed right now just made me want to sink under the table and hide.

'You could always go eat in your room?' Rex suggested, but I shook my head.

However, by the time Ordeth arrived with a plate of bread, cheese, and a fruity preserve that smelled fairly recognisably as some kind of chutney, I was feeling a little braver. The conversation had moved on and nobody seemed to make anything of me being a freaky eater. I cared neither for people fluttering over me nor people mocking me for making a big deal out of nothing. But nobody seemed to mind much at all, so as they tucked into their wild new dishes I had a bit of chutney and cheese and by the end of the meal, I was even feeling brave enough to try a cube of the strange squash, which had a vaguely ham-like flavour and was quite enjoyable.

Only Hanna and Arries tried the bug, everyone else's nerves quickly failing when a crunchy leg was placed on their plate. When Pauline blanched and decided to pass on her serving, Riya reached out with a small hand and transferred it to her plate, snapping it between her hands, as she'd seen Ordeth show the others, and then sucking out the fleshy inside. 'Popcorn flavour,' she said.

'Oh my god, it totally is!' Arries cried.

Riya finished it and placed the shell of the leg back on her plate. 'Did you try some?' she asked me.

'No, and I'm not going to.' I shuddered. 'That looks disgusting.'

'Hey!' Arries turned to frown at me. 'Don't be like that. Riya's doing really well!' He smiled at her, then frowned at me again. 'What if she learns to be a picky eater because of you?'

This seemed completely unfair. She wasn't my kid, as much as she was my responsibility right now. 'It's not picky to not want to eat bugs!'

'I don't want to be like Tar,' Riya said, which stung.

Arries shifted uncomfortably. 'Well ... Tar's really great, there's nothing *wrong* with being like Tar ...'

'Tar stays in the bedroom,' Riya said.

Hanna howled with laughter while Kenta chuckled. I glared across the table at them, where Hanna was now leaning against Kenta as if for support. 'Oh my god, Tar, that kid really has your number.'

Riya smiled at the laughter, then frowned. Her eyebrows pinched. 'That was funny? Was it mean funny?' She looked very concerned.

I shook my head. 'It was only funny because it was so true,' I said. 'It wasn't mean. Or at least, I am not upset.'

She processed this, mouth twisting from side to side. 'Okay. We're still friends?'

My heart ached a little. I wondered how many times Riya had said something that had gotten her in trouble in the past. It had happened to me a lot at her age. 'We're still friends, Riya. You're a good pal. You'd have to be very mean to change that, and you're never mean to me.'

Riya smiled. 'Good. I want to be friends. And I don't want to be mean. It's good you leave the bedroom now though.'

While Hanna and Kenta snickered, I smiled a little. 'I think so too. Maybe just this once.'

Not much else of import happened that day. Kenta and Arries swapped stories of friends from Earth, laughing. Ordeth joined us for most of the afternoon, asking us more about our world. Rex did his best to explain, with Riya sometimes adding odd details like 'you have to eat your vegetables before dessert' and 'there are very tall buildings made of glass where the business people work but a cat would still land on its feet if it jumped' which I really felt revealed more about Riya than they did about Earth, but Ordeth nodded seriously with her every suggestion and said, 'That's very helpful, thank you, Riya!' every time.

Feeling more comfortable after eating and with Hanna now out of the teasing mode of earlier, I mixed more easily with my friends. Kenta and Hanna argued about whether or not North was hot. Arries and Rex found a board game with small coin-like gems on a board of interlocking rings marked like thorny vines and were trying to make sense of the rules, which were in Astral which neither spoke. Eventually Ordeth came and explained.

I sat to one side with Pauline while that went on. 'Is this what beer and board games would be like?' I asked her.

She snorted. 'It's not far,' she said. 'Honestly, it's a little more chaotic, what with a small child and a stranger from another world here with us, but it's not far. We get out a bunch of games and either play one big game together or split into smaller groups. Normally a big game. Hanna gets a bit tipsy. Kenta doesn't drink, because he drives Arries home. Arries never votes on what game to play, because he's happy with whatever and doesn't want to upset anyone. Sometimes we order food if it runs late. It's nice.' She smiled. 'Without B&B and the game, my home wouldn't feel like home.'

'It isn't home if it isn't full to the brim with nerds?' I said, raising my eyebrows.

'Exactly.'

We fell into a comfortable silence. I thought about the game, about waiting all week for it. About messaging my theories to Rex, about planning what to do next with Arries while we grinded quests in A:RO. It had been such a huge part of my life, and these last few weeks it had fallen away. As magical as it was to be *living* the fantasy lives we'd played at for so long ... I missed sitting at Pauline's table. I missed rolling dice and flicking through my notes. I missed the easy camaraderie and the low stakes, as high as they'd felt at the time.

I sighed. 'Is it weird that I wish we could play *Kin* now?'

Out of the corner of my eye, I saw Pauline smile and duck her head. 'Not at all. I was thinking the same thing.' She ran her hands along the arms of her hexclimber. 'Maybe that's something to look forward to. You know, when we get home.'

When this was all over. 'Yeah,' I said quietly.

But I didn't really miss home. I missed the game. I missed carefree time with my friends.

If I was allowed to, I would choose to play right here, in this inn in a crystal city.

But I guess that was the thing; none of us knew whether it was okay to get our hopes up. None of us knew when this magical adventure would end.

Except that it *was* going to end. It had to.

Right?

At night, Rex and I became shy. We shared the bed, each sleeping at the opposite edge. But I could feel his warmth, and hear his breathing, and that was kind of thrilling. Even if it was no different than when we had slept side by side in the tent with all our friends crowded around us.

I didn't sleep much that night. All I could think about was Rex. I kept playing the moment in the park over and over again in my head. *'Sometimes the only clear thought I have is you, you, you.'*

When I woke, Rex was up and out of the room. I joined him around the seats with the others. Riya ran over to me and handed me a picture. It was me and her — or at least, I'm pretty sure it was, given the tufty hair and round shape of one of them

— and above it she'd copied Pauline's script. It said 'Friends aren't mean'.

'I love it,' I said. 'I don't think I have any pizza to give you this time, though.'

'Pauline already gave me a triangle coin,' Riya said. 'I'm going to buy a house.'

'Sounds like a reasonable investment,' I replied, and she nodded like she understood.

Ordeth arrived not long after, looking a little tousled from sleep. He smiled at Kenta, then took the seat next to Arries. 'There's a temple to Sunara here, it turns out ...' he began. Arries looked very interested.

Another knock at the door.

Everything stopped. I had a weird moment of clarity; we were a room of predominantly introverted geeks and we'd all frozen like deer in the headlights at the prospect of unexpectedly interacting with strangers.

Then Hanna gave us all a disgusted look. 'It's just the *door,*' she said. 'I swear to Christ ...'

Ordeth murmured, 'Christ ...?' as Hanna ripped the door open.

North scowled into the room. They were wearing a turquoise cravat embroidered with diamonds and another set of suit-like robes, these ones a pale green.

'Oh good,' they said. 'You're awake.' They looked down their nose at Hanna. 'The arch-mage requests another audience, and it has fallen to *me* to escort you. I trust you won't keep him waiting?'

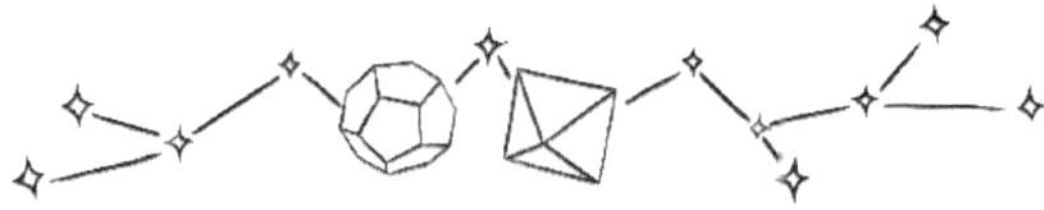

CHAPTER THIRTY-FOUR

We stood on the ground floor of the Verdigris Spire. North turned to face us, having said nothing more than the occasional aggrieved 'Hurry *up!*' the entire journey. 'Your two appointed leaders will accompany me to the arch-mage's suite. The rest of you will be shown to a waiting room as before to await further instruction.'

We all looked at each other. '... Nah,' said Hanna.

North's right eye twitched. 'I beg your pardon?'

'We'll stick together, thanks. The arch-mage wants something from *all* of us, right? Then he can damn well speak to all of us as well.'

North crossed their arms. 'That is out of the question —'

'Not to mention that Tar and Pauline are terrible delegates for the group,' said Kenta. 'Like no offense but P is pretty tight-lipped and Tar gets all squeaky and useless.'

I glared at Kenta. 'I am not *useless* —'

'Can I come?' Ordeth asked. Mileana curled around his feet.

'Of course you can come, you're our *guide,*' said Kenta.

North gritted their teeth. 'Unacceptable. The arch-mage was very clear that —'

'Let them up.' The air behind North's left shoulder shimmered as if in a heatwave, and Vorugar appeared. Today his hair was piled into one tight bun of braids. He looked regal in sweeping green robes with orange patterning.

North quickly spun and bowed. 'Arch-mage.'

'I mean it,' he said, his tone scolding, but with just a tinge of humour. 'I know you don't like it, Cly, but I can handle a rabble of lost extraplanars.'

'We prefer *party,* 'said Hanna.

Vorugar waved a dismissive hand. 'Party, then. If you would follow me?'

His greenhouse-like quarters, which had seemed so grand on our first visit, were significantly diminished by the pack of us crowding into the main room. The smallest of us squeezed onto one sofa — Hanna, Riya, and Rex. Pauline remained in her hexclimber, leaning on one arm with her chin in her hands. Ordeth and I sat on the other, while Kenta and Arries loomed behind us, fists resting on the back. I tried to keep Silky's attention with a treat, but she was soon drifting around the room, snorting at the plants. I looked between her and Vorugar, hoping he wouldn't protest.

Vorugar sat in his armchair, looking just as at-ease as he had meeting just me and Pauline, in spite of the jostling and twitching, in spite of the fast climbing temperature in the room. I wonder what he made of us — seven awkward otherworlders, one of them a child, and their friendly innkeeper guide. Two odd pets. Hardly hard-bitten adventurers he could make use of on some mad quest and hope to see results. But Vorugar looked around at us, smiling and nodding his head, and then sat forward, clasping his hands in front of him.

'So,' he said. 'I've had time to think about what will be required to send you back to your home plane. Without knowing your plane personally, the spell will be more difficult, but I believe I can shift you back given it will be returning you to your home plane. There are certain factors in accessing unknown planes, and having an anchor of some kind is one of them.' He steepled his fingers. 'However, the spell will be costly, both in material resources, time, and energy. I'm sure you would agree that such an undertaking would be unfair to expect for free ...?' He raised his eyebrows expectantly.

And there was the truth of it. No amount of friendly smiles and sympathetic tone could make up for the fact that he was uninterested in our plight except so far as it might benefit him.

Pauline shifted in her seat. 'Of course not,' she said. 'What do you expect in payment?'

Hanna muttered something I didn't catch, but I didn't think it was 'God bless.' She was looking at Vorugar like he was a stress ball she dearly wanted to squeeze.

Vorugar raised his hands, as if to ward off a blow. 'Payment? I am the arch-mage, not a common mercenary. It is more that what I will require for the spell is quite hard to get hold of. And of course, the trading of favours is only polite.'

Silky sniffed toward Mileana, who hissed and fuzzed her tail. I flinched and tried to wave her away.

'What do you *want?*' Kenta said, voice low.

Vorugar sighed. 'There is an anomaly just off the Umalthee Coast. Reports of a vast whirlpool which is stopping trade to and from Mihilit-dalath, as well as most of the region. I have scried it, and to my knowledge it appears to be caused by some kind of planar rift. As to where, and why, I couldn't say. What I *do* know is that planar rifts create deep veins of netheril, which is essential to portal spells as well as much of my work. I need the rift stabilised — no more whirlpool — in order to access it. So you see, you would not only be helping *me*, but also yourselves.' He smiled. 'Netheril is necessary for your return journey, and I get the sense you would be unwilling to sacrifice your ... dice ... to the cause.'

So he had been intending to pocket my d4. It wasn't a huge surprise, but the brazenness of it still rankled. Still, something about this situation didn't sit right. 'Why do you need us?' I asked. My voice was steady, my anger counter-acting my nerves. 'Surely you have plenty of staff who could do this — staff better trained and more suited to the job than us?'

'Certainly,' he said. 'But the political situation between the Spire and the Assembly is ... delicate, of late. We would be better served to have this handled by a third party, and avoid any political unpleasantness.'

The Assembly. The word rang a bell ... I think I remembered that Mistcurl was ruled by a council of sorts. Not based in Mihilit-dalath, where the Verdigris Spire was the dominant presence, but still technically the government of it. We'd just started to engage with world politics in the campaign when all ... this happened.

'What do you expect the challenges of this rift to be?' Arries asked. 'I know I have a big sword and shiny armour, but I've never actually killed anything.'

'Well then, this will be rather throwing you in at the deep end, won't it?' He cocked his head to one side. 'Though I would ask why you are all made up as adventurers and warriors if that is not your calling.'

There was a barb to his words, and I sensed it was more than sarcasm. Did he know there was more to our story than just ... falling in here from another plane? Did he suspect?

Because I knew Pauline was right that we shouldn't let on that this world had been a game to us. I couldn't imagine anyone taking kindly to that knowledge, not least Arch-mage Tellan Vorugar.

He had to wonder why we appeared to be planarkin, like most in this world. Why we spoke the language. He had to wonder why we were as at home here as we were.

Now, he shrugged and leaned back in his seat. 'Invaders from other planes are likely. Most probably beasts of some kind, but people are not out of the realms of possibility. I couldn't tell you whether they will be hostile, but that is usually the way even from known planes like the Glamouring and the Astralar. No world is without beasts, after all. If they can be reasoned with, then by all means reason with them. All that really concerns me is your objective — stabilising the plane.'

'Right,' said Hanna. 'And how do you expect us to do that? I'm a mean hand with a flute, mate, but I know nothing about planes and that level of magic.'

'Naturally, I wouldn't expect a common bard to know the intricacies of planar magic,' Vorugar said smoothly, words so without rancour that the dismissiveness was all the sharper. 'What I expect is for you to be able to follow simple instructions. We have a device which is designed for just such a situation. If you would, Cly?' He looked to his assistant.

North swirled their hands in the air in front of them, creating spinning trails of green light. A large metal disc materialised there and hung in the air for a few seconds before landing heavily on North's open palms.

'Arch-mage,' North said, offering the device to him with a bow.

'This is a Planar Resonance Device,' said Vorugar, turning the large disc over in his hands. 'Or PRD. It will, with the correct tuning, mimic the resonance of the planar rift and will interact with and stabilise said rift in the right location. It's of my own invention, of course.' I noticed North's expression flicker at that, but on closer inspection they only showed attentive interest. 'Have you an arcanist among you?'

Rex hesitated, then nodded.

'Then it'll be you who receives instruction on its use. It does require a modicum of arcane knowledge to operate, but is unlikely to be beyond your capabilities. Can you polymorph? Can you teleport?'

'Yes. And with a circle, yes.'

'Then this will be no trouble to you. If you wouldn't mind remaining behind after this meeting concludes, Cly will instruct you.'

Always trying to split us up. I gave Rex a worried look, but he said, 'Thank you, that would be helpful.'

Vorugar smiled again at that. 'So? If our business now is concluded, Cly will —'

'One more thing,' Pauline interrupted.

Irritation briefly flashed across Vorugar's face, to be smoothed away in another tolerant smile. 'Yes?'

'As you are probably aware, the Order of the Third Eye has been harassing us, and we have no idea how they found us or what their aims are. I'm concerned that we will encounter them again while on our quest.'

'Oh well! That's simple enough. Shall I have them killed?'

His casual words seemed to suck all the air from the room. For a moment I felt light-headed. I pressed my fingers to my temples and before I could stop the words from coming out, I said, 'I'm sorry, *what?*

'The Order of the Third Eye is a small cult. We've been keeping an eye on them, of course, to ensure they don't get their hands on true power or popularity, but if they've become violent or a nuisance, we have the means to remove them.' His eyes were fixed on my face. I stared resolutely at his neck instead. 'I'm quite willing to show that I am invested in you surviving this task, which you are so suspicious of. There's no reason this can't be a mutually beneficial situation.'

He folded his hands in his lap and turned his gaze on the others, expression expectant.

'We don't want anyone killed.' Pauline was firm. 'We just don't want them to be able to find us.'

'Well ... that's a little harder to accomplish, given I have no information as to how they found you in the first place. But perhaps this will suffice — Cly will provide you with a ring that prevents scrying and observation by magical means. That ought to make it significantly harder for you to be tracked. Is this agreeable?'

The same enchantment as the amulet we'd given Kenta. Pauline nodded, though I was still reeling from the casual assassination offer.

'Excellent.' Vorugar stood up and held out his hand to Pauline. After a hair's hesitation, Pauline shook it. 'Safe transportation to Earth,' Pauline said.

☆ 272 ☆

'In exchange for stabilising the Spiral Planar Rift off the Umalthee Coast,' Vorugar replied. And that, it seemed, was that.

☆ 273 ☆

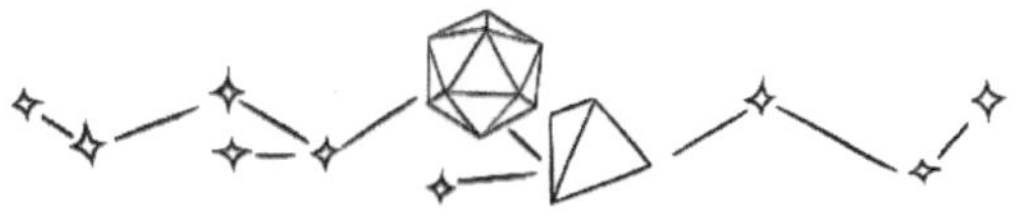

CHAPTER THIRTY-FIVE

From there, everything happened in a rush. North arranged travel supplies and safe passage to the coast. We would then take an airship out to the Spiral Planar Rift. It all sounded very real. I didn't like to think what it would mean, when we finally made it to the Rift. If we even made it that far — there had never been a journey in Pauline's campaign that hadn't led to us being attacked along the way.

But Pauline was taking it very calmly. 'We'll be able to handle this,' she assured me, when I voiced my anxiety. 'We'll find a way out of this. Remember my rule: there is always a non-violent option.'

'Unless there isn't,' I replied, exasperated. 'Sometimes the non-violent option is clearly the "get beaten up and thrown in prison" option, or the "most of your team gets murdered" option.'

'True,' she said. 'But that's the game, and this is real life.'

I wasn't sure that would improve the situation. Pauline set us level-appropriate quests. Vorugar knew nothing about us and I suspected wouldn't blink if we died in the attempt.

I was also suspicious of the Spiral Planar Rift. We'd never heard of anything on its scale during our games, and it was uncommon enough to take Vorugar's special interest. What were the odds that our sudden planeshift to Vanthis and the appearance of this extraplanar rift were unconnected? We talked it through that night, and it didn't sit well with any of us.

But we had vanishingly few options other than Vorugar's quest. So a few days later, we gathered at the southern edge of the city, just outside some rather strange stables from which I could hear all manner of loud and unfamiliar animal cries. North waited for us to stop fussing, their arms crossed. They looked utterly misplaced in this rural environment, with their pink cravat done up tight to the collar of their neatly pressed robes.

To my surprise, though, they didn't rush us. Which was good, because it was time to say goodbye to Ordeth.

'I wish I could go with you,' he said, shaking Hanna's hand. 'Help you get that little girl home, and see what you do next. But I'm even less an adventurer than you. As amazing as this journey has been, it's time I returned to The Honeyhart.'

'Thank you for all your help,' Pauline said. 'I don't know what we'd have done without you.'

'You'd have been fine, I expect,' he said. 'You've picked up this plane quickly enough, and you're a canny bunch.' He knelt down to get on Riya's level. 'And you've got a fine protector here in Riya.'

Riya put her tiny hand in his and shook it solemnly. He looked confused, but pleased.

'Thanks, big guy.' Arries wrapped him in a huge hug, startling a laugh from him. 'You've been a good friend.'

Ordeth blushed, his cheeks darkening. 'I don't know about that. I'm glad I got to meet you all.'

He and Rex exchanged friendly nods, and I smiled at him, though I didn't feel it. I liked Ordeth. He reminded me a little of Arries, in some ways — he was deeply kind, and I was sorry to see him go. Maybe our group had our own history before him, but then it had its own history before me too. It felt right that he'd been with us. 'Do you really have to go?' I asked, trying and failing to make it sound like a light joke. I'd asked before, I just hoped the answer had changed.

Ordeth looked sad and pleased. 'I don't see any other option. What would I do with you, anyway? I'm not some planeswalker. I barely know any magic after a few years of study. It's just — not my world.'

'It's not ours either,' I said, a little quietly.

'Well, you could have fooled me. You are all extremely competent. I don't think the arch-mage would have set you this task if he didn't think you could complete it.'

'I wouldn't be so sure,' Rex muttered, loud enough for me to catch it. I was more than inclined to agree.

'You could stay on the airship, maybe?' I said. 'Watch Riya and Silky?'

The sealorn bleated loudly at her name and started to tug at my tunic with her teeth.

Ordeth paused. 'You trust me with them?' He said it seriously, and I knew he was thinking about my insistence that Riya remained with a member of our party at all times.

I looked at Riya. 'Would you be willing to hang out with just Ordeth for a few hours on an airship?'

Riya shrugged. 'You make good salad,' she said.

Ordeth smiled. 'I do.'

'Will you call the bees?'

'I don't know if there will be any bees,' he said honestly. 'But if there are, I'll call them.'

Riya turned to me and nodded.

'We can pay you for your time,' I said. I looked at Arries. 'We can pay him for his time?'

'We can,' he said. 'We're okay on funds.'

Ordeth turned to Kenta. He shrugged and half-smiled. 'What do you think?'

Kenta cleared his throat. 'You should come.' The words were uncharacteristically gruff. 'I'd — we'd like you to come.'

They studied each other a moment, Kenta not quite able to meet Ordeth's eyes. 'Okay,' he said. 'All right. I'll come.'

I nearly wilted with relief. It wasn't just that I liked Ordeth and didn't think any of us were ready to say goodbye yet — I had really, genuinely been worried about bringing Riya into the Spiral Planar Rift.

As Arries went in for another hug, North cleared their throat. 'If you're all quite finished?' They sniffed and gestured toward the stables.

A few moments later, we were standing in a broad yard with a floor of compact sand and an iron fence lined with hedges. Two tall mounting blocks stood to one side. A blue dragon-like feykin with full draconic muzzle fussed around a moment before herding us into one corner. 'This is your first time?' she asked.

We all made sounds of assent.

'Then just remember to be calm. These are tame creatures, whatever you might think of them. Feykin, just like anyone might be.' A few moments later she led in three large beasts. I sucked in my breath.

I had been expecting ethereal riding bats, like the one Vorugar had dismounted on the balcony of his tower. But these creatures weren't ghostly shadow things, such as were found in the void. They reminded me a little of the chimeras of myth, except they had great goat-like heads with thick lion's manes, scorpion stingers instead of a snake, powerful hind-legs like a big cat, and forelegs that were just ... scythes. Just sharp mantis-like scythes. They shuffled enormous feathered wings, each clawed like a bat's. Their eyes glowed green with eerie light.

I shook my head. Whatever Vorugar wanted, he couldn't expect us to ride these things.

The stablemaster pat the one she was leading. It baaed.

'They can take up to three, ideally two if you want to make good pace,' the stablemaster said. 'This 'un is Fora, and that's Lekka and Mando. You'd be hard-pressed to find a sturdier flying mount than a pankalar, and my pankalars are the best in Mistcurl. You can feed 'em, if you like. Got some fruit here for you.' One of them had a large cage strapped to its back that I suspected was for Silky.

I mouthed the word 'pankalar' to myself, digging in my memory for any mention of them in Pauline's campaign.

Arries must have noticed my anxiety, because he leaned over and murmured, 'Pankalar — vampire goats from the fey plane. No — not vampires like that. They drink juice, primarily. Sometimes a bit of fruit pulp. P told us they're a very common mount in Mistembra, and not uncommon in Vanthis in general. The claws are for cutting fruit from trees and carrying them back to their nests.'

'They're terrifying!' I said.

Arries shrugged. 'They're big bird goats. What's so scary?'

I took a steadying breath. 'Juice. Okay. So why are they called vampire goats?'

'Oh, well they *also* drink blood ...'

Riya walked up, holding an orange in her hand.

'Riya!' I went to lunge for her, but Arries put an arm across my chest, holding me back.

The stablemaster smiled. 'That's it. Flat palm.'

The pankalar looked down at her, snorting. It opened its uncanny, not-quite-a-goat mouth, baring extremely un-goat-like fangs. A long tongue came out and pierced the orange, drinking it down to a shrivelled peel in moments.

Riya giggled. 'Can I pet it?'

The stablemaster encouraged her forward. She pat the enormous creature's neck. To my surprise, it leaned into the touch, like a cat enjoying a scratch.

I was tight with tension. But the pankalar seemed completely disinclined to do any harm at all to Riya, or to anyone else. One of the others bustled forward and nudged Riya's shoulder with its muzzle. She started petting it as well.

'You're the witch, Tar.' Kenta raised his eyebrows at me. 'Animals are supposed to be *your* thing.'

'That's not exactly a housecat,' I said acidly. 'Also, I know very little about animals. As evidenced by *this.*' I tried to yank my tunic free from Silky's grasp. She growled and hung on tighter.

'You're not exactly a house *human,*' he replied. 'You can handle the magical murder goat.'

The stablemaster divided us up into triplets by size. Rex and I were grouped together, but Hanna switched with him. 'Let's not put all the whacko nervous people in one place,' Hanna said.

And as irritating as that was, I had to agree. Rex was looking more than a little anxious himself.

So I was sorted with Hanna and Pauline. Rex and Riya went with Arries. Kenta and Ordeth had the last to themselves, along with Pauline's hexclimber and Silky's cage. I followed Hanna to the pankalar; the only thing keeping me stable was Pauline's grip on my arm. 'Are you going to be okay?' I asked. 'Riding the pankalar, I mean?' It didn't look suited to curling up, and I doubted it would be a smooth ride.

'I'll be fine,' she said. She smiled. 'Besides. The pain will almost be worth it to ride an actual pankalar.'

First, we had to trick Silky into the cage. Though she wasn't frightened of the pankalar, which paid her no mind at all, she was wary of getting close to them. Rex and Ordeth both had pets, and said there was nothing for it but to give her time to get used to them and to offer her treats and praise. When we eventually coaxed her into the box (the stablemaster thankfully had some raw meat available) she started keening a long, low, grating cry that made me wince.

'Sorry, Silky.' I murmured. I tried to reach through the bars to pet her, but she snapped at me. I gave her space.

'Will Mileana be okay?' I asked Ordeth of his cat.

He smiled. 'She'll be fine. She's ... she can be very calm. She'll ride in my lap without trouble.'

After that, Hanna and Pauline mounted up first, ascending a mounting block to settle comfortably on the saddle between the great beast's enormous wings.

I slowly climbed the steps of the mounting block. The pankalar shifted, turning its glowing goat-eyes my way. Somehow they were even worse than a regular goat's eyes, which were already rather disconcerting. It opened its too-long mouth and bared its long fangs and whip-like tongue in what I hoped was a yawn and not a warning.

I tried to remember everything I'd ever heard about befriending animals. As a kid, I'd always daydreamed about having a pet of my own, but between my mother's allergies and me lodging in someone else's house, the opportunity had never arisen. I'd read everything I could get my hands on about animal care and how to befriend various species. The only constants were: not too much eye contact, give them space, be gentle. That all sounded easy enough but you were also supposed to project calmness and I was, at any given time, about one panic away from a full body cramp.

I held out my hand to the pankalar. It sniffed it, its tongue poking out to taste the air, then bumped my hand with the top of its head. I scritched it between its goat ears, its eyes slitting like a happy cat. It shuffled its feet in delight, scorpion tail swinging with the pleased wiggle of its bum.

'Lekka likes you,' the stablemaster said. 'Go on. Climb on up. If you're nervous, you should sit in front. Got a better grip there, plus your friends can steady you.'

Pauline and Hanna wiggled back to make room for me. 'It'll be fine, Tar. It's actually quite comfortable!'

I used the mounting block to swing a leg over and hop onto its broad back. The saddle was well padded, and there were little straps to hook around my legs, which made me feel a lot more stable. Pauline said, 'Okay if I hold onto you?'

'Please do,' I replied. For once, human contact was welcome rather than terrifying. I wanted to be as fixed in place as I could possibly be.

The other pankalars started to wander about, their gaits strangely crawly on the ground thanks to their fore-scythes. One of the rider groups was delighted — Riya was cheering, Arries was laughing, and even Rex had a grin. The other, with Kenta and Ordeth, looked a little more tense. Kenta had his arms wrapped around Ordeth's waist, and had buried his face in the feykin's shoulder.

As they lined up, our pankalar lurched into motion, swaying into place behind the others with no signal or encouragement from us.

Nervously, I called to the stablemaster, 'So how do we steer them?'

The stablemaster grinned, baring her many long, pointed teeth. 'You don't!' She raised a flag striped purple and green. The pankalars trumpeted their baas to the sky, then bounded forward in three awkward hops before unfolding their wings and whooshing up into the air.

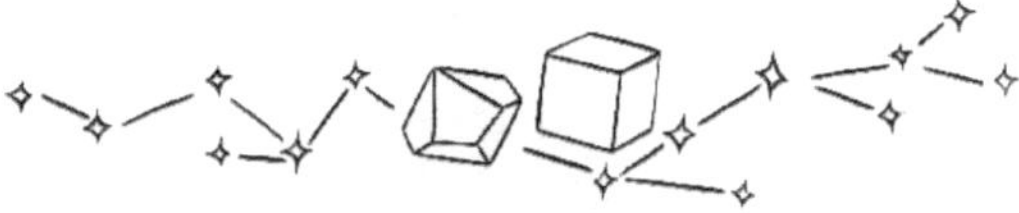

CHAPTER THIRTY-SIX

My stomach dropped. A scream caught in my chest; the only thing holding it back was the choking tension I felt. Behind me, Hanna whooped. I could hear cheering from Arries' pankalar ahead.

Each beat of the pankalar's wings brushed my legs, giving me the uncomfortable feeling that I was about to be shoved off. I yelped at a particularly strong stroke, but the saddle straps had me firmly fixed in place.

'I think I'm going to be sick,' Pauline said. I glanced back at her; her skin was drawn and she looked decidedly uncomfortable, the enthusiasm of earlier fallen away along with the ground.

'How're the vibrations, P?' Hanna called from the back.

'Terrible!' she replied. 'But that's not why I feel sick.'

'How about you, Tar?'

'No talk please.' I felt like keeping my mouth closed as much as possible was a good idea. God, how many bugs were we flying through? Would I get bugs in my hair? In my teeth?!

Hanna's laugh was snatched away in the rushing wind.

But as stressed as I was, there really didn't seem to be swarms of bugs flying into my face. Nor did the awful lurch in my stomach ever lead to us being yeeted off the pankalar's back. As Lekka reached its preferred height, it began to glide, only occasionally beating its wings to keep us aloft. Sometimes, the pankalars baaed to each other as if checking in.

I grew more used to the bob and sway of pankalar flight, and even leaned forward to scratch Lekka's neck. The hair was thick and coarse, but it seemed to appreciate it, making low, contented 'mlep!' sounds while I pet it.

Maybe they weren't so bad, really. After all, pigs were omnivores, and you'd be hard-pressed to find sweeter animals than them. And even fearsome carnivores like cats were incredibly sweet and caring animals, according to Rex.

The world continued to rush past. Finally, I allowed myself to do the unthinkable: I looked down. For a moment, the world spun, and I felt like I would tip over and fall from the saddle, never mind the straps holding me in place. But gradually, the world righted. And as it did, I grew breathless for another reason.

Mistcurl was beautiful, laid out below us like a minutely detailed painting. Mist-shrouded mushroom fields, their glow visible even under the broad sun. The distant, craggy mountains of Stitchfall, spiked and snaking like a dragon's spine. The thick trees and mushroom caps of Turovellis, with their colourful plumage, like splashes of paint on a canvas. And swelling ahead in an expanse of gorgeous turquoise, the Umalthee Coast and Yssamber Ocean.

The speed was incredible, though the air felt like little more than rushing wind. I wondered whether the saddles were enchanted to protect us, or whether that was part of the nature of the pankalars themselves.

As I grew more confident, I leaned back to check on Pauline. She took my hand and gripped it tightly, her other hand resting on Hanna's arms, which were looped around her shoulders. Hanna and I kept up a conversation as best as we could, trying to take Pauline's mind off the ground far below.

By the time we hit the coast proper, the sun had already set. The air was chill, the ground below a mass of shadow speckled with distant mushroom glow. The beas of the pankalars echoed spookily in the darkness, and the pankalars had begun to descend, so that their scythes almost brushed the canopy.

Then we broke out onto a pebbled coast that glittered in the moonlight. A small settlement of a handful of buildings was built there, and a tall tower with a docked airship. It looked like a traditional galleon, but instead of masts and sails, it had a series of translucent wings stretching out to either side. The wood was splashed with a blue and grey paint, giving it the splotchy impression of a rainy sky.

The pankalars landed in a stableyard, sending up clouds of dust and baaing in what was clearly a call for dinner. Stablehands came out, and took them by the harness, leading them to mounting blocks and helping us get unstrapped and dismounted.

I winced as I dismounted. Hours of riding on the pankalar's broad back had bruised my thighs, not to mention that my legs were cramped from being strapped in place for so long. Each step was wobbly and sharp with pins-and-needles. Kenta brought Pauline her hexclimber, but she was taking time to stretch out her limbs as well, each movement slow and careful.

Rex found me. He caught my eye, then touched my elbow with two fingertips. 'You okay?' he asked.

I nodded, turning my head to hide my blush, though my aura gave it away anyway. There was something about having Rex's full attention that was overwhelming and wonderful at the same time. 'I'm fine,' I said. 'Heights are one of the few things that don't terrify me. And it turns out pankalars are just big flying sheep. Who knew?'

Rex smiled. 'Who knew,' he echoed. Wordlessly, he offered me his hand. I took it, and felt him swipe his thumb over mine as our fingers threaded.

'How did you find it?' I asked.

His smile turned mischievous. 'Dream come true,' he said. 'Soaring through the air on the back of a mythical beast with my friends all yelling and cheering around me. I mean ... it was terrifying, but in a good way.' He paused. 'That's not something I thought I'd ever say ...'

'Maybe we should ride together, on the way back.'

He turned to look at me, one side of his mouth quirking up. 'I'd like that a lot,' he said. 'I'd like it even better if we could try it sometime without our friends around.'

I looked down.

Rex exhaled perceptibly. 'Are you blushing? Oh, Tar ...'

'Shut up,' I said trying to turn away.

'You're so red right now!' He pulled me toward him, and I willingly went, burying my face in his shoulder.

'I kind of hate you right now,' I said.

He chuckled. 'No, you don't.'

I muttered into his shoulder, 'You don't know anything.'

His hands settled gently around my shoulders. 'You're really cute, Tar.'

When I pulled away, Kenta was staring at us. 'So that's never going to stop being weird, huh?'

'Ken!' I could feel myself blushing all over again. I walked away rather than face his stare. 'I need to get Silky.'

The sealorn burst from the cage the moment I released the latch. She blared a long, joyous cry, spinning loops in the air, chased by sparkling light. I smiled, my heart a little lighter for seeing her excitement. 'Hey, Silky,' I said, walking over to her with my hand outstretched. She flipped one more time, then watched me suspiciously. Something about her stillness made me worried she was about to bite, and I lowered my hand. 'Silky?'

Slowly, she turned in the air and plopped onto the ground, putting her back to me.

Rex came up beside me, crossing his arms. 'Uh-oh,' he said. 'You're getting the ice treatment.'

Worry pinched. 'She's angry at me?'

'You put her in a cage and ignored her for hours,' he said. 'She won't understand why. She's letting you know that she didn't like that.'

I trusted Rex's experience. He treated his cat like a human with slightly different physical needs, and his cat adored him for it.

And honestly ... if someone I trusted had locked me in a cage for hours, I wouldn't be feeling very charitable toward them either.

'Silky?'

She remained resolutely turned away from me, though her ear fins twitched at the sound of her name.

'Damn.' I looked to Rex. 'Should I give her treats?'

He shook his head. 'This is too important for treats. You need to apologise to her and show her that you're still friends and won't put her in a cage again any time soon. Then, if she accepts that: treats.'

That made a kind of sense.

I crouched down a few steps behind her, gravel crunching beneath my feet. 'I'm sorry I put you in a cage,' I said, as sweetly and sympathetically as I could. 'You're the prettiest, meanest, most wonderful sealorn, and I didn't mean to stress you out.' Another ear twitch; she half-turned her head toward me.

'You're so lovely, Silky,' I said. 'You're so clever and brilliant. I promise I only put you in the cage because I had to, and that I will never leave you alone in a cage like that again.'

She was properly looking at me now, though her back was still turned.

I smiled encouragingly. 'Hi, Silky! I'm so glad you want to look at me again. If you want to bite me, I understand.'

She made a little chuffing sound and started to bounce toward me, her round body moving like a beach ball. When she got close, I held out my hands palm-up for her to sniff.

Her head fin lifted. She sniffed them, nostrils flaring, then gave my finger an experimental nip. 'Ouch!' I said, shaking out my hand. 'Okay, I deserved that.'

She chuckled, a funny, whispery sort of bark, and shuffled forward until she could boff her head against my arm. I gave her a good fuss, noting that she'd messed in her crate and needed a clean. Rex and I flagged down a stablehand for bathing supplies. They seemed amused by our commitment to what was essentially a chicken in this culture, but were happy to help.

While we scrubbed her, Silky spun and chuffed and flipped her fins at us, and only bit us lightly a few times in what was clearly affection.

After, the stablehands directed us up the tower to the airship dock. It was a bare tower with a tight spiral staircase interrupted only by crates of supplies and tools on each floor. The top was open to the night air, lit by brightly-coloured lanterns strung along the rails. A wide gang plank provided access to the ship, which even now a tall deer-centaur-like feykin was striding across, hooves clip-clopping against the wood.

'You're the ones Arch-mage Vorugar sent, are you not?' they said. Their silver skin was almost luminous in the moonlight, a clear astralkin trait. Their outfit was bright but practical — blue leather gauntlets and leg-guards over a green tunic patterned with leaves. A long, raccoon-like tail swished behind them in gentle anticipation.

They bowed to us as a group, hand twisting over their heart, a gesture we returned in various states of surprise. 'You made good time, but then pankalars are nothing if not quick. Still, bit too ... toothy ... for my liking.' They grinned. 'I'm Nahla, quartermaster of the *Singing Drake*. It's an old ship but a good-un — actually, legends say it was a dragon themself that designed it for a human mate. No idea whether it's true, but it's a beauteous ship all the same. Follow me, if you would?'

I was nearly as nervous stepping onto the gangplank as I was about mounting the pankalar, especially when I saw the way it bounced and sprang under Nahla's steps. But it took Arries and Kenta's weight well enough, and after checking in with me, Rex led me across it and onto the sleek airship.

I could believe *The Singing Drake* had been designed by dragons, or at least in love of them. Up close, the carving of the wood hull resembled overlapping feathers. The wings, though stretched with a shimmering translucent material that reminded me at least in part of the crystal of Mihilit-dalath, were spread out to either side of the ship in a way that made me think of a creature basking in the sun. At a guess, they were in some way solar-powered, and that was why they shimmered dully in the moonlight and were spread out so. I'd always imagined the airships in this world to have more bat-like wings, but these wings resembled long, filamented feathers, more artistic than a true wing would be, but nonetheless recognisable.

The deck itself looked like every image of an old ship I'd ever seen. Wood planks, neat railings, lengths of rope coiled at the sides. There was a scattering of crates that looked like they were in the process of being carried belowdecks — there was an obvious staircase down, in front of two narrow cabins at the back of the ship, below an honest-to-god spoked wheel at the helm. It had a lovely steel filigree in places, making the whole thing look as much a piece of art as a functional transport, in spite or even because of how weathered it was.

'The captain's away at the moment. That's Captain Eltan Bol to you. She'll be back before we set off,' said Nahla as we crowded onto the deck. 'We've got a room of hammocks to spare, though you'll need to stack yourselves like books if you don't mind. North sent us the coordinates and we've circled the ... big whirlpool thingy ... more than once, in the few months since it appeared, but the captain will talk you through that. Right now, I'd just like to get you settled and show you what to expect during your journey with us.'

'What to expect' was two cramped but not horribly unpleasant rooms with four hammocks apiece below decks. Each had a porthole window out into the world which, small though they were, I felt certain would be plenty breathtaking. We were told we had the run of the deck day or night, provided we gave the crew their space and didn't interfere with their work.

The crew itself was small and seemed friendly enough — though fortunately not terribly interested in us. I kept to the back of the group, not quite willing to introduce myself personally, though I could almost *feel* Arries' desperation to get to know everyone. There wasn't much else to see — a small mess hall with three tables, an enchanted privvy and washroom. Overall it was a lot more civilised than anything I would have imagined, and I could see how these people had chosen to make their lives and livelihood here.

'We'll take off when the captain returns,' Nahla advised us. 'So stay on the ship. You're welcome to go right to bed, or to wander the deck as you please. I'm sure you're plenty tired after a day on pankalar-back.'

'How long will the trip be?' Kenta asked.

Nahla's head swayed side to side. 'Mm ... a handful of hours, maybe the whole night. We've instructions to remain there for up to two full days while you conclude the arch-mage's business.'

A few days. It seemed like too much. A staggering amount of time to be left in a strange vortex in a world we didn't belong to. But then Vorguar had a much better idea of what to expect out there than we did. Or maybe two days was just to make sure it was foolproof, and we didn't miss our ride home.

Later, when our party had retired to bed, Hanna and I still stood on the deck of the ship, watching the dark waves roll past far below. I leaned against the railings; Hanna had pushed over a crate to do the same. She had her chin resting on her arms, her goat ears twitching with the breeze. It struck me that this was the most relaxed I'd ever seen Hanna. At the table, she was always poised to fight. Honestly, from her messages in chat, it seemed like maybe she was *always* poised to fight.

She glanced at me now. 'What're you thinking?'

'That we're more alike than I realised,' I said. Fight or flight, that was us.

She snorted. 'Don't say that,' she said, but there was no venom in it.

Silence spread between us, something I was unused to with Hanna, but it was comfortable, somehow. I enjoyed it. 'Have we ever been quiet like this before?'

Hanna shrugged. 'I'm plenty quiet.'

'You're always yelling.'

She turned to raise her eyebrows at me. 'You have *never* heard me yell,' she said. 'Count yourself lucky.'

That seemed possible. My mum had often observed that I was oversensitive to tone and volume in conversation.

'And you're always ... saying things.'

Hanna shrugged. 'Maybe we've become better friends.'

I smiled. 'Or maybe you've spent so much time with me these last weeks that you've run out of things to say.'

'A fucking *mouth* on this one,' Hanna said, shaking her head. 'Jesus, you turn into *one* dinosaur and suddenly you're a tough guy.'

We both paused.

'... it's a fucking awesome dinosaur though.'

'It has *feathers,*' I agreed.

'I shoulda taken a few levels in witch.'

Large, winged shadows chased the horizon. I wondered if they were pankalars, or some other flying beast from Pauline's mind. If that was even how any of this worked.

'Do you want to go back?' she asked me suddenly. 'When we stabilise the portal, or whatever the fuck Vorugar said. Do you want to go back?'

I took a shuddering breath. 'I want to see my mum,' I said. 'I want to get Riya home, and say goodbye to Saanvi.'

'But do you want to go *back,*' she said. She was staring at me, I realised. I could feel her gaze like heat on my cheek. I resisted the urge to turn away, and only stared out at the sea and sky, two different shades of black.

'No,' I whispered to the night air.

'Me either,' she murmured. She sounded ... frustrated? I looked at her hands as she straightened; they gripped the rail too tightly. 'Me either.'

CHAPTER THIRTY-SEVEN

I woke to a gently swaying hammock and the ocean rolling past my window. Silky had squeezed into the hammock beside me, and didn't budge even when I tipped the hammock and rolled out. There was a loud buzzing in the air, like white noise. I felt it drumming into my brain.

When I joined the mess, it was to discover the rest of the group already up, except Hanna. 'Get yourself some rice and beans,' said Arries. 'Maybe some veggies as well — Meira did an excellent job on the food, by the way —' he smiled at one of the crew members, who looked pleased.

The ship's mess was surprisingly civilised, comprised of a few long tables and benches, nailed to the floor. The tables were of a solid, varnished wood, though gnarled with age, and the surfaces were scattered with meals in various stages of completion. Ordeth's cat sat at the end of a table, eating something that looked a bit like kibble.

'Are we in a rush?'

My friends exchanged looks. 'We've arrived.'

My mouth popped open. 'And nobody told me?!'

'You needed the rest,' said Pauline. 'Nobody is going in there exhausted.'

I jiggled my legs, tapping out a fast rhythm on the floor.

'Here,' said Rex, sliding a colourful bowl in front of me. The beans and sauce were both pink, though the vegetables looked a little more familiar with some purple cauliflower and chickpeas. This looked a damn sight better than historical ship fare, and I picked up the spoon and started digging in. It smelled spicy and tingled pleasantly on my tongue with a peppery flavour.

Hanna shuffled in, zombie-like, and grunted something unintelligible. Pauline rolled her eyes. 'Is there any coffee here, by chance?'

About an hour later, we gathered on the deck to stare down into Vorugar's Spiral Planar Rift. It was a whirlpool the size of a small village, oddly hollow in the centre and shot through with sparkling light. The roar of it was thunderous. I could feel it vibrating up through the planks of the ship and right through my bones. I covered my ears with my hands, though that hardly helped matters. Beside me, Rex did the same.

Pauline shouted something, lost in the roar. Someone else replied: again, lost.

Arries' hands fluttered in the air in a way I recognised as sign language, though I didn't get what he was saying, and it looked like nobody else did either. He actually rolled his eyes when nobody responded, a level of sarcasm I had never expected from him. I would have smiled if I wasn't being assaulted by sound.

Rex started sketching runes in the air, lips moving though I couldn't hear the words. A moment later the area around us flashed with arcane light; the noise from the whirlpool became muted and muffled, as if it had been thrown under a thick blanket. 'All right,' Rex said. 'The next time anyone mocks me for my spell choices, I'm bringing up this moment.'

Hanna opened her mouth, then closed it. She wanted to argue, I was sure, but it was so clearly not the time.

Personally, for all it was sometimes inconvenient in the *game*, I was very glad Rex had taken more practical spells instead of things that threw acid or fireballs. I had yet to meet anything I wanted to fireball, but we'd been very glad of the packbeast, mirror, and muffle spells.

'So what's the plan?' Arries asked. 'Do we just ... jump in?'

'I am *not* jumping in,' I said. The thought of being sucked into those spinning waves was too much. 'Have you seen the size of that thing? We'll drown!'

'Is it even water?' Kenta said. 'It looks ... kinda off. I don't know, P, what do you think?'

Hanna brightened. 'Yeah! Do the glowy eye thing!'

Pauline crossed her arms. 'I can't "do the glowy eye thing". I don't know what this is or how to study it. I'm not Vanthian Wikipedia.'

'Hey. I'm sorry. It's ... a lot of pressure,' said Hanna.

Pauline smiled tightly, but I sensed she was forgiven.

'I think our options are fly and swim,' said Rex. 'There's enough room there for a winged creature to make it down the centre.' He glanced at me. 'Tar and I could become giant birds.'

Kenta frowned. 'That's some heavy magic, right off the bat.'

'Better we spend some spells than we drown at the first, uh, hurdle,' Rex replied.

Pauline looked down at the swirling mass that was the planar rift. 'We're on a time limit, and we have no idea how large this job might be. Rex is right — let's fly down.'

For a moment, I tried to reach for my magic but my body wouldn't move. I felt frozen by the fear of it all — the thunderous sound, which only Rex's spell was keeping at bay. The enormity of the whirlpool. The eerie light creating an opaque void at the centre of it.

I knew that whatever we were about to face, it wouldn't be easy. That wasn't how things worked in this world. That certainly wasn't why the arch-mage hadn't done this himself. And I was worried what it would mean for my friends.

I felt a light tap-tap at my elbow. Riya was standing there, tugging my arm. 'Yes?' I asked, for a moment torn from my mental spiral.

'Can I come?' she asked.

I glanced at Ordeth, who waited at the other end of the deck. He looked anxious himself, though he wasn't jumping into a giant whirlpool that was also a planar rift. Was he worried about us, I wondered? Or perhaps anxious about being left alone with a child from another world.

'You can't come,' I said to Riya. I didn't want to panic her, so I searched for the right words. 'It's not for kids, what we're doing. It's not safe for kids.'

She considered me. 'Is it safe for grown-ups?' she asked.

The very question I was trying to avoid.

'... No,' I said. I wasn't going to lie to her about this. I had no idea what was about to happen. 'I don't think it is. But we have to do it if we want to get you home to Saanvi.'

Her face scrunched up. For a moment, I thought she was going to cry. 'Come back safe, please.'

'I'll try,' I said.

Then she did something she'd never done before. She hugged me, little head pressed against my hip, bony arms digging into my legs. It was a quick thing, and then she pulled away. She backed up, watching us go. Ordeth came to kneel beside her, but she had eyes only for us.

My chest felt tight again, with a new kind of anxiety. Kids were a special kind of anxiety, I guess. Because now, if we failed, I'd be letting her down. And I didn't know if I could bear that.

We'd better not fail, then.

Silky hadn't emerged from below decks, which made things easier, at least. I didn't want to cage her again if I could avoid it. 'Watch my sealorn?' I asked Ordeth.

'Of course,' he said. 'We'll be fine here. the four of us, right?' he asked Riya.

Riya nodded, slowly.

I looked to Rex, who inclined his head to me, as if we were about to dance and not turn into giant beasts.

'Looks a bit wet down there,' I said. 'Feathers are probably not going to cut it.'

He raised his eyebrows. 'What did you have in mind?'

I took a deep breath and drew three runes. There was no ground to draw power from, but the air around us was moist and full of salt and energy, and I pulled power from it easily. My body glowed and swelled, shifting into powerful leather wings with clawed tips, thick lizard-like legs, and a long thrashing tail. A pearlescent wyvern with an astral glow, a bat-dragon. Dragons in Vanthis were feathered as well as scaled, but there were still dragon-like things that were mostly scaled like our images of dragons back home.

I clawed the deck with my massive wings and turned my long serpentine neck toward the group. 'Yeah, yeah,' said Hanna. 'Give me a sec, I'll climb on.'

She scrambled up my back, the pressure of her hooves little more than a brushing of fingertips against my thick hide. Arries followed, stopping to scratch my scaly cheek. 'It suits you,' he said encouragingly, then climbed up after Hanna. His mass was more considerable, in no small part due to the enormous pile of metal he was wearing. The weight was uncomfortable, but as I shifted on the spot, testing my strength, I was certain I could bear it.

Rex shook his head. 'Always showing off with your polymorphs,' he said, tracing runes in the air. In a moment, he was my mirror image in blue but for the curling ram's horns at either side of his head and voidshadow burning around his eyes.

I laughed, a sound that in a wyvern was a deep chuck-chuck sound, then looked over the edge of the airship. As a wyvern, the depth looked flat and uninspiring, the roar of the whirlpool nothing more than white noise. I climbed up on the edge, hooking my wing-claws over the railing, my head snaking down to test the air with a flick of my tongue.

I was anxious. But I wasn't *as* anxious.

That was a good feeling.

I barked another laugh and launched myself into the air. Hanna whooped; Arries cheered. With a massive *whumpf* of wings hitting the air, we took off into the sky. I angled my wings and we began a downward spiral, following the curve of the whirlpool. I heard a loud chucking sound behind me and turned my head; Rex was behind me, Pauline and Kenta clinging to his back, both wearing identical looks of terror. The legs of Pauline's hexclimber were wrapped around Rex's torso in a spider grip.

The weight of my body was heavy, my wings and shoulders straining with the effort of keeping us all aloft. But it was a good feeling, an exciting feeling, a challenge I knew I could rise to, just as surely as I could rise into the sky if I chose.

Instead, I swept lower down the whirlpool, at times drawing so near to the shining edges of it that with the barest twitch I could have trailed my wingtip through the water. I didn't, though. Wearing a wyvern shape might make me feel like an invincible sky predator, but I was still a human mind nestled inside that body, and I understood caution better than anyone — maybe even too well, if the constant adrenaline and anxiety attacks were anything to go by.

Rex followed my lead. I could hear him behind me, the slow, steady beat of his wings as he traced my path. It felt really good to know I wasn't the only one — to share this bizarre and magical experience with someone I cared about.

As we spiralled deeper, the whirlpool grew tighter. With our wide wingspans, it wouldn't be long before we couldn't help but get caught up in the spinning water. I stopped, treading air, as for the first time since I'd taken this form, anxiety started to peck at my belly.

Behind me, Rex chirped a question. I had no response, my shape robbing me of words. But the whirlpool was pressing in around me, and the eerie white light at the heart of it was so close that wisps of strange smoke curled around my tail, and all I could think was that I had no idea what was through that space — that portal, as it must be. That being a wyvern didn't make me invincible, and certainly didn't make my friends so.

I remembered swimming in a cloudy lake as a child. The silt and muck made it almost opaque. It was fun at first. Splashing on the surface, learning the strength of my own body. But then I felt something brush my feet and I'd frozen in place, trying to choke out a scream. When I'd felt that brush, that slimy tickle against my soles, I realised that I had no idea what might be below me, or how deep this lake went. That I was a powerless interloper into a space I didn't understand.

It was a feeling I would have many more times in my life, but never so powerfully as I did now. I could feel, in my gut, that there was some unseen danger just below the surface of that glow, and that if I were to drop any lower it would have me.

Hanna leaned forward. 'Tar? You in there, buddy?' She was yelling right next to my ear, but even so she was barely audible.

I shook my enormous head, the scales on my neck fanning and rippling.

She laid her hands on either side of my neck. 'Tar ... I know you struggle sometimes, and this is all some pretty wild shit, but Rex is behind us and making all kinds of worried dragon-sounds and I don't think he can help you right now. We need to go into that light. Vorguar thinks it's safe, or he wouldn't have sent us.'

Did he, though? It seemed like he'd sent us because he thought it too dangerous to risk his own people and his reputation. He'd told us so little about what to expect ...

In my mind, I envisioned a huge creature coiled beneath us, winching open a vast jaw, ready to swallow us whole as we descended.

I started to climb higher.

'Tar!' It was Arries now, and I caught myself mid-wingbeat. 'We're all here. It's gonna be okay.'

Was it? How did he know? How could anyone possibly know?

I felt him shift on my back, leaning nearer to my head. 'This is what we're here for. This is how we get Riya home.'

Riya.

I willed myself to move. I couldn't let Riya and Saanvi be separated forever. But the panic fluttering in my chest was growing too strong to be contained. I started to pant — long, hoarse panic-pants of a wyvern. I tried to angle my wings but couldn't bring myself to go lower. I started to growl and squeal with frustration.

'What's happening?' Kenta called from Rex's back.

'Tar's having a panic attack or something!' Arries replied. 'We should go back!'

'It took us an hour to get down here! We don't have time!'

'Can you talk to her?'

'We're trying —'

Hanna leaned close, torso flat against my long neck, so that she got as close as possible to my head. 'Tar. Listen. I know this is all a fucking nightmare. That it's scary sh*t, and that anyone would freak out about it, never mind someone with all the shit you're already dealing with. But we need to go down there. We need to get that awesome, weird little girl home to her mother. And I know, *I know* you can beat this. Do you hear me?'

I wanted to reply but I had no words, couldn't even bring myself to nod my head.

'Tar —'

And then I felt Hanna's weight shift.

I heard her scream, quickly swallowed by the roar of the falls.

I whipped my head around and watched her fall.

CHAPTER THIRTY-EIGHT

Hanna was falling, flailing; a purple streak vanishing into the white glow below.

I had only a split second of panic before I dove, eyes fixed on the place where she'd vanished, my heart a riot of painful beats. Arries was shouting, Rex was roaring, and I could hear the long, high-pitched scream of Pauline before I was utterly subsumed in light.

For a moment, we fell through empty space, utterly silent but for the rush of air against my wings. I could see Hanna, tumbling and utterly untethered. I strained to reach her, grasping with my clawed hindfeet. My toes wrapped around her middle.

Then the light vanished and sound returned — crystalline echoes now, rather than the roar of the whirlpool. I tried to slow my descent as a field of stars opened before me. I frantically beat my wings, only to hit the ground — or rather, plunge into a dark pool, water rushing down my throat. I coughed and closed my nostrils, wyvern instincts kicking in. I spread my wings and flapped them again, slow and heavy in the water. I burst from the surface with Arries' arms wrapped around my neck and Hanna hanging limp in my claws.

We were in a large crystal cave, all sparkling gems and glowing lights. It was this that had made the lake look like a night sky. I could see silver sand ahead; I landed there in a heap, my limbs shaking. As Hanna and Arries climbed away from me, I shed my wyvern shape, becoming a sopping wet astralkin again. Hanna and Arries were equally soaked, and both looked just as shaken as I felt.

For a moment, none of us said anything. I collapsed to the ground and drew my knees up to my chest, barely looking up as Rex landed behind us and dropped his shape as well.

Soft footsteps on the sand approached. 'Tar?' asked Rex, his voice gentle. 'You okay?'

I shook my head and pressed my forehead against my knees. I felt him sit down beside me, heard the shush of the sand shifting. He didn't touch me or talk to me in any way. Was just present.

I tuned out the voices of the others as they marvelled at where we'd landed. I had no headspace for that. All I could think about was the sight of Hanna falling, and the awful, full-body scream I'd felt.

I ought to be checking on Hanna. I ought to be less self-centred. I needed to get out of my head. I needed to be present! But I was trapped by the memory.

At length, I became more aware of the voices of my friends, talking quietly about what to do next. I lifted my head a little, and Rex turned to me. 'No rush,' he said. 'That ... was a lot.'

'That was a nightmare,' I said, and my voice was hoarse from the strain of it all.

He didn't disagree.

I got to my feet. I registered for the first time that I was glowing, my aura lit up like a lantern. Pauline was much the same, though in her case the stars in her hair were bright and shifting, and her third eye and freckles were all alight.

She caught my look and spread her hands. 'It's the Astralar, Tar,' she said. 'We're reacting to it, I think.'

The astral plane. We'd never visited here during my time in Pauline's game. It wasn't much more than an abstract concept to me. Part of the background dressing of the world. An aesthetic.

Well. I looked up at the jagged gems glittering down at me. It was more than an aesthetic now.

There were also ... fish? Luminescent white fish that swam through the air in little shoals of mixed sizes and shapes, few larger than my hand. Their movements and the glittering trails they made in the air reminded me a bit of Silky. They seemed shy of us; the various shoals had all left a wide berth around our group. I supposed, to them, we were a dangerous unknown.

'Uh ... guys?'

We all looked at Kenta. Golden light bloomed from his shoulders.

Pauline's eyes widened. 'Oh!'

The light unfurled into phantom wings, then faded.

'Wait, what was that?' Rex asked. 'Wings? Did Kendallien have wings?'

Kenta reached up and felt his own shoulders, though the light was gone. 'Sort of?'

'Kendallien was astralkin,' Pauline said, solving one of the mysteries of the game. Kenta had always insisted Kendallien was a regular human. 'It was part of his backstory that he sacrificed his wings to Alis-Umor.'

'So ... can she not reach you here? Why didn't we see them before?'

He shook his head. 'I don't know. I tried to bamf them out a few times, but ... nothing.'

'Try now,' said Hanna. 'I want to see you with wings.'

Kenta folded his arms across his chest, shoulders raised. 'It won't work.'

'Try it!' Hanna said, bouncing on the spot.

He closed his eyes. Light flared again at his shoulders, brighter this time. We could see more detail in his wings, the faint outline of feathers. When he opened his eyes, they didn't fade.

'Kenta!' Hanna practically cackled his name. 'Your wings are *beautiful.*'

He looked stunned. He flexed them; they opened wider, then folded again. 'Holy *shit.*'

'Can you fly?' I asked, awed.

'I ... I think so?' He jumped and flapped his wings. In one massive downbeat, they lifted him up to twice the height. He landed heavily, looking dazed. 'Oh my *god*. I can — I — I need to think about this. There's too much else going on.' The wings faded again.

'Aww, Keeeen!' Hanna kicked at the sand.

Kenta shook his head. 'That's enough out of you. It's my power.' He sat down. Gradually, the others sat down with him, forming a circle.

Kenta had wings. It was enough to snap me out of my spiral. He was right though, that there were more pressing matters right now.

'So we're here,' I said. I lowered myself to the ground, joining the circle. 'Does Rex just fire up Vorguar's device now, or ...?'

Pauline shook her head, lips pressed into a thin line.

'It's not as simple as that,' Rex said. 'This place isn't completely in the Astralar — or completely on the Associate Plane, either.' He pulled the device from his bag. The crystal embedded on the top blinked in a slow repetitive rhythm. 'We have to find the heart of it to stabilise it. The crystal will glow solidly when we're near. We aren't near.'

'So now we search,' said Kenta.

'Now we search,' Pauline agreed. Her voice sounded strained, and for the first time I properly took her in. Her skin was drawn, her eyes sunken with pain, and her jaw was set so tight it looked painful.

I wasn't the only one who noticed it. 'P?' Hanna turned to her. 'I'm not gonna tell you what to do, but you look like shit. Did the flight fuck with your pain levels?'

Pauline's eyes widened, then her lips formed into a snarl. 'Did the flight fuck with my pain levels? Yes. Everything in Vanthis has fucked with my pain levels. I am so far beyond "in pain". Moving hurts. Breathing hurts. Thinking hurts. I would do nothing but cry and scream, except crying and screaming also *fucking hurt.*'

I cringed away from her words. They weren't spoken with force, but I had never heard Pauline swear that much — maybe put together. Worse, her voice was raw and tense. The pain she was in was unimaginable to me.

'This is a lot, okay?' she said. Her voice shook; her eyes were wild and shone with tears. 'This is a lot. I didn't *ask* for this.'

'P ...' I began, but I didn't know what to say. What could I possibly do to comfort her? I couldn't fix her pain. I couldn't change our situation. And I was afraid, for the first time, that maybe Pauline could break. And that even if I didn't know what to do, I could have been doing more to prevent that.

But Hanna didn't blink at the sudden force. 'So would it be better if you and I stay behind?' she said. 'We could rest here and you could keep tabs on the group with your Oracle magic. That might even make it easier for them to split up.'

'We don't have time for that.'

Hanna raised her eyebrows. 'We don't know how much time we have.'

'Exactly!'

'Splitting up isn't going to gain us much anyway,' said Rex. He raised the device, with its slowly blinking light. 'I'm the one with the directions.'

Hanna set her lips. 'P. You are fucking awesome and I know you can do this, but I don't *want* you to.'

Pauline glared at her a moment. Then her shoulders slumped. 'I don't want to either. Or at least, not like this. Not right now.' She shook her head. 'Rex, could you summon me the packbeast again?'

He did, and we set off together as a whole group, with Pauline floating among us, curled up on the packbeast, her hexclimber folded at her back. Our path took us around the starry lake and through strange caverns, each lined with multi-faceted gems, where even the air seemed to shimmer with stardust. Each cavern filled with more of the floating white fish. I had thought Mihilit-dalath and its crystal structures beautiful, but that had been carved and tame, a constructed wonder. This was something wild, formed from the stuff of magical stars, and I was awed that I got to be a part of it.

Pauline and I, with our strong astralkin traits, glowed amongst this place. My aura glowed like a flame, while Pauline shimmered, the stardust in her hair now shifting galaxies, the glitter on her skin now shining like there was a star beneath the surface waiting to break free.

Seeing her like this, I could believe that she'd had starlight inside her all along. Pauline was like that: creative, forceful, brighter than the rest of us. But that was a silly thought, when taken to its conclusion; there were no shadows in Rex beyond what he imagined, and certainly no starlight in me. There wasn't a single shard of Alis-Umor in Kenta, even if there had been in Kendallien.

The speed of the light in Rex's device changed gradually but noticeably, dashing my hopes that the source of the rift would be only a few steps away. It was, at least, reassuring that we were getting closer. We passed through a strange crevice lined with veins of gold and silver and into a new cavern. This one was taken up by another starry lake, with no obvious way around it.

'Should we head back?' I asked. Rex walked up to the edge of the lake, holding out the device and watching the flickering gem.

Pauline glanced up at me from where she lay curled on the floating packbeast. Her skin was slick with sweat, and her eyes looked bleary. 'Well, we can't move forward here —'

Rex turned back to us. 'It's definitely this way,' he said. 'Maybe we could make a raft or something, and float across?'

I wasn't sure about that. Our first dunk in the astral waters had been more than enough for me. Besides ... 'Isn't the water in the Astralar ... weird?' I asked. I thought back to when I was planning Astaran for Pauline's game, going through all the lore she'd created.

Or rather: seen.

'Yes. All water on the Astral Plane is ... connected. It can be used to travel between locations if you swim deep enough. But this place isn't quite the Astralar.' Pauline sat up, grimacing. 'This is a pocket of it, or something similar. It's too enclosed; the Astralar is vast and largely open. Caverns like this are rare, and it's stranger still that we haven't seen outside of it at any point.'

'Well, whether it's a pocket or the full trousers, we're still here and we need a heading,' said Kenta. He gestured across the lake. 'Personally, I don't think riding a dingy across the lake is going to get us anywhere. There's nothing over there but sheer wall.'

'Can the device track through water?' I asked.

Everyone turned to look at me and I felt my cheeks heat. I wondered if my aura being activated meant it didn't blush with me like it had on the Associate Plane, or whether I was lit up even brighter in my embarrassment. I crossed my arms and dropped my gaze to the floor.

'No, Tar — it's a good idea,' said Arries.

Rex lowered the device into the water. 'Looks like through might really be the way,' he said. 'It's a little hard to tell without going further in, but I think it could be.'

I didn't like this. Just the sight of him reaching into the water made my chest tight with suppressed panic. 'I don't think we need to do all this,' I said. 'I know it was my idea, but — but we'll have so little control over what we do in there. We won't be able to see; it's a huge open space and who knows where it leads; we won't be able to *breathe* —'

'Tar. Calm down.' Pauline fixed me with a stare from the Arcane Packbeast. 'This is an "unknown dungeon" sort of situation. We have rope. We can tie ourselves to each other so we don't get separated. And we shouldn't drown; water in the Astral Plane isn't really *water* in the same way.'

We tied ourselves up. I didn't feel good about it. It wasn't just the way the water was too still even though the crystals and gems of the cave hummed with so much power that it vibrated through my feet. Wasn't just because it was ridiculous that we should be able to swim with ropes tangling us all up. I felt certain that there was something that would be waiting for us in the water. Something we wouldn't want to meet.

I thought again of the vortex, and the sense of swimming through a lake while unseen things brushed at my feet.

None of us knew what we were getting into.

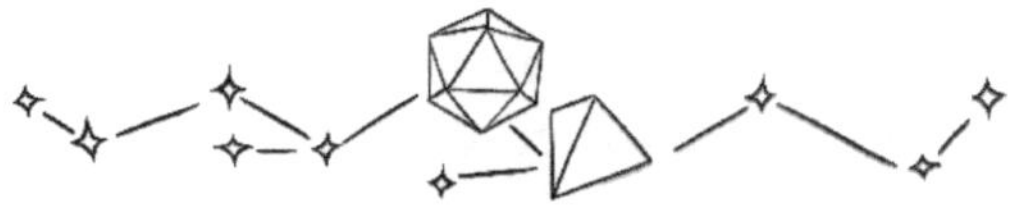

CHAPTER THIRTY-NINE

We lined up at the edge of the water. I watched as a handful of astral fish disappeared below the surface. The rope was taut against my waist. My glasses were packed into my satchel, and the world was blurrier than I liked.

Pauline had her hands on the controls of her hexclimber, ready to spring. Apparently it had a swim function, too. I was beginning to understand why she'd preferred it to a driftchair.

'Ready?' Pauline glanced down the line at us.

Rex squeezed my hand. 'Ready?' he asked quietly.

I nodded.

And then, we all jumped forward to plunge into the dark.

The water was chill and sleek against my skin. Pauline's advice that this wasn't normal water rang in my mind. I opened my eyes, and was surprised to find it as comfortable as open air, if oddly moist. My friends swam alongside me. Pauline moved with octopus like pushes, aglow even amongst this strange, shifting murk. Hanna struggled to keep up, her hooved feet not built for paddling. I pointed back at her and Arries tread water a moment, then tapped his shoulders, signalling her to get a grip. 'Got it?' he asked, his voice muffled but oddly clear. I blinked.

'It's okay,' Pauline said, catching my eye. 'You can breathe here, Tar. I promise.'

Opening my eyes was one thing, but willingly letting water rush into my lungs was quite another. Already though, my lungs were growing horribly thin, the pressure of the water seeming to crush my chest.

Around me, my friends stopped the swim to chorus encouragement. I shook my head and tried to keep swimming, as if I could somehow outswim suffocation in these seemingly bottomless depths.

Rex turned to face me. He smiled encouragingly. 'It'll be fine,' he said. He swam closer, reaching for my hands.

I took them. I was starting to see spots. Panic made my body rigid. If I didn't open my mouth now, I would suffocate either way.

I breathed deep. Water rushed down my throat, and I spluttered, but didn't choke. It felt more like a long drag of winter air: biting and refreshing rather than stifling.

Rex squeezed my hands. I offered him a shaky smile. He continued on, following the light of the device.

It was bizarre down here. The water was simultaneously dark and clear, and filled with sparkling lights like tiny stars. There were astral fish down here, too, as quick and darting as they had been in the air. I enjoyed the weightlessness of the swim, my bulk suddenly lifted. I wasn't much of a swimmer, but I cut easily through the water, almost as if it responded more to my intention than my technique.

As we swam deeper, shadows flitted at the edges of sight, in and out of the glittering clouds. I tugged on the rope ahead of me, getting Rex's attention. I pointed them out.

His eyes narrowed as he considered the shadows. 'There are a lot of creatures that travel the waters of the Astral Plane,' he said. 'Stay alert, but I think the best thing to do is to keep moving.'

We swam deeper. The shadow creatures came nearer, or perhaps we only encountered bolder ones. Some were like fish covered in eyes, others strange beasts made of crystal and gems. Others still were clouds of glittering dust, floating through the water like ghosts, identifiable only by the fiery eyes that followed our movements. Some were no larger than mice, others so vast that I didn't realise it was a creature at all until a massive fin slid past.

It was beautiful and horrifying. Maybe the first place that really made the word 'awestruck' make sense to me. At times, confronted with this vast space, neither ocean nor starscape entirely, I was utterly frozen by the wonder and terror of it all. In those moments, I would freeze up, consumed by the sight, and if not for the insistent tug of the rope around my waist, I might have remained like that. At times, it seemed the others felt the same. This wasn't about anxiety, or broken mental health; it was about the enormity of exploring a world utterly alien to the one we'd known. But together, we kept going; sometimes in silence, sometimes exchanging words of encouragement or soft curses whispered into the depths, but always together.

My limbs grew heavy from the effort of swimming. A dull ache in the muscles that threatened to become something more painful. I pushed on, because what else was there to do?

Rex looked back over his shoulder. 'There's light ahead,' he said. 'I think we're close.' His voice warbled a little in the water, a strangely mystical effect.

At first I wondered what he meant, but then I saw it; a sheet of rippling light that could only mean we were about to break the surface, as bizarre as that seemed when we had only been travelling down, down. I willed more energy into my limbs and kicked after him, wishing I'd opted for a tail or webbed hands in character creation. Pauline had cautioned me against polymorphing to swim here, as we didn't know what we might face ahead.

Rex broke the surface first. As his head went through I felt relief that our journey was almost over. Then, as if snatched by a hook, he shot out of the water and the rope around my waist went tight, dragging me out with him. As I burst into open air, my centre of gravity spun and I started to fall upward into the air. I screamed but only coughed up water in my panic, my lungs emptying in a gout of black liquid. My friends screamed beside me. We were a mess, a tangled mass of ropes and flailing limbs. I tried to reach for them, for anyone, as we fell.

I heard Pauline scream: 'Cast Slowfall!'

And Rex reply: 'It's not working! It's not working!'

I tried to retake the shape of a wyvvern, a giant eagle, anything that could carry us free of whatever death awaited us when we hit the ground, but my fingers created no runes. My magic was gone and dull. I could draw nothing from this air. I could draw nothing from my own pounding heart.

I tugged at the rope around my waist, desperate to pull myself closer to a friend, only for it to disintegrate in my hands.

As I spun, the screams of my friends mingled into an unintelligible mass. I saw Kenta flailing to my left. I reached for him again.

Then everything went black.

☆ ☆ ☆

Time passed. Whether in seconds or hours, I couldn't say. My back was on hard rock. I could feel the edges of it jabbing between my shoulder blades. I opened my eyes to a vast starscape, the shadows of planets looming and seeming to press down on me with their size even at this distance. Standing up was a terrifying prospect, but fear for my friends propelled me. I was standing on ... a planet? An asteroid? A hilly rock large enough that to reach the horizon I would have to run longer and harder than my body was capable, but small enough that I could see the curve of it. Tiny, in the boundless emptiness of this place. The silhouettes of vast creatures, almost whale-like, drifted past; darker shapes against the inky backdrop of this pseudo-space.

I heard a groan somewhere behind me and spun.

Kenta rolled over in the sand. 'Oh God ...' he muttered.

I offered him my hand and hauled him to his feet.

'Shit. That was *wild* ...' He looked around. 'Where are the others?'

My eyes scanned the horizon. 'I have no idea. Do you know how we can call the others?'

Kenta shook his head. 'No clue. We'll have to wait for P to Whisperwind us.'

We found a broad rock to sit on and waited. Kenta crossed his arms over his chest, his eyes cast to the ground. I folded my arms over my stomach and continued to watch the horizon and the sky, with its enormous drifting shapes. I swiped my hand through the air; it left brief trails, confirming my suspicion that this wasn't air as we knew it. At times, we heard distant echoing cries that reminded me of whale song. The hairs on my arms raised and shivered to think of the size of whale that could exist in a place like this.

All the while, the sick feeling in my stomach grew more pronounced. I clenched my fists against a growing tremble.

No message.

Nothing.

At length, I looked at Kenta. His jaw was set, his lips pressed into a thin line. He had to be thinking the same thing as me: they had to be in trouble. None of us would care about anything as much as the safety of our friends. Pauline would have contacted us if she could have.

He had to be avoiding the same thought as me: that they could be dead, and we would have no way of knowing.

Another eerie whale cry echoed across the small asteroid.

I took a shuddering breath. I thought anxiety would strike me now, and I certainly felt sick with it, but also oddly numb. This was too much to process. My head was full of buzzing. I needed to do something.

I stood up. 'We might be able to find them through another lake. P said all water is connected here, right?'

Kenta nodded, not meeting my eyes. Unusual for him.

'I'll scout for a lake or something. You stay here.'

Another nod.

I spread my hands and reached out with my senses, trying to draw power toward myself.

I came up ... empty.

My fingers traced empty air.

I blinked and tried again. Nothing.

There was sand and rock beneath my feet. There were creatures swimming through the air. There was nature here, even if of a different kind than the one I knew.

But I was cut off from it. As trapped within my own head, my own body, as I had ever been before we came to Vanthis.

'Ken ...' I said. My voice shook. My vision narrowed. I sank to my knees, fingers plunging into the sand. 'I can't ... I don't feel it anymore. I don't feel magic anymore! Kenta?'

'Tar. Calm down. I know you need my help but I don't have anything to give right now, okay? We need to stay calm.'

As if I wouldn't if I could. As if I wanted these long gulping breaths that made me feel dizzy.

But he needed me too. I tried to focus on my breathing. That helped sometimes, right? What did they call it — castle breathing? I hated it, but ...

After a moment, Kenta said '... Tar. You aren't glowing anymore. You're not — you haven't been glowing since we got here.'

I steadied my breathing and looked at him. His eyes looked wild.

No aura. No magic.

I licked dry lips. 'Can you spring out your wings?'

He nodded, but nothing happened. His expression turned to one of consternation. 'Why isn't —?'

'It's gone,' I said. 'We're ... we're regular humans again.' I looked at my skin. Still the strange glittering white of an astralkin, but no longer with that glow that really defined it.

I clenched and unclenched my fists, fingernails digging into my palms. My entire body went rigid.

We didn't have magic anymore. We were just Kenta and Tar, nurse and museum assistant. But in cosplay.

And we were on a plane even more dangerous than the one we'd first been transported to.

My breathing grew laboured. I pressed a hand to my chest, starting to double over.

Kenta began to pace. 'Okay. Okay, so we don't have magic. That means the others probably don't have it either, so —'

—*So they are fine?*— A whisper tickled my ears.

I shuddered and flinched away, but when I spun no-one was there. Kenta looked similarly startled.

'Did you —?'

—*They are safe and well?*— came the whisper again. It had a dry quality, like the pages of an old book scratching against each other. I could see nothing in our immediate area. The world around us was as it was before — crystalline, glittering, barren.

Slowly, my eyes moved up. Something was appearing in the sky. Fast approaching, a glowing thing emerging through clouds of space dust and the infinite shadow. The first thing I noticed was the eyes — enormous burning orbs, astral bodies in their own right. Green and flickering.

The next thing I noticed was the hands, each as large as a skyscraper, which settled to either side of us. The force of that slow, gentle touch set the ground shaking, and knocked both Kenta and myself from our feet. Terror gripped me, but my scream was lost in the rumble of the earth we stood on.

—*They are small specks floating in a cosmic sea,*— said the creature. They leaned closer and I saw a humanoid face with a wide mouth that bristled with needle-like teeth. Tentacle hair swimming in space, each strand long enough to wrap around the small asteroid we stood on. A pointed chin and heart-shaped face framed by crystalline green scales. —*They are insignificant.*— Their mouth didn't move.

They could swallow us whole, I realised. They could crunch this landmass like an apple.

'This is bad,' I squeaked to Kenta.

'Yeah.' He nodded, grey with fear. 'Yep. Very bad.'

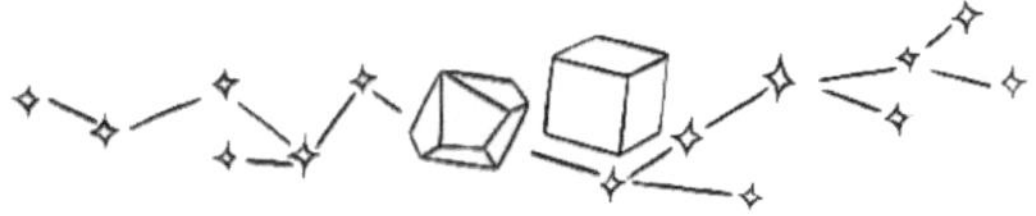

CHAPTER FORTY

We were caught within the grip of a cosmic giant, with no magic and no help incoming.

The creature's enormous hands twitched, claws raking the air. The earth shuddered.

'Who are you?' I asked, because what was there to do in this situation but talk? 'How do you know us?'

'Where are our friends?' Kenta added, his voice grim.

The creature grinned, face cracking open with the width of their smile. An enormous fish-like tail flicked up behind them, then down again. A mermaid, then? Or something?

Not what I'd ever thought of when I'd envisioned them before.

—I am Ekthrentis. I know you because you are here. Your friends are not here, but they are not far. My sibling watches them. But these questions do not interest me.—

Their eyes flared, the fires beginning to spin hypnotically. *—You are not from a plane that touches this one, or the ones that touch it, or the ones that touch those. You are as dust blown from far off lands. You stink of foreign stars and a dry and suffocating space. Why are you here?—*

Beside me, Kenta trembled so hard I could hear his armour jingle. I sidestepped closer to him, leaning my arm against his and nudging his hand. He immediately gripped mine — too tightly, but I gritted my teeth. 'It's going to be okay,' I said to him.

I hoped it was true.

Because we were wholly outclassed here. This creature could likely crush the whole asteroid on which we stood.

But they couldn't know us as well as they claimed, or they wouldn't have these questions.

And we could not be as insignificant as they claimed, or they would not be bothering with us.

There was a way out of this. Our friends were alive, and there was a way out of this, if only we could find it.

Kenta continued to shake but I felt oddly calm. This wasn't a familiar trap, or a familiar fear. This was new, and I was going to deal with it.

So.

Why were we here?

Ekthrentis wasn't all-knowing. It seemed more than possible that we could lie to them. And I definitely didn't want them to know about the real reason we were here.

If only I was any good at lying ...

'We're trying to get home,' I said, because that was true, and felt safe. 'We came here via the Associate Plane.'

Ekthrentis' eyes stopped spinning. They seemed to consider my words. —*This world touches none with your savour. It no longer touches even the Astralar. This was a poor choice of path.*— There was a sense of distrust in their whispery tone. I tried not to shudder at the way their mouth remained unmoving through the whole communication. I suppose we should be grateful that they didn't use their voice on us, which must surely be a booming thing, but it was still uncanny to see.

God, if they sensed we were lying when I told a half-truth, how would I talk us out of this? I wasn't the talker! We needed Hanna, who could tell outrageous lies with complete confidence. We needed Rex, who could think us out of any problem.

—*Try nothing,*— Ekthrentis warned. —*It will go poorly for you.*—

Something about their words struck me as odd.

'We need our friends,' said Kenta. 'We're nothing without them. It will be harder for us to explain without them.' There was an insinuation there that we were ... a unit? Or something? But I appreciated it. As long as we were separated and Ekthrentis' sibling held our friends, there was a chance either of us might say something that put the other group at risk.

—*You seek to regroup and consolidate your power.*— Ekthrentis' voice became a hiss. —*You seek to gain advantage over us.*—

'How can we?' I said. 'We're only tiny. You could squash us in an instant.'

—*I could. You are as a speck of dust to Ekthrentis.*—

'Insignifcant,' Kenta echoed. His hand still crushed mine.

Ekthrentis' eyes narrowed. —*True.*— They sounded suspicious and it struck me again that in spite of their huge size, in spite of this being their home terrain, they could not possibly think us insignificant. But they also clearly didn't want to let on to that.

It seemed *insane* that a creature this powerful could have anything to fear from us, a group of non-magical humans from a non-magical world (Pauline's Oracle powers notwithstanding). But then the unknown was frightening, wasn't it?

And whatever this thing was, they weren't attacking us. They weren't even threatening us. They were just trying to convince us that we couldn't hurt them — much like a cat backed into a corner puffs up its fur and hisses.

Or at least ... I hoped that was the case. It was the kind of thing I could imagine doing, anyway.

I decided to take a risk. 'We don't mean any harm to you, or to your sibling,' I said. 'We just want to find our friends again.'

Ekthrentis' voice took on a barking quality. —*As if you could harm Ekthrentis. I will reunite you with your friends. It means little to me. And Orodantilla will not care, either.*—

Before we could ask what that meant, Ekthrentis drew back, hands lifting from the surface of the planet, causing huge clouds of sand and dust to lift into the air. Kenta and I staggered, clutching each other to remain upright.

Ekthrentis' tentacle hair started to swirl and dance, tracing unknown symbols in the sky with the curling tendril tips. The symbols flashed, then faded, but light gathered all around us as we were swarmed by hundreds of the strange astral fish that inhabited this plane. They swam all around us, surrounding us, creating a hurricane of light and scales. I felt a swoop in my stomach. Momentary weightlessness that filled me with panic. But then the weight of my body resettled, and the astral fish scattered.

Kenta and I released each other. Our friends stood around us, shocked, while Ekthrentis and I assumed Orodantilla, a similarly enormous mermaid-like being with red eyes and grey skin, stared down at us.

'Oh my god oh my god oh my god!' Arries rushed forward, hugging first me and then Kenta.

'Shit! We thought you were dead!' Hanna leapt forward and punched Kenta in the pauldron.

Pauline strode up to us. Her hexclimber was mercifully still intact. 'We don't have —'

'Magic, I know,' said Kenta. 'Funny how quickly you come to rely on it.'

As Pauline moved aside, I saw Rex. His eyes were wide with shock, his mouth trembling. All at once, I felt all the fear of earlier come crashing back to me. The thought that I'd lost all these people, these amazing, perfect people.

He didn't wait for permission this time before crushing me in a hug. I hugged back just as fiercely, tears stinging at my eyes. He cradled my head; I pressed my nose against the space between neck and shoulder. I closed my eyes and imagined we were beneath the trees in the garden in Mihilit-dalath. That we were home in front of Pauline's house, building up the courage to go inside.

'I didn't — I couldn't — I've been a mess,' he said hoarsely. 'We thought, when we were all there except for you —'

'I know,' I said. 'I'm fine, though. We're all fine.'

He only hugged me closer in response.

At length, Ekthrentis' whisper again caressed my ears. — *You are re-united. Now you will answer our questions.* —

Rex flinched at the voice. I pulled back and turned to stare up at the starry expanse and the enormous creatures that dominated it. 'Will you answer ours?' I asked. I kept a grip on Rex's hand, my entire body rigid, my heart beating far too fast. I didn't know if this would work. But I hoped it would.

Orodantilla's head canted ever so slightly to one side. — *What is it you wish to know?* —

'Why the Associate Plane?' I asked. 'Why separate from the Astralar?'

The siblings stared at each other, tentacles twitching, and I felt certain they were communicating in some way we couldn't detect. Ekthrentis bared their teeth and glared down at me. — *What advantage do you seek? What do you care why?* —

'I don't want an advantage,' I said. 'I want to understand.'

'You're running from something, aren't you?' Pauline said abruptly. I shivered, looking at her. The Oracle mark on her forehead didn't glow.

She was Pauline the lair master with added sparkles, not Pauline the Oracle. But she was still more shrewd than anyone I'd ever met. 'That's it, isn't it? Why would creatures as large and powerful as yourselves confine yourselves to a pocket otherwise?'

The siblings both reacted. Orodantilla flinched, hands coming up as if to shield themself, while Ekthrentis bared their countless teeth in a monstrous snarl. — *You know nothing of the Astralar, or the Siblings, or what we have faced,* — they said. — *Understanding will not allow you to defeat us. We have escaped greater fiends and fiercer waters.* —

'Nobody wants to fucking fight you!' Hanna yelled. 'Are you fucking serious? You're big enough to play volleyball with the moon!'

Their tails lashed the space behind them, scattering stardust that floated out into the void. Hard to tell whether it was from anxiety or anger.

But still, they didn't strike us.

Heart-pounding in my chest, I decided to take a risk. This was a stalemate that wasn't going to lead anywhere good for us. I didn't know how long their patience — or fear — would run for us. And it was clear they weren't about to let us go.

'We were sent by a great mage in the Associate Plane,' I said. 'He wants us to stabilise the rift between this plane and his, so that he can explore here and have access to the netheril.' I didn't hold any truths back.

—A great mage?— said Orodantilla.

—He wishes us harm!— Ekthrentis hissed.

Arries shook his head. 'I don't think he knows you exist. He seemed ... greedy, to me. He just wants the netheril.'

—Void-dust is common. This motive is suspect!—

'It's not common on the Assosciate Plane,' said Pauline. Her voice was firm and calm, like she was putting down a player trying to squirm out of a bad roll. 'So rare in fact that he nearly robbed us of the small amount we had.'

'I can't promise he's safe,' I said. 'We don't know him very well. But we know his motive is netheril. And all we're here to do is keep the rift open — a rift *you* created, so I assume that is not distressing to you.'

A long pause while these two cosmic beings considered us. *—We wish the dimensions to remain connected. Stabilising it is beneficial to that goal.—*

Again, they stopped to look at each other, micro-changes in their expressions suggesting some kind of communication we weren't privy to.

—We came seeking a new home— said Ekthrentis. *—The Astralar is dangerous for beings as small as we.—*

As a group, we exchanged looks at the thought of these 'small beings'.

—*We hoped to seek refuge in the Associate Plane. This pocket is familiar, but it is small. We wish to stretch. To see new things and explore—* Orodantilla added.

—*But the rift is too small for us to enter, and we cannot enlarge it without causing damage to this pocket. It is a risk we cannot take.—*

Rex released a shaky breath. 'They really don't mean us harm, do they?' he said softly.

I shook my head. 'Bizarrely, they seem more scared of us.'

He squeezed my hand, then lifted his chin. 'You are likely too large for the Associate Plane,' he said. 'There is gravity there that will weigh you down, and you would crush whole cities with your size.'

As we watched, Orodantilla's brow furrowed. —*We would not crush people that did not threaten us.—*

'You might not realise,' he said. 'Can you make yourselves smaller?'

—*Smaller?—*

'A shrinking spell,' he clarified.

—*That is not a magic we know of.—* Again, Ekthrentis sounded suspicious. I wondered how close they were to just giving up on us and all our strange questions. I wondered if, as timid as they might seem, they were considering killing us rather than putting up with all this. I read people wrong all the time. It was one reason why I'd found my job so difficult, why I struggled to make friends — even leave the house. And these beings were far beyond anything I had ever experienced before. I had no scripts for interacting with them, no list of body language I could try to tick off in my mind to make sense of the interaction.

All I had was that they were scared, and so was I, and I thought that had to be the foundation of *something*.

'It's a common magic in the Associate Plane,' Rex said. 'Though not permanent.'

—And you can cast it?—

'Not yet,' he said. 'Though I'd like to learn.'

Orodantilla leaned closer, its enormous face blotting out the sky. *—You will find us a way into your world.—* Their eyes started to spin again, and I felt myself being drawn into it. Immediately, I closed my eyes, shouting to the others to do the same. *—You have great knowledge. You will find us a way.—*

'You're too big!' Rex said. 'There are mages who could shrink you temporarily, but that wouldn't be enough! And I can't do it anyway!'

I kept my eyes closed. I could feel the heat of their gazes, almost cooking the air, but I didn't want to give in to it.

Psychic powers. I guess that made sense — the voices they were throwing at us were likely telepathic in some way, and I think I remembered that the Astralar was full of weird brain beasts.

'What about if you travelled with us mentally?' I asked.

A pause.

—Mentally?—

I cracked open an eye — both siblings seemed to have settled down again, their hypnosis attempt over.

'As you're talking to us now,' I said. 'Is there a way we could carry your mind with us, so you could see the Associate Plane without physically being there?'

—You offer yourself as a vessel?—

Oh shit. I didn't like the sound of that. 'I mean — no, I didn't — I was just wondering if there was a way —?' I started to panic, struggling to string a sentence together. I wanted to get out of this situation but not if I had to give up my *body* or something.

'What does being a vessel entail?' Pauline interrupted calmly. I fell silent, grateful that she'd stepped in before I could melt-down.

— We will see through your eyes at times, and you will know when. We will have access to your mind but will not be able to

change it or harm you in any way, nor will we have possession of your body. —

It sounded far less bad than I'd first thought, but still I shuddered at the thought.

'Well.' Arries cleared his throat. 'I guess it should be me who does it.' For Arries, he sounded worried, a tremor in his voice that I'd rarely heard.

'Are you nuts? No!' Hanna said. 'You've already got that sun goddess spying on you all the time. You don't need more of this!'

Arries shook his head, gazing up at the enormous creatures looking down on us. 'I like making friends,' he said. 'And you seem friendly enough to me. I'm sorry you had to leave your home. It makes sense that you would hate to be trapped somewhere so small when you had the whole Astralar before. If you need a vessel, it could be me. Though I will not always be in the Associate Plane, so I hope that's okay.'

—You wish ... to be friends?— Orodantilla asked, their whispery voice hazed by confusion.

He gave a shaky smile. 'I just want to go home. If you'll be friendly ... well, I will too.'

'Arries, you can't —' Rex began.

'It should be me,' I said. I hated myself for saying it, but I would hate myself more if I didn't. 'This was my idea. I don't want it, obviously I don't want it, but I can't ask you to —'

'Stop!' Kenta yelled. He glared around at us. 'Give me a moment, okay?' He took a deep breath. 'Siblings. If you were in the mind of someone, could you shield them from other influences?'

Their tentacles lifted curiously. *—Almost certainly,—* they said. *—We are strong in mind, if not in body.—*

Quite a statement from creatures that could bounce an asteroid like a beach ball.

'Then I would like to make a deal with you now,' he said firmly. 'There's someone who ... who lives in my head. She gives me nightmares and sometimes sends me pain, to try to force me to do what she wants. Her name is —' He stopped, licked his lips, and tried again. 'Her name is Alis-Umor, a god to those on the Associate Plane. If you agree to protect me from her, and ... cut her connection to me, then I will agree to carry you with me, on the terms that you will never harm or influence my mind or body, and that you will allow me to block you from my mind and eyes whenever I choose to. Does that seem fair?'

Sends him pain? How much pain? Why hadn't he told us? While I had been freaking out about — about transport, about whether the boy I liked liked me back, Kenta had been struggling with something far larger and far more terrible. I looked at the others to see whether they knew, and I saw that Arries and Hanna looked grim but unsurprised.

Now, Ekthrentis and Orodantilla were silent, studying us with their vast, burning eyes. If they rejected Kenta's terms, then I didn't know what would happen. What it would mean if I or Arries had to carry another entity inside us.

But Kenta looked up at them with something I thought might be hope. My heart ached for him. We should have done more for him than just plan to get him home. I should have done more for him.

—*Your terms are fair,*— Ekthrentis said, *their voice breaking the taut silence. —Your motive is clear. You wish protection, and will give us an element of freedom in exchange. This is agreeable.—*

—*It will be interesting to see a new world from the eyes of a human,*— Orodantilla said. Their head cocked to one side, the tentacles curling about their shoulders as if giving themself a hug. I wondered if it denoted excitement. —*Your desire for privacy is not unreasonable. We will strike the deal.—*

More astral fish gathered in a swirling vortex just ahead of us, a glowing pillar of light and movement.

—*When you are ready, step forth, and we will make the binding complete.—*

'You don't have to do this, Ken,' Arries said. 'I am willing to do this, okay? I don't mind company, I never have. There are other ways of getting rid of Alis-Umor.'

'I know,' he said. 'But ... you don't know what it's like. Every day on what was supposed to be a *magical adventure* had been edged with terror for me. I don't want to hurt anyone. But I *do* want to stay on the Associate Plane. I want to be able to enjoy it. I want to never be afraid that some terrifying torture goddess is going to try to make me hurt people. And obviously, it's bullshit that it worked out this way — that she could reach me, that we became our characters, all of that. But I've got a solution here, and I think it will work.'

He turned his face toward the sky. 'One more thing: we should set a limit. What if this agreement doesn't work? If it makes me or you unhappy, we should both be able to end it. If after six months of mortal time on the Associate Plane, any of us wish to end the connection, we can do so, with no harm to any involved party and no threats. Does this seem agreeable?'

A long pause. — *You seek to escape the deal already?*—

'I want the option of freedom,' Kenta said. 'I think you can understand that?'

— *We do. Your terms are accepted.*— The fish flashed and spun faster.

Kenta looked back at us. 'This is what I want, okay? I'm choosing this. I know some of you are miserable as hell and like to take on blame you don't deserve, but I promise this is my choice. A deal I negotiated myself in a world of magic.' He kind of shook himself, then smiled. 'Besides. Tar, your head is already too full of voices with just your own. And Arries has too many friends. I'm the natural choice.'

'Ken ...' I trailed off, frozen and unsure what to do.

'See you on the other side,' he said, with a smile that was only half-fear. Then he strode into the pillar of astral fish and was consumed by light.

Above us, the Siblings shifted, leaning further over. Each opened their mouth wide. Glittering rays of light shot from their eyes and mouths to strike the column; red from Orodantilla, green from Ekthrentis. As they did, more astral fish began to gather, swimming and weaving around the beams, swirling around our feet.

Then, at once, the siblings' mouths closed. The pillar dispersed, and the fish with it. And then there was just Kenta, on his knees and shaking.

'Holy shit, Ken!' Hanna was the first to move, rushing to her fallen friend. As if her action had unfrozen us, we followed. Arries and Hanna helped him to his feet.

'I'm fine, guys,' he said. 'Just a little shaken.' He looked at us and blinked. His irises had changed. One was a vibrant green; the other was a flaming red. He blinked, and his eyes returned to their normal brown.

'You don't feel ... weird?' I asked. 'Because a moment ago, your eyes ...?'

'Yeah, I know,' he said. 'I could feel it, but it wasn't too weird. It'll take a little getting used to.'

Arries looked worried. 'And Alis-Umcr...?'

'I don't know. I guess we'll have to find out.'

He looked up at the Siblings, who stared back with open curiosity.

—*For us as well,*— said Ekthrentis. —*The world is strange from your eyes. Are we really so big? Is everything so dark?*—

—*The humans are more beautiful than I thought,*— said Orodantilla. —*You must be very dear to each other.*—

'We are,' said Rex.

Kenta cleared his throat. 'So about stabilising the rift ...?'

—*For that, you will need its source. Come. We will show you.*—

The Siblings again summoned the astral fish to move us through their plane. The fish swarmed us, spinning at ever increasing speeds until they were a blur of light and scales. Then the increasingly familiar swooping sensation, followed by falling.

We landed in an open-roofed cavern, the astral fish scattering like a bursting firework as we hit the cold stone floor. The Siblings peered down at us from the sparkling starscape. They emanated curiosity, their frightening smiles vanished, their tentacles squirming with anticipation.

'Some warning would have been nice,' Hanna grumbled. I couldn't help but be impressed that she would gripe even at beings as terrifying as the Siblings.

As I got up, I realised Pauline was glowing again and quickly looked at my own hands. My aura was lit like a flame. 'Magic!' I said. I drew a quick rune in the air, materialising a seed in my palm that started to sprout.

The others echoed my surprise. Rex and Hanna immediately summoned balls of light and juggled them to each other, laughing. Golden wings of light burst from Kenta's back and he leapt into the air.

—*The source,*— said Orodantilla.

'This must be it,' Pauline said. She pointed to the centre of the cavern, where a mirror-like shard, twice as wide as a human and three times as tall, floated inside a cage of glittering blue crystal. Netheril, the same material as our dice, now glowing as if lit from inside.

The cage hovered above a lake. I hesitated. 'I don't think I have more than one polymorph left in me,' I said.

'Me either,' Rex said.

'Good job one of us has wings now,' Kenta said. 'Rex, I'll carry you.'

'Can you carry a whole other person?' Pauline asked.

Kenta shrugged and landed beside us with a whoosh of air. 'Rex is like a third my size. I think I can carry him.'

I looked to Rex. 'And you'd be okay with that?'

'It'd be a bit unfair of me to complain, considering we did the reverse only a few hours ago.'

Rex took out Vorugar's device from his cloak. It was now emitting a steady light; it was reassuring to know we were in the right place. He put it on the ground and activated it, sketching the necessary runes onto the ground around it, which were reminiscent of a simple teleportation circle. Then he picked it up and nodded to Kenta, who wrapped his arms around him and carried him up into the air, hovering just outside the cage.

Rex threw the device into the mirror. There was a pulse of energy that I felt in my chest and stomach as if I'd been pushed, and then there was nothing. I hoped that it worked.

As they landed, the astral fish returned to surround us as the Siblings moved us on again.

They took us to a lake much like the one we'd first entered. —*We do not fit, as you say,*— said Ekthrentis. —*But you carry us with you. Swim down, then up. You will see yourself in familiar waters.*—

I was loathe to enter the waters again after what had happened last time, but Kenta assured us it would be okay. He seemed calmer than he had since we'd arrived, more like his laughing, relaxed self.

So we plunged again into the dark, ropeless this time but more confident of our journey. We swam down, where strange eyes and dark shadows moved further below, then swam up again toward the shining surface.

And this time, when we surfaced, it was to the fading roar of a vanishing whirlpool. White light swirled around us, gentler than it had been on our last visit. The water lifted us up slowly, then steadied and became still but for the twinkling of stardust.

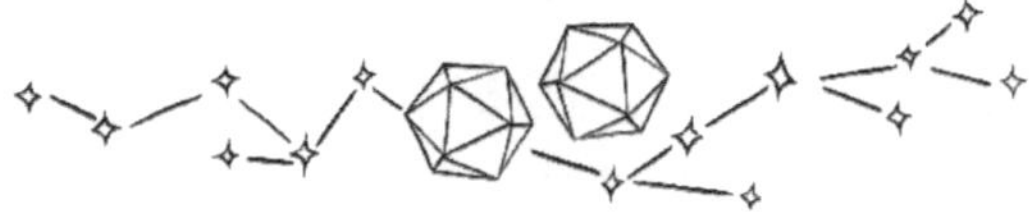

CHAPTER FORTY-ONE

I shivered below deck on the airship, rubbing my hands together and shoving them between my legs until Rex got around to using the drying spell on me. Arries huddled next to me. One of the first things I'd done when I got back was cast a Pathfinder spell. Not because we needed it, but because I wanted to prove that I could. The familiar rush of magic was a staggering relief. In just a few short weeks, magic had become as familiar to me as anything on Earth, and its lack had left me bereft.

And of course ... we'd done it. Our task was complete. Vorugar would have to send us home. No matter how cold we might be waiting for Rex to magically blow-dry us, that was a warming thought.

But apart from the relief of our success, it was amazing to see the change in Kenta. Already, he seemed more relaxed, brighter, quicker to laugh. I wondered whether it was just the knowledge that Alis-Umor couldn't reach him, or whether there was more to it. Maybe she had genuinely been hurting him even with the amulet protecting him. In small ways we couldn't see. Either way, when Kenta bellowed a laugh and slapped me on the back, I wasn't half as annoyed as I'd usually be.

Riya was safe as well. She'd mostly kept Ordeth busy by homebrewing her own game of checkers with coins and a tablecloth. The rules were mostly incomprehensible to me, but Ordeth had been very patient with her.

She was safe, and we were safe, and this last journey would be to get her home.

'She's a good kid,' Ordeth said later, when we were enjoying another warm pink bean dish in the mess. 'Smartest kid I've ever met, actually. Her mother is going to be so happy to have her back.'

It was the one thing about returning to Earth that I felt zero conflict about. 'If she doesn't murder me for having run off with her for weeks,' I said.

Ordeth raised his eyebrows. 'You were magically sucked into another plane. She can't blame you for that.'

'She wouldn't believe it,' I replied. 'Earth isn't ... ah. Trust me. It's ... it's going to be complicated.'

But what wasn't complicated was my gratefulness to Ordeth. In spite of all my worry, in spite of my terror that if we left Riya alone for a moment, she would be snatched away somewhere we wouldn't be able to find her, Ordeth had kept her safe. 'Why have you helped us so much?' I asked.

He blushed a darker silver, rubbing the back of his neck. 'Well ... I wish I could say it's because I'm such a good person, Tar. But honestly, I couldn't miss the chance to be part of a big story. Adventurers from another world trying to reunite a lost little girl with her mother ... I knew I would never forgive myself if I just ushered you out the door and waved goodbye.'

I blinked, stunned by his image of us. 'That's ... a gross mischaracterisation. We're not ... not heroes, or anything.'

He smiled. 'Aren't you? Anyway, Rex let me copy spells from his spellbook so it's not like I've gone uncompensated.'

That thought stayed with me for the rest of the journey home, even when I was sore and clinging to the back of a pankalar. How long had I considered myself an NPC, just a side-character in other people's stories, with no agency of my own?

As we flew, I brought it up with Rex, who rode behind me with his arms around my waist. Silky rode in the crate behind us, having been carefully coaxed in and settled, and receiving frequent treats and attention. 'You've never been an NPC, Tar.' He sounded amused by the thought.

'The first time you met me, I'd nearly bolted away from Pauline's house out of terror,' I said.

'And you went anyway.' He rested his chin on my shoulder. 'Magic didn't make you any more competent than you already were. Or any of us, really. We didn't fight the Siblings — we empathised with them. And you were a big part of that.' He fell silent for a moment. 'How did you know they were afraid?'

I bit my lip. 'Because I know what it's like,' I said.

'And how did you know they would want to make a deal with us?'

I laughed. 'Because I wanted you all to save me too, when I met you. Is that pathetic?'

His thumb brushed my waist. 'Everyone needs help. Everyone needs friends. Even the infamous TarAntula of A:RO.'

I paused. 'Arries talked about me?'

'He *really* wanted you to join our game. He thought you'd fit right in if you could make it through the door.'

I smiled. 'Such a smart guy.'

'You don't need to tell me. He'd been trying to get me to join a party with you on A:RO long before we ever met in-person.'

I frowned. 'He doesn't strike me as much of a matchmaker?'

'I think he just thought we could both use a friend.'

I thought that was more our strength than magic. That we had each other. That we had each of us been through things that made us more understanding of others. It seemed cheesy to say 'Friendship was the real magic all along' but, well ... our TTRPG group had been transported to a magical world. How much more proof did you need?

When we arrived in Mihilit-dalath — rumpled, sore, and windswept — it wasn't long before North arrived to collect us. 'The arch-mage has confirmed the device is functioning. Come with me, and we'll conclude your arrangement.'

What I really wanted right now was to flop into bed in a darkened room, but I wasn't going to argue that point if it would save Saanvi even one less day away from her daughter.

Instead, we made our goodbyes there in the stables among the sand and dirt, with the pankalars bleating in the background. Ordeth stood with his hands in his pockets, shuffling his feet. Mileana sat there, her tail laid gracefully across her paws.

'So this is it,' he said. He smiled to one side, baring his cute tusks. 'You've taken me on a real adventure. I swear I won't forget it.'

Arries transformed into his werefox form to give him a massive hug. 'We'll miss you,' he said. 'You're part of the team, now.'

'You've been kinder than we had any reason to expect,' I said. My throat was tight, and my eyes stung. I didn't feel ready to say goodbye to Ordeth.

Silky nudged my hand, picking up on my tone.

'Yeah.' Hanna held out her hand to Ordeth, who looked confused. She rolled her eyes. 'You shake it.' She gripped his hand firmly, showing him how it was done. 'It's an Earth greeting and sign of respect. Sorry I didn't trust you at first.'

'You were worried about Pauline,' he said. 'I understand that.'

Kenta strode forward, looking ... sad. The two studied each other. 'We're coming back,' Kenta said. His voice shook. 'This isn't the end.' They hugged. Ordeth whispered something in Kenta's ear. He smiled and stepped back. 'I hope so.'

Rex nodded to him. 'Thanks for teaching me magic.'

Ordeth smiled to one side. 'Thanks for teaching *me.*'

'Ordeth,' I said. 'So ... you'll look after Silky?' We'd discussed it on the ship, but now seemed to be the moment.

He nodded. 'Until you get back.' He said the words firmly. Like he believed them.

Silky nudged me again at the sound of her name. I crouched beside her. 'Hey,' I said. 'I'm ... I'm going to go now. You have

to stay with Ordeth for a while again. You like Ordeth, right?'
I smoothed her cheeks. Her ear fins twitched at me. She
stretched her neck up to eye-level and blew hot, fish-scented
breath in my face.

'I'm going to miss you so much,' I whispered. 'You are the
best animal companion anyone could ask for, okay? The best
pet, even when you bite me.'

Silky turned her head to one side, confused by my tone.

I didn't want to leave her, not knowing if we would return.
I'd never had pets; I had been utterly unprepared for how
much I loved her. How special she was, even when she was
being a terror. Especially when she was being a terror. She was
a beastly little thing, but she was *my* beastly little thing. And
she was uncomplicated to love, and loved back with no more
complication than the occasional nip.

But I had to get Riya home. Had to let my mother know
what had become of me.

We would come back, I told myself. We had to come back.

I kissed her on the nose, and she let me. My vision swam as
tears speckled my glasses. I tried to push the emotions down
as I stood up.

'Silky!' Ordeth called. He got out some dried meat. At his
feet, Mileana watched him with rapt attention. 'Silky, want a
treat?'

Silky immediately went to him. Rex took my hand and
guided me away. 'He'll look after her really well,' he said.
'You've seen him with Mileana.'

I nodded, and wiped tears away from my eyes. I tried to
think about other things. This wasn't really goodbye, I told
myself. We had more pressing concerns.

If only I could convince myself.

As North led us to the Verdigris Spire, I fell behind with
Rex and Pauline. 'What do you make of Vorugar? Will he
honour our deal?'

Pauline nodded, her lips pressed into a tight line — though
that was likely more from pain than from misgiving. 'I believe

he will. We've given him enormous riches and power by stabilising this rift. He wasn't lying when he said netheril is extremely precious.'

'But?' I prompted.

Pauline's mouth shifted to one side. 'But we don't know whether he can actually do what he says he can — send us to a previously unknown plane. And we don't know what it will mean to go back, either.'

I wasn't sure what she meant by that, but Rex said, 'You think there could be a time delay between our planes?'

'I think anything could happen. Planar travel isn't simple, not even in the Associate Plane.'

This time, Vorugar didn't meet us in his tower. Instead, North led us into a wide chamber lit by energy pulsing through the crystalline walls. The windows shimmered and shifted, as if made of fractal light instead of glass. In spite of its vast emptiness, it felt incredibly full. Vorugar stood by a little table with a broad leather bag open at his feet. Various chalks, paints, and tools were set beside him, as well as an open book that even from here I took for a spellbook, with its filigree and the shimmering ink on its pages. Today his hair was in thick box braids interspersed with green beads, and his eyes were shadowed with green glitter. His robes were silver-gold and trailed like a wedding gown. He spread his arms wide in greeting as we filed in.

'Ah! Our extraplanar adventurers have returned!' He clapped his hands then rubbed them together. 'I have confirmed for myself that the rift is stabilised. Amazing that you managed to defeat the astral creatures guarding it!'

My stomach dropped; I looked to the others. Kenta looked angry, Arries shocked. Hanna's fingers twitched toward her flute, like she might attempt to spell him here and now.

Stiffly, Pauline said, 'You knew of them?'

Vorugar waved a dismissive hand. 'Early scouts had sent reports — those that survived, anyway. No, no need to look like that. They knew the risks: extraplanar travel is a dangerous business.'

'They knew the risks,' Kenta repeated, exchanging a sidelong look with Hanna. I knew where he was coming from. Apart from the awful callousness of that statement, *we* had known nothing at all going into it.

'Anyway, without them around, it should make extraction go very smoothly indeed. So.' He gestured at the circle. 'If you provide your dice, I can send you on your way.'

North cleared their throat. 'Arch-mage, perhaps a full report would be appropriate?'

Vorugar shrugged. 'The portal is stabilised and these fine people would like to be on their way. I see no point in delaying them further.' He began rummaging through the bag, removing small, capped paint pots.

'We didn't kill anything,' Arries said. 'And neither should you. The Siblings don't have any problem with you mining their netheril as long as you don't attempt to harm them.'

Now Vorugar actually stopped. His hands dropped to his sides. 'You didn't kill the astral beasts.'

'No.' Pauline raised her chin.

He stood up, a muscle flexing in his jaw. 'Then how, pray tell, did you stabilise the portal? By all accounts, they were guarding the heart of the rift quite fiercely.'

Kenta and Hanna both drew closer to Pauline at his approach, their protectiveness evident. Hanna crossed her arms. 'We asked nicely.'

Rex glanced at Hanna. 'We negotiated,' he explained. 'They're very open to negotiation. Which is just as well because you didn't prepare us and we would've had no hope to defeat them.' There was a harder edge to those last words than I'd ever heard from him.

Riya looked between everyone, chewing her lips. She looked so small. I understood everyone's anger but we couldn't afford to make an enemy of Vorugar. We *had* to get her home.

Vorugar smiled, affable again. 'And what was the nature of your negotiation?'

'That's private,' Kenta said with a smile that didn't reach his eyes.

Anger flickered across Vorugar's face, gone again so fast I wondered if I'd seen it. 'Of course. I would never dream of prying. Your dice, please.'

I didn't like this, didn't want to put our lives in the hands of a man who had deliberately deceived us, and now was angry at us, but I didn't see what choice we had. We each retrieved our dice and handed them to Arries, who offered them to Vorugar.

'Thank you.' He tossed them up into the air, where they froze as if trapped in invisible ice. 'These should do the trick. Now I'll require your silence for the next several minutes. The next part requires total concentration.'

I started forward. 'Wait!'

Vorugar stopped, hands in his toolkit. '... Yes?'

'What will it be like?' I asked. 'Time is important. Location is important. We need to go back to our country, ideally not long after we left.'

Vorugar raised his eyebrow. 'I won't know until I make the connection. Time passes strangely between different planes. If you're lucky, it will have travelled at roughly the same time as you've spent here.'

My throat nearly closed at the thought of returning Riya home weeks after she'd disappeared. 'That can't — it isn't —'

Vorugar waved me away. 'Leave me to my work. When the teleportation circle is constructed, *then* we can talk.'

I inclined my head, not looking at him. My chest felt horribly tight, my head full of air.

If we couldn't get Riya back to her mother, there was no point in going back. I was terrified of a faerie story-type situation where we got back a hundred years later or something.

We needed to get her back.

Rex needed to see his family.

Arries needed to see his friends.

And god, I needed to talk to my mother.

Vorugar got to work painting an intricate teleportation circle on the floor. It had branching sigils and arcing lines; part diagram, part artwork. More complex than any we had yet encountered. I supposed planar travel was even less common than teleportation, and with good reason. As he worked, little drifting sparks of ethereal light shed from the paint at moments, so quick it might have been imagined.

Several times, he asked North to check his work. They walked around the circle, studying it intently, but made no corrections. I couldn't decide whether that was reassuring or not. Either Vorugar made no mistakes, or North was making the same ones. I supposed it boded well that Vorugar was even bothering to check — maybe he wasn't about to arrange an 'accident' for us with the spell.

When he finished the circle to North's satisfaction, he stood up and raised his hands. 'I love this part,' he boasted, plucking his fingers through the air like he was playing an invisible harp. The netheril dice, which had been frozen in the air during the whole process, slowly started to spin and weave, a golden glow kindling inside them. He continued to pluck the air, muttering an incantation, before lifting his hands to catch the dice as they came whizzing toward him.

The teleportation circle below flashed, then dimmed to a dull glow. 'One moment.' He knelt beside it, touching his fingertips to a cluster of runes. 'Hmm. It appears time passes at an equivalent rate on your Earth as it does on the Associate Plane. You should only have lost ... was it a few weeks that you've been here? Nothing drastic.' He stepped back and gestured at the circle. 'Assemble on it, if you would.'

Kenta started to move, but I put my arm out to stop him. 'Wait, wait. Is there a way to go back to the time we left?'

Vorugar looked regretful. 'I'm afraid time travel has yet to be discovered. Now —'

'That's not true,' Pauline said. 'Travel between planes has been used many times throughout history for just that effect.'

I watched her sidelong. Her mark wasn't glowing; this was just more lore she'd memorised. She was amazing like that.

Vorguar shifted uncomfortably. 'There are accounts of it, yes. But the knowledge is lost, and it's not something easily or consistently done. It would as likely see you cast adrift in time as not. It's more easily handled with planes that have an unstable time difference with the Associate. Your Earth does not.'

I glanced at North. Their mouth was twisting downwards ever so slightly at the corners. Because they didn't like what Vorugar was saying, or because they wanted rid of us already? Or was I misreading it entirely? Reading facial expressions was always risky for me — I would put too much weight on tiny signals that were meaningless, or miss obvious signs entirely.

But ... and maybe this was foolish of me ... I could not help but feel that North was at least a little on our side. For all their abrasive manner, they had been nothing but helpful to us, and they seemed much more straightforward than Vorugar ever did.

'Is there no point in trying?' I asked. 'We're trying to reunite a little girl with her mother, for fuck's sake.'

Vorugar spread his hands apologetically, too showy to be sincere. 'That was neither the deal nor a possibility. And you are delaying her return by pushing it, are you not?'

I couldn't believe what I was hearing, and I wasn't the only one. The others started to argue, Hanna and Arries quite loudly. But Pauline and Rex stood to one side, talking in low voices. I went to join them.

Rex had his spellbook open and was rapidly taking notes, while Pauline checked over his shoulder. The mark on her forehead was glowing as she looked, occasionally offering notes. It was a direct analogue of North and Vorguar with the teleportation circle, and sure enough a sketch of the circle started to take place on the page.

'Why —?' I asked.

Rex didn't look up from the notebook. 'So we can get back.'

Pauline flicked her gaze at Vorugar. 'But we'll need our dice.'

Vorugar was still trying to calm Hanna and Arries, who were yelling at him and pleading with him by turn.

Kenta was with them, but had a distant look in his eyes. After a moment, his head jerked up and he looked around. 'It'll be okay,' he said, his deep voice cutting through the clamour.

Hanna stopped and frowned at him. 'Did North enchant you or something?'

'I did nothing of the sort,' North said, wrinkling their nose.

'I'm fine, really,' he said. 'It has nothing to do with Vorugar or North.' He gave Hanna a pointed look.

I wasn't sure I was following, but Hanna's eyes widened. 'Shit, really? Okay.' She shrugged and went to stand on the circle. 'I'm convinced.'

Rex and Pauline seemed to have stopped the frantic note taking, though Rex still looked back and forth between the floor and his notes, clearly checking his work over again.

'Ken?' I tried. He glanced at me sidelong. His eyes flashed red and green; he winked, and then they were back to normal.

Hope bloomed. Or nausea.

We could do this our way. We could make everything right.

My gaze fell on Vorugar. We just needed our dice back.

Everyone was busy. We couldn't turn this into a battle, even if we wanted to. There was nothing to do but ask him.

I cleared my throat. 'Uh. Arch-mage?'

He was talking to North and didn't notice me come up alongside him.

'Excuse me — the dice?'

Again, nothing.

I flashed back to the dozens of times I'd been in this situation, fruitlessly trying to get the attention of someone who couldn't or wouldn't even acknowledge my presence.

Every time, I had slunk away, exhausted and ashamed, thoroughly convinced of my own worthlessness.

But I wasn't worthless. And even though my cheeks burned and my aura was aflame, I still raised my voice. 'Arch-mage!' I nearly had to shout it.

Vorugar stiffened and turned, his expression one of shocked displeasure. My throat closed up at it, as if he hadn't put me in this situation, as if I hadn't asked quietly several times already and he hadn't used that to plausibly ignore me.

I tried to find the words. 'You still have our property.'

'I'm sorry?'

'Our dice,' I said. 'You have our dice. They weren't consumed in the spell and we'd like them back.'

He glared down at me.

I built my nerve. 'Surely you can afford to spare us our *own* netheril, given we have provided access to a whole pocket dimension of it?'

'You make me sound like a petty thief,' he said.

I had nothing to say to that, but I raised my chin and willed myself to look braver than I was.

'Arch-mage?' North said, their tone questioning.

Vorugar smiled tightly. 'Of course. I hadn't even realised I'd kept them. I would never dream of depriving you of what is rightfully yours.' There was an odd weight to his tone that I didn't like, and his eyes darted to Pauline as he said it, but he twisted his hand and the dice appeared on his open palm. He tipped them onto mine. 'Well then. If that is all ...?'

I nodded and thanked him, then joined the others on the teleportation circle.

Vorugar activated it, drawing runes swiftly in the air. His sleeve fell back, and I felt like I'd been kicked in the stomach. On his arm, in red ink, was an eye tattoo.

As light blared up around us, he said, 'I won't forget you. *Any* of you.'

I started to shout.

And then we were falling.

CHAPTER FORTY-TWO

It was different to the teleportation circle. Not instantaneous in the same way. There was that feeling of the ground falling away from beneath our feet. There was darkness. I wondered if this was the Void Between Planes, if Vorugar had sabotaged the teleportation circle. In my mind, all I could see was the red eye on his wrist. But then there was a feeling of being hooked, like we were being pulled sideways. Stars exploded into light all around us. Ekthrentis and Orodantilla emerged from the shadows, just as enormous as before. Creatures of scales and fins and crystal.

You will be fine, friends, they said, their enormous hands closing around us, shutting out the stars and plunging us back into darkness.

We landed in Pauline's game room, staggering. A teleportation circle burned into the ground at our feet, light fading like embers. The table had been thrown aside, knocking games from the shelves. But the same bold floral wallpaper. The same smell of cinnamon and roses. I immediately grasped for Riya. 'Riya? Riya!'

Riya hugged my middle. 'Where are we?'

'This is Earth. This is Pauline and Hanna's house,' I said. Riya was in the same fantasy clothes. Her ears were still elven. In fact, looking around, all of us still bore the marks of our time in Vanthis.

Riya's eyes widened. 'We're almost home?'

I smiled. 'We're almost home, kid.'

Riya's eyes filled with tears. She pressed her face into my hip, hugging more tightly. I knelt down and let her hug me properly, stroking her back and trying to ignore the discomfort this gave me. I would bear it for Riya. She'd been through so much.

While I awkwardly murmured encouragement to the universe's bravest seven year-old, I watched the others laugh and embrace each other, or pat each other on the back. Even Rex smiled broadly, his tail gently flicking at the tip in almost feline contentment.

'We made it,' Arries said. 'Earth!' He raised his hands in triumph. 'I missed you, chair!' He righted one of the chairs and hugged it like he was greeting an old friend.

'Hanna, check my phone?' asked Pauline. 'It's next to my bed?'

Hanna nodded. 'On it.'

She rushed upstairs, hooves clattering on every step, to hurry back down with a phone in-hand. '12.01 am, Friday 19th April, 2019,' Hanna said, handing it to Pauline with the screen lit up. 'The same night we left.'

'Oh my god, we did it,' Pauline said. 'No time lost.'

'We did it!' Kenta yelled, to be immediately shushed by both Pauline and Arries.

'It's midnight, Ken!'

'My neighbours are asleep!'

'Right, right,' he made calming motions.

'We couldn't have done this without the Siblings,' Rex said. 'Can you thank them for us? This is incredible.'

Kenta nodded, his eye colour switching to the Siblings' and back so quickly I almost missed it. 'They know,' he said.

I wondered about that — about their help. The deal they'd made had only been to use Kenta's eyes and protect him from Alis-Umor. They had no reason to help us this way — even if they wanted to see Earth, they'd have seen it through Kenta's eyes regardless.

Maybe some people were just kind. Even giant cosmic horror space mermaids. It was a warming thought.

Riya pulled away from me, sniffling. From the look of her, she'd probably gotten snot all over me, but she offered me a wobbly smile and I found I didn't care. 'Can we go now?' she asked.

'Soon,' I said. 'Really soon.'

I stood up and looked at the others. 'So ... illusions? How are we going to explain ... all this?' I gestured up and down at myself, since I was now a glowing sparkle person, then gestured at Arries' fox ears.

Arries' ears twitched. '... We're just really committed cosplayers?' he said.

'I don't think that's going to cut it.' Hanna's mouth twisted to one side. 'Here ... lemme see ...' She picked up her flute and played a short trill that rose and fell. She flickered, like she was experiencing static. Her brow furrowed and she played the trill again. This time, her appearance shimmered, then shifted to her original form: a tall, confident human, with not a glimmer of her satyr-like self from Vanthis. 'Okay that felt ... weird.' She shuddered. 'There's resistance here to Vanthian magic, I guess.'

'Let me try!' Arries said. He started to lean forward, face screwed up with concentration. His back arched. 'Hold on ... almost ... got it ... ahhh!' He straightened, now in his enormous werefox shape, panting happily. 'Oh yeah, that's much more difficult. Doable though.'

'I can't illusion myself,' I said. 'If one of you casts it, how long will it last?'

'A few hours,' said Rex. 'We might need to team up while we visit people for a while, to make sure everyone is covered. Who can cast illusions?'

Everyone but me, Pauline, and Arries raised their hands. Rex looked to Kenta with raised eyebrows.

Kenta looked sheepish. 'The Siblings have granted me ... quite a bit of power. We have it covered.' When Rex didn't lower his eyebrows, Kenta assured him, 'They want to help.'

Rex shook his head. 'Shoulda known being extroverted would pay off for you in Vanthis somehow,' he said, causing Kenta to bark a laugh in surprise.

'But we can't do that ... indefinitely,' I said. 'I mean ... I'm going back. Pauline and Rex, you have the teleportation circle for it, right?'

They both nodded.

I looked at my friends. 'You're going back, too, right?'

Hanna and Kenta nodded, but everyone else looked away. Rex played with his hair; Arries' tail lashed anxiously.

'I've ... got some stuff to work out,' Rex said.

I tried to ignore the tight feeling in my chest, and the sickness in the pit of my stomach. To have come so far together and worked all this out — finally worked it all out! — only to be separated at the end was heartbreaking.

I knew, I *knew*, that there wasn't a single one of us that didn't dream of living in Vanthis. We had a unique chance to start again; to live, actually *live* a fantasy.

And then it struck me, quite hard, that maybe nobody else really *wanted* to start again. Their lives were more together than mine. Maybe Vanthis for them was a holiday rather than a lifeline.

I touched my collarbone, clearing my throat. It was hard to draw air. My lungs felt too full, like they were about to burst. I only nodded.

Rex cast an illusion on me and Riya, making us look like our regular selves. 'Message me tomorrow,' he said, his fingers brushing my sleeve as he turned away.

I felt dumbstruck.

Kenta didn't live far from Pauline; he got his car and dropped off Riya and me at home. As strange as it was, I felt shocked to see Saanvi's house, just a regular terraced house, exactly as I remembered it. I didn't have a key, but Riya dug one out of the flower pot on the doorstep and offered it to me. Quietly, we let ourselves in.

'You've gotta get changed first,' I said to Riya. 'Back into your pyjamas. Can you do that?'

Riya nodded. We went upstairs, but as I let myself into my bedroom Riya didn't head for hers. Before I could so much as whisper a warning, she'd rushed into her mother's room, yelling 'Mum! Mum! I'm home!'

I swallowed hard and closed the door behind me. I could hear their murmured voices. Saanvi didn't sound distressed, and within a few minutes, all was quiet again. No doubt just a mother comforting a child from a nightmare, from her perspective.

I supposed the truth of it all would be out by morning. I didn't know if I knew quite how to break any of it to her. The nerves from that were a tight knot in my belly.

I turned away from my door, taking in the room. The desktop cast gently shifting lights along the wall, filling the room with a gentle rainbow glow. My clothes were still scattered across the floor and bed. A stack of novels was piled on my bedside table, gathering dust. It smelled familiar — my washing detergent, my body spray, the faint after-scent of rain, since I had opened my window to it earlier in the day. It smelled of home.

I flopped on my bed, as careless of the clothes thrown there as I'd ever been.

I had spent so much of my life the last few years between these walls.

Huddled at my computer; curled up with my phone. Laughing as I chatted with my friends; yelling as Arries and I took on some dungeon or other in A:RO.

I had been so unhappy. I had been so happy, too. I didn't think either would change much when I moved my life to Vanthis, but I was more at peace with that than I'd ever been before. I could weather the dark times, with the help of my friends.

It still seemed mad that it had all been real. Lying here on my bed in Saanvi's house, it would be easy to imagine that it was any other night. That the last weeks had never happened — as indeed, in this world, they never had. I held up my hands to the ceiling, studying them. If I focused really hard, I could sometimes catch a glimmer of my astralkin skin beneath the illusion. The barest glimpse.

I wove my hands through the air, trying to draw energy from the earth as I had in the Associate Plane. At first there was nothing, my thoughts straining within my own mind just as it did during an anxiety attack, and for a moment I thought I might scream or cry from the frustration. But then it came ... a trickle of energy, both cool and warm at the same time. I pulled it into me and then pushed it out through my hands as I turned the spell into a snap.

A seed formed between my fingers, small and hard. I rolled it onto my palm and fed it more energy, watching it grow. It started slowly at first, just tiny cracks in the seed's surface, then grew faster, becoming a small seedling before my eyes, reaching for the sky. A flower budded and bloomed. Just a daisy. A simple, Earthly daisy, but my breath caught.

Real. It was all real.

It was all complicated.

I closed my eyes. I'd have to deal with that in the morning.

☆ ☆ ☆

To say that Saanvi took it well would be an understatement, even given that she'd screamed when she'd discovered her daughter's pointed ears, and screamed again when I'd walked out of my bedroom looking like I'd been dipped in white paint and glitter. It took some time to get the whole story out, with me needing to demonstrate my magic multiple times to reassure her it was all real.

My polymorph especially affected her; I guess there was something about your lodger turning into a flesh-and-blood cat that you could physically touch that was more believable than any light or seed I could produce. She hugged Riya close the whole time, her expression during the story sometimes suspicious, sometimes awed.

When I had exhausted all her questions and demonstrations, she took a shaking breath. 'Thank you, then,' she said. 'For protecting Riya. For bringing her home. I can't thank you for taking her away — I don't know if I'll ever be able to forgive you for that. But I understand that it wasn't your intention or your fault. This is ... too much to take in ...' She shook her head, her fingers playing with Riya's hair. They touched Riya's pointed ear-tips. 'So she'll look like this forever?'

'I don't know,' I said honestly. 'I don't know exactly how any of this works. But my friends have more magic than me — we might be able to make her something to hide them.'

'The last thing she needs is more reasons for the kids at school to tease her,' Saanvi said.

'I like my ears,' Riya protested, glaring up at her mother. 'They are very big!'

To my surprise, Saanvi smiled. 'And they look beautiful on you.'

'I'm a Lord of the Rings!' Riya said.

Saanvi gave me a pained look. 'I should never have let her watch that film.'

I shrugged. 'I think it prepared her pretty well, actually.'

We agreed that I would move out — honestly, I think Saanvi couldn't wait to get rid of me — but that before I did, we'd try to make something to hide Riya's elf ears, and train her to hide the small amount of magic she had.

'God,' Saanvi had said to me, leaning in the doorway of my room as I packed. 'I know it's a blessing — a gift, even — to have magic. I'm going to try to think of it that way. After all, Riya has always been special. I just ... can't help but wish she'd remained normal.'

I considered her words. I could understand them from her perspective. To have magic in a magicless world was to be set apart, and that was really hard.

But then again, I'd never fit in at school anyway. How often had I wished that I had magic? That there was some reason for my difference, something that could comfort me? 'I hope she'll feel differently,' was all I said.

We agreed that I would come back to visit a few times a year, if I could, to check on Riya. I promised that I would try to find a way for her to contact me in Vanthis. That was one part of this whole 'move to Vanthis' thing I was still trying to work out. Was cross-planar communication even possible? And if it was, would it still work with Earth, where there was so little magic?

Or *was* there little magic? Our spells still worked here. I was drawing my energy from *somewhere*. And we had never really resolved the question of how we had been transported to Vanthis in the first place.

I didn't know what to make of any of it. I supposed we would find out in time.

I checked my phone often. We had been posting updates to each other in our chat, but it was all very brief, not the lively chatter I was used to. I guess we all needed to decompress from our adventure, but after weeks of being within poking distance of my friends every day, I felt isolated.

I called my mum and arranged to visit her. I decided to drive rather than get the train; long car journeys stressed me out, but better that than my battle with the train. I let everyone know, but got only cursory acknowledgements. I tried not to let that rankle. It felt a little like this was all falling apart. I had proof that the magic was real; I had nothing that the friendship was. That those moments with Rex were.

I remembered sitting beneath the blue-leafed trees in Mihilit-dalath. I remembered his smile, so full of wonder, and swallowed hard. It had only been a week ago, but with the shift back to Earth, it felt like an age. It felt like it was slipping away from me.

I was able to squeeze most of my belongings into my car. What I couldn't take, I arranged for a local charity to pick up. Looking around at my empty room left me with a lump in my throat. This was home. The most at home I'd ever felt on Earth. This was where I'd met Arries. This was where I'd gone over the lore for *Kin*, and made Astaran. It was where I'd started the only job I'd managed to keep, where Saanvi had often offered me dinner when she'd made too much, where Riya had given me her first art of the two of us. I had fallen asleep here reading the messages of my friends. I had cried and laughed and curled up waiting for the panic to fade.

And though I'd dreamed every night of being someone else, living in the skin of my character in Vanthis had proven to me that I would always be me, but that maybe that wasn't the punishment I'd always thought it to be.

Like Rex had said — I could be brave. I was the person who *hadn't* run away. I was the person who kept trying even in the face of being crushed.

And with that in mind ...

I stopped pacing my room. I took out my phone and sent one message:

Tar: Could we meet up?

I waited with baited breath.

Rex: Come to mine tonight. 13B Mercroft Court.

We finalised the details and I held the phone to my chest for a moment, letting both the anxiety and the hope war within me. Then I took a shuddering breath and headed into work to say my goodbyes.

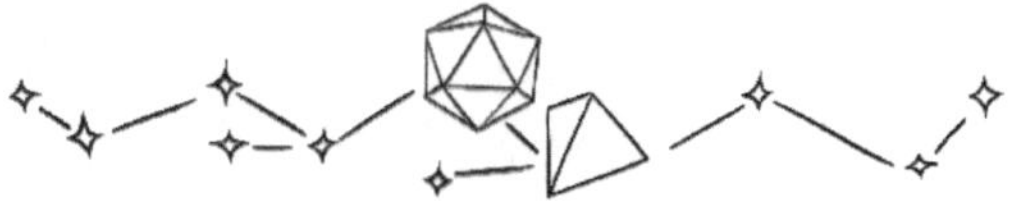

CHAPTER FORTY-THREE

I hurried up to Rex's with my hood up. The illusion Kenta had cast on me had worn off and while I didn't think I'd stand out too much in the short distance from my car to his doorstep, I still felt pretty exposed and was more than a little worried my aura might start glowing. 13B Mercroft Court turned out to be a small maisonette in a nice courtyard tucked away from the busy streets on the edge of town. A number of large blossom trees lined the parking lot, leaving the entire court blanketed in a quilt of pink petals. The houses here were clad in dark, warm colours.

13B had a little shrub sitting outside that looked well-tended. I brushed its soft leaves with my fingers, then knocked on the door.

As the seconds ticked by, I imagined that I'd gotten the wrong house, and checked the messages again. That Rex had accidentally given me the wrong address and I was about to be confronted by a stranger. That I'd gotten the day wrong, somehow, and a myriad of other miscommunications that left me breathless with panic. But I waited.

When the door opened, though, it was only Rex. He wore an illusion that made him look like his Earth-self, though I noticed he'd decided to include blue chalk in his locs, reminiscent of his Vanthian form. He offered me a flimsy smile, not quite looking at me. 'Hey, Tar. Come on in.'

It was a small ground-level, one-bed flat. The walls were decorated with A:RO posters and fantasy art prints. D20-

shaped cushions decorated his sofa. I could just see the kitchen, which was tucked around the corner. But what really struck me was that everything looked undisturbed. The sofa and TV were still in place, as was the PC desk in the corner. My stomach lurched with dread.

He wasn't planning on going back.

He stood in front of me, thumbs in the pockets of his jeans, rocking back and forth on his heels. 'Uh ... can I get you a cup of tea, maybe?'

I shook my head, promptly forgetting the thousands of times my mother had scolded me that refusing a drink was rude. 'No thanks.'

Now I couldn't look at him either. Pressure was building behind my eyes and my throat was tightening. God, was I going to cry? That was the last thing I needed right now ... I wished my hair was long and loose, as it had been when I was a teenager, and that I could tip my head forward and try to hide my face with it.

Rex gestured to the sofa. 'Sit. If, you know, if you want.'

I perched on the edge of the seat. It was a worn, old-style sofa with green leaves embroidered on it. It would probably be quite comfortable to lean back against but that felt too vulnerable a position. I put my hands between my knees.

I didn't want to have this conversation. I didn't want to lose Rex. I didn't want to confirm what I was so frightened of: that in the cold light of reality, Rex had realised that he wanted neither a world of magic nor me, though I'd have given up the former if he'd asked me to.

'So ... what, um, what did you want to talk about?' he asked. His voice was hard and closed off. He leaned forward in his seat, his arms crossed like he was guarding his belly.

I cast around for what to say, my eyes going everywhere but to him. From this angle, I could see into his bedroom. The mattress stood up against the wall. Cardboard boxes crowded around it.

I stopped, words halfway to my mouth.

'Tar?'

I looked at Rex, who still stared down into his own lap. Maybe he really was having doubts about me, but maybe I had given him this weird energy. I wouldn't know until I asked. 'I thought you weren't going to go back to Vanthis,' I said. 'Or ... or that you've been avoiding me because you were having second thoughts. About.' I cleared my throat. 'Me.'

Rex's head jerked up in surprise, his eyes locking with mine. 'What? No! I mean ... I didn't *mean* to avoid you ...' he trailed off. 'I just thought ... what with being back on Earth, maybe *you* were having ... doubts ...'

I was grinning at him and he couldn't help but grin back. He turned his head to the side, rubbing the back of his neck. 'Stop that.'

'We are absolute fools,' I said. 'We're ridiculous. You can see how ridiculous this is?'

'I think we might need to work on our communication skills.' He laughed shakily.

'And your self-confidence,' I said. 'It would be like spitting in luck's eye to break up with someone as amazing as you.'

'*Luck,*' he said, shaking his head. 'Maybe we *both* need to work on our self-confidence then.'

We were sitting closer now. So suddenly I wondered how it happened. He touched his fingertips to mine, so I took his hand. He leaned close to me, eyes flicking down to my lips and back up to my eyes. I could feel his breath warm on my face but it didn't bother me. 'I would like to kiss you now,' he said. His voice was very soft.

I swallowed hard, my mouth suddenly dry. 'Please do,' I replied hoarsely.

He leaned in, pressing his lips to mine with a gentleness I found almost dizzying. His fingertips brushed my chin even as my hands came up to cradle his face. It wasn't how I remembered kissing, which had often felt invasive. This was warm. This was comforting and thrilling at the same time. All I could think was that this was *my* life. That for reasons I might never understand, the elusive Rex had chosen *me,* wanted this closeness with *me.* That I really, really wanted this. Not sex, but closeness. Intimacy. The feeling of a connection that was only between us.

Our bodies pressed closer, his chest flush against mine. One of his hands went to the small of my back, pressing the soft indentation there. He pulled back after a moment, smiling at me with a look of dazed wonder. 'You are *everything,*' he said, his voice hoarse now as well. He looked so soft and flustered that I kissed him again, his startled laugh sweet against my mouth.

When I pulled back, his smile was crooked. 'That. Was good.'

'Very,' I agreed.

'We should do it again sometime?'

I nodded vigorously, and he laughed again.

We slumped on opposite ends of the sofa, just smiling at each other.

'So does this mean you're my boyfriend?' I asked, a little anxious just to say the words, but comforted by the glitter in his eyes.

'*God* yes,' he said. He looked at me almost reverently in that moment. 'Does this mean you're my datefriend?'

'I really, really hope so,' I said.

He nudged my foot with his, grinning. 'Just us?' he said. 'I know you might prefer —'

'— Just us,' I said quickly. I had loved very little in my life, and every time fiercely devoted to only one. And Rex ... my feelings for Rex were so large I almost didn't feel big enough to hold them.

He looked relieved. 'Good. Okay.'

'Okay.'

He nodded. 'All right.'

'Fine,' I said, grinning.

'Great, even,' he said, laughing.

When we'd recovered from the intensity of it all, he introduced me to his cat. Khara, named for the giant cat creatures of Arcadia: Redux Online, stared at me with wide eyes from under the mattress. She was just a shadow with orange eyes until Rex coaxed her out. 'It's okay,' he said. 'Tar is a friend. I really like Tar and I think you are going to love them.'

I hoped it was true.

Khara slunk out from under the bed, sniffing toward me curiously, shoulders tense and poised to flee. I instantly recognised myself in her stance, and held out my hand for her to inspect. She wasn't grey, as I'd first thought, but a gorgeous tortoise-shell of ginger, tabby, white, black, and grey. 'You're beautiful,' I whispered. 'You're like every colour of cat at once.'

She sniffed my hand very carefully, then rubbed her cheek against my fingertips. I held in a squeal of excitement. She climbed into Rex's lap and narrowed her eyes at me in a slow blink.

'That's a smile,' Rex told me. He scratched her shoulders and she started to rumble with the deepest, most menacing chainsaw purr I had ever heard. 'It means she likes you.'

'I like her, too,' I said. Though seeing her with Rex made me miss Silky terribly.

Khara would be going back to Vanthis with us. I wondered whether she would meet Ordeth's Mileana, and what they would make of each other. I would certainly have to make Silky behave with her.

After that, I helped him pack. It was mostly moving boxes around for me — he'd genuinely boxed away almost everything — but since I was big and strong and he was significantly leaner and more waifish, I felt like I was still contributing. He warned me that his parents and one of his brothers were coming around later with a van. 'Do you want to meet them?' he asked. 'I mean ... I know it hasn't been long for us, but we're going to Vanthis soon.' He gave me a worried look.

Khara popped out of a box, looking confused. Rex went to get her out.

I tried to even out my breathing and properly consider what he was saying. I did want to meet Rex's family. It was a big family and he was really close with his siblings. But also the short notice made my chest really tight, and also I was *really bad* at meeting people. I couldn't always speak very well — sometimes it was just a squeak. I would be awkward and struggle to make eye contact and they'd all think I hated them or I was rude.

I must've spent longer than I thought mulling it over, because I felt a touch at my wrist.

'Hey,' said Rex. 'It doesn't have to be today. But since we'll just be moving stuff into the van, I thought it might be a low pressure way to meet some of them, so maybe it'd be easier in a more formal meeting with more people next time. It's just an idea. I won't think less of you if you say no, or want to wait for another time.'

The urge to say no was strong, if only because it was always easier to not meet someone than to meet someone. But this was Rex. Rex, my *boyfriend.* It would be worth any discomfort to know him better, or to make him happy.

I took a shuddering breath and gave him an anxious smile. 'I'd like to try,' I said. 'I might not be able to stay long, but I'd like to try.'

He searched my face. 'Yeah?'

'Yeah.'

'You know my family is black, right?'

'I was able to surmise that, yes,' I said, but I knew that wasn't really what he meant. 'Will they mind? That, you know, I'm white?'

He shook his head, and for a brief moment I saw a flicker of void energy at the corner of his eyes. 'They'll be really excited to meet you, it's not about them. But ... Earth isn't like Vanthis. There're things we need to talk about, if we're going to be in a relationship.'

I wanted to say that I understood, that I was prepared, but realistically how could I be? I'd spent most of my life trying to unlearn the racism I'd been taught by other white people. I probably still had a long way to go. I couldn't know.

'Okay,' I said, swallowing hard. 'Let's talk about it.'

So we spent the next few hours doing so. The first of many conversations, he said, and I could feel the truth of that.

As it happened, his parents were warm and friendly. His dad strode up to me and shook my hand, all smiles. His mum hung back a little and didn't quite meet my eyes, but was very kind regardless and honestly that was kind of a relief. Both resembled Rex, in different ways — Rex's father had Rex's sharp cheekbones and jawline. Rex's mother was a similar height and her elegant mannerisms and withdrawn behaviour immediately reminded me of him. His brother arrived not long after. A slim man of much the same build as Rex, but with rounder features more like their mother, and with a broad smile more like their father. He wore a loose t-shirt and jeans so neat they looked almost ironed, a far cry from Rex's preferred ripped skinny jeans.

We didn't talk a lot, busy as we were with moving Rex's furniture, but they were helpful and thoughtful and didn't seem to dislike me. I stayed longer than I thought I would last, but when they invited me for pizza with the family afterwards, I felt like I would cry. Rex swooped in and said I had my own errands to run and encouraged me to go home. His parents both hugged me and asked me to come visit before the big move. My magical nature didn't come up — I assumed Rex hadn't broken the news to his parents yet, or else they weren't sure whether I was in the know.

Later that night, I called Rex from my mum's living room. 'I made it,' I said with a shaky voice.

'You made it,' he said, with a tone of such genuine relief that it made me feel better about the whole thing.

'I really like your parents,' I said. 'They seem like good people.'

'The best.' I could hear his sincerity. 'I'm going to be staying with them in a few days. They want you to come for dinner.'

I nodded and bit my lip. 'I think I can handle that. Do they know about Vanthis?'

'They do, though my siblings don't yet. I'm taking them a couple at a time so I don't get too badly outnumbered. My sisters are going to be *furious*. They'd kill to go on a fantasy adventure.'

'Do you think we'll be able to do that?' I asked. 'Bring people with us, I mean?'

'At some point,' he said. 'As long as we get back okay this time. We can alter the spell, get better anchors for everyone ... I think it's doable.'

I considered that. We still didn't completely understand what it was about the dice that had pulled us through into Vanthis — or why it had made us look like our characters and given us magic. But if travel between our plane and others was possible, who was to say whether other people hadn't found their way there — or whether others from Vanthis hadn't found their way to Earth.

The universe was so much larger and stranger than any of us had guessed. Even Pauline, with her vision of distant worlds, had never considered that ours might be part of the vast spiderweb of Vanthis' reality. That the Associate Plane might also be connected to Earth, of all places.

We still didn't know how the Order of the Third Eye had known about Pauline. Or how netheril had ended up on Earth. Netheril shaped like poly dice, which had somehow fallen into our hands.

When we talked about going to Vanthis to live, it was to start quiet lives. Well — I thought Arries might actually go out and do some hero work, but certainly most of us just wanted to become NPCs, as it were. There were still mysteries yet to solve before we could do that safely.

The idea, for once, didn't terrify me.

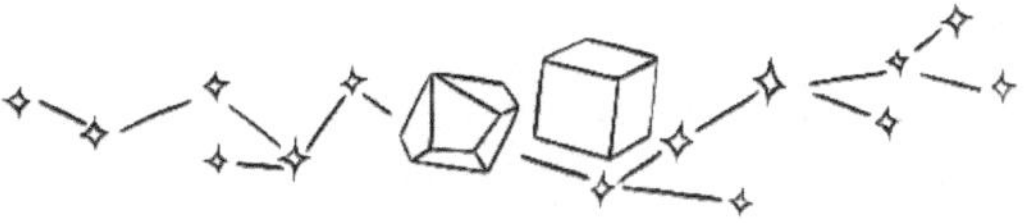

CHAPTER FORTY-FOUR

It took a lot of emotional build-up for me to tell my mum, but my illusion wasn't going to last much longer and I knew I had to tell her soon if I was going to tell her at all. You'd think it would be easy, given the amount of strange things my mother believed in. She had made believing in things a lifelong calling. She'd even started a part-time business doing astrology and palmistry, and putting crystals in people's gardens on the weekends. Not enough to quit her admin job yet, but impressive all the same.

But there was something very different about me, Tarot, her very logical and level-headed child (well, apart from the anxiety) coming to her and saying 'magic is real, let me show you'. What if she thought I was a liar? What if it scared her? She believed in all kinds of evil spirits and stuff like that. I just had no way to know how she would take it.

But most of all, I didn't want her to see me differently. We hadn't always seen eye-to-eye, but the thing she believed in most was *me*. She'd never backed down from her story that I was meant for great things. That I was special in some way. And I honestly couldn't say whether she would think this whole 'magical world' stuff would confirm that, or disprove it. After all, I wasn't special. Pauline was the one who had seen that other world. And the powers I had been granted there were not uncommon. I was, at best, an interdimensional bystander.

But I knew Rex didn't like me to think of myself that way, and honestly I didn't really like it either, so I let it go. I tried to centre myself. To find the same courage I'd found to explain everything to Saanvi.

It just ... felt very different with my own mother.

So the second day at my mum's, when I'd folded the futon back up and gotten dressed, I waited in the kitchen for my mum. My white hair was still damp and glittered like it had been dipped in sparkles. My aura was a faint glow I couldn't quite push down — I think my nerves were making it worse. My eyes were unquestionably golden where once they had been dark brown. So even in my favourite turquoise A:RO hoodie and slouchy jeans, there was no denying that there was something supernaturally different about me.

I paced the kitchen, waiting for my mum to come downstairs. I rubbed my eyes under my glasses, and tugged at the bottom of my hoodie. God, I wanted this to be okay. I wanted this to be normal. I didn't know what I would do without my mum.

When she arrived, her hair in a loose bun, wearing a silk dressing gown covered in flowers, it was all I could do not to blurt everything out there and then. Mum paused at my appearance but didn't say anything about it. Instead we ate breakfast together, while my mum talked about the day before, and the clients she'd had visit the small office she'd set up in the garage. 'This week was palmistry,' she told me. 'You wouldn't believe the fascinating things you see on people's hands sometimes. Nothing dramatic, just — making a new friend, getting lost in a familiar place, things like that. I'm really looking forward to the next time they visit so that they can tell me how it all worked out. That's always the most rewarding part of my job.'

I nodded along, twisting my hoodie up in my hands below the table. 'Anyway,' she set aside her porridge bowl. 'What was it you wanted to talk about?' she asked. 'You've been very tense all morning, darling.'

I took a deep breath. 'Mum ... you've probably noticed ... this?' I pointed to my face, now white and sparkling. I held out my hands, which had a faint glow.

My mum gave an even nod. 'I didn't want to make you feel self-conscious. You always hate it when I comment on how you look. But you do look fabulous, Tarot. Are you off to a party or something?'

My mouth went dry. She was willing to accept a mundane answer to this — which was no surprise, really, because what other kind of answer could there be in this world? But I didn't want to go to Vanthis without her knowing the truth. Honestly, it would make it easier to come home and visit and find a way to communicate between the worlds if she was on board. 'Mum ... it's not dye, or glitter. I, um — I'm magic.'

I sketched a rune in the air and reached for the vase she had on the table. The flowers there were beginning to wilt. I summoned a spark of magic up through the soles of my feet and pushed it into the flowers. A bit of a strain, on Earth, but it went through. The flowers straightened, petals blooming and flushing with colour. The leaves became plump and vibrant. Roots started to grow from the stems, seeking purchase against the glass.

My mum's eyes widened as she looked from the vase to me. She didn't say anything.

That alone gave me pause.

'It's not a trick, mum,' I said, my voice a little hoarse. 'It's not all I can do, either. Do you want me to show you?'

My mum put her hand to her temple. 'Not yet, please. I ... need a moment. How did you learn this? Only a few weeks ago you were telling me you were going to your friend's birthday party and now ... magic?'

I licked my lips. 'It's kind of a long story,' I said.

'Well, let's hear it.'

So I told her everything. About the dice, Vanthis, and Riya being sucked through with us. Our journey to the arch-mage, and his demand that we do him a favour in return. Meeting the Siblings, and how they'd protected Kenta and then all of us on our return to Earth. Cheeks flaming, aura flaring bright, I even mentioned Rex and our feelings for each other, though I was quick to move on. For maybe the first time in my life, my mum listened with minimal interruption, only asking every now and then if we could pause for a cup of tea, and to ask me to demonstrate some of the spells, especially Polymorph — each time she would touch my fur or my feathers with shaking hands, as if to reassure herself that she wasn't hallucinating.

But when it was all done, she smiled. Her eyes shone, almost with tears. 'I always said you were destined for great things, didn't I?'

I stared at the table, running my fingers along a score in the wood. 'All mums say that about their kids.'

'But only I *knew* it,' said my mum. 'Not because I'm psychic — you know I'm just a studier of these things. Not because I read it in your stars. Because of *you,* darling. Because of how beautiful and brave you are. Because of how kind you are. Because of how fiercely you have survived in a world that wasn't made for you. I know I haven't always understood, but I've always, always been rooting for you.'

I glanced up, reassured by the warmth in her voice. She was positively beaming with pride, but her mouth trembled. 'Thanks, mum.'

She reached across the table and gave my hands a quick squeeze, before pulling away. 'So when do you leave? And for how long?'

I took a shuddering breath, tears stinging at my eyes. 'At the end of next week. For how long? I don't know ... we want to come back and visit but I think ...' I trailed off.

'You think you want to move there permanently,' my mother said gently. 'And who can blame you? You dreamed of fantasy worlds since you were a little child. Never did have your feet nailed to the ground, like me.' She sounded completely serious, but I chuckled all the same. We'd never been in agreement on which of us was the more realistic.

'We're going to try to find a way to communicate with family here,' I said. 'I think Rex has something specific in mind.'

'Ah yes, the mysterious Rex.' My mum raised her eyebrows. 'Now why don't you tell me more about this young man you're so fond of?'

I groaned and buried my face in my arms. '*Mum ...*'

It was both hard and easy to talk about Rex. As excruciating as it was to talk about relationships with my nosy, prying mother it was also just ... nice to talk about him as a person. How he was smart and shy. How we helped each other through our anxiety. How he didn't seem to expect anything more from me than I felt able to give. How he was handsome, on Earth and on Vanthis. How unbelievably lucky I felt to have gotten his interest.

'And you're meeting his family properly? Before you go?' my mum said.

I nodded. 'Yeah. I mean ... that's the plan. They might hate me, they might —'

'Nobody could hate you, darling,' my mum interrupted me. 'Nobody worth knowing, anyway. And your Rex seems to really love his family, so I'm sure they will love you too.' She leaned back and crossed her arms. 'Now Tarot ... when are you going to bring *him* to meet *me?*'

I laughed, shakily, but a little of the tension bled out of me with it.

I texted Rex under the watchful eye of my mother. He was reluctant to meet her — at least as reluctant as I had been to meet his parents — but he was willing all the same. For my sake.

✩✩✩

As it happened, both meetings went smoothly. His family were prepared to meet their son's magical datefriend, and my mother was only mildly embarrassing (after I gave her a thorough list of cringey bullshit she wasn't allowed to bring up). She seemed immediately charmed by him, for all he was quite withdrawn and struggled with eye contact. Rex was polite and intelligent, and he was obviously doing his best to be as friendly as possible given how uncomfortable he was.

As for Rex's family, his parents wanted to know all about my life on Earth, while his siblings were more interested in my time on Vanthis. His youngest sister was especially fascinated, and with Rex's permission, we went outback and I turned into various animals for her amusement, even letting her ride me around the yard. Rex swore he would find a way to bring them to visit as soon as he was able, to which his sister was simultaneously delighted and disappointed. I understood her feeling; how impossible must it be to know that a magical world existed and that you could one day travel to it — but not *yet?*

At the end of the second week, we gathered again at Pauline and Hanna's house. It was now bare of most of their furniture and ready to spend a few years fallow. In the games room, Rex had drawn the necessary circle in chalk and paint. On Earth, it didn't glow in quite the same way, but every now and then a rune might spark, so quickly it almost seemed to be a trick of the eye. It would take us, not to the Spire and Tellan Vorugar, but to the Loten-Tooth in Lundanar. To Ordeth, and Silky, and the Honeyhart.

I looked around at my friends gathered there. Hanna, the 'non-geek', who had loaded up her laptop and game supplies as some of the essential items she would bring with her. Kenta, who had been so anxious on our first visit but now seemed extremely calm. He caught my eye and gave me a wry look. Arries, so excited he looked like he might burst, but who only last night had cried down the phone to me about saying goodbye to so many friends. Rex, who dusted off his hands then threaded his fingers with mine, meeting my eyes with an expression half-fear and half-mischief. And Pauline, the source and centre of all that had happened. Maybe the most magical person in two worlds. She tied a scarf across her forehead, and winked at me.

'Looks like we're all here and ready to go,' said Arries. He was nearly vibrating with excitement.

'No last minute business?' Pauline said. 'You've all said your farewells, and sorted out your houses? All packed and ready?'

Rex snorted. 'Has everyone had a potty break?' he imitated her voice, and Pauline attempted a scowl at him, somewhat ruined by the grin tugging at her lips.

'I'm ready,' I said.

'I don't feel ready at all,' said Kenta. 'But honestly ... this feels right. And besides: I have a promise to keep.'

Hanna raised her eyebrows at him. 'So serious.'

'Shut up, Hanna. It's a momentous occasion!'

Hanna shrugged. 'We're just *moving house.* It's whatever. I'm ready.' She hoisted her pack higher on her shoulder.

We all stood around the circle and, without prompting, without really needing to, we all joined hands.

'We're really doing this?' I whispered.

'We're really doing this,' Rex said.

I took a deep breath. Rex freed his other hand and sketched the rune that activated the circle.

Then together as one, we stepped forward into the rest of our lives.

ACKNOWLEDGEMENTS

Hey, you read my book! And you made it through to the end! Wow, that's extremely cool of you. Thank you for the gift of your attention. All published authors crave it (for our work, anyway).

It's wild that we've made it to this stage because, like *Books & Bone* before it, I couldn't afford to publish this book. But thanks to the magic of crowdfunding and human kindness, here we are. In fact, it was so successful that I can hardly process it at the time of writing. I had always thought that something like *Non-Player Character* was a niche book. If it is, it's a fucking supportive niche full of awesome people.

In many ways, this was the hardest book I've yet written. Like Tar, I am not great at 'IRL stuff', and writing about it is no exception. Writing about it in a pandemic ... well. It was tough. And then writing candidly about autism and anxiety and the constant gnawing stress of living where people can see you ... it was an emotional book, for sure.

But enough about that.

I want to thank Joh for being my constant sounding board and first reader (I know I don't make it easy for you). I want to thank Angelica Fyfe, for being my excellent beta reader and proofreader (something I am badly in need of).

I want to thank Grim (@renardroi) for doing the first character concepts of the Amethyst Hand. You were a delight to commission. I want to thank Vanessa Schiefer (@hellebardedraws) for this stunning cover art and for responding with enthusiasm and even excitement when I came to you with a huge cover art commission on a tight deadline. I'd also like to thank Tais Yastremska for the gorgeous chapter header illustrations. You were so quick. so skilled, and so pleasant to work with.

I want to thank Gwenfar, Sario, Tak!, chimerical girls, Lara, Waldweg, Samantha and my monthly supporters who are not listed here for helping keep this author business afloat but also for being an unending source of emotional support.

I want to thank all the people working hard every day on TTRPGs big and small. You are an inspiration.

And of course, I want to thank everyone involved in the Kickstarter campaign, whether backing or sharing or spreading the word. This would not have been published without you.

SPECIAL THANKS

This book could not have been published without the generosity of these wonderful folk:

AJ Knight, Alana Post, Albert Cua, Aleta van Riper Mendenhall-Turner, aletheridae, Alex Dubois, Alex Q, Alice Oxford, Alistair Winters, Amelinda Webb, Andrew Dwoinen, Andromeda Taylor-Wallace, Angel Malachi, Anna Mickelsen, Anne Ferrard, Annie Larkin, Arcane Malcolm, Arlene Benningfield, Ashe Lyn, ashes, Astrid Portner, Aura ❀ V, Axolotl fragiadakis, Azaliz, Becca L, Ben Hamill, Benita K., Bookwyrmkim, Brighton Bloss, Briony Woodman, Britt H, Brooks Moses, Bryanna Hitchcock, C. Fahey, Cadfael P., Caitlin Ward, Catsafae, Cerys Rose Anderson, Chelsea Hammink, Chickadee, chimerical girls, Chris Mobberley, Chrissy & Mickie, Ciel, Constantine Jaffe, Cora Anderson, Craig Campbell, Cyberfossil, D. Moonfire, Daniel Silver, David Frahm, David Jaxon, Denise Atwood, Desiree Jung, Dill N Holman, Dixon Reuel, Dr. Sean M, Dzmitry Kushnarou, Edel, Elaine Chandras, Elizabeth Hollyburn, Elizabeth Sargent, Elliot Rose, Emet Rosmead, Emily Willis, Emma Maree Urquhart, Emory Black, Evelyn, Faxe MacAran, Filip H.F. "FiXato" Slagter, Fool's Moon Entertainment, Inc., Frank Hatcher, Georgina Coates, Ginger Bear, Gordhan Rajani, Gordon Goblin, Gordon Milner, Grayson Schultz, Grey Shisler, Gwenfar, halfsickofshadows, Hugh, Ingrid Saliste, Jacen Leonard, James Lucas, Jamie Bliss, Jamie Mendenhall-Turner, Jantien Schoenmakers, Jasherel Turner, Jean-Philippe

Dufraigne, Jennifer Polley & Rose Brannon, Jens Van Neyghem, Jerrie the filkferengi, Jinx, John Cater, John Fiala, Joke Van Driessche, Jon Auerbach, Jonathan "Buddha" Davis, Jonathan Allan Maurer & Lexington Witherspoon, Jonathan Veguilla, josh giesbrecht, Julia Lia, Julian Macias, Kade Sharp, Karranda, Kat L., Kate Lindstrom, Katherine R, Katie Fouks, Ken Finlayson, Kiji Marie Anastacio, Kim C.J., Klaus MacDubhghall, Kris M, Kwaku Ananse, Kynerae, L. Gonzales, L. Rowyn, Lara, Laser, Laura Shull, Lauren E. Mitchell, Leo Zaghis, Leucosia, Libellus Drakena, LilFluff, Lily Morgan, Lindsey Hunt, Lisa Padol, Liv Fleur-ange, Liz Neering, Liz Siewerth, Logan Franklin, Lore, Lukas Feinweber, Mallowsap Proudburrow/Oatley Maltshake, Marc Grondin, Marcy J. Chiera (She/They), Marjo Hämäläinen, Marjon, Mark Sabellico, Mars, Marsh J. Lynx, Maya Coleman, MCP, Meg, Mega, Mia Tylia, Mihail Braila, Miller, Milouchkna, M'liss Garber, monstergrrrl, Morgan Tenhouse, namtari, Neil Hart, Nentuaby, Neo & Sio, Niklas M., nittofulaks, Noam Bergman, Noelle Leigh, of a feather, Olivia Montoya, Owen Strawbridge, Paige Kimble, Paige Lisko, Paradox, Phoenix Ta, prin, Rachael Edmonson, Rachel Christensen, Rain & Aidenn, Ransom Meltzer, Raven Song, Rebecca Crawford, Rebecca Shipp, Reese Polilla, Regan, Riley Cruickshank, Rin Seilhan, Riot Fae Dice, Rixska Sorsa, Rob & Jenny Haines, Robin Hill, Robin Lee Sanford, Rommudoh, Rowen Kade, Ryn Helter, S "Jazz" Mattson, so, Sabine V, Sajesh Cherian, Samantha Vente, Sambience, Sarah Troeh, Sario, Scott Bryant, Scott V A Hunter, Sentinel Ark, Sergey Kochergan. Seth Scott, Shadu Murasaki, Shahazadei, Siavahda, Simba P. Maliki, Simone "OldMariner" Carlini, Skye Lowell, Socheata Chan, Sophie Jane, Stephanie Zella, StephDragon, Susan Tarrier, T.J. Franks, Tascha, tastytea, The Selkie Delegation, Thea Flurry, ThemFatale, Tina Marie Maes, Tom and Sarah Stanton, Tom Zurkan, Tony & Lilette, Torie Washburn, Trip Space-Parasite, Tuetenclown, Tuula Turto, Vhalesa, Vic H, Vik-Thor (Lirleni) Rose, Werekat, Wes Frazier, Willard Goosey,

William C. Tracy, X. Rouxinol, xap, Yncke, Yuu Gamon, Zarak, Zatty, and Zeta Syanthis.

And of course, thanks to all the other supporters of the *Non-Player Character* Kickstarter campaign not named here.

ABOUT THE AUTHOR

Veo Corva writes things and reads things and reads things out loud, and sometimes they get paid for that, which is nice because it means they can feed their cat.

They live in Wiltshire with their partner and their furry familiar and as many books as they could fit in their small flat.

They are anxious and autistic and doing just fine.

To find out more about them and read more of their work, visit https://veocorva.xyz

SIGN UP FOR PUBLISHING UPDATES!

If you'd like to receive an email every time a new Veo Corva
book is announced or published, you can sign up to
their newsletter here: https://tinyletter.com/witchkeyfiction

No spam, no extraneous updates; just letting you know when
a new book is available.